ONE SHATTERED CROWN

REBECCA ZANETTI

HEADLINE ETERNAL

Published in the United States by Kensington Books, an imprint of Kensington Publishing Corp., New York. First published in the United States in 2026

First published in the UK in 2026 by Headline Eternal
An imprint of Headline Publishing Group Limited

1

Content notice: *One Shattered Crown* contains themes that may be distressing to some readers, including violence, nonconsensual groping, sexual & emotional dominance, manipulation, spanking, erotic humiliation, coerced exhibitionism, toxic families, organized crime, and gun violence.

Cataloguing in Publication Data is available from the British Library

Paperback ISBN 978 1 0354 1795 7

Offset in 10.67/14.55 pt Stempel Garamond LT Std by Six Red Marbles UK, Thetford, Norfolk

Printed and bound in Great Britain by Clays Ltd, Elcograf S.p.A.

MIX
Paper | Supporting responsible forestry
FSC® C104740

Headline's policy is to use papers that are natural, renewable and recyclable products and made from wood grown in well-managed forests and other controlled sources. The logging and manufacturing processes are expected to conform to the environmental regulations of the country of origin.

Headline Publishing Group Limited
An Hachette UK Company
Carmelite House
50 Victoria Embankment
London EC4Y 0DZ

The authorised representative in the EEA is Hachette Ireland, 8 Castlecourt Centre, Dublin 15, D15 XTP3, Ireland (email: info@hbgi.ie)

www.headlineeternal.com
www.headline.co.uk
www.hachette.co.uk

This one's for the curious.

Curiosity always has
consequences . . .

ONE

Ella

Justice . . . yeah, he *looks* dangerous. Jet-black hair, broad shoulders stretching the seams of his suit, gaze constantly scanning the room. I feel a little sorry that I tried to kill his brother not too long ago. Thorn survived—barely—and the only reason I'm still breathing is because he'd bend reality to keep Alana safe, and she loves me. My death would hurt her, so I get to stay alive.

Which is a good thing, because there are more guns in this opulent pavilion than actual people.

I tear my gaze away from Justice and take a sip of champagne. The expensive brew is a crisp, floral, bubbly delight that tickles the roof of my mouth as I try to count how many bodyguards are lurking around the place. I give up after twenty. This is ridiculous.

Then I purposefully avoid looking at Justice and glance over at Alana. My best friend. The newly crowned Mrs. Thorn Beathach.

Her beauty practically fills the whole room, like light

refracting off a diamond. She has sparkling eyes, thick, dark hair cascading down her back, and cheekbones that are sharp yet feminine. She's glowing. Literally. Maybe it's the chandeliers catching her earrings, or the champagne catching up to me. Could go either way.

Her man is danger in a suit with a scar across his face that's a clear warning sign.

They're a striking couple: beautiful and terrifying in equal measure. Like a rose with steel thorns and a body count.

She holds up her phone and makes a post, probably on her family's social media platform, Aquarius Social. She's the biggest influencer in the country, with a platform that allows people to share emotions. Considering she's radiating happiness, she's spreading a lot of love right now.

Soft music winds through the air that sounds like delicate and expensive strings. My shoulders roll back, irritated by a persistent, uncomfortable itch down my spine. My quite bitchy stepmother must be nearby. And, bingo. There she is with the stepsisters, loitering near the buffet where most of the bachelors are filling their plates. My stepmother and sisters are just pretending to pick at things. Performance dining.

I shake my head.

"You really could smile a little," Rosalie says beside me, her voice warm and dry with amusement.

I half turn to take her in. Rosalie wears a deep sapphire gown that hugs her like it was sewn on by angels. The color makes the impossible blue of her eyes even more shocking. Ethereal, but in a way that says she could still stab you with a heel if it came to it.

"I am smiling," I tell her.

We match tonight in the same gown, same shade. Except I'm many inches shorter, and mine doesn't quite flow as gracefully. But my blonde hair is curled just right around my shoulders, and my makeup's on point. I feel acceptable. Like I might belong here. If I squint. "I can't believe you're here talking to me all by yourself."

Rosalie rolls her eyes. "Don't be silly."

I scan the room again. Glittering gowns brush the marble floors, and tuxedos prowl past like sleek predators. Laughter hums just under the music. I catch sight of Alexei Sokolov by the bar. He's partially turned, but his gaze flicks in our direction. Direct. Calculating. Possessive.

"Oh, there he is," I murmur. "I'm surprised he let you out of his sight for long."

Rosalie laughs, soft but rich. "He is a mite overprotective." Right. Like the leader of the Russian mob is just *a bit* protective.

"How many guns does he have on him, anyway?"

"I don't know," she says.

I glance toward the exits, from doorway to doorway, cataloging shadows and broad shoulders. I count at least two mafia guys at each exit. The Russian half are Alexei's, and the Irish ones are Thorn's. Then a few more are scattered throughout.

Yeah. Glitter, music, silk, and enough firepower to start a small war. Just another Saturday night.

Alexei and Thorn own two of the most powerful social media companies in the world and also run mafia-like organizations with enough reach to make FBI agents cry into their keyboards. Charming, really. Alana's family owns the third out of four major companies.

Technically, I should own the fourth. *Should.* But my stepmother's still clinging to it with her clawed fingers and Botox-smoothed smugness. That's temporary, though. The clock's ticking, and she doesn't even hear it. Unless she finally succeeds in getting me killed, and then she wins.

I can't let that happen.

A couple dances past us, the woman's golden gown billowing out and catching innocent ankles like a weaponized fabric storm. Strings hum from somewhere above like music's just floating down from the cosmos, or a luxury sound system pretending to be heaven.

I'm ready to get out of the gown and into my yoga pants. Even though I grew up an heiress in one of the wealthiest families of all time, my stepmother shipped me off to a boarding school in the middle of nowhere, with no fancy celebrations or even cake. I'm more comfortable by myself in comfy clothes with a computer in front of me. But I know my role, so I smile for anybody looking or filming. "I'm still surprised Thorn agreed to have the wedding reception on Alana's father's property." The pavilion's gorgeous, sure, but Thorn doesn't exactly scream *let's compromise*. The man radiates control-freak energy in his sleep.

Rosalie snatches a champagne flute from a passing tray and takes a healthy sip. "Do you really think he'd have people over to his place?" she asks. "The guy has a moat. A real one. Like, with water and probably crocodiles. He doesn't want strangers anywhere near it."

"Good point," I say. This location works for me, however. I've got a little side mission that will include hacking into Alana's family servers. I mean, it's not like I'm going to hurt anyone. For sure, I'd never harm Alana, but I do need access, and this party is a perfect distraction.

Rosalie looks around at the sea of glittering gowns and streamlined, gleaming tuxes. "Everyone from Silicon Valley is here," she murmurs.

"And both mafias," I add.

"Ella," she hisses. "We're not supposed to talk about that."

"You're not supposed to talk about it. I don't give a hoot." The word "hoot" feels stupid the second it leaves my mouth, but I commit to it anyway. A shiver crawls up the back of my neck like a cold fingertip. Not just nerves—something heavier. A shift in the air. I pause and scan the room. Yep.

He's watching me, and I hope he didn't notice me staring at him a second ago. Something tells me he notices everything.

Justice Beathach. Thorn's brother and enforcer. For years, nobody even knew he existed, but when Thorn and Alana went public, he was found out. I believe he's now the most eligible bachelor in the world, which is probably something he hates. I kept the article and pictures, just for research purposes. Of course. Currently, he's standing by the window like a predator in a designer tux, staring through the crowd like he's memorizing everyone's weak spots.

Rosalie follows my gaze and manages to remain quiet for half a beat. "He watches you a lot, and I can't say there's any amusement in his eyes."

"Oh no," I agree. "He hates my guts." Yet, I try not to notice how disgustingly good he looks. That tux hugs his broad frame like it's been tailored perfectly for each muscled inch. He has dark hair and brown, copper-flecked eyes sharper than razors as well as shoulders wide enough to block the sun . . . or a bullet. And he's still staring at me like he's deciding if tonight's the night.

"You *did* try to kill his brother," Rosalie murmurs.

"I didn't know Alana was going to fall in love with Thorn," I snap, trying to look casual. Like I'm not deeply aware that Justice is probably the most dangerous man in this room.

Forget the "probably." He *is* the most dangerous. And he really, truly wants me dead.

I glance down at my citrine-encrusted heels, which sparkle like tiny suns caught in a death trap. Absolutely stunning. Completely useless if I need to run. But the citrine grounds me.

Every human has an affinity with a specific crystal, whether they know it or not. Most people never bother to learn, never take the time to actually engage with that pull humming just under their skin. But some of us know all about the energy exchange. We feel it. The strongest ability to *harness* the power only belongs to particular bloodlines, I'm fairly certain. Those of us at the top? We were born into it.

The owners of the four social media giants are not there via coincidence. We all come from long lines of crystal-bound bloodlines. Old power. Ancient tech, dressed up in modern servers where crystals run computer systems with more electrical power than imaginable. Everyone thinks social media platforms are run by codes and data. They're not. We're using amplified magic.

Right now, diamonds are powering the servers at TimeGem Moments, a social media company that allows viewers to share memories, and one that should be mine. TimeGem is my birthright. My company. My network. But diamonds aren't the right crystal for our system. They're all flash, no flow. My stepmother charges them with her abilities in a simple energy exchange, sure, but it's all brittle. Citrines are better. Stronger. More intuitive. And they're mine. I can exchange power with citrines by placing my hands on those crystals and moving energy between us in a way my stepmother can only dream about.

Citrine is my key back in, assuming I survive long enough to reclaim what's mine and the assassins don't get to me first. "Rosalie, I'll be right back." I turn slightly. "I'm going to run to the restroom."

Her eyes drop to my heels and then rise with one dark brow arching. "What are you up to?"

"Nothing bad," I say, a little too quickly.

Rosalie sighs, slow and theatrical. "Come on, Ella. It's Alana's wedding. Can we please just enjoy ourselves and not cause any problems?"

"I'm not causing problems," I protest. "You know I'd never do anything to hurt Alana."

She shifts her weight. "That's not the same as not causing problems."

"I just have a little business to conclude. Trust me."

She studies me like she's trying to see through to the server room hiding behind my eyes. "I always trust you."

Warmth floods through me. It pools in my chest and lights up my bones. She means it. Just like Alana does. They trust me, even knowing what I can do, what I have done. Even knowing I've hacked places I absolutely shouldn't have. But it's my one true talent, and I don't want to let it go.

Rosalie glances around. "Where's your date?"

I spot Wesley Whisper at the cake table. "Over there."

He looks good in a suit. Really good. His blond hair is freshly cut, and his frame's more muscular than anyone expects from a code junkie. Wesley isn't just any programmer: He works for Alana's family and is the genius behind their algorithm. We've been seeing each other on and off for a few months now.

I really like the guy.

He looks up, catches me watching, and waves. He looks sober. Grounded. Present. I smile, humor bubbling up in my chest.

Rosalie's watching me with a suspicious glint. "Please tell me you're not using him just to get into the Beaumont servers."

"I'm not." I lift my chin. "I really like him. He understands code. He can talk about it for hours. It's . . . nice."

"That is what one wants in a man," Rosalie says dryly.

I glance across the room to where her man is standing—by the orchestra, arms crossed, watching her like she's the only person in the room. Alexei Sokolov. Leader of the Russian mob. Pure, unfiltered danger in a tux. I'm honestly surprised the tux hasn't grown sentient just trying to keep up with his raw energy. Black hair, obsidian eyes, and a body hardened by seven years in prison. When he and Rosalie decide to set the world on fire? It'll burn. "It looks like your man wants you."

She follows my gaze. Her lips curve. "He always wants me."

And she sounds so damn happy.

I like that but wouldn't have picked Alexei for her, not with the whole kills-people-professionally résumé, but the man loves her. He'll protect her against anything and anyone, and she needs that. I mean, who doesn't? "You better go dance."

"I think I will." Rosalie leans down and presses a sweet kiss to my forehead. She smells like gardenias and something dangerously expensive. "Try to have some fun, Ella. We'll go after your stepmother the second you're ready. I promise."

I have her support as well as Alana's. And probably, even if reluctantly, their terrifying men. But this thing? This war? It's between me and the woman who stole my birthright. "Thanks," I say. "I appreciate it."

Rosalie exhales, the sound soft but weighty, and then she turns and walks away with the kind of grace that could make statues weep. Heads turn as she glides across the floor toward Alexei.

I drain the rest of my champagne in one go, and the last bubbles tingle up my throat. Then I move—casual, nonchalant, totally-not-doing-anything-suspicious—toward the restrooms. When I get there, I veer right.

There's an exit behind the hallway. Not many know about it, but I've studied the floor plan of this pavilion like it's a level in a video game. It shouldn't take me long to slip into the control tent, which has to be connected to one of the Beaumont mainframes. Everything's networked. Always has been.

But just as I pass the last column, a voice cuts through the air—deep, dark, and so close I nearly jump out of my skin.

"Where are you going?"

I manage to turn just a little, keeping my expression flat.

Justice Beathach stands in front of me like a wall made of malice and sculpted bone structure. Looking down. Always looking way down. What is he, six foot four? Six five? He's freakishly tall and infuriating about it.

I'm petite. Like, professional pixie height. And while I can fight, somewhat, size and strength still matter. A lot. "None of your damn business, Justice," I snap, my spine going stiff, my fists clenching on instinct.

His chin lowers and an odd warmth slides through his eyes. "That's where you're wrong."

That's it. That's all he says.

"Excuse me?" I demand, already calculating if I can knee him in the balls and survive the attack.

He tilts his head slightly, watching me the way a hawk watches a field mouse who's trying very hard not to look like prey.

I set my shoulders. One hand curls into a fist. I know I won't do much damage, but I'll aim strategically.

Then he smiles.

I'm not ready for that. The sight hits me like a sucker punch.

He's handsome in a completely lethal way. The kind of man who definitely owns a dungeon and not in the cute romantic metaphor sense. No, this one's probably got shackles bolted to the walls. "I think we're going to dance, Ella Rendale."

"I don't think so," I shoot back.

He doesn't argue. He doesn't need to. One arm slips around my waist like he's done it a thousand times and lifts me against him like I weigh nothing, because apparently the laws of physics just surrender when Justice decides they should.

"What the hell—"

"Behave yourself," he murmurs, his voice going low and sounding almost bored. "If you're a good girl, we'll just dance. If you're bad, well, you're going to moan as you dance." With that, he carries, *carries*, me back through the pavilion like it's no big deal. Through the crowd, past the chandeliers and the murmured gasps and the clink of crystal.

Right onto the bustling dance floor.

TWO

Justice

Ella's lighter than she should be. I lift her without effort. She stiffens in my grip, like she thinks she can intimidate me into putting her down. Cute. Not happening.

Not when this room is a live wire. When every tux hides a weapon and every smile could be the start of a war. Thorn's wedding or not, this place is a powder keg. And she . . . she's the lit match.

I set her down on her three-inch and deadly looking heels.

The orchestra starts playing *Clair de Lune.* Of course it's *Clair de Lune.* The kind of song that turns rooms intimate without permission. Makes people say things they shouldn't. Feel things they can't afford. The moment she opened her mouth in the hallway, my skin electrified. In a good way. No pain, just pleasure.

I want to hear pleasure come *from* her. More than anything else in the world right now.

My hand rests at the small of her back. I take her other

hand and draw her against me. She fits perfectly, which pisses me off. Her body is warm, tense, dangerous. My own personal landmine in lipstick and heels.

Her cheek brushes my chest, and she shifts to breathe, like I'm smothering her. I might be. I hope I am.

"What do you think you're doing?" Her smile stays fixed for the cameras, but her voice . . . her tone slides under my skin like silk laced with static.

Her voice soothes through me. Calms me. I'm accustomed to every voice causing a reaction inside me—from everyone. This one is new. Soft. Sweet. I'm intrigued against my will, and my dick goes rock hard. If she had any idea what her voice actually does to me, she'd have a weapon that could shred me. I definitely don't trust her with anything, much less that. "Keeping you where I want you," I say. "Away from trouble."

Her sigh presses into my chest, warm and soft. I feel her frustration before I hear it. Then she tilts her head and looks up at me with those storm-lit eyes. "Listen, Justice. I'm sorry I almost killed your brother, okay? But I didn't know things were going to turn out the way they did."

There it is. That slight tonal shift. The true sorrow in her sweet voice. The tone flows down my throat and settles like warm cider in my gut. Her voice is a drug. Smooth. Addictive. The tenor calms the static for one damned second, and I hate that too. I hum without thinking. The note inside me starts low and soft, then darkens, thickens into something closer to a growl. I feel it move through my chest and into hers. She blinks like I short-circuited something in her. Her balance slips. My grip tightens. I keep her upright and make it look effortless for the many eyes on us.

"What was that?" she breathes.

"None of your damn business." My voice emerges lower than I intended. Rougher. She doesn't flinch. Doesn't smile either.

She glances over her shoulder, scanning for allies. Alana. Thorn. An exit. She wants out. And I get it.

I scan too. A waiter's pattern stutters, someone near the bar holds their drink too long, a flash of metal catches my eye near the back corridor. Threats are everywhere, and I have to track them all while she burns against me like a fever.

"You're making a scene," she says.

The woman is lucky I'm not, because a scene would involve my tossing her over my shoulder and escaping this glittering hell. "I'm just dancing," I reply. "While keeping you out of trouble."

"I wasn't going to get in trouble."

A chuckle escapes me, sharp and sudden. Her lips twitch. She wants to argue.

Instead, she relaxes. Just slightly. The tension in her frame shifts and softens. Her body leans into mine like she might trust me. Or like she's tired of fighting me for one moment. Either way, it sets fire to something under my ribs. A low, slow burn that's been building since the first time she opened her damn mouth and made me feel anything at all.

We dance one song. Then another. Her rhythm syncs to mine, and her breath evens out. Her body fits. She even starts to enjoy it.

That's the problem.

Because if she keeps looking at me like that, if she keeps feeling like this in my arms, I might forget how dangerous she is. She tried to kill my brother, and I'm the enforcer for our entire organization. I have to make sure she can never do so again. Plus, I need her help, which is a fact I strongly dislike.

But when she speaks, her voice slides inside me, and I want to return the favor. Bury myself so deeply inside her that she forgets all about attacking her enemies.

The thought shocks me, but the woman is a mouthwatering temptation.

And she has no fucking clue how precarious her position is right now.

I shift my gaze past her shoulder, surveying the room again. Thorn stands near the edge of the ballroom with Alana tucked safely at his side. He's tense, even when he smiles, and his hand keeps ghosting toward his inner jacket pocket. His instincts are screaming, same as mine. They're too exposed here. Too many angles. Too many windows and too many cameras. I need them out of town by morning.

My eyes lock on Alexei Sokolov, who's lounging near the orchestra, as still as a predator between strikes. He tips his glass in my direction when he catches me looking. Not a threat. Not now. But Alexei's the kind of man who chooses chaos the way others choose a tie. As the owner of Hologrid Hub, a social media offering that uses holographic options, he may not be planning anything at the moment, but that doesn't mean he won't tomorrow.

Ella shifts slightly in my arms, her soft scent pricking my instincts wide awake and centering them fully on her.

"Have you always been drawn to computers? To code?" I want to hear her voice again.

She tilts her head. "Since I was eight. I broke into a

private school server to change a grade and was caught, but they couldn't kick me out since I wasn't on scholarship."

Her voice hits differently this time. Lower register. Light sarcasm, like warm electricity winding through nerves already frayed raw. The softness sparks something in me I can't control. Not anymore.

I grit my teeth.

The thing crawling inside me that makes simple voices somehow physically injure me, that's coiled under my skin and burrowed deep in my veins, calms when she talks. I don't know why or how. It's like she's figured out how to hack me, and a part of me wonders if she has. If she can hack into crystals and cause chaos that can infect people, why not in a direct line to men? Her voice cuts through my usual pain with an erotic slide of heat. Not perfectly, but enough to take the edge off. This is the closest we've ever talked, and my cock is brick solid, taking me out of my pain for a moment.

No one knows the mess that has descended upon me. Not Thorn. Not anyone in our organization. I tried to save my brother and ended up screwing myself. I'm good with computers; not as good as Thorn, but I should be able to figure it out. The static in my vision is one thing, but voices hurting me worse than before, as bad as bullets, is pissing me off. There's a heat in my spine that never cools down, and it's Ella's fault. Completely. But now she's making me feel better.

She doesn't know what she's done, I'm fairly certain. No way has she hacked me—that was a fanciful thought now discarded. So she has no clue that she's harmed me. That's the dangerous part. If I ask for her help, she'll know my weakness. Know she's more powerful than she thinks.

So I don't ask.

Not yet.

But if this illness gets worse, and it probably will, I may not have a choice. I might have to kidnap her, which would solve two of my problems, really. It'd take her out of commission when it comes to harming Thorn, and I could make her heal me once I have her locked down. Yeah, I want her under my control. Completely.

She looks up at me like she's about to say something else. I pray she does and brace for it. For her voice. For the tone that heals my pain and also fires my body alive in a primitive way that's new.

God, I want her to talk again.

Even if it ruins us both.

Ella

I want to stomp on his foot. I really do. Except his foot is huge, and his leg is between mine. In fact, his entire body is too close, too hot, too steady. It would be like trying to kick over a statue. One with excellent posture and a superiority complex. What did he mean about my moaning on the dance floor? Can he tell how my body reacts to him?

Hopefully he can see how my brain does—with a plan to destroy.

Then his hand shifts at my back in just a small movement, with light pressure guiding my next step. His touch feels invasive, controlling. Like he knows where we're going even when I don't. My nipples harden, and I hate how much I respond to him.

My breath escapes in this ridiculous, involuntary little sigh that I want to shove back into my lungs and set on fire. "I'm totally innocent here."

"Ha. Baby, you left innocent behind several firewalls ago." His eyes flick to mine. He sees me. Of course he does. But he doesn't smirk, doesn't comment, and just watches me like he's logging my every move, my every weakness. Like this is all part of some mental file he's building in case he has to put me down later.

It probably is.

Justice Beathach knows I'm the enemy. I know it, too. I've tried to kill people he's sworn to protect, and I've breached systems he was ordered to keep locked. If we weren't wearing formal wear, we'd be armed and bloody by now.

"You really think I'm that dangerous?" I ask, even though I know the answer. I want to hear him say it.

"I know you are." He says it like a fact. No heat, no praise. Just truth.

The heat that pulses low in my body is unwelcome and completely infuriating. I feel my knees start to betray me again, so I pivot to cover it. Clean step. Controlled. Almost elegant. I'm proud of it until his hand adjusts with me, just enough to keep me from actually falling. Like he anticipated the slip before I did.

I hate how easily he can hold me like this. I hate how warm he is. I hate the smell of his cologne. Expensive, complex, a little sharp. Like black pepper and sin. "There's a running theme in my head about you. It's called hate." I might as well give him the truth.

"Really?" He slides one hard thigh between my thighs and presses up.

Electricity arcs between my legs and through my body. I gasp, my clit pulsing. What is he doing? "Stop."

"No." His hand flattens across the small of my back, and he pulls me toward him, pulsing up with his leg. His very strong, muscled, unrelenting thigh.

Oh, God. Tremors begin to shake inside me. "Justice."

He forces me to ride it, turning with the music, holding me close. Does anybody know what he's doing to me? I clutch his lapels tight, digging my nails in. Liquid pools in my panties. My teeth grit. "You are such— "

"Watch it, princess." His hand slides down to cup my ass and then squeezes, just as his thigh muscle tightens.

My body jerks and my nipples sharpen, scraping against the soft fabric of the dress. Even that small sensation is overwhelming.

My head drops toward him. Live wires uncoil inside me, and erotic sparks zing up from my clit. I blink several times. My breath starts to pant. Panic takes me along with the need to let go. "Justice," I breathe again, needing him to stop. Now.

"Say please."

I swallow. People are all around us. His gaze drops to my hardened nipples. "Last chance."

"Please." I can't orgasm in front of everyone. How is this happening?

His leg slides back and he twirls us. "Good girl."

I want to hit him. Kind of. I also want to finish what he just started. That's not like me. Not at all.

He studies me. "You look lovely tonight, Ella."

It sounds like he means the compliment. "Are you always this nice to your enemies?" I keep my tone dry, but I hear the edge in it. The nerves. The pull.

"I'm not nice," he says. "This is containment."

"Charming." I stiffen.

His hand spans my entire lower back. "You should keep talking," he adds.

This throws me, and I don't want to challenge him again right now. Not with people all around us and my vagina weeping for him. This confuses my brain. My body seems to have a plan of its own. "Why should I talk?" I whisper.

He's quiet for a beat too long. "Your voice helps me think."

It's a lie. Or it's not. I can't tell. I can't read him. For someone like me, that's terrifying. I narrow my eyes. "I know your brother has a form of lexical-gustatory synesthesia and can taste people's words. Do you have it also?" The condition is real but enhanced with Thorn and makes him have a taste in his mouth any time somebody speaks. When Alana talks, he tastes honey.

Thorn apparently loves honey.

Justice stiffens and then relaxes. Crap. Maybe I shouldn't have said that. "How the hell do you know about Thorn?"

Heat tinges my face. "Alana told me. Thorn knows I know." Anything that will keep Justice from snapping my neck right now is a good sentence to say. "I'll never tell anybody. I promised her." I will never break a promise to Rosalie or Alana. Regardless of the consequences. "Do you have it, too?"

"No. I just like your voice," he says, and his thumb presses lightly into my lower back again, steadying me mid-turn. "If you're talking to me, you're not trying to kill anybody I care about."

I laugh, breathy and sharp. Do I believe him? Maybe.

He sounds sincere, but he wouldn't tell me if he had a weakness, would he? I angle my head back to look at his rugged face. "I've already apologized. Are you going to take revenge?"

He doesn't smile. His jaw flexes. He says nothing. But his eyes say *yes.*

This is not comforting. "You're making me nervous," I say, and this time I mean it.

"Good." His voice is too even. "You should be."

He's not threatening me. Not directly. But he doesn't have to. The truth is worse than a threat. I'm the enemy, and I'm completely caught in his arms.

We dance another full song. Somehow, I move against him naturally, my body wanting more. A lot more from him. His hands are steady, his rhythm flawless, and every time I breathe in, I get that mix of expensive cologne and skin-warmed heat that makes my head spin. His touch never falters. Not too tight, not too soft. Controlled. Intentional. Deadly.

Which is exactly what I should be focusing on. Not the pressure of his palm, or the way he moves with me like we were made for this. Or the fact that part of me, a part that absolutely needs to shut up, is starting to enjoy the feeling of us plastered together.

Then someone taps a knife against a champagne glass. A soft *ting ting ting* echoes through the pavilion, pulling all attention toward the cake table.

"Oh, it's speech time." I'm breathless and a little dizzy. "Aren't you the best man?"

"I really am," he says, and there's something deeply unfair about how good that sounds in his voice. Smooth, confident, unshakable. My brain short-circuits just a little.

He takes my hand, whether I like it or not, and I very much don't. I have a date, who I can't even see right now. Where is Wesley? Then Justice starts leading me through the crowd like I'm a very fancy, very glittery flight risk. People part like the sea for Moses. Only this time, Moses is carrying a hacker hostage in heels.

At the table, he snags a flute of champagne with his free hand like this is just another night out. This man is about to toast the bride and groom, and I'm still trying to remember how to breathe. The moment no one's looking, I wrench my hand free and vanish around the other side, heading straight for Alana. Still trying to catch my breath, I grab a fresh glass of champagne, trying to act as if I wasn't just dragged across the ballroom by Justice Beathach like his personal property.

From the other side of Thorn, Justice gives me a look. A *behave* look. The one that says I'm a project, a file he's keeping open, a mess he's determined to clean up. Since when did I become Justice Beathach's hobby?

I glare back.

My stepmother moves closer. At around six feet tall, she looks elegant and lovely in a silver-toned ball gown, her thick brown hair up and her deadly blue eyes perfectly accentuated. The hair color is fresh with new highlights. Her longtime boyfriend, Horace Whimple, is at her side. She lowers her chin, her gaze hard on me. "Hello, Ella."

"Hey, bitch," I whisper.

Stacia chuckles from my other side, and I jump. I didn't see my stepsister arrive. I turn to see her in a pretty pink gown with a rather cheap-looking silver sparkle purse, amusement in her dark eyes. Corinda is next to her, a tall and stunning blonde, and she looks over my head at Justice. "He's hot. Not your type, Ella."

"I know." I don't want Justice. "But he likes them smart, Corinda. Not your type, either."

Her blue eyes flare.

Yeah, I can hit back.

I try to appear bored and shift my attention to the speeches. Rosalie steps up first to toast Alana, and the speech is beautiful. Poised, elegant, sharp. Exactly what I'd expect from a lawyer who can out-argue a senator and seduce a judge in one breath. Alana's eyes glisten halfway through. Mine might have, too, if I wasn't still coming down from the contact high of dancing with a man who can snap my neck with one arm and ruin my life with the other.

Then it's Justice's turn. He's speaking for Thorn, and I'm not prepared. He's quiet. Honest. Nothing flashy. No intimidation tactics. Just simple, brutal truth. A brother who loves fiercely. A man who protects what's his.

Proving once again exactly why he's dangerous.

Because underneath all that cold precision is something raw and deadly.

I shake myself out of the fear and concentrate. Watching Justice and Thorn, I wish I had a sister. But I've got Alana and Rosalie. We're just as tight. Maybe tighter. Blood's not the only thing that binds.

Justice turns to clap Thorn on the back.

That's my window.

I move fast to slide behind Alana, weave through a tangle of well-dressed guests, make it to the bathrooms, and slip out the back exit. One quick turn and I'm in the tent containing the control room.

Two guys are sitting in front of a bank of screens, surrounded by wires and gear like they're backstage at a high-budget concert. Both wear black uniforms and have the nervous twitch of those taken away from the latest *Call of Duty* game.

"Hey," I say breezily. "Alana wants this played." I type in a couple of commands. Hopefully we're connected to the servers at the main house, which should be connected to the ones at Aquarius Social, their social media company.

One of the men starts to object, "Wait, what—?"

"The bride wants this," I interrupt, dropping sharpness into my voice. "She owns this place."

He blinks, looking confused. "Oh. Yeah."

"It'll just be a second." I type fast. Command line open. Fingers flying. Music begins to play with a decoy track I loaded in advance. The guys relax.

Idiots.

While they nod along to the tune, I slip the payload into the system, opening a clean back door into the Beaumont mainframe. Just a crack, just enough. I don't need much.

"Thanks," I chirp, turning and breezing outside the tent before they can question a thing.

Cool air hits me like a reward. My chest swells. That was almost too easy. I pivot to head back toward the pavilion—

And there he is.

Justice.

Leaning against the building like the embodiment of fury itself, glare locked on me like a missile. I freeze. Panic. Pure, stupid panic. Then I bolt.

I turn, heels slamming against stone, dress flaring out. I make it four steps before, damn it, I trip. Hitting the ground, being well acquainted with gravity, I roll and come back up with one shoe and zero dignity, and keep running, hitching along with one high heel.

He's behind me. I hear him. Heavy, fast, relentless. But this isn't his playground. It's mine.

I know this estate. I've been to Alana's father's place too many times to count. I dart left through a patch of decorative brush, ducking onto a hidden trail only a handful of people know about. His footsteps falter behind me. He's lost.

Two more sharp cuts, and I'm clear. Out front. I sprint toward the nearest parked car, which is some kind of sleek black town car, with its engine humming and the driver slouched over. I yank open the back door and launch myself inside. "Hi! I'm a bridesmaid. You have to go. Now."

The driver blinks once. Shrugs. Starts driving.

Bless him.

I glance out the back window and see Justice reach the Italian tile drive just seconds too late.

He stops.

His suit's dusted with dirt, shirt slightly open at the collar, and fury is written across every inch of his face. Lightning cracks in the distance, of course it does, and for one horrifying second, the flash paints him in stark silhouette.

Panic takes me. I have to get to a safe house.

He doesn't look like a man anymore.

He looks like retribution.

THREE

Justice

Fury lances down my spine as I watch the car vanish down the gravel drive, taillights bouncing like they're mocking me. How the hell did I let her get away again?

Ella Rendale is too damn clever, too fast, and too fucking cute for her own good.

She thinks I want her dead. I should. Except I don't. I want to trap her at my house in the woods and have her sing. Talk. Joke. Hum. Any sound out of her magical mouth.

I'm not good. But I'm not evil either. I don't like the idea of killing a sprite. Not even a volatile one with champagne on her lips and code in her blood. However, I'll do my job and lock her down to protect my brother.

Right now, I want her under me. For an entire night. One good night to fuck her out of my system is all I need. And I'll get it.

I turn and head back through the trail. Brambles slice at my pants and dirt sticks to my boots. My mood doesn't improve. Then I see something in the mud.

Sparkles against the sludge.

I take three more steps and find her heel—citrine-stoned with the spiked heel half hanging off as if it snapped when she was running. I pick it up and laugh under my breath. Of course it's hers. No one else would weaponize jewelry and sabotage in the same night. I keep moving, brush the worst of the forest off my clothes, push open the door, and step back inside.

That's when he hits me.

Not physically. Vocally.

One of the IT techs, some kid in a suit too expensive for his social skills, steps directly into my path. "Mr. Beathach," he says, too loud, too sharp, too wrong.

His voice scrapes through my nerves and explodes in my elbow like a sucker punch of cold pressure. I bite back a grimace, rolling the joint once like I'm adjusting a cufflink instead of trying to force sensation back into the limb. Every word this guy says feels like sandpaper grinding bone, and unfortunately, affects me physically. "We had a woman come into the tent. She typed something into the system, and the guys think it was just a change to the music. I'm not sure."

I nod. "Do a deeper dive and then send me the logs." His instincts are good, but I doubt he'll uncover what Ella did. She's too good. I'll check it out later. It's not like I haven't hacked into Aquarius Social before.

He hesitates, clearly wanting to keep talking. I narrow my eyes. He gets the message and clears out.

Inside, the ballroom looks unchanged. Champagne pours. Music flows. I spot Thorn near the cake table, surrounded by men in suits who pretend not to carry knives. He turns the second I approach. "What was that?"

I lift a shoulder and keep my voice low so his bride doesn't hear. "Best guess? Ella hacked into the servers."

His gaze sharpens, and the air tightens. "Should we shut it all down?"

"Not yet," I say. "I'll dig later to see what I can find. She'd never hurt Alana, so I'm not horribly worried." Curious, though.

Alana appears beside him, fingertips brushing his arm, and effectively halts our conversation. She leans in and whispers something. He bends his head to listen.

I watch. The moment is private, and I shouldn't care, but I do. There's something in that kind of closeness that makes the rest of the room feel fake.

Alana looks at me, soft and confident, like she sees more than she should. "That was a lovely speech, Justice. I have to tell you, I've missed my brother so since his untimely death. It's nice to have a brother again."

I exhale. Some of the fire in my chest cools. That's Alana's gift. Her voice lands like a feather. No bruising. No sparks. It doesn't hurt to listen to her. "I'm proud to be your brother." It's true. I'd easily die for her . . . and now kill for her, if necessary.

Ella, though?

Her voice ensnares and caresses, and I'd love to have her mouth around me. Can already see it in my mind. I feel the broken heel in my hand. The citrines on the shoe hum in my pocket, and I don't have a connection to citrines. But she does, and I sense it.

Alana moves to speak to other friends, and bodyguards shift positions subtly in every corner of the room.

Thorn looks around, back to business. "Should I be concerned about Beaumont's servers?"

"No." I follow his gaze, scanning the ballroom. The security's solid, the perimeter holds, but I can still feel the static under my skin. Ella's out there. Loose. Brilliant. Unstable.

"I love Alana," Thorn says, and his voice drops just slightly when he adds, "She's mine. And her father does own this company."

"I'll look into it," I say. "You've earned this six-week honeymoon. You need to take it."

His brow creases deeper. The scar down the side of his face tightens when he frowns like that. It runs from temple to jaw, a permanent reminder of our difficult childhood. It makes him look just as deadly as I know him to be. "I don't know," he says. "If something's going on . . ."

"No," I cut in. "I've got it. I can charge our servers, run Malice Media, and handle our people. Seriously. Go."

He watches me. I feel him weighing it, the responsibility, the risk. Then he says, "I know you're capable. But if we're facing another attack . . ."

I shake my head. "Why? Ella doesn't want you dead. Not any longer."

Thorn snorts. "Maybe not me, but she looked ready to spit fire when you made her dance earlier. She might want you drowning in your own blood right now."

That makes me laugh. "Yeah. She might."

"I don't want to harm Alana's best friend," he says, softer now. His gaze drifts to where she ran. "But if Ella keeps pushing, someone's going to get hurt."

"I'll handle it," I say. "She won't get near to hacking our servers."

Not again. Somehow she snuck code into the garnets and infected our entire platform with a computer virus.

When Thorn laid his hands on the crystal to charge the system, he caught the virus and started to freeze from the inside. The thing morphed from energy to rewriting him. She didn't create it, but she managed to get it uploaded. The code almost killed him.

She didn't mean to nearly murder him. At least, that's what she said. She also assisted in bringing him back from the edge and helped us find a way to undo the damage.

That doesn't make her safe. She could still cause damage if she chooses.

Thorn's attention shifts to Alexei Solokov, who is dancing with Rosalie Mooncrest, Alana's other best friend. The Russian moves like a panther on a leash, his gaze always somewhere else, like the music is just an excuse to stay within striking distance.

Thorn doesn't say it, but I can feel the thought between us.

Alana's best friends are ticking clocks. Brilliant. Dangerous. If either Ella or Rosalie gets hurt, we're the ones who will bleed.

I know something else, too. Ella is a threat. A beautiful, burning threat with code in her blood and secrets in her eyes. But God help me, after her voice rippled beneath my skin, I don't want her erased.

I want her under control.

If I have to lock her down myself, I will.

I don't want to go to war with Alexei. Which might happen if I take Ella away from here. Or . . . maybe not. Maybe he'll be grateful that I took care of the threat and he can still appear innocent to his woman. Well, as innocent as he can seem. Hard to tell with him.

Those three women—Ella, Alana, Rosalie—they're

tight. They're twisted into each other's lives like rope. If I hurt Ella, even by accident, it won't just be Alexei who wants my head.

Alana will come for me.

Rosalie, too.

Which means my brother's life gets caught in the fallout.

"Leave Ella to me," I say, and I mean it.

Thorn knows me better than anyone else walking this planet. He looks at me like he's reading more than I want him to. "Are you interested in her?"

"God. No." The denial comes out too fast. Too sharp. I clear my throat. "Yes, she's beautiful and brilliant. But so is the black widow spider."

He doesn't say a word. Just raises one brow.

So I shut up.

He really does need a vacation, and I need him gone so I can figure out what the hell is going on with my health and the fucking garnet that seems just fine running our servers now. No longer diseased, which confuses me since I'm definitely having issues. With him out of the way, I have options. I can take Ella out of play. Quietly. I'll handle it myself. I won't risk someone else screwing it up.

I don't want the blowback to touch Thorn. I can live with Alana hating me. I can live with Rosalie's fury. I can even live with Alexei sending his entire organization after me.

But I can't live with letting anything harm my brother.

I can have Ella dropped on an island in the middle of nowhere with no signal, no server, no keyboard, no power grid. Just sun, water, and books. She'll have to take up reading. Gardening. Maybe swimming.

The image of her on a beach clicks through my brain. Her bare feet in the sand. Her skin golden under the sun. Naked. Wild hair down her back. No phones. No firewalls. Just Ella skinny-dipping at night.

My whole body tightens instantly.

I shift my stance and clench my jaw.

This is a problem.

A real one.

FOUR
Ella

I'm in.

The Aquarius Social firewall gives way, but not easily. This is the third layer, and it's built to hide something. Not protect. Hide.

I should feel guilty, maybe a little, for hacking into Alana's company. Or her dad's, anyway. I'd almost too easily sent the code through the system that opened up doors for me. Those poor idiots in that tent. It had been child's play. But I also know that Aquarius Social has been working to gain entrance into TimeGem's servers. Wesley had let that little fact slip while we'd been miniature golfing, and I'd shrugged it off on the surface while already planning. Yeah, I feel guilty about it, but not enough to stop.

As far as I'm concerned, TimeGem is mine. I'll protect it, even if I don't have control yet. Lines of code scroll across my screen as I infiltrate Aquarius Social. I isolate the threads connected to the aquamarine crystal protocols.

These aren't just random encryption strings. They're tied to resonance-based shielding systems. The kind integrated for high-clearance data. The system should be clean.

But something's wrong.

There's a pattern embedded in the subcode. It's close to the crystal resonance profile, but not exact. The frequency is forced. Someone has tried to mimic the aquamarine interface, and they've come close. Too close.

Someone has been inside the Aquarius system. Someone who shouldn't be—besides me, that is. I easily find the hack from Wesley trying to get into TimeGem. He's not even close, and I have to wonder if he's noticed the trail in his own system.

My phone buzzes on the table. I ignore it. It buzzes again, and I look down to see notifications from posts on Aquarius Social and Malice Media. Sighing, I lift the phone to see Alana posting on both platforms about her wedding. She's beautiful and has a million likes on both platforms, even though they have different functions. Then TimeGem Moments buzzes with a notification, and I click over to see Corinda dishing about the event. My step-sister gives a couple of digs to Alana, hints that Justice Beathach made a pass at her, and then flirts with the camera.

Rolling my eyes, I go back to my computer for a few more minutes until my phone dings with a call this time. I answer without looking away from the screen. "Yeah?"

"Ella, it's Wesley. You disappeared on me. Is everything all right?"

I forgot about my date to the wedding. "I had to deal with something for work." I catch another flicker of the false crystal code. This didn't come from

Aquarius—somebody has hacked their system. An outsider. It's not just an intrusion. It's a rewrite. If they manage to blend this synthetic pattern with Aquarius Social's original structure, the entire shielding network could be compromised. Dang it. I can't let this hacker take down Alana's platform.

"I was heading to the diner," Wesley says. "Didn't eat at the wedding. Want to meet?"

My stomach growls. I haven't eaten all day. I hesitate, watching the diagnostic algorithm begin to crawl through the compromised sectors. It'll take at least twenty-four hours to complete the scan. Should I tell him somebody has infiltrated his system? He'll patch it and I won't be able to use my own hack to tunnel toward the TimeGem servers. I'm starting to dislike myself. "Yeah, I can be there in twenty minutes."

"Perfect."

I end the call and lock down my equipment, stash my encrypted drives, and slip a static disruptor into my bag. The diner's only a few blocks away. It's secure and located on neutral ground. I'm not in the mood for surprises, but if they come, I'll be ready.

There's no time to overthink. I throw on a pair of jeans, a plain black T-shirt, and an old gray hoodie. My knife goes into the front pocket. It's well-balanced and easy to reach. I don't carry anything I can't use quickly.

I lock up the safe house, moving fast through the soft rain with my hood covering my head. I've got several cars stashed around Silicon Valley, all scrubbed and clean. I head for the closest, which is an unremarkable gray Volkswagen Bug parked in a back alley two blocks away. It starts on the first try.

I drive through the quiet streets of Palo Alto, heading south toward the edge of the industrial district. At this hour, everything has a washed-out, artificial glow. Most of the Valley is asleep. The real work happens under it.

The place isn't just a diner. Not really. It's called Plot Twist, and it's a twenty-four-hour techno bar hidden behind a fake bakery front. You don't find it unless you know the entry code and the right way to knock. Inside, the lighting is dim and ambient, the tables are old steel server racks repurposed into booths, and the place always smells faintly of ozone and fried eggs.

Pumpkins and fall leaves decorate the interior of the place, giving it that cozy autumn vibe.

I hustle in and spot Wesley right away. He's seated at the back in a semi-private booth, facing the door. Tugging off my hood and shaking rain off my arms, I move toward him.

He smiles. There's an ease to him that makes it hard not to relax, even now. He's always been fun to be around, but tonight I like him more than usual. There's something steady about him, even when everything else in my world feels unstable. I wish I could tell him the full truth.

I hurry toward him and take a seat, slightly breathless.

"I missed dancing with you," he murmurs.

"We danced." A couple of times, but the only songs I remember are the ones I danced with Justice. What is it about that guy? My clit perks right up at the thought of him. What is wrong with me?

As if reading my mind, Wesley frowns. "Is there something going on between you and Justice Beathach?"

"No." I sigh. "I'm sorry I danced with him." My clit throbs in total protest, but I ignore that bitch. "He was rather insistent. It won't happen again." Not that I owe Wesley an explanation. We just started dating and spend more time talking code than kissing.

The waitress bops up, smiling at Wesley, nodding at me. We both order the breakfast special and she takes off on high-tops, her legs long beneath a short skirt. I don't love how she looked at Wesley, but I like her pink hair a lot.

"She's cute," I murmur.

"Who?"

Okay, that's sweet. He didn't even notice the waitress. Wesley deserves somebody better than me, considering I'm hacking into his system right now. Maybe that's why we haven't taken this thing very far. Instinctively we know it's a bad idea?

He takes my hand. "We need a vacation. A destination one. Somewhere sunny with tropical drinks and nude beaches."

Nude beaches? This is a surprise. His hand is warm on mine. "We both have a lot going on."

"I want more. Between us. Everything." He smiles. "Don't worry. I'll plan the entire week." His phone dings. He pulls it out and reads the message. "Damn it."

"What?" I ask.

"Somebody just tried to breach Aquarius Social's servers. Our automated perimeter scan flagged an internal access attempt."

I freeze. My brain does a rapid check of the breadcrumbs I might've left behind. I was careful. I was *very* careful. But the algorithm I used was a variation of the one I've used a few times before. If it bounced wrong, it might've tripped something in the larger system. "Do you need any help dealing with the problem?"

He looks at me across the table. His expression is calm, but I can tell he's weighing every word. "You know we don't cross that line."

I blink, trying to keep my expression neutral. "I don't know why not. Alana's my best friend. I'd be happy to help."

"Yeah," he says quietly, "but we both know you're going to take over TimeGem Moments the second you can, and I'm going to help you do that."

I raise an eyebrow.

"Once you succeed and own the platform again," he continues, "we become competitors. And that's fine. I'm not afraid of the fight. But we need to keep our personal and professional lives separate, at least for now."

I nod slowly, but my mind is still on the breach. If it wasn't me, then someone else is in the system, moving through the same digital tunnels I've been testing. Which means this thing is bigger than I thought, and it just got a lot more complicated. I let out a quiet chuckle. "Fine. Fair enough. I'll get the bill."

"You will not," he says. "I'll pay on my way out..."

I start to argue, but he raises a hand. I let it go.

He watches me for a second, his brow drawn tight. "I can give you a ride," he says. "I don't like you out alone this late."

"Please," I reply. "Nobody knows I'm here. I'm in jeans and a hoodie since I changed out of the ball gown hours ago. I look like half the women in the Valley. No one's going to recognize me."

He looks down at me, jaw tight, then shakes his head once. "You really don't know, do you?"

I blink. "Know what?"

He doesn't look away. "Ella, you're very memorable. You're probably one of the most beautiful women I've ever seen."

For a second, I don't react. Then I laugh, quiet and reflexive. "All five feet of me?"

I think of Alana, with her model height and mythic bone structure. Rosalie, with that slow-burning elegance that turns heads just by walking into a room. I'm cute. Efficient. Quick on my feet. I've never thought of myself as the one who draws a second look.

"Wow," he says. "You really don't see yourself." Before I can respond, he leans over and kisses me. His lips are warm and steady, not rushed. His hand brushes my jaw, and it's a sweet touch that doesn't go behind my chin. Nowhere near my zones that had lit earlier for Justice. Wesley pulls back just enough to speak. "I'd invite you over, but if we were hacked tonight, I'll be stuck working for hours."

"I know," I say, settling back. "I actually need to get back to work shortly." I have to make sure I wasn't the one who triggered the alert. If I wasn't, then whoever planted that other code is back, and I'd love to trace the hack back to them.

If they're even one step ahead of me, we've already got a problem.

I think about calling Justice because his servers might also be in danger. For half a second. Then I shut the thought down. That would be a disaster. He'd want answers and would start pulling levers I don't want touched. If he discovers what I've been working on, he'll make a move before I have a chance to finish.

"Be careful," Wesley murmurs, his attention already

drifting to whatever system he's mentally dissecting. "I'll plan that vacation where we can get serious. About us. Not computers." His fingers twitch like he's pulling code apart in his head. He moves away, already lost in thought when he reaches the door.

Maybe I shouldn't be dating someone who thinks like I do. The overlap is too much. There's no balance. Just two people quietly trying to outmaneuver the same world. Besides, do I want to spend a week nude on a beach with Wesley? I can't even think about that right now.

My food arrives, and I dive into the eggs. They're decent—hot, salty, and solid. I barely get three bites in before the air shifts.

A shadow cuts across the edge of my plate. Every nerve in my body lights up. I don't have to look up to know who is now sitting across from me.

I lift my gaze anyway.

"Hello, Sprite," Justice says, his voice gravelly low. "You and I need to have a little talk."

FIVE

Ella

I flush. Heat sears across my chest, climbs up my neck, then fades, leaving me cold. Then it hits again, a wave of something else that's stronger than nerves and sharper than fear. It's heat again. No, it's hunger, and not for the eggs in front of me.

Justice fills the booth across from me like he was built for it—broad shoulders pressing against the vinyl, legs spread in a way that dares me to look anywhere but at his eyes. Wesley has size. This is different. Justice *owns* space. He controls it. Every inch of him is measured power, wrapped in something too dark to name.

I stab my fork into another bite of eggs, but they taste like cardboard now. Figures. "How do you know about this place?" I keep my tone casual, even though nothing inside me feels remotely calm.

One of his dark brows arches, slow and deliberate. He studies me like he's considering where to sink in his teeth. "I know every place in this town."

I believe him.

For years, he's been the shadow behind Thorn. The invisible hand no one talked about because no one even knew he existed. Not most people, anyway.

I did.

I'm a hacker. One of the best. I was born into one of the four main families, and information is what we breathe. Even so, I'd only seen traces of him in digital echoes that didn't make sense. But nothing prepared me for the man sitting across from me now.

He's lethal in a way no code could predict.

The kind of danger you don't see until it's already in your bloodstream.

I cough. "As one of the most eligible bachelors alive, shouldn't you be out and about? Getting your picture taken?"

His chin lowers. "I'm having trouble finding the miscreant who nominated me to that magazine, and more importantly, sent the picture they used for the spread. When I find that person, they're going to bleed." He sits back. "It wasn't you, was it?"

I snort. "I wish. I've spent so much time in the shadows I wouldn't have thought to drag you out of them." But I'll shake the hand of the person who did. If they're ever found.

"Humph." He wears black like it's part of his skin in a simple shirt stretched across his chest beneath a battered brown leather jacket. It's a definite departure from the tux he wore earlier, and yet, both seem at home on his muscled form.

His hands are relaxed now, but I've heard of his capabilities with them, and not in a good way. The man is a killer. His copper-flecked eyes don't bother to hide that fact, but his cut features, sharp and strong, would steal any woman's attention.

Not this one. I can't afford to lose my edge with him. Trying to appear casual, I brush my hair away from my eyes. Blonde strands fall forward again anyway—too soft, too light for a moment like this. I lean into the seat, spine straightening. "All right, Justice. Let's have it out."

My voice sounds steady. Too steady. My heart's crashing around my ribs like it's looking for an exit.

"Gladly," he murmurs, low and deliberate.

The word settles somewhere between my stomach and my spine. I take a breath and know I'm going to need help getting away from him. So I shift my weight, drop my hand, and press a button on my phone that's programmed to do what I need. "Are you going to try to kill me?" Wanting to read him, I meet his gaze. Direct. Unblinking. I don't flinch, even when I notice the odd metallic glint in his irises. Not just reflection. Not lighting. Something real.

"That's a direct question." He's human. Definitely. But human doesn't mean ordinary.

I studied eyes once when I became obsessed with the way power interacts with biology. Why some people can draw charge from crystals, why others can't. I mapped out pigmentation, rare mutations, and anomalies.

"So answer it. Do you want to kill me?" I can't quit studying him. Justice's eyes shouldn't exist. They hold layers. Depths. Power that doesn't just reflect but stores. Why hasn't he put me out of commission? It has to be because of Alana, his new sister-in-law. I hope.

"Do you think I want to kill you?" His voice sounds

flat. Not bored. Not curious. Just steady. He could be asking about the weather or what kind of coffee I like. No threat in his tone. No comfort either. But he watches every twitch of my expression, and I'm giving him too much. "Ella?"

I need to get my face under control. "I have no idea." I keep my tone steady. "But if you are going to attempt my murder, could you at least have the balls to tell me?"

He doesn't blink or shift in his seat. But something changes. I feel it. Not in him, but in the air between us, which is denser now. Tighter. Maybe it's the word *balls*. That one always hits. Men either flinch or smirk.

He does neither. "If I decide to kill you, Ella, I promise that I'll tell you beforehand."

My breath catches. Just for a second. I ease it out with a slow exhale and pray my chest doesn't give me away. "So you'll tell me a week in advance? A day? Two seconds?" I let the sarcasm bleed through.

He almost smiles.

The hint of humor does not comfort me.

He rests his arm on the back of the booth, stretching his impressive chest. "I don't know. What do you want? Twenty-four-hour notice?"

"I'd like a week."

"I'll give you two days." He drops his arm and leans forward slightly. "If I decide to kill you, I'm giving you that much of a warning." His words are a quiet promise, spoken with complete certainty. His lips twitch again. The movement is barely noticeable but enough to confirm he finds some part of this exchange entertaining or useful. That's good.

I'm fine amusing him if it keeps him off my back, but I do like to know where I stand. "Is this about revenge? Because I almost killed your brother?"

"No. My brother survived, and you helped save him." Justice's voice lacks gratitude, and his tone is final. His expression remains unreadable. "It's a protection issue," he says. "I can't have you doing it again."

"What if I promise I won't?"

"I don't believe you."

Fair enough. We don't really know each other. I chew the inside of my cheek. I don't lie often. Not because I have any moral high ground. I just prefer control, and lies unravel control. "I don't trust you, either."

"Let's see if you can be truthful. Why did you hack into the Aquarius Social mainframe after the wedding?" His gaze sharpens. "You care about Alana," he says. "She is still connected to Aquarius, even if she married Thorn."

"I'd appreciate it if you didn't tell her." The last thing in the world I want Alana worrying about while she's on her very deserved honeymoon is the oncoming threat for us all. Somebody else has definitely infiltrated her system. If I take care of the breach before she returns, she never needs to know about it.

Justice leans back without breaking eye contact. He's still reading me. Still tracking every shift in my breathing.

The waitress appears beside our booth. She's slightly out of breath and clearly overwhelmed, yet has plenty of time to run her gaze over Justice's body. She hums. "Sorry for the wait. The five-top in the corner is keeping me busy. What can I get you?"

"Coffee," he says. His attention never leaves me.

She reaches for my plate, *her* attention not leaving him. "Are you finished?"

"I am," I say to the side of her head.

"Great." She collects the plate and disappears again.

I don't trust Justice. Not now. Not ever. He'll always act in the best interest of Malice Media. If the other three media companies collapse, I'm sure he'll treat the devastation as useful data. Yes, I'm tempted to tell him the truth about a fifth player making a move against Aquarius and probably the rest of us as well. But he might use that against my company if it serves his interest.

He taps his fingers on the worn table. "Ella? I'm not going to ask you again. Why are you hacking into Aquarius Social when your best friend is on her honeymoon?"

I love that Alana is safe and know that Thorn will destroy anybody coming for her. "I'm not going to discuss Aquarius Social or Alana with you."

"You are," Justice replies. His certainty moves through me with impact, and his statement sounds more like an observation than a threat.

"No, I'm not. Not right now."

His expression doesn't shift. His presence weighs on the space between us, and his attention drills into every breath I take. There's no point pretending I'm unaffected.

Heat builds in my cheeks. The warmth hits before I can stop it.

He tilts his head slightly. "Why are you blushing?"

"I'm not. I'm warm."

He rubs his shoulder, clearly annoyed. "Quit lying to me. I don't like it."

"I don't like it either," I admit. "But you and I aren't on the same side."

"We could be."

I stay quiet. It's the only move that doesn't backfire immediately.

"What if I hired you to work at Malice?" he asks.

"You're going to give me access to your servers?"

His eyes glitter. "No. I need a personal assistant."

I rear back and then note the glimmer. I really *am* amusing him. "I didn't know you had a sense of humor."

"I'm hilarious." He reaches into his pocket and pulls something out—my damaged heel. The one I lost when I hit the ground and didn't look back. "I suppose you want this back."

I take it from him, turning it over in my hand. Sequins still cling to the strap, but the heel is bent nearly sideways. "Yeah. I think I can fix it."

He frowns like that's the most impractical thing he's heard all week. "Why don't you just buy a new pair?"

"Funds are tight." I shrug. "My stepmother finally managed to cut off my trust fund. At least for now."

"Bribed a judge?"

That seems the most likely scenario. "I think so."

"Do you want me to take care of it?"

My mouth dries instantly. I swallow once, twice, and take a long sip of water to cover the third. "In exchange for what?"

His gaze drops—slow, deliberate. I feel it track over the hoodie and down. "I think we could come up with something."

Was that an offer or a threat? My body can't tell the

difference. Electrical sparks zing through me. I need to get them under control.

Two of my best friends are tangled up with the most dangerous men alive. I don't need to collect a third. Especially not when I'm still dating Wesley. I have to keep remembering that. The fact that I have to remind myself isn't a great sign.

"What did you get from Aquarius's servers tonight?" Justice asks.

"Nothing," I say honestly. "Yet. I'm in, but I haven't found what I want."

He glances at the five-top near the far wall. "What do you want?"

"I'm not going to tell you that."

"You are, sweetheart."

The waitress sets the coffee down between us and lingers for a moment, finally turning away when he doesn't acknowledge her.

He takes a long sip, then pulls a fifty from his pocket and slides it under the cup. "All right, Ella," he says, voice low and even. "Let's go."

"I'm not going with you." I keep my tone flat, not letting him see the way my pulse kicks. Where is my backup? I pressed the code in minutes ago.

He grins, slow and lazy, then glances around the diner. "You think anyone's going to stop me? You can walk or you can be carried. Totally up to you, princess."

"Why?"

"I'm locking you down." His voice is calm. Almost polite. Like this is standard procedure. He even sounds a little sorry about it, which somehow makes it worse. He's absolutely confident.

My head snaps up. "No, you're not. You're not locking me anywhere."

"You going to fight me now?" He perks up slightly, like he'd enjoy it.

The door opens, and two police officers walk in—young, fresh-faced, and too clean-cut for this neighborhood. Finally. Geez.

Justice doesn't flinch, but his gaze flicks toward them. Measuring.

I sigh and look toward the officers. They're not seasoned, not like the ones who left when the city started to rot from the inside. But they wear the badge. The first walks over to a waitress and whispers something.

She looks around and shrugs as if there's no problem and she has no clue who called them.

I did. Well, I sent a coded message that there was a problem in the diner. They'd taken longer to arrive than I'd expected. "Excuse me, officer," I call out, voice pitched just right, not with fear, but with concern.

The guy next to the waitress looks up and heads toward me. He can't be more than twenty-two and has dark hair and blue eyes. He's clean-cut in a textbook way. "Did you send out a distress call, ma'am?"

I don't look at Justice, but anger swells across the table.

Ma'am? What a cutie patootie. "No, I haven't called anybody." True statement. "But since you're here, I'm hoping you can assist me?" I open my eyes wider.

His hand on his holstered weapon, he turns and scans the entire diner before focusing back on me. "It looks like our call was a false alarm. What can I do for you?"

I shrug as helplessly as I can. "Well, I heard there were a couple of robberies around here. I was hoping one of you would walk me to my vehicle. I mean, since you're already here."

His gaze shifts toward Justice. "Of course." He squares his shoulders.

"Thank you. My friend isn't finished with his coffee." I look at Justice.

His eyes glitter. I know how dangerous he is and can even see the math in his potential movements. He could take out everyone in the room if he decided to make a statement. Yet that would cause all sorts of problems for him.

"Nice move," he mutters under his breath.

"Thank you." I stand, slipping the damaged heel into my pocket.

He doesn't move. "I'm going to see you real soon, Ella. I promise."

My smile wavers. "Looking forward to it." I turn before I can hesitate, stepping toward the cop. "I really appreciate this, officer."

"You can call me John." He gives Justice one more look and then gestures toward the door. "I'll walk you out, miss."

"Thank you." I keep my steps quick but steady. I have a healthy fear that Justice will be behind me the second that door swings closed. I'm not ready for what will happen when he catches me.

SIX
Justice

I knock back the last of the Irish whiskey, let it burn its way down, and place the glass on the older wood. The sound it makes is sharper than I intend, but Fergus doesn't look up from the other side of the desk. He keeps typing, fingers rattling over keys like he's beating them into submission.

We're in the back office of the Blood Garnet Pub. The air is thick with old smoke, wood polish, and whatever the hell soaked into the floorboards over the years. The radiator coughs like it's dying in the corner, but it still pushes out heat that settles under my skin and stays there. The walls are stained paneling, yellowed at the corners. There's a file cabinet with a dent the size of a fist and a ceiling fan that clicks in slow circles, doing nothing but reminding me how long it's been since I fixed the place. I built the pub to be a front, but it's been too profitable to ignore.

Fergus is hunched over his laptop. He's sixty-five,

maybe older, but looks closer to ninety. His skin's worn down to the grain, and his comb-over is offensive in a way that feels intentional. Like he's daring someone to bring it up.

He glances at me without pausing in his work, his eyes squinty and bloodshot, the blue faded to that color plastic gets when it's been in the sun too long. "The pubs all look good. We're going to show a ten percent increase in profits from last year."

I nod, but I'm not hearing him. Not really. I'm still in the diner. Still watching Ella walk out with a cop and a lie pasted across her face. I could've stopped her. Dragged her back, cleared the room, made a point no one would forget. But the timing was wrong. Too many witnesses, too many risks. And she knew that. She played me clean.

The problem is, I don't know if I'm pissed at her for outmaneuvering me, or at myself for letting her. I'll deal with her before Thorn comes home.

"Justice? I'm thinking we should open at least twenty more pubs this year. I know you thought we'd just use them as fronts, but we're making real money now." Fergus speaks in Gaelic, and with the softer sound of the language, nothing in my body hurts from listening to his voice. That's rare.

"Fine by me. I assume you have locations?" I invested in my first pub before I could legally drink and moved on to the next, then the next after that, each one a piece of structure, leverage, and shelter. These pubs span across cities and countries now, and every one of them serves more than alcohol. They provide cover, information, and access. But apparently the alcohol is making me even wealthier. Who knew?

"I have several proposed locations, about fifty of them. But the smart play is to open twenty at the most this year." He pushes his spectacles up his nose. "You'd need to look at each location, and I don't want to pull you from Malice Media if Thorn is going to take some time away from the company."

"He'll be back in six weeks." Which gives me a limited time to figure out what Ella's virus did to me and fix it. Malice Media runs on neural interface technology capable of transmitting emotion, memory, and raw experience across distance without delay. It can take a thought in one city and deliver it fully formed in another. My brother created the architecture, and it's brilliant.

Garnets have always responded to me, and the fact that Ella has fucked with that is pissing me off again. She somehow disrupted my current with the gemstone.

A knock hits the door, hard and fast.

"What?" I call out.

Bronco, my chief driver, pushes the door open and steps inside. "Hey. We just got word that our shipments have been delayed by about a week."

I stare at him. "Which ones?"

He doesn't flinch. His black hair frames a rugged face with Irish blue eyes. If we need to send someone in to seduce a woman, we send him. "The garnets and alexandrites coming by sea. Bad weather and nothing else, it seems. Still, I wanted you to know."

I stand and step away from the desk. My spine locks into place. With how I'm feeling, I need those stones sooner rather than later.

We keep garnets fresh, stocked, and accessible because they anchor every system we run. But alexandrite is rarer, less stable. Its energy is different. Our R&D teams are still studying the neural response patterns, but even early trials have shown results. If we can use the alexandrite to extend garnet charge time or even amplify output, it could change the pace of interface use entirely.

The science is still early, but I've seen the preliminary data. Faster emotional compression. Sharper memory echoes. Extended cognitive sharing. I'm sure the other social media companies are also conducting similar research.

"All right. I want to check on our properties," I say. We head toward the front door. One of my men is already waiting, standing to the side and ready. He hands me my Glock without needing to be asked. I take it and slide it into the holster at my side.

I check my watch. The data feed lights up as expected, synced with the surveillance reports. I scroll through two updates quickly. "Ella's back at the house on Elm?" I ask as I step outside into a suddenly drilling rain.

"Yes," Bronco says. He moves ahead of me and opens the back door of the town car. "She arrived twenty-three minutes ago. I have a man on the house."

"Good," I say. "Have him call if she moves."

He nods and taps something on his phone.

I slide into the car and shut the door behind me. I don't like how easily I tracked her. She either wants to be found or she doesn't understand the stakes.

Neither option sits well with me.

For now, I have to act like the head of the Irish mob and hold everything together. It'd be a hell of a lot easier if I were at full strength. I need to get everything in order so I have time to heal myself . . . with Ella Rendale's help, whether she likes it or not.

Ella

The click of the keys is sharp in the quiet. I type fast, my gaze locked on the stream of code climbing across the screen. I'm deep inside Aquarius Social's mainframe now, chasing threads Wesley probably didn't think I'd find. I spot his signal ghosting mine, and for a second, I let him think he's gaining ground.

Then I flip the switch. Reroute. Bury. Move deeper.

He's good. One of the best.

But I'm better.

I should feel bad about this, considering we've been on a couple of dates and all, but I don't. I like the challenge. It's like playing chess with someone who actually knows how to think three moves ahead. Most people don't. Most people only see what's right in front of them.

My mind shifts to Justice and the anger in his eyes as I'd left earlier with the police officer. Oh, I know Justice could've stopped us. But he didn't. Getting in trouble with the law the second Thorn leaves town would've been a bad move.

I try not to smile.

Rain starts a pattern against the windows, soft and rhythmic. I barely register the sound. This is one of my favorite safe houses, tucked into a cul-de-sac on Elm Street. Every house around me has that worn-down charm that says its residents don't have neighborhood picnics. Retired couples. A few single professionals who work from home. No kids. No teenagers. A couple of lazy dogs. Maybe a cat or two.

I've been thinking about getting a cat, but I need to make sure I'm going to live long enough to take care of one. Between my stepmother and now Justice coming after me, it doesn't feel like the right time to add responsibilities.

Plus, I've found life is easier without ties or love. Yeah, I have Alana and Rosalie, but we formed ties as kids. That's different. It's too late not to love them.

Wesley makes a move that's both sneaky and clever. He reroutes traffic across three fake nodes to distract me, maybe hoping I'll get cocky and follow. I don't take the bait. I tap out a quick counter, slipping into a shadow relay he left open by accident or out of arrogance. I'm not sure which. It slows him down just long enough for me to go deeper. Past the firewalls. Past the audit logs. Into the bones of the system most people don't know exist. Does he have any idea he's chasing me?

This is Aquarius Social's mainframe, Wesley's territory. He built a lot of this, but he didn't build all of it, and some of what's here doesn't look like him. My earlier hack has finally uncovered more of this one.

I pause.

There's a cluster of code tucked deep inside a rarely accessed corner. It's not his style and seems too modular, too insulated. Tendrils of data branch off like veins, pulsing with activity. But it's not just timestamp manipulation or data masking. This is something else. A high-level relay, maybe. Something designed to cross domains.

A path.

My eyes narrow. The encrypted pathway is hidden and running from Aquarius into a completely different system. TimeGem Moments. *My* company.

This penetration is farther along than I expected, the

hacker expertly manipulating the Aquarius Social servers to infiltrate TimeGem. It's genius, really.

Oh, my stepmother thinks she owns the infrastructure, and she guards it like a dragon hoarding gold. No one touches it without clearance, and even then, access is layered in redundancies and biometric fail safes.

I just found a way directly into TimeGem's systems. I've been working on a way for years, and here it might be. My breath catches. I lean forward, fingers hovering over the keys until I expertly create a firewall strong enough to hide this path from Wesley. Who is this hacker? I need to decrypt the signature and confirm the path. Maybe extend it.

The air around me changes.

I pause, fingers stilling.

The feeling around me is subtle. There's a drop in pressure or a shift in the air current. We all have instincts forged by our ancestors in order to survive, and even now, they kick in for us—if we pay attention.

I lift my head to listen. The house is a single level with one bedroom, a small kitchen, and an open living room with creaky floorboards and a vintage couch I picked up for eighty bucks. The bathroom is my favorite part. It has a massive clawfoot tub, deep enough to drown in. I spend a lot of nights in that tub when the world feels too heavy.

But something's off now. I stand slowly and reach for the knife block next to me on the counter. My fingers wrap around the steel handle, second from the right. The weapon is balanced, sharp, and easy to throw.

Standing as quietly as possible, I take careful steps toward the bedroom.

The rain gets louder.

A window is open. I know I shut it. I always shut it.

"Shit," I whisper, pivoting to run.

A man lunges from behind the door with brutal speed and weight, his movement sudden and overwhelming. He's tall and broad, wrapped head to toe in tactical gear. A black balaclava covers his face. His eyes shine violet through what I assume are tinted contacts, and he smells faintly of mint.

No warning. No words. I want to scream but don't waste the air.

His arms wrap around me, and I react on instinct. My knife slices up, aiming for his shoulder. He jerks away just enough to avoid a fatal hit, but the blade sinks into muscle. Warmth splashes across my hand. He grunts, low and surprised.

I twist, elbow him in the throat, but his arm comes around fast, his closed fist hitting my shoulder. I fly into the wall. Pain flashes through my ribs. My shoulder knocks a ceramic dragon off its hook, and it crashes to the floor. I barely register the damage.

He charges again.

Panic rips through me and I kick. My foot connects with his shin, and he stumbles, giving me just enough time to rip the knife free of his arm and stab again. This time I duck and go lower, catching his thigh and tearing out the knife. He hisses and backhands me across the face.

My vision explodes into stars. Pain blooms in my temple. I smash into an end table, knocking off the contents, and then hit the floor, breath whooshing out of me. My jaw throbs. He's fast. Strong. Professional. There isn't time to talk and see if there's a way out of this mess.

I roll as he lunges again, and my hand connects with the base of the now-broken lamp. It's heavy. I grab it and swing upward with everything I've got. The base cracks against his head with a dull, wet thud. He stumbles and staggers back.

My entire body hurts, but I move fast. Panicking. I push off the floor, my legs barely cooperating. I'm dizzy, bleeding. My cheek's swelling, but I don't care. I limp through the house, knife still in one hand, the other clutching my side. I can't afford to slow down.

The rain pummels me as I burst outside, grunting and sobbing. It's cold and relentless, soaking me to the skin in seconds. I half run, half stumble down the driveway, past the hedges I trimmed myself last week. I have to get to one of the hidden cars. My feet hit the edge of the concrete, and my knees give out.

I drop. Holy ouch, damn it.

The pavement is hard beneath me. Rain splashes against my back and soaks my hair. My palms scrape the asphalt, and my breath comes in ragged bursts. I try to get up. I can't. Fear tastes sharp and metallic on the back of my tongue. Everything tilts.

My body pitches forward, and I fall hard, cheek planting against the wet ground.

Pulling in breath, I push to my hands and knees to crawl around the side of the hedges.

Crashes come from inside the house. I might've slowed the attacker down, but he isn't out. Tears slide down my face, blurring my vision even more. I have to get out of here.

The front door hits the wall.

Gasping, I lunge away from the small shrubs and scramble toward the street, where I smash into a hard body out of the darkness.

Crying out, I fall onto my back, my head clunking against the torn driveway. I'm going to die.

The body moves, and a shadow crosses over me. A heavy hand touches my shoulder. "Sorry about that. Are you all right?" a voice asks, dark and calm.

I blink. There's water in my eyes. Rain and tears. My vision swims. I look up just enough to catch a face—dark hair, blue eyes. The voice has an edge to it. Not American.

"He's coming," I croak.

The man looks up, draws a weapon from his side, and fires three times. Small pops. Barely loud enough to cut through the rain. Did he just save me? The question barely goes through my brain when a broad hand brings down the butt of a gun onto my savior's head. His eyes widen and blood slides down his face. He falls to the side.

How many attackers are out here in the stormy night?

I struggle, fighting the darkness, but with the rain slamming against me, I close my eyes again and then actually feel my body go limp. Unconscious.

SEVEN
Ella

A smell awakens me, and I'm in a comfortable bed. The scent is sharp and oddly comforting, a strange blend of minty air freshener and lavender. I breathe out evenly, unsure why that combination makes my brain twitch.

Beep. Beep. Beep.

A high, mechanical chirping bounces above my head. I crack my eyes open.

Everything around me is white. Not the sterile white I'd expect from a hospital, but a soft, designer white. The walls and counters are beige and gold-trimmed, like someone decorated this place for a magazine shoot and decided to toss a wounded woman into the middle of it for drama.

I glance down. A plush white blanket covers me, warmed and tucked. My head feels like someone used it for bocce ball practice. My vision swims, then slowly sharpens.

My stepmother sits in a chair next to the bed, ankles crossed, perfectly still, and her floral perfume wafts my way. Her nails are flawless, manicured in pale pink. Her expression is one of mild amusement, like this is a casual brunch and not a hospital room where I just woke up with half my brain rattling loose.

My lungs spasm. I gasp.

"Relax." Sylveria Rendale lifts one of those perfect hands in a dismissive wave. "If I wanted you dead, you'd be dead."

She's not wrong. I fumble around until I find the remote attached to the side of the bed and smash the button. The motor whines as the bed creaks upright, and I press a shaking palm to my temple, trying to catch up. "What the hell happened?"

Sylveria tilts her head like she's examining a piece of fruit she's not sure she wants to buy. Her newest hairdo is a straight brunette cut with not a strand out of place, and her suit—a pink linen number, pants and jacket with a matching shell—looks like it stepped out of a *Vogue* spread. Unwrinkled. Immaculate. How does she wear linen without causing one wrinkle?

"Apparently someone tried to kill you," she says. "Another man waiting for you shot him. My guy hit that guy in the head and brought you here. It seems like you have more than one enemy after you. You're welcome."

I blink. It's rare for me to be speechless, but right now, in a luxury hospital suite with Sylveria fucking Rendale lounging next to me like this is normal, I find myself struggling for words. I swallow. "I'm going to need more than that."

"That's all I've got, dear." Her tone is syrupy and smug.

I narrow my eyes. "Didn't you try to have me killed just a short time ago?"

She waves a hand, somehow managing to look elegant even as she brushes off an attempted murder. "Oh, please. It was one little hit. I don't think there's any reason to get too upset. It failed, as you know."

"Yeah," I mutter. "I'm still here." Though honestly, it feels like my body went five rounds in the NBA as a basketball.

Why would Sylveria save me and then sit here in the hospital as if watching over me? She hates me. A diamond necklace clings to her throat and matches the six-string bracelet on her wrist as well as three thick rings glittering on her fingers. Sylveria Rendale truly loves her diamonds. She wears them like armor.

I shake my head and immediately regret it. Pain lights up my skull like someone cracked it with a bat. "Why did you have somebody bring me to the hospital? We both know you want me dead."

She tilts her head. "Oh, dear. Would you stop being so dramatic?" She sounds like she might be frowning, but her Botoxed forehead stays unlined. No movement, no expression. Sylveria is a gorgeous woman. Still in her forties, her eyes are a piercing, unnerving blue, and her bone structure is straight out of a sculpture. I'm almost certain she's had some work done, but not the overdone kind. Just enough to make her face unforgettable.

I can see what my father saw in her.

Too bad she's also a monster. As beautiful as she is poisonous.

My gaze drops to my arms. No straps. No restraints. But I'm not stupid. If I know Sylveria, and unfortunately I do, there are guards just outside the door. She wouldn't risk letting me wake up without backup. I try to banish the reasonable fear coursing through me. "What do you want?" My voice shakes, but not enough to count me out. I'm in a hospital bed after being knocked unconscious, so I figure I get a pass.

The memories slam into me without warning. The man in my safe house. His shadow, the hit, the scuffle. Blood. Darkness. Then the guy outside shooting him.

I gasp. My heart kicks against my ribs. "What happened to the guy who attacked me in the house?" I try to read anything in that cold, lovely face. "Is he dead?"

"No. You didn't kill him, and neither did the bullets he took outside," Sylveria says, her tone flat, almost disinterested. "My people have escorted him somewhere secure."

I stare at her, waiting for more, but she just smooths the leg of her linen pants like this is all routine. "Great. I don't suppose you'll tell me what you discover after they torture him." I fold my arms over the blanket. "I'd really like to know who he is, considering it clearly wasn't you who sent him. Who else wants me dead?"

She smiles, but it doesn't reach her eyes. They remain as cold as polished sapphire left in an Arctic freezer. "I assume quite a few people want you dead, Ella, so let's not play that kind of game."

I don't know what game she thinks we're playing, but I'm in no condition to argue. Especially not while wearing a hospital gown and nothing else, sitting under high-thread-count sheets, while Sylveria probably has three concealed weapons tucked inside her designer purse.

The bag is unmistakably Hermes in a limited edition, no doubt. Pale rose leather, sharp-edged and impractical. I have to admire it, even though I hate that I do. I'm not up to leaping for it and grabbing a weapon, so I look around the room. There's no clock. No window. No way to gauge time. I pause, then give in. "How long have I been here?"

"You've been out for three hours," she says, her voice lowering just a tad. Am I inconveniencing her? "It took my associate maybe thirty minutes to get you here. The doctor said you have a mild concussion and quite a lot of bruising." Her tone softens, not with compassion, but interest. "I'm impressed. You put up a good fight."

I don't answer her. I'm absurdly glad I didn't kill the guy. Oh, most folks think I'm a murderer, or an attempted one, anyway. I'm not. I actually didn't mean to hurt Thorn to the degree I did.

She taps a ring against the chair arm once before adding, "We will find out who he is. My people are . . . very thorough."

I don't doubt that. Sylveria Rendale doesn't waste time or resources. If someone tried to kill me and it wasn't on her orders, she'll dig up everything. "I want to know."

"Of course. For now, I obviously saved your life." Sylveria brushes the diamond choker at her neck. "So you owe me."

My mind blanks for a second. I try to rewind, to find something in the fog behind my eyes. Then I see the moment with the rain slicking the driveway, a figure outside the house, a hand on my shoulder. He asked if I was okay in an Irish accent.

Was he one of Justice's men?

If so, who attacked me inside the house? It doesn't make sense. My gut says it wasn't Justice. If he wanted me dead, he wouldn't send someone. He'd show up and do it himself. I glance at Sylveria, who's still fiddling with her necklace. "Wait. You didn't take the guy from outside the house, too, did you?"

Her eyes flick briefly toward the window shade. Then back to me. "No."

Ah, I get it. "Your guy checked him out and found, what? An Irish mob tattoo on him?" I try to smile even though my whole face feels like it's been hit with a brick. "You didn't dare take one of Justice's soldiers."

"That's neither here nor there," she says. "As I said—we saved your life. Now you owe me." She shifts in the chair with an aristocratic grace that would fool most people. Not me. I know exactly where she came from. Sylveria Rendale might look like old money, but she crawled out of the backwoods of Kentucky. Beauty bought her a ticket to Silicon Valley, and my father, for reasons I will never understand, bought everything she was selling.

And here she is. Smug, polished, and smiling like the Queen of Versailles while I lie half broken in a hospital bed.

Curiosity has always been my downfall. "What do you want?" I haven't had time to fully hack the TimeGem system yet, so this isn't about that.

"It really doesn't matter." Sylveria straightens her jacket like this is a done deal. "Because as soon as the doctor releases you, you'll be coming home with me. I must make sure you're all right." Her voice is softer now, with that artificial calm she uses when she wants to sound maternal. Except she sounds more robotic than concerned. What is going on?

"Listen, Sylveria," I say, my voice cold, "if you were falling off a cliff, I'd record the whole event so I could replay your death over and over again when I need a little pick-me-up."

She exhales through her perfectly pink painted mouth. "You do need to grow up. I saved your life. You owe me, and you're coming with me. I have guards on the door and downstairs. You don't have a choice. So instead of throwing a fit, why don't you just behave for once?"

My fingers curl around the blanket. This is becoming tedious. She wants something, but I still don't know what, and the longer she stalls, the more that unknown gnaws at me. My brain spins with possibilities. "Don't tell me the diamonds aren't charging the TimeGem servers anymore, like they have for the last ten years."

"Of course they are," she replies with that fake-bright smile. "Diamonds are a girl's best friend."

I feel an almost physical urge to slap her just to see if her face will actually move. She's so tightly Botoxed, I doubt it. "Citrines are stronger," I say flatly. "TimeGem was built on citrine crystalline symmetry. Everyone's running AI now, and that means more drain. More demand. More power. You need citrines. You need me to charge them." I'm guessing, of course.

She doesn't deny it, but nothing in her expression confirms my hunch, either.

An image hits me like a punch: me chained to a server core, locked in a freezing room, forced to push energy through stone and wire forever while Sylveria and her board rake in the profits.

I'd rather starve.

Her eyes drift around the plush hospital suite. "We'll discuss it once we get you home. I do want to leave this unfortunate place."

My dislike sharpens into something uglier. But behind the anger is unease. What does she actually want? "Don't you think we should discuss the fact that you sent a hitman after me a few months ago?"

"I truly don't know what you're talking about," she lies without hesitation. "But for the record, I'm quite happy you're still alive. You do owe me for paying for your schooling all these years."

"Bullshit." I sit up straighter, ignoring the throb behind my eyes, and scan the room. There's no closet. No chair with my things. No indication that I ever had clothes here in the first place. My skin prickles. "Where are my clothes?"

She doesn't answer and just watches me with a slight smile.

"My father's trust paid for my schooling." I'm feeling ready to fight. "And just so you're aware, you'll be hearing from my attorney any day now."

That gets her attention. Barely. A flicker shows in her eyes.

"So far I've held Rosalie off from suing for the corpus," I continue. It was because I want access to the servers and don't want Sylveria to see me coming. This little kidnapping negates that plan, so I might as well put my cards on the table.

Her smile curves upward, smug and unbothered. "My attorneys are prepared."

"Mine's better."

"I'm not entirely sure it'll matter." She checks a diamond-encrusted watch on her wrist.

I hide a shiver. That doesn't sound good.

She clears her throat. "Your clothing should be here any

minute, along with your discharge papers. How annoying that they're late. I might have to have this doctor taken care of."

"Shut up," I mutter, not wanting my absent doctor to be hurt. I throw the blanket off my legs, the hospital gown shifting awkwardly around me. I don't care. "I'll walk out of here like this if I have to. I'm not going anywhere with you." My voice is sharp, but beneath it is fear. Real, cold fear.

The door opens and we both pause as Corinda and Stacia walk inside, coffees in their hands. Corinda gives one to her mother.

Stacia smiles at me. "I brought you one, but it's truly crappy."

I shake my head.

Corinda looks lovely in a green dress with Louboutin heels, while Stacia appears comfortable in a blue sweater with stylish jeans and cool brown boots. She still has the glittery silver bag over her arm. Must be her favorite.

Sylveria sips the coffee, grimaces, and turns to put the cup on the counter. "Gross. I was just telling your, ah, sister that she needs to come home. For her own safety."

Corinda places her cup next to her mother's and pulls out her phone. "We should post this."

"No." I hold up a hand. "Don't even think of posting me in this gown."

A loud thud echoes from the other side of the door. We all freeze. Slowly, in eerie unison, we turn our heads toward the sound. Another thud. Heavier this time. Closer.

Sylveria reaches into her purse.

The door instantly explodes inward. It's kicked open

with so much force it slams into the wall, bounces off, and nearly swings shut again from the impact.

Justice steps through.

He's tall, muscled, and bleeding from the corner of his mouth. The deep brown of his eyes glitters with what appears to be anger. Maybe rage. His dark hair is a mess, and his gaze locks onto Sylveria like she's the reason the world is on fire.

Corinda and Stacia both move toward the window and away from Justice.

I sneeze three times. Hard. Nerves?

Sylveria pivots, fast, pulling a silver handgun from her purse and aiming it at his chest.

He doesn't flinch. He tilts his head slightly. "All of your men are down," he says, voice flat. "All of mine are in their place. You sure you want to shoot me?"

EIGHT

Justice

I am far too relieved to see Ella standing in that ridiculous little pink hospital gown, legs bare. She's such a tiny thing. Long legs, though. Bare, bruised, scraped. Toes painted—neatly, even now. I clock the details, the fragile angles of her face, the ice-blue eyes, the ugly bruise riding her cheekbone.

Stacia and Corinda hover by the windows and out of my reach. Smart. Wait. Corinda has her phone out. "Put that away, or you won't like where I put it."

Her eyebrows rise, and then she slowly drops the phone into her purse. Good.

Then I shift my focus back to the gun pointed at me. "Put that away."

Sylveria Rendale looks far too comfortable holding it, no hesitation in her grip. She was probably born with a pearl-handled weapon in her hand. "I don't think so."

Her voice scrapes along my shoulder blades and oddly cuts between my toes like somebody trying to sharpen a knife there. It fucking hurts. I shrug once, remaining calm because I've already decided how this ends. "All your men are down. You shoot me, you die. It's truly pretty simple."

She frowns, but she's calculating, not panicking. "Are they dead?"

"No. You left mine alive at Ella's little safe house. I returned the favor."

"Oh." She keeps her composure. I'll give her that. Impressive, considering I'm one wrong twitch from putting her on the floor. Without a word, she slips the Smith & Wesson back into that absurd designer handbag like it's part of a brunch outfit. Elegant, polished, venomous. "Well," she says, schooling her features, "I saw no reason to kill your man. I believe he was trying to help her. I am worried about my stepdaughter, as you know."

Bullshit.

I truly don't have time for this. "I know you put a hit out on her. That failed. What I don't understand is why she's still breathing right now."

Stacia gasps, and Corinda cocks her head. Yeah, they're not in their mother's world.

Ella nods from next to the bed, sharp and emphatic. "Exactly. I'd like to know the same thing."

Sylveria lifts one toned shoulder, all casual elegance and fake concern. "As I said, she's my stepdaughter. It's my duty to protect her."

I shift my weight, noting how my shoulder blades feel better. Why? Even so, blood is drying on my jaw, and my patience is shot. The room smells like antiseptic and whatever designer crap Sylveria wears. "My man reported there was a fight in the house." I turn my full attention to Ella, my voice flat. "Who hurt you?"

She looks too pale in that thin little gown, her skin almost translucent under the soft light. I don't like seeing her this way. So fucking defenseless. I need to remember how much danger she actually poses. But every protective instinct I've got is wide awake and clawing through my ribs, and I really hate that she does this to me.

She lifts both hands, helpless. "I have no idea. If it wasn't your guys, and it wasn't Sylveria's, I'm truly not sure." She glances down and to the side on the word "sure." She's lying. Or not lying, exactly—just not saying everything. She has an idea, but she isn't certain.

"Who have you hacked lately?" I ask bluntly.

She pulls back like I slapped her.

I raise a hand. "Don't." I'm not in the mood. My jaw still aches from the third man of Sylveria's that I dropped in the hospital. The bastard had a decent right hook. He's unconscious now, which mollifies me slightly.

"I'm not lying." Ella strides away from the bed. Her movements are stiff but determined. "Where are my clothes?" She hovers there for a second. Small. Still half dressed in hospital linen, bruised and tired. But not broken.

"I told the doctor to bring you scrubs so I could take you home," Sylveria says, brushing imaginary lint off her sleeve.

I straighten. "She's not going anywhere with you."

"I say no." Ella frowns, crossing her arms like she thinks that settles it. She looks adorable and tousled. "I'm not going with either of you."

She's wrong, but I'm not about to argue with her. Her feet catch my attention again. That bubblegum-pink polish. My eyes keep drifting down to her toenails, and I hate that I keep noticing. I've never been a foot guy. Ella Rendale could change that. The thought is uninvited and irritating.

I straighten my shoulders, forcing my focus back where it belongs. "Ella, we're leaving. Now. We don't have time to wait for clothing." I have no doubt Sylveria has more men coming. I brought three of my own with me, but I'd rather not end up in a shootout at this overpriced, glorified hospital.

Ella's small chin firms. "I'm not going anywhere."

"All right." I stride forward, done playing nice, and I'm gratified when she instinctively takes a step back.

Smart girl.

I grab the white blanket off the hospital bed—that's some luxury cashmere thing that probably costs more than most people's rent—and toss it around her shoulders, pulling the ends shut at the front.

"What are you doing?" she snaps.

Even that harsh sound feels like a balm to my skin. This is so not good. "Making a burrito." I wrap it snugly around her. The moment flickers with something almost warm until she blinks, her gaze landing on my mouth.

"Are you all right?" I dip my head, checking her eyes.

They're clear. Not glassy. She's aware. She's been in a fight, no doubt. The bruise along her cheek's blooming purple, and I don't like seeing it. I hate knowing someone got that close.

I look over my shoulder at Sylveria. "Where's the guy who hurt her?"

"We have him," she says, calmly. "We'll figure out who he is."

Good. He needs to bleed. "I want him."

"No." Sylveria watches Ella try to escape the blanket.

Her one word scrapes my skin. "Yes."

Sylveria lifts her chin with that same smug confidence she wears like perfume. "All right, you can have him. But I'm keeping Ella."

Ella continues struggling to get out of the blanket. "Nobody is keeping me."

"Wrong, princess." I duck my head and lift her as gently as I can over my shoulder. She's light, and while the doctor's notes said she's mostly okay, I can feel how tense her muscles are under the hospital gown and blanket. She's putting on a brave face, but her body's not convinced. I don't want to hurt her, but I'm also not giving her a vote.

"Hey," she starts, trying to worm her arms free from the wrap.

"Behave yourself." I wrap one arm over her legs and turn toward the door. She keeps squirming, but it's half-assed, more out of protest than real escape. She knows I'm not letting go.

Sylveria's already reaching into her purse again, slow and theatrical. That same polished calm.

"You reach for that gun," I say coldly, "I'm going to make you eat it."

She pauses, hand still, mouth pressed into a line. We lock gazes. She steps to the side, just enough. "I am quite the witness, Justice Beathach," she says. "If Ella ends up dead, I'll make sure every newspaper and authority in the world knows it."

"She's not going to end up dead. Not today, anyway." I shift Ella's weight slightly, tightening my hold on the wriggling bundle over my shoulder. She's still not yelling.

She's not pleading. She's saving her breath for something that actually matters.

That's another thing I like about her.

God, she's irritating.

I stride past Sylveria and nod to my men at the door. Sylveria's guards are still unconscious in two separate heaps. We hit the hallway, then the stairwell, all the way down to the car waiting outside.

Ella lets loose with a spew of truly impressive language—creative, vicious, and borderline poetic in how violently she strings the words together.

I've heard a lot of swearing in my life. This is new. I'm impressed. I fight the urge to smack her ass just to interrupt her, but I don't know how badly she's hurt, and the last thing I want is to cause more damage. She might be a thorn in my side, but I don't want her bleeding.

We reach the car. I flip her around and lower her into the back seat, following close behind. She immediately explodes into motion, struggling like hell, her hair flying in every direction.

I grab a strand as it whips across my face and shut the door just as my driver peels away. "Your hair is soft," I murmur.

She freezes for a beat. "You are a fucking asshole. Get me out of this stupid blanket."

Amusement slips inside me. It's unwelcome, but there it is, cutting under my skin like adrenaline. I don't get intrigued often. I definitely don't get amused when someone's this pissed at me. But with her? It's different. Her fury doesn't push me away. It pulls something to the surface, and somehow, her words don't harm me. In fact, I feel better than ever.

Yeah, I need to fuck her out of my system. Once she feels better.

She flails again, and I've had enough.

I pluck her up and set her on my lap, locking her in with one arm. "Would you please behave yourself?"

"Behave myself?" she spits. "You just kidnapped me!"

"I saved you from your evil stepmother."

She narrows her eyes at me, clearly recalibrating. She doesn't trust me—not remotely—but she's doing the math.

I decide to save her the trouble. "I'm the biggest threat."

"That's what I figure," she mutters. "Why are you kidnapping me, Justice?" She sighs like she's run out of an entire day's worth of patience.

"We'll discuss that later. I'm having my doctor take a look at you. I don't trust your stepmother's."

She shifts slightly. "Why do you even care?"

"I need your help," I say simply.

She blinks once, then twice. The blue of her eyes cuts through the shadows inside the car, sharp against the dimness. Rain taps against the roof like fingers drumming in warning, and the windows begin to fog. The air's close now, tight. "My help?" she asks cautiously.

"Yeah. First, I want to know why you're hacking into the Beaumont servers."

"Not going to tell you."

"I didn't think so." I can make her talk. I've made worse people give up bigger secrets. But right now, she's warm on my lap, wrapped in that blanket like a stolen thing, and I'm not in a hurry.

She shifts again and then freezes. Her eyes widen

slightly as she no doubt brushes against my erection. I don't apologize. I just watch her.

"I'm not going to hurt you," I say.

She goes still. Utterly still. Not in fear, but calculation. She's trying to decide what I am. Cute, though. I'll give her that. Even when she's glaring like she wants to bite someone. "That's not what you said before."

I nod. "I've decided you're forgiven. But if you try to kill my brother again, we're going to have a real big problem." Yeah, I might have to neutralize her away from computers, but she doesn't need to know that tonight. First, I require her help.

"I already said I was sorry," she snaps. "I can't believe you're still pissed about one little virus."

Truth be told, I'm not feeling particularly pissed at the moment. I could be wrong because I want her. Badly. Her words don't cut me. Her voice heals. I'm curious. And very aware of her weight, the way she fits against me even when she's doing everything she can not to. So I turn her attention elsewhere. "I want to know exactly what you did to the garnet to poison it—and then Thorn."

Even through the blanket, I can see her cross her arms. She might not be able to get free, but she sure as hell makes the movement anyway. That defiance. Always. She winces slightly.

"What hurts?" I ask instantly, every nerve on alert.

"Just my shoulder from the fight with the asshole in my safe house." Now she looks a little pouty.

Unable to help myself, I reach out and run a finger down her flushed face. Her skin is even silkier than her hair. Warm. Soft in a way that makes my jaw tighten and my erection harden further. I curse myself silently. Not the time. Not the place. But damn, she's something.

Her eyes go wide.

"I said you're safe, right?" I murmur.

She mutters a barely audible "yes," but there's something layered behind those eyes. Interest. Intrigue. A light blush touches her cheekbones, and I know this tension between us is mutual—and unwanted by us both.

I don't trust myself around her. My alliance and my loyalty belong to Malice Media, to my brother, and to the organization we built. I won't let that slip. I won't let her make me weak. But a quick fuck? Maybe a few times? That we both need.

She glances toward the window, voice low. "Where are we going?"

"My place," I say simply.

She huffs out a breath. "I take it your guy was the one who got hit in the head in the driveway? The one who shot the attacker for me?"

"Yep." Wynd has a hell of a headache.

"How'd you find me?"

I settle her more comfortably in my lap and ignore the fact that my cock tries to punch through my zipper. "Wouldn't you like to know?"

"I really would," she hisses. "Considering there was a jerk in my house, your Irish dude in my driveway, and then Sylveria's stooge who kidnapped me."

It's irritating so many people found her safe house. "We had a tracker on your car. My guess is we're going to find a few more."

She sits up a little straighter, looking genuinely affronted. "You all found my car?"

"Yes. There's CCTV everywhere, Ella. You should know that."

We picked her up a couple times on camera—clear shots of her walking behind the car. I don't tell her that. Don't tell her we're watching closer than she knows. Nor do I tell her that we also found four of her other vehicles scattered around town. I've got a team searching now to see if anyone else has tagged them. If not, I'm leaving my trackers in place.

I know she has more cars stashed around Silicon Valley than those. She's clever. Paranoid. Quietly thorough. But I'll find them.

Her gaze drops to my mouth. "Why are you so interested in me?"

"That's not why," I say before I can stop myself.

She jolts, like she didn't expect me to deny it. She squints at me, scrunches her nose, and I swear to God she's the cutest thing I've ever seen. And that? That's a problem. A huge one.

I lean in and tangle my fingers into her hair. She freezes, but not with fear. She doesn't even try to fight, doesn't twist out of the blanket.

"Justice," she whispers.

"Yeah." I lower my mouth to hers and take one taste. It's a mistake. I know it instantly.

She tastes like wild berries and pure maple syrup, like late summer heat and danger and something I should never touch. But I go deeper, and she kisses me back like she's drowning and I'm the only breath in the room.

The world goes quiet. My thoughts vanish. I growl, low in my chest, and she shudders, melting into me. I'm two seconds from ripping that blanket off when reality punches me in the throat. I pull back, breathing hard.

She looks dazed. Lips swollen. Eyes that impossible, unnamable shade of blue—like they were made just to wreck me.

I could spend the rest of my life trying to name that color.

The only word that comes to mind is *mine*.

That blue is for me and me alone.

Shit.

NINE

Ella

I can't believe Justice Beathach just kissed me as I sit wrapped up in a blanket on his damn lap. My lips sting and the rest of me heats to match. This can't be normal. His eyes glitter, steady and unreadable, and I keep looking because breaking the line feels worse than holding it. This is a disaster.

The way he carried me out of that hospital room keeps playing in my head. He threw me over his shoulder. He'll pay for that. Even so, his grip stayed careful. He read every injury and moved like he refused to add another one. The memory warms places I should lock down. Truth be told, I feel good. Not safe. Not calm. Good.

I need time with a citrine. A big one. I want the pulse that comes with it, the clean push that sets my spine straight. He doesn't have one. I'd bet on that. I've never tried pulling from a garnet, and the idea sits wrong in my bones. I shift to get leverage and brush across his erection.

A sound climbs my throat and I swallow it. My breath comes back rough. Heat spikes through me again and my focus blurs, then snaps tight. "I'd like to get off your lap now," I say.

"No."

The arrogance tugs at my temper. I tip my head back and lean away as far as he lets me. It isn't far. He cradles me, one arm under my knees, the other across my back, and his body doesn't give. I feel the strength in it, and self-preservation holds me in place when sense tells me to squirm.

"You don't want to mess with me, Justice."

He shows his teeth. The expression passes for a smile and does nothing for my nerves. It feels unwise to remind him that I nearly killed his brother, so I lock that threat away. I don't think he'll actually kill me. Alana is family now, and that draws a boundary I can use. I don't trust what he'll try inside that boundary.

His scent closes around me. Male and warm, with a spice I can't name. It slips under my caution and lingers. Another shiver runs through me, and I hate that he feels it. Something shifts in his eyes. They're brown, deep as old wood, and threaded with lighter flecks that weren't there a second ago.

I finally release my arms from the blanket wrap, and his arm tightens a fraction. He's tracking every twitch. I match him breath for breath and refuse to give him the flinch he's waiting for. I set my hands on his chest because there's nowhere else to put them.

He leans in again. His nose nearly brushes mine.

A shudder rolls through me and it zaps straight to

my clit. When God gives a man this face and this body, anyone would heat up. Maybe it isn't God. Justice carries the flavor of the devil.

"Definitely," he says.

Crap. I said that out loud. "Let me go." I forget self-preservation and push against him, struggling for all I'm worth.

He lets me.

I don't move. Damn it. Fury careens through me, and I punch him in the neck. The sound echoes around the car. I suck in a breath.

He casually, way too easily, captures my wrist, manacles it to my other wrist, and secures them at the back of my waist with one hand. The blanket falls down to my hips. "That wasn't nice."

"I'm *not* nice," I gasp out.

His free hand wraps around the front of my throat, his thumb on one side and his fingers on the other. He tightens his grip. "It's a good thing I don't *like* nice." With just that hold, he pulls me toward him, his mouth taking mine again.

Hard.

Fast.

Deep.

I can't breathe. As his tongue slips between my lips, the taste of fine Irish whiskey fills me. He growls low, pushing me down to the left, his mouth brutal on mine. I fight to free my wrists, but his strength far outmatches mine. I thought he'd kissed me before.

Not like this.

There isn't anything like this.

My mouth opens under his, and I take him in. Rough

callouses brush my ribcage, and I jerk, realizing my hands are free.

He caresses up my ribcage, a hard press, and cups my breast.

I murmur a protest into his mouth, and he pulls at my nipple. Not hard. Not gentle, either. I gasp and my body takes over, pressing against him. Right against his cock, which seems to be trying to escape the confines of his pants.

He moves to the other breast, and the tug this time holds more pain.

Enough to shoot lightning through me and wetness from my core.

His chuckle into my mouth is dark. Filling me, taking over, just like the rest of him.

He releases my throat, and I have a second of relief, until he tangles those long fingers in my hair and jerks my head back, his mouth unrelenting as he takes from me. But the heat he gives, oh God, it's all encompassing. Everywhere.

He isn't gentle as he scrapes down my abdomen and slips his fingers into my panties.

I jolt, but he kisses me harder, stealing any sound I might've made. Then he's inside me. One finger. Two. Then three. Stretching me. The need inside me is so great I can't breathe.

A horn echoes. Somewhere.

I jolt, remembering the driver.

I push against his chest, maybe, but I remain locked in place. One hand in my hair, the other inside me. Those three fingers begin to move, in and out, showing no mercy.

I pant, kissing him back, knowing I shouldn't. But my body is moving against him, with him, like it has its own goal. I know what it is. Damn it.

"We're getting close, boss," the driver says.

A roaring fills my head, and I push harder against Justice.

He bites my lip.

The sharp sting goes through me, somehow erotic. I moan.

"Then I'll hurry," he says against my lips, letting me breathe for a moment. I suck in oxygen, and his words penetrate. I pull in more air to protest, and he kisses me again, driving deep in rhythm with his fingers.

It's too much. Live wires explode inside me. He scrapes his thumb across my clit, and I explode. The climax burns, careening across every nerve inside me. He releases my mouth just in time for me to cry out. Loudly.

I shut my eyes.

The waves take me and I ride them out, pressing my lips together to keep from crying out again. A small whimper still escapes. Finally, I come down, sagging against him.

He releases my hair and then my pussy, which protests and tries to grip him. "So this is how to gain your obedience."

I blink and look up at him, my vision clouded. Heat spirals into my cheeks, and I can never look at that driver again. "I hate you." My words slur.

"Then you're gonna want me dead after I fuck you a couple of times." He sounds almost cheerful. Then, keeping my gaze, he licks his fingers clean. "Delicious."

I don't have the energy to punch him again. "Gross.

Just gross." Yeah, I'm cradled against him, snuggled into him in a way I can't afford. I can't trust any man, anybody beyond Alana and Rosy, so this can't happen. "I'm going to kill you slowly," I mutter.

"Maybe we should go again." He rubs his thumb across my bottom lip.

I tear my gaze from him and pretend to study the world outside of us. It's about two in the morning, the hour when downtown Palo Alto shows both polish and rot. LEDs glow on glass towers, and a street sweeper sends water across broken cups and napkins. A delivery bike runs a red light and vanishes. A man sleeps under a silver survival blanket near a bench lit by a boutique's sign. The city throws sparks and shadows in equal measure, and our car swims through both.

I mark the route. University. Ramona. Bryant. We slip past late offices with screens still on and cafes that never close. The air inside the car holds whiskey, leather, and *him.* My pulse won't settle. "Where are we going?" I whisper.

He turns his head so close that his breath warms my mouth. "Wherever I want." He leans toward the front and speaks to the driver in Gaelic while his hand settles at my waist. The cadence is sharp and quick. Alana taught me enough to recognize the language, not enough to pull meaning from the words. I track the driver's small nod and the way his grip tightens on the wheel. We avoid each other's gazes.

We keep moving toward the city center, which argues against a body dump, at least for now. I'm sure he'd bury me out in the middle of nowhere if he wanted me dead. Right now, anyway.

Wait a minute? Why would we head into town? "Are we going to Malice Media?"

He ignores the question but still holds me tight. Heating me.

Movement erupts at the edge of my vision as two black SUVs barrel out of opposite alleys and box our lane. Our driver swears and cuts for the curb, and the grille of a Mack truck fills the street ahead, dead center. Brakes slam. My stomach flips and I yelp before I can stop it.

Justice pulls me tight and locks my hips to his chest, then lifts his chin toward the front. "Go back," he orders. The driver throws the car into reverse and hammers the pedal. The car jerks hard and surges backward, tires screaming while the lane opens for half a block. A second Mack rolls out behind us and drops its broad nose into our path, killing the escape. The driver stabs the brakes, and the chassis shudders under me.

I twist enough to see past Justice's shoulder. The driver shouts a string I can't interpret and slaps the horn while he checks both mirrors. Sweat beads at his temple. His breath rasps. "Punching in a 911 to the men," he mutters, tapping against the dash.

Justice stays calm and holds me steady against him. His heartbeat presses against my shoulder in a slow, fixed rhythm. I push closer because my body wants the steadiness, and I hate that I need reassurance from him. My hands grip his shirt to anchor myself.

Gunfire cracks the night and stitches the air with a hard rhythm. I scream before I can stop myself. Justice folds over me, covers my head with his jaw, and keeps his arm firm across my back. The driver throws another curse and rides the gas, then the brakes. My teeth rattle. The door shivers near my hip. The window haze blooms and spreads.

Gunfire patters.

Glass shatters.

Justice slides me onto the floor. "Keep down." He kicks his door open while pulling a pistol from his side. Cold grit bites my bare knees. The car reeks of oil and cordite. My mouth tastes of metal. I press my spine to the seat base as fear crawls up my throat and tries to choke me.

He leans out with the gun. "Shoot everyone, Rick," he mutters as the driver shoves his door wide and rises into the frame. Glass breaks again and rains over my arms. The street noise tilts into a roar. My ears ring so hard I can't hear my own breath.

Gunfire erupts everywhere. The rhythm is too fast and too even. "They have automatic weapons. You only have a handgun," I yell.

Justice drops into a crouch, braces, and fires three sharp shots.

The sound multiplies. A new wash of bullets tears across the block from two sides, then another answers from the rear. If we're close to Malice Media, there should be guards moving right now. With Thorn out of town, Justice is the head of the Irish mob in this slice of the world. What would anyone be thinking to hit him here? My hands shake so hard my fingers ache. I press my palms to my temples and swallow down panic.

A lone voice cuts through everything and shouts, "Give us Rendale!" The words land wrong and cold. I look up and catch Justice in profile as he pivots, fires twice, and resets. A yelp breaks from the dark. Metal echoes. Something heavy drops out of sight. More gunfire surges around us and drives me lower. I cover my head and clamp my elbows to my skull.

The hood buckles with a deep, torn sound. Heat punches through the vehicle.

Justice leans in. "*Dar fia.* The thing's going to explode."

The words punch through my gut and open a pit under my ribs. I reach for him.

He grabs my wrist and yanks me into the rain, then shoves me behind his body so he takes the line of fire. My bare feet slide on glass. My stomach lurches. The night tastes burnt and wet.

I look past him toward the front of the car and see bodies on the pavement, sprawled in angles that don't move. The strobe of muzzle flash keeps lighting them and erasing them. Gunfire still erupts from every direction. My heart hammers so hard it hurts.

He jerks his head. "We'll move closer to that brick building and duck down out of sight. In the alley." He still sounds calm. How the fuck does he sound calm? I make myself small behind his body and let him cover me, his arm steady as he fires in controlled bursts. We angle for the building. The sidewalk is wet from the unrelenting rain. My pulse runs hard enough to blur the edges of my sight.

His body jerks.

"Justice," I gasp.

He drops to one knee.

"Justice." I grab the collar of his button-down and haul him toward the wall, feeling exposed in the hospital gown. Heat leaks through his shirt and coats my palm. A man cuts in from the curb and sprays rounds past us toward the truck behind, protecting us. "Down." I shove Justice flat as another burst hits the street and bites stone from the curb.

"I'm fine." He looks more pissed than hurt, but blood blooms across his white shirt. It's deep red and keeps spreading.

Another man rushes up with scars laddered across his face. "How bad?"

"Shoulder," Justice murmurs, and he glances across his forearm. I edge into the mouth of the alley and press to the brick, trying to breathe. "Stay put," he orders, and I nod while my legs fold.

I crouch and pull myself tighter. The concrete is cold on my bare skin. Gunfire ripples up the sidewalk between us and I yelp and duck farther into cover. The air shakes. Grit sprays my cheek. Justice sits up and both men return fire in a clipped, controlled rhythm. Casings tinkle on the pavement. Someone cries out across the street and then stops.

How many bullets do they have? My throat closes. I count breath in fours and fail on three. The alley smells of wet cardboard and bleach. A drain gurgles. Sweat stings my eyes. I wipe it with the back of my hand and smear dirt across my face.

I freeze and then really look around. I'm in an alley. No headlights. No footsteps. No one's pushing in on this line. Finally, my instincts take over. I pivot on my heel, jump up, and run.

"Ella," Justice bellows from the curb, voice hard enough to make me want to stop, but I don't.

I've been in survival mode since my dad died so many years ago. I clear a pile of garbage bags and my bare foot slips on a wet label. I ignore the pain. A rat scurries from under a crate and vanishes between bins. I keep moving, my lungs burning from the cold.

I go deeper into the alley and turn right at the next building, blinking rain from my eyes. It's still dark. I'm small and fast, and I know these streets better than anyone. I memorized the map years ago. I thread through a run of service corridors, cut behind dumpsters, pass locked gates, and keep my steps quiet. The gunfire fades. Even the chasing steps drop off. My breath evens enough for me to think. Justice Beathach isn't going to be happy about this. I've slipped him twice now.

Hopefully that gunshot to his fine body is as through and through as it looked.

An old Chevy Caprice waits under a dead streetlight, paint sunburned to chalk. The lot is empty. I slide in, drop low in the seat, and check the mirrors. Nothing moves. My hands know what to do without looking. Plastic bites my palms as I tear it away. The column is rough under my fingers. The air tastes of dust and copper and stale cigarettes. I work the old wires together, holding my breath. When the starter catches, the engine coughs and settles into a tired idle. I keep it gentle so it doesn't stall, ease it out of the space, and roll.

I keep well clear of the blocks near the gunfight. I hit green lights and empty lanes, drift through the skeleton of downtown, and point west. The road climbs toward the hills. The city thins, trades glass for scrub and low buildings. Fog hangs over the ridge in a light band. I push past the last strip mall and head more toward Half Moon Bay.

My heart rate finally slowing, I park in a narrow pullout that smells of eucalyptus and salt. I kill the engine, ditch the car, and move on foot for about ten blocks in and out of cut-throughs and quiet streets—avoiding all cameras. I keep to hedges and shadows, pass behind a mural wall, wait under a fire escape while a dome camera pans, then cross when it looks away. I mapped every CCTV in this pocket years ago. I follow the gaps I made for myself, hit an isolated laundromat, and quickly yank on jeans and a sweatshirt, as well as a mismatched pair of tennis shoes, from the lost and found bin.

Then I head back out.

Dawn lifts at the edges first. The sky goes pale and the streetlamps blink out one by one. The Cinderfalls Community Home rises at the end of the block, low and wide with a fenced field and a cracked blacktop. I stop and breathe until the shaking in my hands backs off. The retirement home won't open for hours.

That's fine.

My tree waits at the front edge of the property. Roots push up the soil, while the bark is rough and familiar. I climb to the middle third of the massive tree, where the trunk splits clean and a set of branches hook just right. I settle with my back wedged into the pocket and my feet braced. Another branch crosses at my shoulder. I've slept here more than once. The leaves hold the morning light and soften the wind. I tuck my chin into my collar and listen for engines, for boots, for voices that don't belong. Nothing comes. My eyes burn. I let them close, just to count to ten.

I take several deep breaths and let myself drift. The branch holds. The leaves hush the street. Sleep nips at the edges and I give it a little space.

The day wakes slow. Light picks out rooflines and

fence posts as the traffic builds, first a few cars go by, then a steady stream. My bruises still ache. I need an energy hit and have to get to my citrines.

Across the way the shift change starts. Night nurses in navy scrubs file out with tired eyes and slight limps while orderlies tug hoodies over polo shirts and bump shoulders on the sidewalk. A janitor with a red cart locks the maintenance door and checks each pocket for keys. Physical therapists arrive with gym bags and tape peeking from side pockets. A social worker in flats calls a ride share and rubs her temple. The rhythm of it says morning, not panic. It has to be around eight.

I yawn and blink until the scene stops doubling. Then I wipe dust from the too-large jeans. My hands are filthy. I rub them on the inside of the faded pink sweatshirt.

The retirement community sits next to a field, neat and proud. Fall hits the front walk in an honest way. Pumpkins line the path in mismatched rows, some smooth, some warty, some painted with cheerful faces. Mums crowd big clay pots in burnt orange and wine, while a wreath on the glass door holds dried leaves, small pinecones, and cinnamon sticks tied with rough twine. Someone tucked plastic turkeys into the hedges and a plastic crow into the planter by the bench. The whole place looks tended.

The morning staff has the door propped open with a rubber wedge.

It's time to see my godmother.

TEN
Justice

Fury runs through my veins with the precision of a laser strike.

Sirens rise and fade while my crews clean the block. Men in dark jackets sweep brass into canvas sacks, roll hoses, and rinse the curb. Two fold a tarp and lift a body to the van. Another checks for pulses that aren't there and tags wrists. Phones are already out to the right sources in the police department, but we only have a few more minutes until they have to arrive. My men will get it done.

I stalk into Malice Media's main hub, so angry my ears burn. My white shirt drips and clings to my skin. Blood runs warm down my ribs and cools in the air of the lobby. Security clocks me without a word. The two men who brought me in hold the elevator and keep their eyes forward. We ride down in silence. The car hums. Fluorescents buzz. I breathe through the sting in my shoulder.

The doors open and Kaz looks up from a bank of

monitors. He's our resident computer genius. "What the fuck happened to you?"

His damn voice slices across my ribcage. "Firefight. Didn't you hear it?" My voice is even and low. Copper sits at the back of my tongue. I taste dust and cordite and stale coffee from the elevator.

"Yeah, but I didn't think you got shot. I got the 911 and sent our soldiers." His voice grates, like usual, but I don't wince. My brother relies on him, which is why he's still breathing. He looks at my bloody shoulder. "How bad?"

"Stop talking. I'm fine." I brush past him. "Ella Rendale was with me and escaped through an alley, somehow losing both of my men pursuing her. Find her by the time I get back." My teeth grind.

I reach the far wall and work the locks in sequence. Keypad. Card. Palm. Retina. The green bar crawls to full and relays click until the magnets release. I pull the door and step inside. The room breathes at fifty-eight degrees and fans move in a constant wash. Ozone and cold metal and a faint hint of lemon cleaner hang under the noise.

The wound is high on my shoulder, so I strip out of my shirt to study it. Entry and exit are both shallow. Good. It's nice to know I gauged it correctly, although the wound is aching like a bitch. Inhaling, I cross to the pedestal at the center, where light panels bathe the stone from four sides. The garnet sits in milled steel, a mass of dark red with crisp facets, the color deepening toward the core. It's the size of a bowling ball. The air around it feels warmer by a narrow degree. Power pools in the space like an electrical field I can feel on my skin.

My shoulders drop, though one burns. I reach the stone

and place my palm on it. The contact quiets the noise in my head. My breathing evens, and the heat at the edges of my sight cools. How have people not figured this out?

Of course, even if they have, not many can reach our level of expertise. It's probably something genetic that hasn't been mapped yet.

I close my eyes, take a long breath in through my nose and release it slowly from my mouth. I push a steady hum through the heel of my hand. The garnet brightens, takes the current, and returns it on a higher pulse. Air catches in my chest as the flow enters, runs across my clavicle, rides my brachial plexus, crosses to my spine, and settles along the ribs. The pattern holds. The stone and I meet on the same frequency and lock. Maybe that's the key. We've got theories and partial proofs. We don't have the full map. Matter carries energy. Energy carries information. The fit between my field and this crystal stays true every time.

Finally, my eyelids open. The tear in my shoulder knits from the inside first. Heat climbs, then eases.

The pain is excruciating, and I should take several hours to fix myself. I don't have time. Ella hasn't given me that time. So I push to get it done, my knees weakening from the agony.

Pain flares hot and cutting for too long before dropping to a dull throb. Ceiling fans pick up a few cycles, and the room adjusts to the load without complaint. The garnet dims by a notch, so I ease more of my own energy store into it, not just surface current but the deeper charge that feels personal and specific. Essence, if that word must stand. The transfer stabilizes the crystal, and a dark red color returns to her center.

I hold contact and keep count. Ten breaths. Twenty. A

minute. I'm going to spank Ella's small ass raw for this. God knows what kind of damage I'm doing to my body by rushing the healing process.

The pulse under my hand and the rack hum fall into a clean ratio. I add my second hand to the facet and test for resistance. None presents. The stone still has headroom, so I give more. My shoulder tightens once and lets go. I lower my arm and stretch it carefully, noting that my range of motion returns without instability. The edges of the wound seal. A band of heat remains. Functional is enough.

Hopefully I didn't just give myself permanent damage. I'll find out later.

I think about the day I worked the damaged crystal that was killing Thorn. It never bound to me and didn't push back. Although it drained me and led to the mess I'm in right now. The sensitivity in my auditory cortex somehow went from nuisance to pain. Voices that only irritated me before now turn into knives on my nerves. We pulled Thorn out with energy workers in a circle, a timed sequence, and a set of stones that weren't supposed to share a room. Chance and pressure made it hold. I don't think we'll ever reproduce that again, which sucks for me.

This garnet still answers me. That means something. The hole in my shoulder is closed now but still aches beneath the muscle. The stone has given what she can on this pass. I lift my hands. The glow steadies at a lower value, and the server noise eases my pulse. Static clears from my head.

I then open the server room door into the main floor. Cold air spills out and thins. Kaz looks up from the console and lifts a hand to stop me at the threshold. "All better now?"

"The only thing I want from you is Ella's location." I walk past him.

"Why do you have to be such a dick?"

Fire runs from my shoulder into my biceps, stretching a muscle with pain. "Would you just shut up?" I snap.

Kaz blinks once and tilts his head. He keeps his hands on the edge of the console and watches me without moving.

We're rarely alone. I avoid him when I can. When I can't, Thorn usually sits between us and tells us both to shut up.

"What's your problem?" Kaz says, eyes still on me, voice rough from too much coffee and not enough sleep.

"I don't like you, and I don't like when you talk." It is as close as I'll give him to the truth. Sound grinds in my head when it comes out the wrong throat. His is the wrong throat.

"Your brother likes me just fine," he says, rolling one shoulder as he drops into his chair.

"That's because you're the best computer programmer in the city. In the world." Maybe Ella's better. I don't say that. "Did you find Ella Rendale?" My palm actually heats with the need to meet her ass. Hard. I can't believe she ran away during a fucking firefight.

He mutters under his breath. I think about putting a bullet in his head. Thorn would be pissed if he came back and his top computer guy was a stain on the floor. Shit happens. Kaz catches the thought on my face or reads the angle of my shoulders and drops his gaze to the keys.

"She's fascinating," he says, fingers moving. He tiles

feeds across the far wall, pulls license plate hits, lights up a geofence, and pushes audio to my left. "She hotwired an older car outside the IHOP on Sixteenth." He scrubs back, zooms, and tags the model.

She hotwired a fucking car? The woman who can hack into anything modern also has old school skills? I stand there shirtless, blood drying across my ribs, and shake my head. "Where did she go?"

"I've been searching all available cameras," he says, softer now, voice leveled out for my cars. His hands blur. Window after window opens. He tracks alley cameras, pulls a private garage exit, sorts a license plate list, and kills three false positives. "She went south. No. Southwest." He reads off street names and time stamps. He circles a frame. "Here's the car."

Good. Where the hell is she? "And then?"

"Then," he says, typing hard. He flips to a city grid, overlays transit cameras, scrubs the stream, and tags motion vectors. "She's gone."

I still. "What do you mean, gone?"

"Her trail's gone. Wherever she was, she avoided CCTV." He taps the desk once and locks the view.

I hold still and listen past the fans and the hiss of the HVAC. Sirens skid across the edge of my hearing and fade away.

Kaz keeps working the computer. "I'm not finding her."

Oh, I'll find that brat. I drop into the chair at the console across from Kaz and start typing. I take his feed, pull street grids, then hack every CCTV endpoint within two miles. I strip out every camera cone and leave only the dead zones. I map each gap, block by block, alley by alley.

I scrub the last fifteen minutes on every surviving feed. She never crosses a lens. She's in one of these holes.

I reach for my phone and take it from my back pocket. The screen lights. No cracks. No bullet took it. "Any idea who attacked us?" I keep my eyes on the map and mark the dark pockets in red. I have to find her.

"No." Kaz pushes his chair in and widens a grid. "We kept three attackers alive, but two are bleeding pretty bad. They've been taken to the Boathouse."

The Boathouse sits in the cliff below Thorn's place cut into the rocks above the ocean. I'll head there after I find Ella Rendale. Two of the three captives will probably bleed out before I reach them. Not my problem. One talking mouth is enough.

I glance over at Kaz. "Call our competitors. I want a meeting sometime soon." I send the search teams to the red blocks and tag a route I'd take if I were her.

"No problem." Kaz pivots to the comms desk and starts dialing. He sounds cheerful, which grates on me. My head doesn't like his register and never has.

I stand from the console and roll my shoulder. "Let me know if you find Ella. I'm sending teams to sweep each zone." I mark assignments and set check-in times. If she never hits a camera outside these pockets, she's staying inside them. My gut says southwest, so that's where I'll go. "Put out the word. If anybody lets Thorn know what happened this morning, they'll die bleeding from the eyes."

My shoulder now itching, I cross the room and ride the elevator up to my penthouse apartment. The doors open on clean tile and cold air, so I head straight to the shower and rinse the blood off until the water runs clear.

Afterward, I pull on a dark shirt and jacket that will move with me, holster my Ruger and Glock, sheath the knives where my hands expect them, and load spare mags into an inner pocket.

Back in the elevator, I thumb the ops channel open on my phone. Ella Rendale and I are going to settle this today.

ELEVEN

Ella

Raindrops hang on the leaves, but the sky has somewhat cleared this morning. I grip the tree branch and let out the call in a sharp, high-pitched note, once, twice. A bird whistle. I do it again and then count to twenty in my head. That should be enough.

Dropping down, my mismatched tennis shoes smack the grass, and I force myself into a casual stride across the lawn, aiming for the main walkway. The building looms, brick and glass softened by the climbing ivy, but it's the heavy door I want. I slip inside, head down, and sign the visitor log with a name I make up on the spot. No one's at the desk. Figures. This isn't the kind of place where the residents run off.

I hum under my breath, needing to steady myself. I should be freaking out after the firefight in the middle of Silicon Valley. Nope. My body still tingles from Justice, and that won't do. He played my body like we've been together for years.

Shaking myself out of it, I head down the corridor. Right, then left. The hallway smells faintly of bleach, and I keep walking, acting natural. At the far end, a suite door is already propped open. Glitter sprinkles across the carpet like a warning. Pink, of course.

"Perfect," I mutter, pinching my nose. My allergies have had a long week too. I push the door open all the way and step inside. Three credenzas line the wall, cluttered with monitors, papers, and bowls of wrapped candies. Between them sits a low table covered in tiny glass bottles from their online business with perfumes, oils, and candles in squat jars, their wicks blackened from use. The air thrums with rose, sandalwood, and something sweet that makes me hungry.

"There you are, my beautiful goddaughter," Aurelia Mendoza says without glancing up from her monitor, her voice warm. Her name fits her, although she goes by Aura normally. "I heard the whistle. Took you long enough. You getting slower in your old age?"

I snort and instantly regret it when glitter dust drifts up my nose. Coughing, I cross the room fast, bend down, and kiss her cheek.

She's seventy-three, rocking a neon pink tracksuit that sparkles from ankle to chin. Not manufactured sparkle, either—every rhinestone glued on by her own hand. Bedazzled, weaponized, unapologetic.

I straighten and glance at the other two women waiting, their eyes twinkling like they already know what trouble I've brought with me.

Joslyn Park and Magdalena Palmita sit in front of the computer banks, both in their seventies, sharper than most people half their age. The computers can be hidden in the credenzas if anyone wants the room neat, but right now the screens glow with tabs, numbers, and streaming data.

Mags wears a light blue tracksuit with crystals stitched neatly down the sides. Not subtle, but not blinding either. Jos has gone in the opposite direction with jeans and a pressed white shirt, every button closed to the collar.

"Sorry about the glitter," Jos says, brushing her strawberry-blonde curls back over her shoulder. She's softened the color as she's aged. She yanks open a drawer, fishes out a bottle, and tosses it to me. "Claritin. You'll need it. Your godmother and Mags turned this place into a glitter bomb."

"We did not," Aura says, lifting her chin. The rhinestones on her tracksuit catch the light like tiny beacons. "We just wanted to brighten things up a little."

She's not lying. Glitter dust coats the carpet, and blinking star-shaped lights are strung across the doorway, wrapped around the window frames, even outlining a couple of paintings like halos. The whole place twinkles with defiance.

I pop two pills and dry swallow. My throat burns, and I cough. Allergic to glitter. Lucky me. It's only the cheap stuff that bothers me, because I'm fine with sequins. I collapse into the sofa facing one of the credenzas. "How's it going?"

"Very well," Aura answers, tapping fast across her keyboard, her gaze on the screens.

Mags glances at her own monitor. "Birthday calls are logged. Kindness tips, too. Five dollars sprinkled here and there. No loose ends." She keeps it efficient, like she's reporting in. That's her thing, sending unexpected thank-yous and thinking-of-yous across the city. I don't have the time to help, and she doesn't need me.

She reaches for a small bowl of wrapped caramels. "Fuel," she says, unwrapping one.

Aura leans back and grabs a vintage atomizer from the perfume table. She sprays a fine mist into the air, the scent warm and floral with a bite underneath. "So glad you like the blinking stars." Her smile flashes as she nods at the lights above the door.

I don't answer since I'm accustomed to her changing subjects. Her mind's a thousand-watt circuit that never slows.

Aura was my mother's childhood best friend, and she's taught me most of what I know. She worked switchboards back in the day and then outwitted phone phreakers after that. She broke down billing systems a decade later, trained others to do so, then steadied voices on crisis hotlines for a spell. Now she calls it retirement, but she runs scam-proofing workshops for seniors and still manages to send goodwill out to strangers, one message at a time.

The glitter on the floor, the perfume, the blinking lights wrapped around everything—this is Aura's doing. Her suite. Her command center.

The trio has been at this retirement home for about six months, and once they get it into tip-top shape, they'll move to another one. It's a good hobby for them.

Jos looks up from her screen, her expression tightening. "There've been two animal cruelty calls in the last couple of days. One's already handled. The other is a Rottweiler out in the country that needs help. He's chained up and starving."

Of course she'd bring this to me. Jos never lets an animal slip through the cracks, and I can't say no to her.

She taps another key, her gaze flicking across the feed. "I think we may have a litter of cats out there too. I've seen some CCTV footage from a barn."

"There are barn cats," I say.

Jos smiles faintly. The woman is nuts for animals. That's one of the reasons I love her. The other is her brain. She started as a catalog clerk in her youth, working the stacks and learning every system libraries had to offer. Public records came next, then genealogy, and eventually a deep dive into newspaper archives. Now she's neck deep in open-source intelligence, picking apart information that's legally available to anyone with the patience to dig.

Mags gives me a long once-over. "Why don't your tennis shoes match?"

"Long story. It's what all the kids are doing," I say easily.

"Uh-huh." She leans over and lights a tree-shaped candle beside her computer to bless her machine. I've never understood it, but I don't argue. A stack of paper manuals sits on the same table, and when she notices my stare, she lifts her chin. "It's ambiance."

"It's kindling," I mutter, standing and grabbing the candle. I move it across the room and set it on top of the antique cupboard near the door.

"Oh, whatever." She waves a hand and then looks back at her monitor. "We've got a line on a child trafficking ring in the inner city."

I move toward her. "Now that's more like it. Give me the details."

"I've been running it through the dark web," she says, her voice calm, like she's talking about the weather. "We should have names or directions to hand over to the authorities soon. Is Merlin up for helping?"

Merlin's a member of my other band of do-gooders. He's an ex-hacker, and when we had time, the two of us plus Rosalie and Alana did some good for the world. I'm sure we'll get back to it as soon as things calm down a bit.

"I can probably get Merlin to help us. Alana's on her honeymoon, and Rosalie's still tied up building that house with Alexei." The one with the extra space for her seven borders, including Merlin. "I'll reach out."

Aura's cheeks color in a faint but noticeable hue against her jeweled tracksuit.

So it's like that? At her age, she's still got someone who makes her blush. My godmother, queen of glitter and strategy, is not as untouchable as she pretends. Interesting.

"Wonderful," she says quickly.

Mags rolls her eyes.

I grin. Mags has always been blunt. She started in family radio and TV repair when she was young, and eventually shifted into large-scale systems remediation. Now she spends her time tracking human traffickers online. Once she or Aura uncover something solid, they pass it to the authorities in a neat bundle.

"Let me know the second you've got anything useful," I say.

Mags nods. "Of course. I'm digging now. We'll have locations soon."

"Good. Thank you." I glance at the clock.

Aura fixes me with that steady godmother stare. "Is it

time for us to go after your heritage? I'm getting older, and I won't be here forever."

"Yes." I tell her about Sylveria visiting me in the hospital.

"Well, that's interesting," Mags cuts in. "I wonder what she wants from you. My guess would be that with the advances in AI, diamonds aren't cutting it for her. TimeGem was built on citrines, with their different energy cadence, whether she likes it or not."

Yeah, no kidding. I swallow. "Speaking of TimeGem, I've been working a backdoor through Aquarius Social to reach my servers."

All three women turn toward me.

"Seriously?" Jos asks.

I nod. "Yeah. I found a backdoor already in place, and I don't know who left it there."

Aura pivots back to her keyboard, rhinestones glinting. "Yep. Already knew that."

"What?" My body stills. I don't need them running parallel hacks.

Jos straightens her already straight collar. "Please. We taught you, remember? We've been keeping tabs on Aquarius, Malice Media, and Hologrid while tracking TimeGem. Aura found the new signature last night."

I sigh. "You've found evidence of the new hacker?"

"Yes," Aura says, her eyes gleaming. "It's one party with a definite signature hacking into the four other systems. I'm running a list of up-and-coming social media companies and trying to cross-reference those with the hacking signature and any large purchases of some type of crystal. Haven't found anything yet."

Anticipation lights through me. "I was so busy tracing them from Aquarius to TimeGem that I didn't check the others. So they've hacked all four of us? Fascinating. We have to find this party. Maybe align with them in taking down Sylveria." Or take them out. Who knows?

Jos nods. "While you two run down that rabbit hole, we need to get serious right now. There was a gunfight in the middle of Silicon Valley last night. Most of the CCTV was scrubbed, but one camera slipped through. You were on it."

My stomach drops. "Please tell me you erased it."

"Of course I erased it." Her voice goes sharp, and she leans back like I just insulted her.

Aura reaches blindly for a pair of glasses and slips them on. She doesn't need them for the screen, only for distance. "What were you doing in a firefight?"

"Somehow, I walked straight into somebody else's war with Justice Beathach." I shake my head. "He was just giving me a ride home after the hospital."

Mags's jaw drops. "Are you kidding us right now?"

"I'm not." Heat rises up my neck. I see no reason to give them the full truth about my night.

Mags turns to Jos, her voice tight. "A gunfight is unexpected. Bad timing? Should we get Ella out of town?"

Jos nods, calm as ever. "We can. Private plane, whenever we need it."

"No." I lift a hand. "I've got this. You three need to trust me. We've got more important things to worry about. Like a child trafficking ring. And that poor dog—what's his name?"

Jos exhales. "We zoomed in on his collar. It says Killer."

I roll my eyes. "Okay. Send in animal control."

"No," Mags says. "The owner has papers. We need you to get him. Unless you want us to get you out of here?"

It's a threat. Seriously. Yeah, they could have me kidnapped. I'd get free but I don't have time to waste. "I don't have time to save a dog."

Jos gasps and holds her chest.

I exhale. Now I've done it. "All right. Sorry. I'll make the time. Think of another name for him. We'll give it to him before I drop him off at one of the shelters."

"Be careful," Jos says, narrowing her faded blue eyes at me. Somehow, even with age clouding them, she still looks right through me.

Each of them has talismans—Mags with her smoky crystal pendant, Jos with a topaz locket that never leaves her neck, and Aura with her citrine stones tucked under the rhinestones and glitter.

"I will," I promise. "I know what I'm doing." I mentally go over the cars I've stashed in the area, running through which one will serve best.

Mags tilts her head, studying me. "You really blushed when you talked about Justice."

I arch a brow. "He's very sexy."

Her voice flattens. "He really is." Then her chin drops. "A good man is a challenging one."

I fold my arms. "I'm not getting involved with a mobster. He's just the brother-in-law of my best friend." That's all I give them. I push up from the sofa. "All right. I'll go get the dog." Which I really do *not* have time to do.

"Do you need money?" Mags asks.

Frankly, I always need money. "No. I'm good." The lie rolls out easy enough.

The three of them exchange a look and then turn back

to their computers. Keys clatter in fast rhythm until Jos hits a button with a flourish. "Your accounts are fully funded now."

I feel like an ass. "I don't need your money."

Jos waves a jeweled hand like she's brushing the idea away. "We have so much of it. We play the stock market for fun."

She swivels back to her monitor while Mags digs into her candy bowl. "She's right," she says, unwrapping a caramel with sharp fingers. "I made a killing yesterday. Tech stocks are insane."

"Got to know when to sell," Jos adds without looking up.

"Got to know when to buy," Mags finishes, her mouth full.

I slide my phone into my pocket. "What I really need is to stay out of Justice Beathach's line of sight."

Aura chews on her lip, glances at the others, then fixes her gaze on me. "All right. The question has to be asked. Do you want us to have Justice Beathach taken out?"

I drop back onto the loveseat. "No. I don't want him taken out."

"We might have to," Mags says, voice calm but pointed. "You did try to kill his brother. His brother's now out of town. If Justice wants you removed, now's the time."

"I'm aware of that," I say. "I don't think he actually wants to hurt me." Well, not really. Maybe a little. I lift a shoulder. "Okay, it's possible. But if he wanted me gone, I'd probably already be gone." Maybe. Thorn just left town, and Justice was probably waiting for that.

Aura tilts her head, her smile softening. "Maybe Justice is looking for a mate. He is very handsome." Of the three, she's the romantic.

"Yes, he is," I admit, remembering that orgasm. Justice is dangerous to me in too many ways. A girl has to protect herself. "But one of us might have to kill the other."

Mags coughs. "No, no, no. We'll take care of him if you want."

"I don't," I say firmly. "I really don't."

The last thing I need is these women anywhere near Justice's crosshairs. They're in a good place in life, and they've spent their lives giving—to animals, to strangers, to me. They sent me love even when I was locked away in boarding schools, sending it from a distance when they couldn't be near. It's my turn to protect them.

I stand, forcing a smile as I cross the room. "All right. I'll take care of the dog. Keep the cameras off, and blank anything between me and that animal. I know you can't get everything, but do your best."

At the closet, I tug out a wide cowboy hat and a green bedazzled jacket, light enough to move in but lacking actual glitter, so I'm safe from an allergy attack. I pull them on, catching my reflection in the mirror. Best disguise I've got for now.

"How much danger are you in?" Aura asks quietly.

I pause, the words pressing at my throat. Three groups have already tried to grab me, right out of what was supposed to be a hidden safe house. The truth is, it doesn't look good. Instead, I turn back to her and lie with a smile. "I'm fine. Don't worry." I definitely need to give them a task. "While I go rescue this dog, will you do another deep dive on Sylveria and her daughters? We haven't checked in a while, and I want everything."

Mags pushes her glasses onto her head, eyes bright. "Really? It's time?"

"Oh, it's time," I say. "I want to take everything."

Their squeals of delight fill the suite. It should sound dangerous. It doesn't. But I'll work with what I've got. Now all I have to do is rescue a dog named Killer, figure out who all wants me dead, and avoid Justice Beathach, who is most certainly on the hunt for me right now.

Yeah, he's the biggest threat.

I shiver before kissing the cheerful women goodbye, hoping it's not for the last time.

TWELVE
Justice

Thirty minutes. That's all it's been since I caught Ella on the feed. One grainy camera out of Silicon Valley that whoever scrubbed the others missed. And there she was—Ella—in a cowboy hat and a damn glittering green jacket, striding through a storm like she belonged onstage.

I'd been behind the wheel before the clip even finished playing. Drove hard, cut through traffic, didn't care about the red lights or the cops who looked twice and thought better. Every second felt like an edge digging under my ribs.

Yeah, they know my car.

Now her beat-up van sits crooked in a dirt yard, headlights dark, rain sluicing off the windshield in heavy sheets. The same van from the footage. She doesn't cover her tracks half as well as she thinks.

I roll my shoulders.

What the hell is Ella Rendale doing in this dump?

She's a hacker, and this is no place for her. Nobody

is going to end her life until I've fucked her out of my system.

I roll my eyes at myself. Yeah, my plan is solid, but even then, I won't let anybody kill her. Even when I'm done with her.

So I stride out of my Bentley Mulliner Bacalar and check the road. Vacant and sad. There's an empty lot to one side and an abandoned, boarded-up home to the other.

The place stinks before I'm even inside. It has a sagging porch, wood black with rot, and beer cans lined up on the railing like trophies. A broken swing creaks in the wind. Rain pours through the holes in the eaves, drumming against the muddy ground. Somewhere close, a dog barks rough and desperate, the chain rattling with every pull.

Energy careens down my arms, and the garnets set into my watch start to glow blood red.

I take the steps fast, each one groaning under my weight. My hand flexes at my side. Ella's voice, raised inside, nearly stops me.

What the hell?

A man yells back, his voice slurred.

My jaw tightens. I don't knock.

I lift my leg and nail the door with my boot. The worn wood shudders and bursts wide, wood cracking against the wall. The stink of booze and grease spills out, hot and thick.

Crossing a filthy living room with a ripped sofa and stacks of what looks like kiddie porn on a chair, I barrel into the kitchen to see grease stains, rotting food, and a stack of bottles on the counter. And in the middle of it—Ella. Bedazzled jacket plastered to her from the rain, cowboy hat tipped low, her arm twisted back in the fat hand of a red-faced slob. His gut strains against a stained undershirt, his knuckles white where he grips her.

Her eyes snap to me. Defiance, always, but there's strain under it, too. She's fighting.

"Get your hands off her." My voice comes low, steady.

The man stares, sways, and doesn't let go. His eyes are bloodshot and his pupils dilated.

I take another step in, rain dripping from my coat, boots hitting the linoleum with a solid crack. The dog outside keeps barking, chain rattling, the sound mixing with the storm.

The man mutters something ugly and tries to drag Ella closer. His voice, dark and evil, ripples across my skin and bruises my fucking elbows. My vision narrows until all I see is her in his grip.

Absurd. Sequins and rhinestones in a filthy kitchen. But there's nothing funny about the fury boiling in my chest.

"Fuck you," the asshole mutters and yanks Ella tight against him like she's his property.

That's it.

I move before he can blink and grab his beefy wrist. The bone snaps in my grip, breaking with a sharp crack. He screams, high and panicked, and Ella tears free. I shove her behind me, never taking my eyes off him.

He staggers, clutching his useless hand, and swings with the other. Pathetic. I catch his arm, drive my knife up under his ribs, and push until his mouth opens in a wet gasp. His eyes go wide, confused. He didn't see me go for one of my knives.

No words. No warning.

The blade slides free and his knees buckle. He crashes to the filthy linoleum, bottles rolling across the floor, blood soaking through his stained shirt.

The only sounds are the storm pounding the roof, the dog still barking outside, and Ella's sharp breath behind me.

I wipe the blade clean on his shirt and straighten. Cold rage still burns steady in my chest, but the job's done. He won't touch her—or anyone—again. Blood spreads fast, mixing with the grime already ground into the linoleum.

Behind me, she inhales sharp and quick. Tennis shoes, one blue and one purple, scrape against the tile as she backs away.

"Justice . . ." Her voice shakes once, then steadies with sheer will. "You didn't have to kill him."

I turn just enough to see her, the cowboy hat tipped low, sequins catching the weak light. She looks furious, but her eyes—wide, startled—betray her.

She doesn't understand. Of course she doesn't.

The man touched her. He doesn't get to breathe after that. Neither of us needs to question the why of that. Not right now, anyway. Seeing that scum try to hurt her had awakened something primal in me.

Something I don't want.

Rain pounds the roof. The dog outside thrashes against the chain, barking hoarse. I slip the blade back into its sheath, the motion automatic, my pulse already steadying.

"He laid hands on you," I say, my tone flat. "That was enough." I'll have someone burn this entire place to the ground once I get her to safety.

Her mouth opens, then shuts. She shakes her head, hat dripping water onto the floor, and takes another step back.

Shock rolls off her in waves, but I don't move toward her. Not yet. She needs space to realize what kind of man I am.

What kind of man she's facing.

The storm hasn't let up. She turns and runs out of the back kitchen door. Curious, I follow her. Does she actually think she can escape me?

Again?

Rain sheets sideways, hammering the sagging porch as we step outside. The door bangs against the wall behind me, left open to the stink of booze and blood.

Ella doesn't look back. She pulls the hat lower, her sequined jacket dripping like a beacon in the dark, and heads toward the sound of the chain. She's pale, lips pressed thin, but her stride doesn't falter.

Why is she wearing a bedazzled jacket and cowboy hat? If she wanted to disguise herself, she failed.

She's still in shock. I can see it in the tremor of her hands, the stiffness in her spine. I killed a man for laying hands on her, and she doesn't know what to do with that truth.

The dog knows we're coming. He barks, raw and hoarse, yanking against the chain. When we round the corner of the house, he's all teeth and fury, ribs showing through wet fur. A metal collar digs into his neck, too tight, rust flaking under the strain. He looks to be part Rottweiler and maybe something else. Too skinny.

Ella stops short. Water runs off the brim of her hat, down her pale face. She lifts her chin, but she doesn't take another step.

"Let's go," I tell her, keeping my voice even.

She flicks a glance at me, defiant even now. Her fists

clench at her sides. The rain drills her, sliding down the feminine angles of her pixie-like face. "I'll make you a deal."

I ignore the rain smashing on me, intrigued. "Go on?"

"We work together for today. It's obvious you want something from me. I'll give it to you if you help me." Her eyes are so blue, something in my chest hurts. Hard. And her words cause more pain—right to my cock. She'll give it to me?

"What if I want you dead?"

She rolls her eyes. Actually rolls her fucking eyes. "Then I'd already be dead."

Yeah, she's not wrong.

She lifts a hand in the rain, toward me, before I can argue. "I know. You probably do have plans to kill me at some point, but right now, you need something from me. We were going somewhere last night, so I figure you need computer help. I am the best." She shrugs, looking ridiculous and uncomfortably appealing in the sparkling jacket.

Again, her instincts, or raw intelligence, are spot on.

The dog whines.

"Why are you here, Ella?" My patience is about gone. It's shocking I have any left.

She glances at the animal. "For him."

I blink. Barely. "Explain."

She shrugs. "Somebody called in an animal cruelty report, and nothing was done, so I came to take him."

Is she bullshitting me? "You came here, knowing you're being hunted by not only me but somebody who sent an assassin after you last night, to save a fucking dog?"

Pink bursts across her high cheekbones. "Yes."

I don't know what to make of that. Kindness,

sweetness, even vulnerability aren't attributes I want to find in her. She definitely isn't my type. I date women who want a hard and fast—often painful—fuck. That's it. "Explain better," I snarl.

She wipes rain off her nose. "That's the entire situation."

"What do you get out of it?" This doesn't make sense.

She sighs, her sapphire-colored eyes softening. "A safe dog. He can't protect himself, so here we are. Do you want to make a deal or not?"

We both know I can take her out of here in a second if I wish. Yet, having her cooperation will be helpful. Plus, I'll never admit it, but I'm damn curious about what she wants. "All right. Give me your terms."

She perks up, looking like a rare lily in the gray storm around us. "Excellent. All right. So, you're going to help me save, um, Leo here."

"Leo? His tag says Killer."

She moves closer to the dog and stops when I shift my weight. "Not anymore. He's Leo. It's a strong and admirable name with ties to Citrine because of the astrological sign." Her voice lowers to a purr. "Right, boy?"

He cocks his head, his focus on her. Then he gives a short whine.

She bunches as if to move toward him, and I shake my head. "Stop. He's dangerous. So I help you with . . . Leo, and then you'll help me?"

"Sure. I'll give you twenty-four hours of my hacking skills, with the provision and your word that you let me go afterward. That you take twenty-four more hours before coming after me again, if that's your choice. And that under no circumstances, no matter what, do you try to kill me."

No circumstances? What exactly does the woman have planned?

The dog lunges again, chain rattling hard enough to snap.

I keep my focus on the woman. She guessed I need her hacking skills, and she's mostly right about that. Yet she can't call all the terms. "I'll help with the dog, and you're mine for forty-eight hours." If she can't fix it in that time, I'm fucked, anyway. "And during that timeframe, you're mine in any way I want you."

She takes a step back and slides in the mud. "What does that mean?" Her voice quivers just slightly, and my cock tries to punch out of my pants. Again. For her. At her.

"Exactly what you think it does." I'm tired of ignoring this pull between us. A couple of hard fucks, and she'll be out of my system. "I'm not gentle or even kind, princess. I want to see you beg, and I want to see you cry. Before you agree, understand exactly what you're getting into."

She swallows. "If I disagree?"

I glance around. "You're coming with me, anyway."

Her chin lifts, and pure challenge filters across her face. "Fine. But I like a good fight, and I'll give it to you. May even kill you." Those eyes darken. "Either way, after forty-eight hours, you let me go and give me the same amount of time before you come after me."

"No. You get the twenty-four."

"I may kill you, Justice." She glances at the dog. "All right. Deal."

Something settles in me, and I take note of how her voice hasn't harmed me. Not once. I stare at the dog.

He's wild, desperate. I step forward, my boots sinking

into mud, and crouch low to meet his eyes. He snarls, lips peeled back, but I don't flinch.

"Easy," I murmur. My hand goes to the chain first, not him. He jerks, teeth snapping inches from my arm, but I keep steady pressure, shifting his weight until he's forced to stumble closer. His growl cracks, confusion slipping into it.

Ella makes a soft sound behind me—low, steady, the kind of noise you'd use with a child. Her voice carries under the storm. The dog hears her and freezes, ears flicking back.

My knife cuts the lock off, and the chain drops, the sound sharp under the rain. The dog stumbles free, muscles coiled. He lunges once more, but this time toward me, pressing his weight against my legs instead of tearing them apart.

I steady him with a hand on his neck, my palm against wet fur. His tail gives a single, uncertain wag.

Ella exhales like she's been holding her breath for hours. She takes a step forward, cautious, her hands open. The dog's head turns, eyes catching hers. He doesn't growl this time.

She kneels in the mud without hesitation, sequins flashing in the rain, hat tipping forward until her face is shadowed. "Hey, boy," she says softly. Her hand hovers an inch above his muzzle. He leans forward, sniffs once, then presses into her touch.

"Keep your fucking face out of his reach," I snap.

She leans back and smiles at the beast. Even pale, even shaken, that kindness radiates off her like heat.

I keep my hand on his collar, ready to pull him back if he changes his mind. But he doesn't. He pushes closer, ribs sharp under his coat, soaking her with rain as she strokes his head.

I let go. He doesn't lunge. He stays right there with her.

"Come on," I say. "Let's get him out of here."

Together, we guide him to my car. Great. It's going to smell like wet dog now. He stumbles a little, weak from hunger, but keeps pace between us. When Ella opens the passenger side door and slides inside, tugging him toward her, he hesitates only a second before jumping in, curling on her lap like it's the first safe place he's had in months.

They're too big for the space.

Her jacket drips across the seat, sparkle dull under the rain. Her face is still pale, eyes shadowed, but her shoulders loosen as she strokes the dog's head. Then she reaches into her pocket and brings out a couple of plain burger patties wrapped in paper.

He scarfs them down as if he hasn't eaten in days.

I close the door and walk around to the driver's side to slip inside. The storm's eased only slightly, rain steady on the windshield as the engine turns over. The wipers smear water into streaks as I pull onto the road, wanting to get out of this depressing neighborhood.

Ella leans against the dog, murmuring to him, her voice soft but sure. He presses closer, eyes half closed, his whole body trembling.

I glance at her, just once, then back to the road.

"You didn't have to do this," I say.

She looks up at me, surprise flickering through the pale mask of her face. "He would've died out there."

"So?"

Her lips part, like she can't believe I asked. "So I couldn't leave him."

I don't answer right away. The tires hum over wet pavement, the storm muttering low against the roof. I flick another glance at her. Her hand never stops stroking the dog. Her face is still pale, but the shock has shifted—her focus is on the animal, not the body cooling in the kitchen we left behind.

"You always do this?" I ask finally.

"Do what?"

"Save strays."

Her mouth curves in not quite a smile. "Somebody has to."

The dog groans low in his chest, curling tighter against her. She murmurs something I can't catch, her voice dropping into that same soft cadence that calmed him outside.

I grip the wheel tighter, jaw hard. Thirty minutes ago I'd seen her sparkling like a fool on a security feed. Now she's sitting pale and stubborn in my passenger seat, a half-dead dog leaning on her like she's his anchor. "What shelter do you want?"

She looks longingly at the dog. "Eastside. They're a good one."

I'm surprised she doesn't try to keep him and then remember she'll be on the run soon. She might have a softness for dogs, but her brain is always calculating.

The shelter's not far. A low building on the edge of town, lights still burning in the storm. I pull into the lot, cut the engine, and sit for a moment, watching her stroke the dog's head.

I study her profile, pale skin, damp curls clinging to her face under the cowboy hat. "I'll take him in."

Her bottom lip trembles.

Cold rage is easy. It burns clean, sharp, leaves no

questions. What I feel looking at her—mud on her knees, sequins catching light even here, kindness bleeding out of her when it shouldn't—that's harder to name.

I kill when I need to. So does she. She nearly took Thorn away in a brutal and slow death. I have to remember that fact.

She lifts her head, her eyes filling. "Can we keep him?"

THIRTEEN

Ella

We slip into Malice Media's private garage, and the air changes, becoming too still and cold. Shadows stretch long against the concrete, and inside them, men wait with guns half hidden. They don't move, but I feel their eyes tracking me.

A shiver races up my arms before I can smother it. I clamp down on Leo's leash, holding him close, grounding myself in his warm, solid weight. My dog. Mine. I still don't understand why Justice let me keep him. He doesn't strike me as a man who leaves anything to chance, especially not something alive, something that eats and breathes and requires attention. But here we are.

Leo pads beside me without a sound, big head swinging left and right. He doesn't like the shadows either, though he doesn't cower. I think he can feel the freedom that's now his.

Earlier, we'd stopped at a vet. Leo had been scrubbed down until his coat smelled faintly like oatmeal and disinfectant. He's gotten shots, a checkup, the whole nine yards. The verdict is that he's underfed but otherwise healthy. I didn't even know vets gave baths, but then, Justice has a way of bending the world until it gives him what he wants.

We picked up food. The good kind, the stuff that costs more than I usually spend on groceries for myself. We also walked Leo on a thin strip of grass by the parking lot, a scrap of normal life tucked into a day that was anything but. That moment had lodged in me, stubborn and dangerous.

Dogs don't belong in apartments. Not big ones like Leo. He needs space, dirt under his paws, and a fence to patrol. I'll have to buy a safe house with a yard, and soon. Assuming I live long enough to go house hunting.

I kept my gratitude locked tight back at the vet's office. I didn't gush. Didn't thank Justice more than politeness required because I'm freaking the hell out. Why would he let me keep the dog? He couldn't be so much of an asshole that he'd use the animal against me, could he? Did I just take on a weakness?

I hope not but won't bet on it.

Now, in the elevator, the silence is thick.

Leo tugs on the leash, and I loosen my hold. He pads over and sits on Justice's foot, panting happily.

Justice looks down. "What are you doing?"

I swear, the dog smiles. Actually smiles and then nudges Justice's knee with his nose. Pure adoration.

Justice just looks confused.

As am I. Dogs are supposed to have good instincts when it comes to people.

Men like Justice don't keep things, or people.

The elevator opens, and I brace myself for cold chrome and hard edges. Power on display.

Instead, warmth spills around me.

The penthouse is wide and bright, floor-to-ceiling windows offering a glittering sprawl of Silicon Valley. The sofa is cloth—cloth, not leather—deep brown with throw pillows that look like someone actually uses them. The coffee table is mahogany, polished but cluttered with books. Not business manuals. Not glossy magazines. Books with cracked spines and bent corners.

I edge closer. Mysteries. Christie, Grafton, newer names I don't know. Dog-eared. Read and reread. My chest tightens, because the last thing I expected here was comfort.

Justice says nothing. He just turns down a hallway with that lethal grace of his, not checking if I follow. Of course I do. My shoes whisper against the floor—wood, thick and knotted, glowing like it's been burnished by fire. Not marble. Not slate. Not cold.

Who is this man?

He opens a set of double doors, and the suite beyond is lovely. A king bed dominates the room, the navy cover thick and inviting, accents scattered through the room in the same deep blue. But it's the stones that catch me.

Garnets. Everywhere. Set into the chandelier, the drawer pulls, the handles of the dresser. Their deep red glows in the light, dark fire staring back at me. My pulse stutters. Of course he surrounds himself with them.

Another glimmer catches my eye. A heavy clock on the dresser, sleek black stone. "Onyx?" I ask, leaning closer.

"Obsidian," Justice answers, voice like low velvet.

I step back quickly, and he gestures toward two side

doors. Does he also have a connection to obsidian? That makes me shiver. I don't know why.

He points to a wide double door across the room. "Closet. I'll have clothes brought for you. Bathroom's the other one. There's a tub. For you. Not the dog."

The corner of his mouth twitches in almost a smile. Almost.

"I hadn't planned on scrubbing him again," I mutter, crossing my arms.

"I'll have his food and dishes sent up. Keep them in the bathroom. Not my kitchen."

"Fine," I say, maybe too quickly. Truth is, I like Leo close. He's pressed against my side now, brown eyes soft but wary. He keeps glancing around like he's waiting for the world to collapse. I know the feeling.

I glance back at Justice. He hasn't moved from the doorway. What game is he playing? "Justice. Why am I here?" Besides the explicit remark earlier. I do not look at the bed. Yeah, he's hot. Deadly sexy. But I have to keep my brain intact.

"You're here because you created a deadly computer virus that infected our garnets and my brother. Get the dog settled and then come out. We haven't eaten. We'll talk while we do."

Leo jumps up on the bed, circles twice, and flops onto the duvet. His sigh is so heavy it ruffles the covers. I wait for Justice to order him off, but he doesn't. Not even a glance. That rattles me more than if he'd snapped.

I pat Leo's head and whisper, "Good boy." My hand lingers longer than it should. Then I straighten. "I'll be out in a minute." I seriously doubt there are any weapons to find in here.

"Good enough."

The mirror isn't kind, but I brush my hair and wash my face anyway.

When I walk down the hall, I hear it first—oil spitting in a hot pan, metal scraping against metal. Then the smell rolls through, warm and sharp. Garlic. Butter. Lemon. My stomach knots hard enough I have to slow down.

I stroll inside and stop.

Justice is at the stove. Sleeves rolled up, forearms shifting as he tilts the pan. Chicken sizzles in a sauce that sends up curls of steam. The briny hit of capers cuts through the air, and asparagus glistens on the counter, waiting.

"Sit," he says, not looking up.

I move to the marble island and drop onto a stool. The surface is cool under my hands.

"Red or white?" he asks. "Chicken piccata. Asparagus."

"White."

He already has the bottle in hand. Rombauer Chardonnay, chilled. He pours with precision and places the glass in front of me. His fingers brush mine.

Heat fills me. My heart kicks up. Darn it. This is bad. I can't fall for this guy. Is that his plan? He's smart, I know. He also probably really knows women.

I pull back too fast and take a sip to cover it. The wine is crisp and buttery and unfairly good.

Justice plates the food without comment. The chicken is golden, the sauce glossy, and the asparagus bright green. He slides it across to me. My stomach growls, loud and humiliating. His mouth curves, faint amusement flickering and gone.

I cut a bite and chew slowly. The taste is lemon sharp, garlic warm, with the butter melting into everything. It's perfect. I should be planning a way out of here. Instead I'm sitting in his penthouse, eating dinner he cooked, every nerve wired tight.

Maybe he isn't so bad?

He eats standing across from me at the counter, fork in one hand, eyes flicking between his plate and me. Halfway through, he reaches for an unlabeled glass bottle filled with something dark. Without asking, he shakes a dusting of spice over his chicken, then leans across the counter and adds more to mine. "Try that."

I hesitate but take another bite. The flavors sharpen—heat, smoke, a bite of something I can't name. It's better, although it was already good. My head reels, not just from the food but from the sheer wrongness of sitting here, eating dinner with Justice as if this is anything close to normal. No wonder he's the most eligible bachelor around. The magazine got that one right.

He glances at his watch.

"Justice," I say quietly, laying my fork down.

His gaze lifts, pinning me in place. Dark, unblinking. "Here's the deal, Ella. I don't like that you created that virus, and I want to know everything about it. Show me how it works."

I grimace. "I thought we all agreed that the knowledge should be buried? That nobody should be able to do that."

"If you can, somebody else will be able to do the same thing, so we need to work on countermeasures," he says calmly.

My gaze narrows. He's not telling me everything. "What else?"

One dark eyebrow rises. "With the computers? Nothing."

I gulp. "Is there something outside of the computers?"

"Yeah. You and me. Forty-eight hours. I plan to be inside you most of the time."

My clit jumps. Seriously. "That wasn't the deal." So much for the couple of romantic thoughts I had about him. He only wants sex and my computer skills. Asshole.

"Sure, it was."

I hadn't been specific, now had I? "Whatever." I can be such a pain in the ass he changes his mind. Maybe. "For now, let me at your computers, and I'll try to re-create the code." It's a bad idea, but the countermeasures do make sense. I'd like to be able to protect Alana, since she charges the aquamarines that run Aquarius Social. "Okay. I mean—I have the code. I can look at it. But I'll need access to your system."

"I'm well aware." He checks his watch again, this time with impatience.

"Do you have somewhere to be?" I ask.

"I really do," he says. "A couple of men need to be tortured. Probably killed."

My fork clatters against the plate. I gulp, the wine sour on my tongue now. "Your honesty is not refreshing."

His mouth curves faintly.

"Fine," I mutter. "I'll just get to work while you're gone."

"No."

The single word is sharp enough to cut. Then something flickers in his eyes—amusement. The realization makes me blink. He's enjoying this. Us. The whole kitchen scene. Why? Is he lonely, or does he just like to play with his prey?

"You're not going anywhere near my computers unless

I'm in the room," he says. "I'll be back later tonight. Then we'll discuss the second part of our arrangement."

Heat coils through me at the phrasing, spiraling low in my belly. I hate the response, hate that my body betrays me. "I don't believe I agreed to that."

"I believe you did." His voice drops an inch lower, steady, certain. "You're blushing again."

I press my palm flat against the counter to ground myself. He's dangerous in too many ways. Still, the fact that he wants me might be leverage. He gave me twenty-four hours to run *after* I help him, which is a decent window. He has no idea how good I am at disappearing.

I'll need to check in with the ladies before I vanish. But first . . . curiosity edges out fear. If there's a back door from Aquarius Social into TimeGem Moments, there might be one buried inside Malice Media, too. I want into his servers. Bad.

I look up at him. "Have you hacked Aquarius lately?"

"No." His tone hardens. "We haven't touched their servers since Thorn and Alana—" He stops, jaw flexing.

"Combusted the world together?" I finish for him.

His mouth pulls tight. "Something like that. Why do you ask?"

"Just curious," I say, though my pulse spikes. "Trying to see where everyone stands. Things are shifting."

"Yeah." His eyes darken further. "I feel it too."

The elevator dings, echoing across the penthouse. Justice pushes his half-eaten plate toward the sink

He levels one last look at me. "I'll be back, Ella. Be ready."

FOURTEEN
Justice

Blood and torture aren't my thing. Neither are voices that lie and scratch my skin like ribbons. My legs are killing me. I slice the neck of the final guy standing, or rather sitting tied to a chair, in the torture room dug into the rocks. The ocean rolls almost happily in the darkness beneath us, and I can smell the salt and spray through the copper scent around me. I wipe the knife on the now-dead thief, making sure the obsidian and garnet accents on the hilt are clean.

Oh, he's evil. Not just a moron who shot me and tried to take Ella. There's a local gang that hires out for jobs when they're not trafficking women and kids. So many kids. He's high up in 21 Purple and has more blood and lost innocence on his hands than I do. By far. Killing him is doing the world a service, although that isn't exactly my thing, either.

Thorn likes to mete out punishment to enemies.

Sometimes needs to feel his fists pounding his anger away. I do it for the job. Because it's necessary.

I'm not mellower than my brother, not by any means. I'm just colder. I have to wonder if that's why the virus in the garnet tried to freeze him to death and is just working to drive me insane. I'm already too cold to freeze.

Sheathing my knife, I turn and forget about the three dead gangbangers immediately. I reach the outside ledge and look down, barely seeing the spray as ocean waves smash against the rocks. Clouds mostly cover the moon, and a light rain falls.

Wynd reaches me, solid and quiet at my side. "Did they give anything up?"

"No. They were hired to take Ella but don't know why." They would've told me. I'm good at my job.

Wynd sighs. "Bodies?"

"Burn and scatter the ashes far out in the ocean like usual," I murmur, his voice mildly brushing my skin but not causing any damage. I wonder if Ella can fix my problem. Then I banish thoughts of her. While she's the enemy, her small pixie-like face doesn't belong in my head that's still filled with screams of pain. "I don't like that they had no clue who hired them."

"Probably Alexei," Wynd replies, stretching his neck. "He's still consolidating power after retaking Hologrid Hub."

"Maybe." But I think Alexei would've kidnapped Ella and not just hired a local gang. That isn't his style. He likes to get his hands dirty. I've heard he's busy updating the servers at Hologrid, which is a social media platform that allows users to meet in holographic form at any time and in any place. Plus, his home compound is almost finished, and my contacts at the granite supply store tell me that Rosalie is driving him crazy with finishing touches. The idea amuses me. "Have Rick and Jocco take care of the bodies."

Wynd nods and doesn't ask questions. He's a distant cousin and understands loyalty.

I turn and stride up the rough stone steps and pause at another landing, this one with a roaring fire going, to toss in all of my clothes. Blood burns away. Trying to wash it out of fibers is a rookie mistake that ends with prison.

Then I move toward the far edge of the rock and hit a button so water cascades down over me. A quick rinse with soap, and I'm clean. Of the most recent blood, anyway. I grab a backpack off a ledge, take out a towel, and dry off before donning jeans and a T-shirt. Not my usual fare, but keeping a suit wrapped in a backpack is just stupid.

I climb up more rock steps that can't be seen from anywhere but the sky and reach my Bentley to slide inside, uncaring of the increasing rain since I have the top up. I know my men don't like me going at it alone and prefer for me to take a town car, but I need space. From voices that bite. From all voices, really.

Except for Ella's. Why hers doesn't hurt me is a mystery, and I'd love to hear her in a second of true emotion. Real passion. That brat can probably heal with her voice if she wants.

Too bad she wants me dead.

My lips twitch, and something that might feel like amusement filters through me. I'm not sure. It's a new sensation.

I drive too fast away from the ocean and back into the

city, parking behind the Blood Garnet and going inside. Fergus is lounging on an older sofa in the back room, a black-and-white movie on the plasma TV in front of him. I'm not sure if he ever sleeps. But at his age, perhaps sleep isn't something he wants to waste time doing. "Hi."

"Hi." He swirls an amber brew in a crystal glass, glancing up. "Your delivery came. I put it in your office." That's it. No questions, no concerns, because he doesn't have any. Doesn't worry about anything but making me more money.

It hits me that he's more of a father to me than mine ever was. Maybe that's why his voice doesn't grate or cause bruises. "Thanks. Get some sleep."

He shrugs, looking casual tonight in a Dodgers sweatshirt and matching sweats. "I'll sleep when I'm twelve feet under." He pauses, his dark gaze probing. "I do want to be buried. Don't go burning me into ashes and scattering them."

We've never talked about his death. "All right."

He takes a deep gulp. "Just in case I ain't dead. Don't burn me."

"I'll make sure you're dead if I bury you," I offer. "But I promise. No fire." I suppose we'll all see plenty of fire once we're gone.

He nods. "You and Thorn need to procreate to continue your line. You should get on that."

I pause. He's probably the only one of my men who'd say such a thing. Take such a risk. "That's Thorn's job." Not mine. I'm the enforcer and the one to jump in front of a bullet for my brother. My mind slides to Ella and how cute her babies would be . . . What the fuck? I don't care about that.

Plus, my job is probably to make sure she doesn't

have enough time in her life for babies. "Go back to your movie." Irritated now, I stride out of the room and toward my small office, noting the box on the desk. I cut it open with my knife and look inside.

Two large, melon-size crystals lie there. One obsidian and one a light yellow citrine. Dark and light. Good and evil? Both strong and dangerous. The obsidian hums softly, and I reach out, placing my hand over it.

Power thrums through me.

I look around, but I'm alone. I shouldn't have this connection to any stone but the garnet. It's not part of my family. I can't explain it and don't want to share it. But I love this stone. Feel like it's a part of me. There's no historical record of my lineage having a connection with any stone but garnet. Through my father's side. My mother's side didn't have any crystal knowledge. But here it is.

I stare at the pretty citrine. Yeah, if Ella's going to do the work for me, she needs power. Plus, it's a nice gift to keep her happy.

A happy Ella is easier to manage than a pissed-off sprite who looks like Tinker Bell but acts like the Terminator. If we lived in different times, in different places, we might've gotten along. Even liked each other.

This world makes us enemies, and no matter how alluring she is, I can't forget that. Although I meant my words. There's an attraction between us, and she feels it, too. We're going to act on it. Get it out of our systems. Mine, anyway. If I can somehow manipulate her with sex, I'll do it. She's a softie sometimes, and I think that might be a way to gain her acquiescence.

Or I'm just an asshole with an ego. Well, that's definitely true.

I should probably check that with her. She could try to take advantage, and I should be aware. She might be adorable, but she's a fucking genius. Our energy exchange with crystals through our genetics, for centuries, has most certainly affected brain patterns and abilities. I close the box and lift it, walking out of the pub without saying goodbye to Fergus. The guy probably wants babies to play with or teach math to or something like that. I wonder why he's never had kids.

Probably didn't want the weakness.

Neither do I.

Thorn and I were kidnapped while young and used against our father, and he didn't really give a shit about us. I might have to make some new plans for Thorn's protection soon, especially if he starts popping out little mafia dons. Or beauties like Alana. That idea stops me cold. Thorn now has weaknesses. At least one with Alana. Oh, he needs to carry on our line, so it makes sense, but now he's vulnerable in a way I hadn't anticipated. He didn't marry for logic.

The guy actually loves her.

Weakness.

I shake my head, load the box, and jump into my baby. The only one I'll ever have. I drive through town, enjoying the rain, and enter my parking garage. The guards are in place. Good.

Taking the box, I ride the elevator and enter the penthouse. Something's burning.

I turn toward the kitchen and stride inside, halting in my tracks. "What the actual fuck?"

Ella looks up, flour on her face, pots and pans and disaster all around her. "I tried to make cookies."

Burned chunks of blobs sit on several surfaces. A light smoke still fills the air. She's wearing one of my older T-shirts over her jeans, and it's covered with shit. Flour, maybe part of an egg, some sugar. Her hair is a wild mess around her head.

"Why?" I ask.

She shrugs and looks around my demolished kitchen. "I was bored. You had the ingredients. I figured, why not?"

I place the box on the counter. "All right. Let's deal with your boredom."

"Not like you plan." She puts both hands on her hips and turns to face me fully, irritation in her too-blue eyes. "That's part of the kidnapping code. We are *not* sleeping together."

"Who said anything about sleep?" I move toward her. "Are you forgetting the moment in the car? I think you screamed my name."

She lifts her chin in pure defiance. "You can't be looking for a girlfriend."

Amusement ticks through me. "I'm not."

Red spins into her cheekbones. "So you just want sex."

"Yes." I find honesty is the best move with her. "Let's get it out of our systems."

Does she look disappointed? No. Pissed. She draws in a breath. "Drop dead, Justice."

That's it. I grasp her arms. "Fine. We'll just shower together and see how long you last. My bet? Won't be long until you're begging for more."

She pushes me, hard, but now I'm pissed. I lift her just by the arms, and her legs dangle. One of her eyebrows arches.

"Don't kick me," I murmur. "You won't like the result."

She pauses. Good. I want her to take me seriously.

Something hints in the air. I pause and look toward the wall of windows beyond the breakfast nook. Rain slashes against them. But something—

A wisp through the air echoes before a flash of light. Brightness flares before a missile pierces the glass. I drop to the floor, flattening Ella beneath me on the hard tile.

Then the world explodes all around us.

FIFTEEN

Ella

The tile is cold beneath my cheek, and Justice's body is inferno hot and stone hard. A fire starts to roar above us. I shriek as panic slams into my chest, but I can't move. He's a solid force, locking me against the floor. Glass explodes somewhere behind us. Gunfire rattles through the night outside, each burst sharp and controlled.

"We have to move." Justice rolls off me, still covering me with his body, and then pulls me forward. The pressure is gone but the urgency spikes to my nerve endings. I launch into motion on instinct, my body reacting to the rhythm of gunfire.

Was that a real missile? If so, another could be on its way. The elevators won't be safe.

I gasp, and before I can warn him, Justice shoves me toward the living room.

His eyes snap to the wide wall of windows. He swears, grabs my hand, and yanks me forward. "Run."

We tear down the hallway. Justice whistles sharply, and

Leo darts out of the open doorway, panting, tail up, eyes alert. He barks twice toward the blown-out kitchen, teeth bared in a silent snarl, then sticks tight to Justice's side.

"They could've infiltrated the elevators," I choke out, my voice high.

Justice glances at me but says nothing, scanning every shadow.

A helicopter thumps the air outside, blades cutting deep and loud.

"Is it yours?" I whisper.

He doesn't answer. My stomach knots.

Then the chopper tilts, nose down.

Gunfire erupts and shatters the living room windows, bullets ripping into the furniture. The shots punch through walls, spraying drywall dust through the air.

I scream and grab Justice's arm.

"Not ours," he says, low and brutal.

Leo growls deep in his throat, teeth flashing white.

Justice drags me forward. "Go!"

We sprint the rest of the way. He kicks the wide double doors open, revealing his bedroom in tones of black and red.

I have no time to take it in. He pulls me into a walk-in closet lined with suits and rows of polished shoes. At the far wall, he shoves shirts aside and presses his palm flat against the unmarked surface.

The wall slides open.

He yanks me into a narrow chamber, and Leo leaps in behind us. A dim light flickers on overhead. The door seals behind us. My breathing is ragged.

Justice's arm clamps around my waist, holding me steady. "Hold on."

The chamber is metal, every edge perfect. He shifts me behind him with one quick motion, keeping my body shielded. His palm presses against another mirrored wall and it unlocks, revealing an arsenal stacked tight. He grabs two weapons, one for each hand.

The elevator drops without warning. My stomach flips, and I yelp. The chamber is a hidden elevator buried inside the skyscraper, carrying us away from the burning wreck above.

"I can't believe this thing exists," I gasp against his back. This box isn't on any plans and nobody knows about it. We're dropping way too fast for an elevator.

"Hold on to me." He braces his feet.

I clamp my eyes shut and wrap my arms around his waist, plastering my body to his. The landing is going to be rough.

It is.

We smash onto the floor, bounce, slam again. Metal screeches. My teeth snap together, pain shooting up my jaw. I nearly lose my grip but force my arms tighter around his waist, refusing to be thrown.

I let go only when the chamber stills. Going on instinct, I reach into the storage compartment. My fingers find a weapon, heavy and certain. A Glock. I rack the slide. A round spits free. It was already chambered, but I want to be sure.

"Don't shoot me," Justice says, voice clipped.

The building trembles, rolling with muffled blasts.

Explosions. The ground shakes and I nearly fall but regain my stance. Someone just attacked the Malice Media headquarters with a missile. How many more do they have?

Gunfire echoes above us. Shouts rip through the night. His men are holding the line.

The chamber opens into a hidden garage with room for two vehicles, but just one is here. Not just any car. A Rezvani Tank, matte black, angular and brutal, armored with clean lines and military-grade plating. Rare, modern and built for survival as well as dominance.

"Get in," Justice snaps.

I don't hesitate. I run to the passenger side, let Leo jump in and move to the rear, and then throw myself inside.

Why isn't this space under attack already?

Then I see it. Thick walls surround us that are reinforced and seamless, with no visible door. "How do you plan on getting this out of here?"

Justice drops into the driver's seat and punches a sequence on the console. The floor dips forward, grinding open into a downward ramp.

"Holy crap," I mutter.

The engine roars alive. He drives hard, tires screaming against polished concrete. A tunnel stretches ahead, walls tight on both sides.

We're flying.

I shake my head. I've studied the schematics of Silicon Valley my entire life, hacked into servers and systems most people don't know exist. There is no record of this tunnel. None.

What kind of power does Malice Media really have?

The tunnel veers. Justice takes a hard right, then a left. The incline shifts and we're climbing again. A detonation slams through the passage, deafening. I twist in my seat, panic seizing my throat.

Leo barks twice. Sharp and loud.

Through the back window, fire surges forward. A roaring wall of flame, racing straight for us.

I scream.

Justice climbs farther, slams the brakes, and throws the vehicle into a hard spin to stop abruptly. I smash into the dash and bounce back.

"Get out!" he yells, grabbing my hand. He flings his door wide, drags me across his side, and yanks us both into the open to drop fast.

Leo launches out right after us, nails scraping concrete.

We land hard in a smaller garage. I hit with my knees and keep my grip on the Glock as Justice jerks me to my feet. Leo circles once, ears pricked, then bolts for the door at our side. We chase him out into the night.

Trees. Wet earth. We're in a wooded area, nowhere I recognize.

Justice sets a punishing pace, boots driving into mud. Rain slashes down in sheets, soaking us instantly. I gasp, coughing on the cold air.

The fireball explodes behind us. The SUV, the garage, everything erupts. Metal shrieks. Shards of glass, wood, and more metal whistle through the air.

Justice barks a curse, tackles me, and drives me down behind a tree. His body covers mine as burning debris rains past. Leo growls low, teeth flashing, and crouches against us. A hubcap slams into the ground a few feet away, making him growl at it before he steadies again.

Rain pours into my eyes, blurring the ruin and beating the fire easily.

Justice looks back, jaw tight. "Nobody is coming for us through there. We're safe but need shelter."

I push to my feet, brushing pine needles off my jeans. His chin is split, blood mixing with water. He wipes it away, fury glittering in his eyes. That's twice he's thrown himself on top of me. Twice he's taken the brunt. He must really need me alive.

I glance around. "Where are we?"

"Just follow me and move fast." He ducks low, maneuvers under branches, and takes a trail at a brutal pace.

Leo runs close at my side, muscles bunched, his coat slick with rain. I pat his head as we push forward, needing the touch of something steady. His ears are up, his tail flicking like he knows this is life or death. He barks twice toward the wreck behind us, sharp and warning, then focuses ahead again. The dog is fine. More than fine. This is an adventure for him. His belly is full, his eyes bright, and he looks like he's ready to fight.

I clutch the Glock tighter. I could shoot Justice. But I don't. He saved me twice. I have no clue where we are and need him right now. Probably. More noise comes from behind us.

We walk for what feels like hours. The rain pounds us, cold and steady, and my legs ache. I'm soaked through, exhausted, and my breath comes in ragged bursts. Justice doesn't slow, just drives forward with that relentless stride until we take another turn and—there's a cabin.

I stop. This is the best safe house I've ever seen. The cabin is built into the rock itself, invisible from above or from any angle. From the path, it looks like shadow and stone until we're right on top of it.

"Come on." Justice stomps up the short steps and shoulders open the door.

Leo bolts past him, nails clicking on the wood as he bounds inside, tail wagging like he owns the place.

I drag myself up after them at a slower pace. My clothes are heavy, my hair plastered from rain and debris, and my body screams for rest. I'm wet, I'm freezing, and I'm stranded in the middle of nowhere. "Where are we?"

Justice shuts the door behind me and flicks on the lights. He's dripping rainwater onto the floor, dark hair plastered to his head. His jaw is cut from stone, his bone structure sharp, his mouth hard. Muscles stretch tight under his soaked shirt, every line carved and unyielding. His dark brown eyes are cold, pissed, and alive with power. He's currently serving as the leader of the Irish mob while his brother is out of town, standing in the shadows of a cabin, and somehow he looks like sex and danger wrapped in one. "Safe."

The place is small but solid and has one bed, a kitchenette, and a bathroom I can see off to the side. A sofa and two chairs are arranged in a square that looks like they've never been sat in. There's no warmth or clutter. This place is temporary and utilitarian, obviously here as a true safe house. "This doesn't make any sense." I scan the bare walls.

Justice moves past me into the kitchen, crouches, and reaches under the counter. He pulls a hidden lever. A trap door near the bed slides open, revealing stairs leading into shadow. The steady hum of electronics rises up to meet us.

That sound lifts something in my chest. "Now that's better."

Justice doesn't move right away. His gaze locks on the Glock in my hand. "Give me the gun."

"No." I tighten my grip, daring him. "I'm not defenseless anymore. You have two guns and I'm keeping this one."

His jaw ticks. "Hand it over." He steps in close, all hard muscle and authority, his hand closing over mine. He pries my fingers back, ignoring my struggle, and yanks the weapon free.

"Don't," I snap, fury flaring hot inside me.

"I don't take risks I don't have to," he says, sliding the Glock into the back of his waistband. "And you, Ella, are a risk."

Leo growls low from where he's settled near the sofa, ears forward, tail twitching. Justice doesn't even glance at him. He just turns for the trap door, commanding without effort. "Let's find out what's going on."

I glance toward the kitchen to see if there's a knife block. Anything I can use for a weapon. Nothing. I can run, but the way I'm feeling, I won't get far.

But downstairs? There are computers. Humming. Yeah. Those are weapons, too. He shouldn't let me near them.

"Come on," he says.

Gladly.

SIXTEEN

Ella

In the cabin's underground computer room, I stare at a screen showing a news crew at the smoldering skyscraper housing Malice Media. This place is high tech and delightful. Leo has long since gone upstairs to sleep—no doubt on the bed. Justice types next to me and then finally sits back. "They hit the penthouse and not the social media hub on the main floors."

Yeah, I noticed. I turn to face him in the swivel chair, noting he doesn't look tired. Not like I feel. He appears pissed off and ready for revenge. "You think they want you or me dead?" People know he took me out of that hospital, and it's easy to find his apartment.

He shrugs powerful shoulders. "Who knows. Maybe both?"

A two-for-one. Smart. This isn't good for him, not by any means. It's public. Thorn's out of town. If Justice doesn't strike back at somebody fast, he looks weak, which in the mafia, Irish or Russian, is bad. He'll have enemies coming for him. There's no chatter on the web. "I can't find who ordered this."

"Neither can I." A muscle in his jaw clenches. He has a tough guy jaw. We're both in danger, and he might be in more than me.

I yawn. "I need to use the bathroom. I don't suppose you have dog food anywhere upstairs?"

"No, but I keep steaks in the freezer. Take a couple out and thaw them in the microwave. We can feed him one."

I like that. Leo needs to be fattened up. "Fine." I yawn again and stand, wobbling slightly. Mud has dried on my jeans, making them stiff. "Extra clothes?"

"In the bathroom cupboard. Nothing will fit you." He's already turned back to one of the three computers.

"Great." I limp to the stairs and chug up them, reaching the main room to see the dog snoring in the middle of the bed. I hesitate. He's a good dog and I want to keep him. Hopefully Justice won't hurt him.

I cross the cabin to the bathroom, use the facilities, and look for clothing. Yep. T-shirts and jeans. The shirt falls almost to my knees, and I have to roll up the too-large jeans. A lot. Then I move into the kitchen area to quietly open the fridge and take out steaks before going through the few drawers. There are a couple of good knives, and I filch them.

I need to get away from Justice. He'll force me to give him the code to create a computer virus, and nobody should have that. It's too much power, and he might use it against Alana's family or Rosalie's man. It's what they all do. The four families have a lot of blood on their hands.

And we all know there's someone else on the board. A

fifth player who has yet to make a real move. Unless they have, and we haven't figured it out.

Somebody wants me dead. A lot of people want Justice dead. While I don't think he wants to kill me, he does want to have sex with me for the near future. My body is totally on board with the idea, and my brain knows better. Probably because my heart keeps going all pitter-patter because the asshole keeps protecting me with his life. Jerk.

I have to get away from him, and this is probably my only chance.

With one last sad look at the sleeping animal, I tiptoe across the living room, open the front door, quietly shut it, and start to run.

Seconds later, heartbeats really, I hear the door crash open.

Fuck.

I duck my head and run faster, dodging between trees and ignoring the punishing rain. It's as if nature wants to stop me.

He's getting closer and not being quiet about it. Why would he? This is his territory and he knows it. Plus, he's faster and stronger.

But I'm smaller.

I duck between two younger trees, crouching to avoid their branches, and keep low.

He's coming.

Branches slam into me as I run, lungs burning, mud sucking at my shoes. The brambles jab against my side. My chest aches, but I keep moving.

Justice is behind me. No stealth. Heavy boots, breaking branches, closing fast.

I duck under a branch, cut left, then cut right. My breath tears out in gasps. For a second I think I bought space.

I didn't.

His hand clamps my arm. Hard. He yanks me back and spins me. My feet lose the ground. My back slams into a tree, bark scraping, air exploding out of me.

He's here. Too close. Rain drips from his face and plasters his black hair to his head. His dark eyes lock on mine, glittering. His arm bars across my chest, pinning me. His other hand braces by my head.

He's all cut muscle, soaked shirt plastered to his body, chest rising and falling steady while mine jerks. Heat rolls off him even in the storm. He looks like power carved sharp. Dangerous.

My chest heaves. I shove at him with both hands. His body doesn't budge. "Let me go," I rasp, voice shredded from the run.

His jaw flexes. His mouth is hard. His breath hits my cheek, rough. "Are you insane? You don't even know where we are right now."

I push harder, palms against his chest. Nothing. He doesn't move. "The forest is safer than you are."

His laugh is short. Cruel. He leans in closer. The bark digs harder into my spine. His body presses, unyielding. His mouth is near mine now, heat cutting through the cold rain. "The forest at night is much safer than I am," he agrees, low and certain. "You'll never outrun me."

My breath comes too fast. My hands stay flat on his chest. I could shove again. I don't. My heart slams hard enough to hurt.

His eyes flick down once, then back up. Fury still

burns in them, but it's not just anger. There's hunger in those orbs. For me.

I swallow. My legs tremble but I hold his stare. My voice shakes but comes out. "Maybe I don't have to outrun you. Maybe I just need to fight."

His lips twitch. Not a smile. A warning. His grip on me tightens, like he's daring me to try.

Rain pounds harder, running over both of us. The storm rages, but all I hear is his breathing and mine.

My pulse hammers as I glare up at him. His arm pins me, body pressed tight, rain dripping between us. The knife digs into my hip where I hid it. My fingers close around the hilt.

I rip it free and slash upward.

Justice catches my wrist before the blade can rise past my ribs. His grip crushes, iron strong. His eyes narrow, fury flashing. "Really?" he rasps.

I twist and fight, my muscles straining. He holds me in an unbreakable grip. Man, he's strong. I slam my knee up, but he blocks with his thigh. The knife trembles in my hand, but he forces it down.

"Let me go," I hiss, wet hair clinging to my face.

He rips the blade from my grip and flings it into the mud. Before I can lunge, he spins me, slams me chest first against the tree. Bark bites through the fabric of my borrowed shirt. His palm cracks across my ass, sharp and hot.

I gasp, rage and shock colliding inside me. "Bastard."

His mouth is at my ear, breath hot. "You pull steel on me again, I'll make you regret it."

I shove back hard. He presses tighter, his body pinning mine. His hand grabs my wrists, slams them above my head. His other hand digs into my waist, holding me against the rough bark, and he secures the other knife. That, too, flies through the air.

"Get off me," I pant, straining.

"Not a chance." His voice is pure gravel, steady while mine shakes.

I buck against him, every muscle burning. He drags my arms down, spins me around, and presses my back into the tree this time. His hand locks around both my wrists, pinning them above me. His chest crushes mine, hot, soaked, all carved muscle and fury.

Dark eyes bore into me, alive with anger, with something more.

"You think you can fight me?" His voice cuts low.

"Yes," I rasp.

His lips twitch, dangerous. "You're fighting yourself more than me. That's why you ran, baby."

There's too much truth in his statement. But that's not the only reason. I can't give him the code to create that computer virus. I just can't. "Not a chance, asshole," I hiss.

His mouth crashes onto mine.

The kiss is merciless, claiming, and hard enough to bruise. His grip locks my wrists high, unbreakable, his body pressing me flat to the tree. Heat rolls off him despite the storm, his tongue demanding, forcing me to match him.

I bite his lip, sharp. He doesn't flinch. He growls low in his chest and kisses me harder, swallowing the sound of my defiance. Desire roars through me, louder than the blood rushing through my veins, stronger than the storm gathering around us.

My nipples peak and my thighs tremble. I'm so wet

already that it stuns me. I'm *craving* him. Yeah, maybe this is why I ran.

Rain beats down. Bark digs into my back. His mouth is hot and rough, his body iron, and I can't move—except to kiss him back.

Pinned. Furious. Alive.

The tree digs into my back. His weight pins me there, chest to chest, his hand locked around my wrists above my head. His breath is hot against my mouth. My chest heaves against him, furious, my pulse a fist pounding inside me as he releases my hands and pulls me closer by the waist. Such need scares me, but it's too late. I don't think. I grab his shirt, soaked and plastered to his chest, and yank. The fabric clings then rips up over his head. Rain hits bare muscle, every line cut, chest broad and hard.

My breath stutters.

He seizes the opening, slams my wrists back up, pins me again, mouth crashing onto mine.

The kiss is brutal. Teeth, tongue, fury. His body crushes mine, my spine grinding into the tree, rain dripping between us. His hand grabs my hip, fingers biting deep, dragging me against him.

I should shove him off. I don't. My body answers before my head can scream no. My hips shift forward, grinding into his. My fingers claw at his shoulders when he frees one wrist, nails digging into hot skin.

"This doesn't make sense," I rasp against his mouth.

"Nothing about us makes sense," he growls, voice raw. "Doesn't mean I'll stop."

I lunge up, kiss him, mouth open, hungry. He meets me with equal violence, devouring.

His hands tear at my clothes, pulling down the fabric

and shoving it aside. The cold storm slams my bare skin but his heat burns over me.

I yank at his jeans, and the wet fabric is rough against my palms. He jerks them down halfway and kicks them off. His mouth devours my neck, my collarbone, back to my lips.

Every move is a fight. I shove, he pins. I claw, he captures. I buck, he drives me harder into the bark. My defiance makes him fiercer. His control makes me wilder. The storm disappears. The danger, the chase, the knives, the guns—gone. Only this. My naked body lit, my thoughts burned away. Even sound.

He lifts me, both hands gripping my ass as I wrap my legs around his hips and my arms around his neck. His mouth owns mine, his body crushing every line of me.

I gasp his name. He growls mine.

Then he slams inside me. I'm more than ready, and I don't understand that. Sex and fighting have never gone together before now. But I feel him everywhere. I gasp, arching, completely taken over as he holds me against the tree, my legs around his hips, his cock pulsing inside me. All the way.

I like it more than I should. More than I want to, but I don't care. Later, I will, but that's a concern for tomorrow. Right now, I'm finally out of my head. Out of my fear of the future, of the enemies coming for me. There's only right here and now. I grip him tighter as he starts to pound, his hands protecting me from the bark now. Spread across my back. I dig my nails into his skin, gasping and climbing. Fast. Desperately. He shifts slightly to the left, brushing my clit, and I explode.

Crying out his name, I bite into his shoulder, silencing

myself. He keeps hammering, a long time, way past the aftershocks inside me. I climb again. How is this even possible? His teeth latch onto my shoulder. Pain and pleasure mix wildly inside me. I teeter on the edge again and then fall, my entire body gyrating against his much larger one. His hotter one. The guy is an inferno.

When I've come down, he stills. His body tightens then he erupts inside me, jerking wildly.

Holy crap.

His teeth release their hold. I gasp, trying to breathe.

The rain pummels us.

He leans back, his gaze intense. Shielded. Dark. Then he slowly withdraws from me. My body shakes, trying to hold him in, and more aftershocks slake through me.

I can only stare at him. Bemused.

One of his dark eyebrows arch. Then, in a too smooth movement, he shifts and tosses me over his broad shoulder, buck-assed naked, before striding back the way we came.

To the cabin.

SEVENTEEN

Justice

I watch her sleep. Blonde hair springs in curly directions, and her body is barely discernible beneath the comforter. She snuggles into the bed with the dog splayed across the bottom, no doubt pinning her feet. I took her hard against the tree outside and then again inside the cabin, and she'd been all in. A fireball in such a small package. Consent from both of us had been clear, and I'm sure we'd both like to change that fact. Not the consent, but the fact that we'd been unable to stop. Truth be told, I almost lost control.

Never in my life have I wanted a woman more.

She's wrong for me. All wrong. An enemy with a mission of her own. She's a killer as well. Attempted, anyway. Allowing such a threat to continue breathing goes against my very DNA. Against every cell still multiplying or dying in my body. I've fucked her twice, and she's nowhere near out of my system.

It might take a week.

A buzz sounds and I move to the kitchen, opening the

bottom drawer and ripping out the false bottom to grasp a burner phone. Neither the woman nor the dog move.

I pad barefoot across the cabin and outside to sit on the porch, my legs extended to the bottom step. "You shouldn't be calling on your honeymoon," I answer.

"Who attacked us?" Anger rides Thorn's tone. So much for his relaxed vacation.

"Don't know." The rain has ebbed but water drips loudly from the tree branches around me. "The hit was to the penthouse and not the servers, so—"

Thorn swears. "You were the target. Take you out while I'm gone." He exhales. Loudly. "I'll have the pilots clear a flight home."

I stiffen. "Nope." My jeans are clean but my feet are still dirty. I should shower. "If you come back right now and don't trust me to handle this, then you're cutting my legs off beneath me." It'd be seen as a sign of weakness. "I have to handle it myself."

He's silent. Yeah, he knows I'm right. Might not like it, but there you go. "Do you think it was Ella Rendale?" The question makes sense because she did try to kill him.

"No."

"How can you be sure?"

I glance at the silent cabin behind me. "I had her in the penthouse at the time. She might've been the target." I do like that none of our men told Thorn about Ella. So his sources are from outside the organization. Our men are loyal to us both. "She's safe."

"You kidnapped Ella Rendale?" Thorn snaps.

I grin. "Maybe she came willingly." Actually, she'd just *come* willingly. I doubt Thorn would appreciate that statement.

"Justice, I said I want her alive. Not dead."

Yeah, he had said that. "You're safe, brother."

He growls now. "I'm not worried about blame. If she dies, Alana is hurt. Bad. I can't let you do it."

"I'm not going to let her die," I snarl.

He's quiet. "Wow. That's a tone from you."

"If I have to lock her down, I will. But I won't kill her." Damn, I sound reasonable. What tone? I can smell her on me and still hear her sighs while I moved inside her. I have to remember always that Thorn is now compromised because of Alana. Not weakened. Just not thinking as pragmatically as he once had. I'll never let anybody get that close to me and my motivations. A shuffle sounds and I reach back to let the dog out.

Leo looks at me and then saunters down the stairs, running into the trees.

Allowing her to keep him wasn't a weakness. Maybe I'm totally full of shit. Could be. "Thorn? Stop worrying. I've got this." My tone stays level. I let her keep the dog because now she has a vulnerability. Simple as that. Yeah, I'm lying to myself.

"What the hell is going on?"

Perhaps my tone wasn't as level as I thought. At least he hasn't heard about the attack in the middle of the street. The first attack. "Nothing. At the moment, I'm trying to figure out who just shot a missile into my penthouse. Someone is making a move, and you have to stay there."

He's silent for several long moments, no doubt trying to get around my logic. He can't. "You need to hit somebody and hard. Now."

"Already in the plans," I say calmly. Even if I'm wrong, I have to strike out. That's easy enough. While

I'm calm, I'm pissed. Cold fury is so much more effective than heated fire, usually. "I'm not hitting Alana's family, so don't worry about that."

"Alexei might've made a move since he probably didn't know Ella was in the penthouse."

Very true. A good statement would be to hit the Sokolovs and Hologrid Hub. Our people are prepared for a mob war with the Russians, and Alexei is probably ready as well. I don't like the idea of the streets of Silicon Valley running red while Thorn is out of town, but I'll do what I have to do. "Thorn? Get back to your bride and make me a nephew. Or niece. I don't care which." So long as the kid can charge garnets. "You might need a few of those." There's a good chance their kid will charge aquamarines like Alana does, so they'll have to keep going until they get a garnet charger.

He coughs. "Don't get ahead of yourself. I just got married and am not bringing a kid into this until we get things settled down." He clears his throat. "Why don't you have a kid or five? Ella is a genius, and she'll make kids who can charge stones."

I inhale so fast I almost choke. "Shut up."

"You shut up. I'm going to ask you again. Why was Ella Rendale in the penthouse?"

I can't let him know about my illness, so I take the easy way out. "I want her."

He's quiet.

I roll my eyes. "It's temporary. There's something between us, and we're dealing with it."

He snorts. Actually snorts. "I see. You giving it a number of fucks or a number of hours?"

I think he might've attached "dumbass" to the end of

that sentence, but I'm not sure. There's wind through the line. "None of your business. Just don't worry about it."

His chuckle sounds lighter. Amused. Good. "This might be fun, brother. Ella Rendale, huh?"

That's it. I'm done. "I'll be in touch. Say hi to my new sister for me." I end the call.

The dog returns just as my phone buzzes. "Yeah."

"It's Kaz. The servers are safe, but we did have a back-door attack when the missiles were flying."

Makes sense. "Did they get in?"

Kaz coughs. "There was a zero-day in your API gateway. Looked like a TLS downgrade at first, but they piggy-backed it into a privilege escalation inside your SSO. If it had landed, they'd have root on every user profile inside Malice Media. They'd own our authentication keys. Every call, every handshake, spoofed."

I blink. "Somebody is feeling brave."

"Apparently. They could've hijacked every identity on the platform. Every politician, every celebrity, every account. They'd be inside the system anytime they wanted."

I grind my back teeth together. "Did you stop it?"

"Of course. I built a decoy environment last month. Full mirror of your production. Their exploit tripped my canary accounts. They thought they were rooting the real servers. In reality, they were trapped in my sandbox."

Excellent. I like that. A lot. "What'd you do to them?"

Kaz chuckles. Low. "I injected a poisoned payload. Their central command should be fried, every machine in their cluster hard-locked. Whoever ran it won't be sleeping tonight. I left them a little note. Nothing they'll enjoy."

"Good job, Kaz." He's so jacked right now that his voice isn't grating on me. That's interesting.

"Thanks." Yeah, he sounds surprised. "They wasted rockets and hackers and got nothing."

I wish that were true. "Not nothing. They tested our response time. They measured how long it took you to move assets and how quickly I countered. Next time, they won't send amateurs. This was recon. There's another attack coming, Kaz. After they regroup. Get ready."

"I agree. Also, hate to tell you this, but that wasn't the only cyber attack. There was another push from that signature we've been watching the last couple of months. Just a push."

Ah. The fifth player. "Keep trying." I end that call. Maybe Ella has a line on the new player. It's possible.

The door opens and a sleepy Ella Rendale stands there wearing one of my T-shirts that reaches past her knees. Her eyes are cornflower blue, her legs toned, and her toes cute and pink. "We need to talk."

Ella

I don't like feeling off balance, and dealing with people sucks, which is why I prefer computers. Code. Numbers. Not hot-bodied males who can fuck like machines against a tree with a storm beating the wilds all around us.

Leo yips and runs toward the porch.

Justice partially turns, his dark eyes raking me. Head to toe. I swear, I can feel that gaze like a touch. A rough one. "So talk."

Irritation clacks through me. Along with vulnerability. Even though he's sitting and I'm standing, and even though I have a knife tucked into the back of my underwear beneath the borrowed shirt, I feel anything but strong. The sun has risen in the east, painting the bottom of the clouds pink. My mouth opens and nothing comes out. What in the world can I say? "Okay."

His hair is tousled and his feet bare. Man. Even his feet look tough. His toes are scarred, the skin rough, like he's used to gravel, to fights, to never being comfortable. The shirt he's wearing is thin and clings across hard muscle, every line cut and unyielding. He looks carved into that porch, the boards straining faintly under his weight. "How about you lose the knife and then we talk?"

I blink. How in the world does he know? "Um—"

"Don't lie. We're past that." He holds out a hand. "I don't want to come and take it from you."

There's a part of me, a rather large part, that'd like to shove that blade through his palm. Rolling my eyes, I yank it free and hand it over. "You're kind of a jerk."

"Just kind of?" He pats the worn wooden porch next to him.

I feel shy. Darn it. So I lift my chin and walk to him, sitting on a plank. The wood is warm from the sunrise, and I notice the grooves cut deep into the boards, like someone sharpened knives here. His heat radiates through the space between us. Leo licks my face, snorts happily, and then jumps off the porch, bounding into the trees. His tail wags once before he disappears, ears high, already on guard.

Maybe I can be honest with Justice. "I'm not going to give you the code for the computer virus." At least not until I figure out a cure for everybody if it gets loose again. I feel guilty enough about that already. Causing a world-wide problem would suck.

"You'll give me what I want."

What a complete ass. Maybe I can change the subject. "Forget that for a moment. Why do you need my help, if it's not for that virus?" It's a safe topic, much safer than talking about sex the night before, so I latch on to it.

He looks into the trees. "It's about that virus. You apparently know that my brother has lexical-gustatory synesthesia and he gets a taste in his mouth when people speak to him?"

I nod. All right. Now we're finally getting to it. "Do you have that?"

"A variation of it. Voices can irritate the hell out of me." That makes sense. He does seem cranky. "When you tangled with the garnet and nearly killed my brother, I thought I could help. I tried to charge the stone myself and take that virus into my body, hoping it would leave Thorn's. He doesn't know. Won't know."

I swallow hard. "Are you dying too?"

"No. I don't think so." His tone is maddeningly calm. "If I am, it's slower than it was with Thorn."

My stomach twists. "Oh." The word is flat, useless. I try not to grimace but fail. "What is happening with you?"

"Ever since I tried to exchange energy with the garnet you infected, voices can hurt me a lot worse than before. It's always been difficult, but now voices can bruise or cut me easier than before."

Holy crap. No wonder he wants me dead. "I didn't mean to hurt Thorn," I burst out, surprising myself. "Or you. Honest. I thought I could cause a disruption. Not a death." It's the truth, but I don't expect him to believe me. "I wanted to test it out on Malice Media, perfect the virus, and hit TimeGem Moments to retake my company."

Using the diamonds, of course. Not the citrines. I'd never infect the citrines.

He cuts me a look. "I don't know whether or not to believe you, but I think I do."

Because we had sex? "Why?"

"Lies cut." He looks away again.

So now the guy is a lie detector? This might not be good for me. Although I am telling the truth about Thorn. This at least explains why Justice wants me near his computers. Perhaps I can cure him without giving him the code. "How can I help?" To heal Thorn, we healed the garnet and Thorn at the same time. So why wasn't Justice healed as well?

"I don't know. Do you still plan to infect your family's crystals?"

"No."

He winces and rubs his neck. The muscles in his shoulders roll under the shirt, thick and coiled. "When I tell you not to lie to me, listen carefully. I will retaliate."

Crap. I really don't like this. "Then don't ask me questions I don't want to answer." Should I lower my voice? Soften it? I don't want him to retaliate. "I'm glad Thorn didn't die, and I'm sorry you were also infected."

He glances at me, apparently unharmed. Yeah, that's the truth. "Can you fix it?"

"I have no idea, but I'll try. Will you promise not to kill me?" I hold my breath. Oh, I won't make it easy to kill me, but I don't like my odds against him.

"I promise."

I still. He just promised. "Um, okay. Because we, ah, slept together?" Curiosity has always been a problem of mine.

"No," he says softly.

All right. That may hurt a little bit. "Then why?"

"I never planned to kill you."

How does that make sense? My mind scrambles. Wait a minute. Dread slams into my stomach. "Do you also promise not to lock me down somewhere away from computers?"

He doesn't answer.

Damn it. "If you do, you might as well kill me." It sucks that we don't trust each other, considering the sex was, well, amazing. Beyond so. The thought sends anger through my blood. "Have we screwed each other out of our systems yet?"

Without warning, he partially turns and plucks me off the porch, settling me on his hard thighs. His arm is solid around my waist, his chest hot against my shoulder. He smells like smoke and rain and iron. "Not even close. Did I hurt you last night?"

I try not to relax while surrounded by so much heat. And muscle. "Do you care?"

"Yes."

Well. All right, then. "No, you didn't hurt me." Not in a way I didn't appreciate. I glance down to see the back of his hand shredded. The grooves are deep, skin raw, blood dried in the cracks. I gingerly run a finger over one of them. He protected my skin from the bark and injured his own. While he had me up against the tree. "I don't want to be your enemy, Justice."

"Good."

Yeah, but that wasn't my brain speaking. Not even close. My body leans into him without asking my permission, and his hold tightens just slightly, like he noticed.

A rumble echoes through the trees, and a black SUV drives around the side of the rock formation. Its tires grind on gravel, engine deep and quiet. Justice stands, still holding me way too easily. Too casually, like I belong right here, cradled against his chest. His dark eyes flick at the vehicle, and I once again can't read him. "Our ride is here."

EIGHTEEN

Justice

Bringing Ella into the Malice Media hub tightens every muscle in my body. I don't like having her here. She's too dangerous.

I fed her an early lunch, so at least she's in a good mood. The woman has a penchant for cookie-dough milkshakes.

The elevator doors slide open, and we step into the quiet hum of the floor. Cold air breathes out from the vents and smells like metal and lemon cleaner. Screens glow along the far wall, code racing in columns that reflect off the polished concrete.

Kaz looks up from his work and stills. He's got both hands going on different keyboards, fingers moving so fast it looks like he's playing two pianos. He doesn't need to look down. Thirty and all lean focus, dark blond hair that never quite cooperates, green eyes that miss nothing. His chin juts like it wants an argument, with a stubborn dimple dead center. I noticed it when we were kids and it still reads like Cary Grant, whether he likes it or not.

Yeah. It's rare for me to bring anybody in here, much less a woman in my T-shirt, jeans, and dirty tennis shoes.

"Hi." He stands and comes toward her, hand out, clear interest on his face. "You're Ella Rendale."

"I am." She takes his hand, smiling, and the room brightens like somebody bumped the dimmer.

Kaz grins back and shifts his feet on Italian loafers. "I'm Kazstone, but everyone calls me Kaz. I wish I had nicer clothes to offer you." His gaze lifts to me with his eyebrows arching in a clear question.

I don't answer, as this is none of his business.

The walls show faint scuffs where a fight got too close. Cleaned. Sterile again. Of course Kaz handled it. He gets twitchy if a cable isn't coiled right, and having part of the building crumble after a missile attack probably kept him up all night.

"Ms. Rendale, what can I do for you?" His tone sounds friendly. Too friendly.

I answer before she can. "I'm taking her into the main server room."

He draws back a fraction. Shock flickers across his face. "You're . . . you want to take her where?"

"It's a long story, and it's none of your business," I say.

"Fine." He snaps the reply off and turns back to his screens. His fingers fly harder, like he can out-type his temper.

Heat bites along my clavicle, and a bruise blooms up fast. I wince. Ella tracks the movement and then looks away without comment. Her hair has dried into curls I didn't expect, brushing her shoulders. She used to wear it shorter, cut to flare out. I like the longer length. It gives me something to hold onto. The thought hits hard and I shake it off. I need to get my head on straight.

"Come on." I take her hand. Her fingers are cool. I lead her to the blank wall and press my free palm to the sensor. The plate warms, reads me, and the seam opens with a soft hiss. I'm rather disappointed the missile attack to my penthouse destroyed the citrine I purchased for her.

Cold air spills from the server room and smells like dust and ozone. Rows of towers blink in patient lines, status lights pulsing like a heartbeat.

Ella steps in and draws a sharp breath. Her excitement vibrates through her and into me, clean and bright. The hum around us seems as calming to her as it is to me, and that pleases me.

Fascinating.

"Oh, this is awesome," she breathes.

"Yeah. It is." I follow her inside as the door snicks closed behind me, sealing us into the server room. The air is tinged with the sharp scent of heated metal, carrying the steady vibration of power. The hum isn't loud, but it's constant, a low thrum that works its way under my skin.

Ella moves forward, steps quiet, almost reverent, her gaze locked on the garnet in the center of the room. The gem sits on a black pedestal, bathed in a narrow shaft of white light that fractures into crimson sparks across the polished floor. The stone itself is huge, flawless, the deep red facets alive as if fire is trapped inside.

"What a beauty," she whispers, and pride tightens my chest. It shouldn't matter. But this garnet feels like mine.

"Thank you," I murmur.

Her attention slides past the stone to the cupboards lining the far wall. "Backup garnets?"

"Yeah, and some small alexandrite. I'm trying to get my hands on bigger ones."

She nods, eyes narrowing in thought. "I've read the data. I haven't tested them much myself, but from what I can tell, they accelerate the processes of the current gems. More like fuel than competition."

Clinical words, sure, but the way she glances over her shoulder ruins it. She's too damn distracting in my T-shirt, wearing too-large jeans, curls wild around her shoulders.

She circles the garnet slowly, fingertips trailing through the air near it, eyes fixed on the pulsing glow. "This one's perfectly healthy," she says at last. "Have you exchanged energy with her?"

"Several times."

"And it hasn't helped you?"

Wouldn't that be ideal? "No."

She presses a finger against her mouth, thoughtful. "I'm not sure what to do. Your condition hasn't killed you yet, but it could. Especially if the wrong people realize how to exploit it." Her gaze lifts, blue eyes bright and sharp, pinning me. "What would happen if too many jerks attacked at once? If they hit you with their voices together?"

The question slices too close. I've worried about damage to my internal organs—my heart or even my brain. My jaw tightens. "I don't want to think about it. Only you know about my condition. I don't want Thorn to know."

"That puts a bull's-eye on me."

"It does." I step closer, the garnet's glow brushing heat along my arm. "So keep that fact to yourself."

She rolls her eyes at me, like I'm overbearing. Her lips curve, faint but there.

Not afraid. Not of me.

That's not good.

She glances at a clock mounted high on the far wall, just beyond the rows of blinking server lights. Her brows pull together. "We can't leave Leo in the car too long."

Of course. She's attached to that dog. "I know." I study her, waiting. "Any thoughts here?"

She shakes her head, curls shifting around her shoulders. "No, but I promise I'll start digging. Quietly. Under the radar. I need to research your condition more, even if there's nothing written about it. Sometimes the key is in the underlying problem, not the name of the ailment. I also want to recheck everything we did for Thorn. Something in that process should have helped you too."

"Yeah, but we were focused on Thorn," I say, jaw tightening. "I just haven't figured it out yet."

"I know." Her voice softens, and the weight in it punches straight through my chest while my cock hardens. That sweet, soft sound might kill me. "I know it's my fault. But I will help you." Then she tries to negotiate. "But since your apartment was blown up, maybe we meet in a couple of days? Somewhere neutral?"

A low chuckle escapes me before I can catch it. When was the last time I laughed? Genuine amusement slides through me, hot and unfamiliar. "You're fucking adorable."

Her head snaps up, eyes flashing. She doesn't preen. She knows exactly what I mean.

I guess I need to be more direct. "No."

"Justice, come on—"

"Nope. If you think I'm letting you out of my control, you've lost your damn mind."

She looks like she might stomp her foot, and hell, it's cute. Too cute. "Listen, buddy—"

"Nope." I cut her off again, slow and deliberate. "Don't argue with me, Ella. You won't win."

Her glare could scorch a weaker man. "Fine. Then where exactly do you plan on putting me and my dog?"

"You'll see." I reach for her hand again.

She narrows her eyes, suspicion etched across her face. "I guess I'm not being clear. It's time to make a deal. I'll save you, and you let me go. Full stop."

"No." I'm done. I yank my shirt up over her head before she can move.

She hisses, hands on her hips, gorgeous tits tightening in the cold.

Fuck, I like that she doesn't cover herself and looks like a sex kitten.

Instead, she slides one leg back and barely drops into a fighting stance. If I wasn't watching her so closely, I would've missed it.

Heat spirals down my spine and flicks my balls wide awake. My blood thickens and heats through my veins.

Her chin lifts, and challenge fills her blue eyes. Then she screams. At an ear-splitting decibel.

I frown, waiting until she stops. "You know this room is soundproof."

Her face falls. "That didn't hurt you? At all?"

The little brat. She tried to shred my skin with her voice? As an experiment, it isn't bad. Mean, though.

"No. Guess you can't extort me that way," I murmur. Fascinating. The screech had just annoyed me. No pain involved. Why just with her?

Her mouth quirks. "Darn it." She's disappointed?

I'm caught between being pissed and amused. "Don't try it again."

Her eyes light. Wait a minute. Does she think she hurt me? She opens her mouth and shrieks at an even louder and higher tone.

My ears protest like any human's would. So I dodge forward, lift her up, and plant her over my knee. She struggles, and I lift my leg to the round base of the pedestal, giving me better leverage. Then I smack her ass.

Hard.

She yelps and squirms like a fish on the line.

The clothes are in the way. I tear them off and then smack her several more times. Her ass turns red, and my handprint looks perfect there. Absolutely fucking perfect.

She lets loose with an impressive list of threats and curses, so I start spanking her in time with her words. Finally, she stops with a soft whimper.

I smack her three more times. "Are you done being a brat?"

"I fucking hate you," she breathes out, face down, her blonde hair brushing the floor.

"Guess not," I muse, swinging again. Her butt is beet-red, and I can smell her arousal. I'm hard, but this is a lesson that needs to be learned. And acknowledged. I give her five more, noting how hard she's panting. "You done, baby?"

Her body tightens, and I can feel how hard it is for her not to swear at me again. So I give her another good smack to help her out. "Yes," she blurts, still struggling. "Fine. Yes."

Good enough. I palm her ass and feel her shudder. Then I slide my hand down between her legs, where she's so fucking wet my brain almost explodes. I tap her clit, and she moans.

Not good enough.

I flip her over, plant her on the cement floor, drop to my knees, and bury my face between her legs.

Her hand lands on my head. "No, Justi—"

Then she's coming. Hard and fast, her body gyrating against my tongue. She slaps both hands on the hard floor now, arching into my mouth. She tastes like every good dream I've ever had with a hint of spice. I murmur against her as she comes down, licking her. That was fast. Too fast.

She gives a half-hearted struggle, and I use my shoulders to widen her legs before swirling my tongue around her clit.

The sound she gives makes me chuckle against her, inside her, and she arches again. I slip two fingers inside her and crisscross them before going at her clit again. God, she's responsive. She tries to hold back this time, her legs tightening by my shoulders. Perfect. I turn and bite into her thigh, not gently, and she gasps.

Then I return to her clit and suck it deep into my mouth, lashing her with my tongue.

She emits a strangled cry and comes hard, her thighs clamping on my shoulders. Her entire body goes lax when she comes back down, and her hands flop on the floor.

I lift up, setting my chin on her pubic bone. "I could do this all day."

"You are trying to kill me," she breathes.

I smile, feeling light. Oddly so. I'm starting to wonder if my plan of sexing her out of my system is going to work. I push up on my knees and flip her over, pulling her up onto her hands and knees with one arm while releasing my cock with the other.

One hard push and I'm inside her. She's wet and swollen around me, and I can feel her nerves firing somehow. I clamp a hand on the back of her neck, the other on her hip, and start to pound.

Hard and fast, my vision blurs. Nothing in my entire life has ever felt this good. A warning echoes in the back of my mind, but then her body is clamping down on me. All around my cock, as another climax rips through her, caressing ferociously around my dick, and taking me with her.

I shudder as I stiffen, holding her to me, and come so hard I see stars.

Holy fuck. That was fast. I'm a guy who can go all night. Can make sex last hours. Was that even minutes? Yeah, she took me with her, and she got off three times, but still. I withdraw and her body trembles.

My gaze catches on the clear imprint of my hand on her ass.

I breathe out and somehow get the clothing back on us both. She stands next to me, her blue eyes dazed as I brush her hair away from her face. "Come back. Concentrate," I say, my voice gritty.

She swallows and shakes her head. "I'm fine."

I open the door and lead her back into the main hub. The air feels warmer here, buzzing with static from the server racks. The hum greets us like a pulse, steady and cold. Screens flicker across the wall, lines of code streaming too fast for anyone but Kaz to follow. He looks up from his chair, eyebrows lifting.

"Done with your date?" His tone drips sarcasm, enough to make my jawbone ache with the sting of his voice.

Ella turns toward him before I can say anything. "Would you be nice?"

The words stop us both cold.

Kaz blinks, clearly caught off guard. He isn't used to being challenged.

Apparently her brain has returned. That was fast.

Ella doesn't back down. "I'm serious. Your voice is disrespectful, and you need to do a better job. This is supposed to be a safe, happy place. The computers can hear you."

I blink. What the hell? Computers can't hear anything. But she just warned Kaz to watch his tone without giving away my secret. Clever.

And Kaz—Kaz actually blushes. He glances at me, then back at her, clearly off balance. "I'm sorry," he mutters, his words clipped. "Justice and I have our own mode of communication."

Ella plants her small hands on her hips. "Well, that needs to stop. You're making the computers unhappy, and if you really know what you're doing, you understand that."

Kaz's jaw tightens like he wants to argue, but he doesn't. His fingers twitch near the keys, restless. The man who types faster than machines has no idea what to do with her.

It's pure bullshit, but she sells it like gospel. And damn it, something warms inside me. She's protecting me.

Standing up for me. Nobody does that except my brother. Not really. The last time I remember someone speaking up for me, I was too young to fight back myself. That's when Thorn's face got scarred so badly.

A sensation winds through me, hot and unsteady, making me want to reach for her when I shouldn't. It's getting harder and harder to imagine locking her down without her precious electronics. "Come on, Ella. Let's go. I mean it."

She lowers her chin like a queen about to scold her subjects and marches toward Kaz. "You have to start using a nicer, softer voice. Do you understand me?"

Kaz actually leans back in his chair, rolling a few inches away as if afraid of the little sprite in my shirt and dirty jeans. His fingers tap against the armrest. "Yeah," he finally mutters. The glow of his screens paints his face pale green, and the blush spreading across his cheeks is almost comical.

"I didn't know computers—" He glances at me, searching for help. I keep my expression flat, refusing to throw him a lifeline. Kaz can sink or swim on his own. He swallows, shoulders drawing tight. "I'll do better."

Holy shit. He *is* doing better. No bruises sting down my back, and no cuts slice across my skin. His tone is controlled. A man teaching himself restraint because Ella demands it. That's new. That's power.

Ella whirls on me like a storm about to break. "You could be nice to him. Both of you should set a better tone."

Now she's lecturing me. Head high, eyes sparking, as if she owns the damn room. The worst part? She kind of does. The servers hum around us, cold and constant, and somehow her voice feels stronger than the machines.

Kaz's mouth ticks in the briefest flicker of a smile before he wipes it away. He's enjoying this.

I shake my head, reaching for Ella's hand. "Aren't you afraid of me?"

"I'm still afraid of you," she mutters, her voice steady even as her fingers tremble against mine. "Just . . . not as much."

So much for spanking her into submission. She's losing her fear, and that makes her dangerous. Because once fear is gone, there's only trust—or defiance. Neither bodes well for me.

My grip tightens as I pull her toward the elevator, the doors sliding open on a rush of cold air. The scent of metal and lemon polish escapes, sharp and sterile. Ella glances up at me, chin stubborn, eyes unyielding.

Well, that attitude won't do at all.

NINETEEN

Ella

Justice's burner phone feels small and cheap in my hand, the kind that's meant to be disposable, to disappear without a trace. I turn it once between my fingers, weighing my options. He drives with that same maddening calm, eyes forward, hands loose on the wheel like he owns the road. Leo snores in the back, a soft, steady rumble that makes the silence heavier.

"What if I promise not to leave town?" My voice is quiet, meant more for myself than him.

"No. Put the call on speaker."

The words snap like a lock clicking into place. He doesn't even look at me when he says it. My butt is tender, and I want to smack him. The guy spanks hard. I bite back the retort rising to my lips and instead punch in a number, pressing the speaker button.

Rosalie answers on the third ring, voice tight. "Hello?"

"Hey. It's me."

"Where in the world are you?" Relief bursts through

her tone, tangled up with annoyance. "I've been looking everywhere. You need to stop hiding in those stupid safe houses. It's not safe, Ella. Just come to my place."

My forehead presses against the glass, the window cold against my skin. The road blurs past, sunlight striking in flashes. "I'm working, and I'm fine. Quit fussing over me like somebody's grandma."

"Did you just call me old?"

I grin despite myself. "How's the house construction coming?"

"Perfect. I've set up a whole suite for you. An office too. You'd have space."

"I appreciate it." The words come easy, but my gut knots. "I don't really want to live under Bratva lock and key."

"You'd have freedom, Ella," Rosalie says.

Yeah, just like the freedom at that boarding school my stepmother had shipped me off to for my childhood. There was no escape, and every time I got in trouble, usually by taking apart computers to figure out how they worked, I ended up on cleaning duty. If I never have to clean another filthy kitchen, I'll die happy. "Thanks," I say. "If I need a place, you'll be the first I call."

The hum of the SUV fills the pause. Justice doesn't look my way, but I feel the weight of his awareness. He hears everything. He trusts me not to give Rosalie the truth, or he thinks it doesn't matter if I do.

Rosalie clears her throat. "There was an attack on Malice Media last night, and it wasn't from Alexei and Hologrid Hub. I can't imagine that Alana's dad would attack his new son-in-law's building, so it's probably not the group from Aquarius Social. That leaves TimeGem."

"It's possible," I allow. "But I don't think Sylveria

is dumb enough to come at Justice directly." But who knows.

Rosalie breathes out.

I stiffen. "What?"

She sighs now. "I don't know, but what if Sylveria is trying to start a war in which you get caught? She wants you dead. If it's known that the Rendales and the Beathachs are at war, at least to those in the underground, then your death wouldn't be blamed on her. She could have you killed and then scream bloody murder about Justice or Thorn taking you out."

It's a good hypothesis.

Justice glances at the phone and then back at the road. Yeah, Rosalie is wicked smart.

So I don't tell her I was present for the attack and explosion. Has my stepmother made a move? "I'll keep that in mind. Try not to worry."

"I can't help it. Also, and I have no idea if this is related, but Horace Whimple has gone underground. Sylveria has put out feelers to find him," Rosalie says.

I can't see the connection between Sylveria attacking me or Justice and the loss of her boyfriend. "He probably smartened up and left that witch."

Rosalie chuckles. "That was my first thought, too. So, Justice is there?"

"Yes. Rosy? Have you heard from Alana?" I change the subject.

"Not really. She's on her honeymoon. I doubt she has time to talk."

Very good point. "That tracks." I lower my voice into a teasing drawl. "Speaking of honeymoons, are you still planning to marry that Russian mobster?"

"I told you to stop calling him that—especially on the phone. I am an officer of the court," she snaps, but there's no heat behind it.

True. She is a lawyer. "Right. Sorry." I'm not sorry, but I let the apology stand. I glance at Justice. His jaw's set, but his lips twitch like he's holding back a grin. He doesn't give me much, but that almost-smile . . . it does something.

It's too bad he's so good in bed. That confuses me.

I want to talk to Rosalie. Really talk. About what happened in the forest, or the server room, about the mess in my chest every time Justice looks at me, about the urge to run, and the thrill of maybe not running. But with him sitting right here, heat radiating off him like a storm contained in a human body? No. Not yet.

"Ella." Rosalie's voice sharpens again. "No more safe houses."

"We'll see. I have to get back to work but will be in touch soon. Say hi to your gangster for me." I end the call before she can push, thumb pressing hard against the button. The screen goes black, and I hold the dead weight of the phone in my lap.

Outside, the land stretches wide, and the sky is pale and endless. Every turn in the road is another possibility. I start mapping exits, routes, and places to vanish. Freedom isn't just about survival. It's the challenge, and if I can beat Justice Beathach at his own game? That's worth every risk.

I glance at him. "Where are we going?"

He doesn't answer. Typical.

Outside, Silicon Valley fades behind us. The glass and steel towers give way to low commercial blocks, then thinner neighborhoods, until the road narrows and the trees take over. My butt feels heated and my clit tender. I'm kind of in a continuously aroused state.

Butthead.

Pines line the ridges, tall and dark, throwing shadows across the asphalt. The air sharpens, cooler, tasting faintly of salt. Mountains rise in the distance, green and gray with the hint of early mist, and the road curls upward through them before dropping toward the ocean. The water appears like a bruise on the horizon, slate colored and rolling, its whitecaps flashing as we descend.

We reach a long, private driveway cut between thick stands of fir. Justice turns in without a word, gravel crunching beneath the tires. At the end of the drive stands a three-story wooden structure. It's too massive to be called a cabin, but it has the bones of one with logs stacked and fitted with precision, wide eaves, and glass windows catching the gray sky.

Another freaking safe house? It's bigger than the cabin we hit last night. This is a massive home. "Hey," I say, leaning forward. "We're by Thorn's place."

"We are." Justice pulls to a stop, kills the engine, and opens his door. "Come on."

"You have another house nobody knows about?" I step out onto the gravel, shoes crunching, and take it in. For years nobody knew about Justice. It's impressive, really, in this time when every idiot has a digital footprint trailing behind them.

Leo bounds past me when I open the back door, barking joyfully before tearing into the trees.

"Is he safe here?" I ask.

"He's not going to leave you. He's not dumb. He's a

smart dog," Justice says dryly, already hefting too many bags for one man.

I shift my weight. "Do you need help?"

"I've got them." He shoulders the bags like they weigh nothing and heads up the steps. The wood gives a faint groan under his boots. The porch smells like cedar, sharp enough to sting the back of my throat. He unlocks the door without pausing, like he's done it a hundred times.

I glance at the tree line, that prickling instinct crawling higher. "Shouldn't there be Irish mobsters patrolling?"

"Oh, there are." His tone is flat. "You just can't see them."

That shiver? Yeah, it runs straight down my spine. Invisible guards. Perfect. I tug the hem of his T-shirt lower on my jeans and follow him in.

The place instantly charms me, as it's not what I expect. Honey-colored logs create thick and solid walls that don't feel new or staged. They're scarred a little, worn smooth where hands have touched them over years, with beams across the ceiling, the kind wide enough to sit on and hide. The smell is layered. Wood smoke clings stubbornly to stone, the bite of salt air creeps through cracks, and the scent of leather softens the notes.

Windows eat up the far wall, and beyond them the Pacific heaves, gray and restless. A stone fireplace waits, logs stacked beside it. Couches sag with use, blankets tossed like afterthoughts. A low table is scratched all to hell. Books crowd shelves in the corner, spines cracked, some stacked sideways because there's never enough room. It's messy. It's lived in. It hums with life. Not the sterile kind of hideout I expected. A home. Which makes no damn sense with Justice standing in the middle of it.

He doesn't give me time to stare and just heads down a hall, boots echoing on the boards, to shove open a set of double doors.

The bedroom is more country than city. A heavy quilt in red and cream spreads over a large bed surrounded by oak furniture built to last. But it's the stones that stick out. Obsidian chunks sit in a bowl on the dresser, along with polished pieces gleaming on the shelves, as well as sparkling garnets set into the base of lamps. Little shadows and sparkles in an otherwise cozy room. A reminder this is his space. Not soft. Not safe.

He dumps the many bags on the bed and looks back at me. "Take a shower. Pick something to wear. I'll put the groceries away."

The words are simple, but they hit with weight. Justice in a kitchen isn't domestic—it's deliberate. Another move in a game I don't know the rules of. He doesn't have to feed me. He doesn't have to soften the edges. So why does he? To get under my guard? To remind me he can be both the hand that starves and the hand that gives?

"Tomorrow," he adds, "I'll take you to the computer hub in the basement."

I perk up. "You have a computer hub?"

"Of course I have a computer hub." His voice is even, brooding rather than amused, the weight of it settling heavy in the room. "We'll see what we can find out about the illness." He pauses, his gaze flicking to the garnet bookends on the shelf, then to a chunk of obsidian catching the weak afternoon light. Shadows carve harsh lines across his face when he turns back to me. "I'll help you take down TimeGem Moments in exchange."

I take a step back, pulse leaping. Him actually helping

me could get this thing done. It's too big, too dangerous, too . . . real. "They'll come after us," I say.

"I'm planning on it." His answer is simple, ironclad.

A bark sounds from outside, sharp and happy. Justice exhales, almost a growl, and rakes a hand down his jaw before he says, "I'll let your dog in. Then we'll meet in the kitchen."

Anticipation lights through me, sparking quick and bright like electricity. If he really helps me, this could work. But the stones glimmer dark in the corners of the room, garnets glowing faintly, obsidian swallowing light, and I can't shake the sense that they're watching, listening. Like him.

My stomach twists, heavy and cold. What happens when we succeed? What happens if we fail? Even if I find a way to help him, what does he plan to do with me afterward? "I'd like an agreement in writing."

He snorts. "No."

All right, I'm definitely going to escape. Sure, there are guards out there, but I didn't see a moat like at Thorn's place. No monsters circling in black water, no castle walls. Just trees, ocean, and a road I can vanish down if I get the chance.

As if catching my thoughts, Justice moves. One step, maybe two, but it feels like the air shifts with him. Suddenly he's there, right in front of me, close enough the heat rolling off his body skims my skin. My back straightens on instinct.

His eyes pin me. They're dark, unreadable, and the kind that don't just look at you but cut through skin and bone to something deeper. They drag across me, slow and sure, and my pulse stutters like I've been caught doing something wrong.

Heat filters along my every nerve ending. I swallow, my throat dry. "Um."

Justice doesn't bother to answer. Instead, he lifts a hand, deliberate, his knuckles brushing against my temple before sliding into my hair. His fingers are warm, rough, threaded with strength I can feel in every careful stroke. He pushes a stray curl behind my ear, then lets his hand linger at the side of my face.

My body betrays me. A shiver ripples down my spine, every muscle tightening. The brush of his thumb near my cheekbone sends sparks low in my belly. I should move. I should push him away. Instead I'm rooted to the spot, my chest rising fast, heat pooling where I don't want it.

He leans closer, not touching but filling my space until I can't breathe without drawing him in. His voice is a rasp, low and rough. "Planning something?"

My heart slams against my ribs. He knows. Of course he knows.

I shift my weight, but his hand slides, slow and possessive, down the side of my neck. The pressure is light, almost tender, but there's nothing gentle in the way he does it. It's control. A warning. A reminder that escape won't be easy.

I shudder, and his dark eyes narrow, catching it. Not missing a single reaction.

"You're shaking," he murmurs, his breath warm against my skin. "Afraid of me?"

Yes. No. Both. My body hums with it, fear and want tangled too tight to separate. "I need to take a shower." My voice shakes.

His phone buzzes. Saving me? He releases me and tugs it from his back pocket to read. "I have a meeting soon that'll go late, but have time for an early dinner first. Be in the kitchen in fifteen minutes, or I'm coming for you. Shower or not."

I stand there. "Um, okay." We're playing house now?

"You can write out the code for the virus while I'm gone. I want to have it. Maybe I can take it and find a cure for myself."

There's no cure just in the code. It's about energy. At least it was with Thorn. "You'll use the virus to harm the other social media companies." He won't be able to help himself.

"It's up to me how to use it." He turns and walks out of the room.

I stand there, my mind spinning and my body firing. The truth coils sharp and quiet inside me. I have no idea if I can help him, or what he'll do with me when the work is finished, if it ever is. I can't give him the code. I also can't stay with him. Because, even though I know better, it's not just my body wanting him now.

I can handle a good spanking.

I can't handle a broken heart.

I don't know how.

TWENTY

Ella

I don't want to leave Leo. That's the problem and the weight in my chest even as the house creaks quietly around me at two in the morning. Justice left for some meeting after I went to bed, after cooking for me like we had some type of relationship, after warning me about the guards in the trees and the animals hunting the grounds. I believed him. Of course I did. But there isn't a moat out here. No killer trench filled with beasts like Thorn's place. That means I have a chance.

I feel a little guilty but I can't stay here. We kind of have an agreement, but this is too much. I'm falling for the guy, and I can't afford that. Worse yet, he'll make me give him that computer code, and I think it's almost his responsibility to take down the other companies—and families. It's in his damn DNA, which I can understand. I have it, too. It's a good thing women are so much more evolved than men. I know the virus should be buried forever.

His loyalty will always be to his organization. Not to

me. This has gone too far already. Running is what I do best.

My instincts scream that he pretty much owns my body now, and I'm not ready for that. But I can't stop feeling him all around me. Inside me. I have to run.

He's just too . . . Justice.

Plus, and I can admit this only to myself, I like the challenge of outwitting him. It's dangerous, and I'm sure foolhardy, but adrenaline still flows through my veins. The idea actually turns me on.

I am so screwed up.

I wait until the clouds smother the moon before I crouch next to Leo. His head lifts instantly, eyes glowing in the dark, ears cocked like he knows the plan. "Okay," I whisper, curling my hand into his fur. "Let's go."

He wags his tail like I just promised him steak. He's stronger than when we first pulled him from that hell. Loyal in a way I don't deserve. My throat tightens. "You realize I don't have a life for a dog, right? I like you, but I'm always running." He licks my hand, tail wagging harder, calling me a liar without words. What have I gotten into?

We slip out the back door onto the wide wraparound porch. The cliff falls away beneath us, the Pacific hammering at the rocks below. Spray leaps so high it catches my face, cold, wild, and salty. The night air tastes alive. For a second, it feels like freedom.

Leo pads beside me, tongue lolling. I stick to the shadows, circling the far edge of the house. Instinct says not to risk the front. Cameras and motion sensors are probably all around us. I don't see them, but I feel them. Justice wouldn't leave a blind spot.

Justice. Just thinking his name slows me down. He left hours ago, but his presence lingers like smoke. I should be running faster, but all I can picture is the way he looked at me. The way he kissed me. The way he cooks like it's second nature and then turns around and threatens to kill somebody in the same breath. I should hate him. I should fear him. I do. But not enough. Not nearly enough.

If I'm smart, I'll keep moving. Freedom's right there. But my feet drag. My chest knots tight. Out there, it's nothing but woods and darkness. Alone. On the run again. With a dog that already owns my heart.

Wait a minute. There has to be an easier way. Man, I'm off balance. Where's my brain? I tug Leo back inside, pulse pounding. The house is silent, every shadow too thick, every corner alive with secrets. We pad toward the kitchen, floorboards whispering beneath our feet.

We reach the garage door, and I freeze. My hand hovers over the handle. Freedom is one tug away. But the thought of leaving feels heavier than staying. I've never hesitated like this before. Yeah, the sex was great, and there's a computer hub somewhere near me that I want to reach. But I can't find the basement door.

I whisper to Leo, more to myself than him, but still open the door to the garage. "What the hell am I doing?"

Silence.

No alarms. No buzzers. Nothing. The quiet is wrong, pressing in on me, heavier than sound. My skin crawls. "Okay," I whisper, gripping his scruff. "If there's an alarm, it's quiet. We run."

We slip into the garage. The air smells like oil and rubber. The space feels too empty, too clean, like it's waiting. And then I see it.

Silver. Low to the ground. Curves that look poured, not built. The car's hood bears a red prancing horse, and my stomach lurches. It's a LaFerrari Aperta. I've only seen one in pictures. Limited edition. The kind of car collectors hoard and show off at auctions. It shouldn't be here.

A laugh bursts out of me, quick and shaky. "That's a nice car."

Leo's tail thumps the floor as I hurry to the car and open the passenger side door. He bounds inside, claws clicking against the leather, circles once, and drops to sit.

I slide into the driver's seat. The leather fits my butt like it's molded just for me, warm and luxurious. The console glows faint blue, waiting. The keys sit in a tray, casual, like Justice could walk in and leave again at any second.

I grab the fob and press the start button. The engine doesn't purr—it detonates. A roar tears through the garage, vibrating in my ribs. My hands shake. Fear spikes inside me, but exhilaration crashes over it, fast and addictive. For the first time tonight, my lips twitch into a grin. "This is going to be fun." The garage door grinds up, and I throw the vehicle into drive. Rain spits in, streaking the windshield in crooked lines. This car doesn't deserve storms, but we don't have a choice. Leo pants beside me, eyes bright, and I know he's all in.

"Yeah," I mutter, pressing the gas. "We're really doing this." I can't let Justice have the code to the virus. Or my heart. Definitely not my heart.

The main drive stretches out, slick black under the rain. Flashlights blaze between the trees, jerky beams searching. Guards. Of course.

I slam my foot on the accelerator. The Ferrari launches forward like it's been starving, tires gripping the asphalt with a precision I've never felt. Justice didn't pave this driveway for comfort. He paved it for speed.

The end of the drive comes too fast. I stomp the brakes, tires shrieking, and the car fishtails before correcting. A wrought-iron gate blocks the exit, hidden in the trees until now. I didn't see it when we came in. No wonder he felt just fine about leaving me here alone.

"Damn it." My fingers fly across the console, hitting switches I don't recognize. Nothing.

Leo growls, low and warning, his body braced.

A shack to the right bursts with light. Men pour out, flashlights slicing through the rain. I can't see their faces, but I feel their attention, sharp and focused.

My pulse pounds so hard it hurts. "Shit." I stab another button. The gate groans, jerks, and finally starts to slide. Too slow. Way too slow. "Finally." My chest is tight, hands welded to the wheel. Adrenaline rips through me, hot and sharp, and I don't look away from the opening. "Now hold on, Leo."

The men surge toward me, boots hammering on wet pavement, their flashlights jerking through the rain. The gate is almost open enough when a black SUV tears around the corner, its engine howling. My gut drops. Oh, crap. They opened the gate—I didn't.

I press the gas pedal down hard. The Ferrari leaps, bucking under me, and then shoots forward. The SUV keeps coming, big and black and steady. Justice. Damn him. I flick my lights to high. He cuts his off. Of course he does. Power move. My stomach flips but I push harder. He swings sideways, blocking the drive in one smooth arc, the road locked tight between steel and trees.

"No." I hit the brakes. The Ferrari skids across the

slick pavement, tires shrieking, and smashes into a tree. I jolt against the belt so hard my chest aches. No time. I rip free and shove my door wide. "Come on." Rain slaps my face as I hit the ground running. Leo bounds beside me, ears back, tail streaming.

We dive into the trees.

Not again. Seriously. I'm not made for running through forests.

The forest swallows us fast. Branches whip my arms and my face. I just wrecked Justice's Ferrari. Run. I have to run. He really is going to kill me.

Roots grab at my boots. My lungs already burn, but I push harder, weaving through the trunks, hoping Leo can see better than I can. Mud slides underfoot and nearly takes me down twice. I curse every step, curse Justice, curse myself for not being faster. My boots are heavy, waterlogged, but at least they're tough. He bought them. The thought makes me want to rip them off.

I duck left, too slow. My shoulder smashes into a tree. How am I running through trees again? Pain detonates across my arm and I spin, staggering, half blind from the hit. Bark scrapes my cheek. I shove off the trunk and stumble forward, sucking air. No time to stop. Keep moving. Leo growls low, urging me on, and I follow the sound of his paws pounding earth.

Behind me, Justice's voice cuts through the storm. "Ella. Slow down."

My heart spikes. He's closer than I thought, his tone low and furious. He's in the trees with me. I hadn't even heard him leave the SUV. Adrenaline rockets through me, washing out the pain, so I run harder, pushing my legs until they feel like they'll tear apart.

I turn another bend because there's a slight trail and run smack into him. Panic heats through me as I bounce back and land on my ass in the mud. He's just there, solid as the trees, rain dripping off his hair, eyes burning. He reaches for me, but it's too late. I'm already scrambling back, palms sliding in wet leaves.

"You wrecked my car," he snarls.

"I hit one little tree," I protest, breathless, mud soaking into my jeans.

He towers over me, bigger than the shadows, and every nerve in me screams vulnerable. Kind of mad, kind of scared. Leo plops down like this is nothing, tail wagging, tongue lolling as he looks at both of us. Traitor. I want to shout at him to attack, but I doubt he will. I think he considers Justice a friend.

I shove up to my feet. "Kidnapping's a crime."

"You wrecked my car."

Yeah, guys have a thing for their cars. And that one was . . . a pretty cool car. I throw up both hands. "When I retake TimeGem Moments, I'll buy you a new car."

The forest presses tight around us, my pulse hammering as I edge back a step at a time, looking for any gap. He's blocking the narrow trail, broad shoulders filling the available space, but there's an opening in the trees to my left. My muscles tense.

"I honestly thought you'd stay here and that we'd reached an agreement," he warns, his voice low, edged like a growl.

"Ha." I wipe rain and hair from my eyes, crouch low, and leap for the opening. I don't make it.

He snags me around the waist mid-stride, hauling me up.

"Damn it." I punch him in the throat, pain exploding across my knuckles.

"You are a pain in my ass." His voice is flat, irritated, not even winded. He tosses me over his shoulder, easy as hefting a bag of feed.

"Put me down." I slam my fist into his kidney. The smack he delivers to my tender ass echoes in the trees before the sting blooms hot across my skin. "Hey." I squirm, knees bunching as I pound them against his chest, my fists punching his back with everything I've got. My jeans slip against him, my hair whipping as he walks like I'm not even fighting.

"You are such a fucking brat," he mutters.

Gravity shifts and I'm gone. My stomach lurches, and I yelp before I realize it's not me falling. It's him—no, it's both of us. One graceful move and I'm flipped, dumped face down across his knee like a kid. Rain splashes my hair, mud grinding into my palms when I reach for balance.

"Hey," I snap, kicking hard. Not again.

He doesn't answer. My jeans rip down with one vicious tug, not even bothering with the button. Thank God they were too big or that would've hurt. Cold night air licks my skin a second before his palm cracks down on my bare ass.

The sound is sharp. The pain sharper. Heat radiates out in an instant, shocking, humiliating.

"Justice." I jerk, but he's iron hard under me, and when I move, he hits harder.

"I'm fine with a spanking a day, you little brat. Maybe two. Or fucking five." His hand lands again, harder, and my cry breaks loose. The sting builds until I can't separate pain from the hot pulse flooding lower. My body betrays me, traitorous and confused.

I reach back, desperate, but my fingers grab bark and wet dirt, nothing to anchor me. I am *not* fine with a spanking a day. My butt is already too tender. "Let me up, you asshole."

Leo yelps like this is fun, tail slapping mud. Useless dog.

Justice spanks me again, slow this time, deliberate. The strike burns deep, and heat slides into something else, something needy—unwanted, humiliating. I grit my teeth, trying not to make a sound, but the next blow tears through my control. A moan slips out, half pain, half something darker, and I hate myself for it. I'm wet and aching, and I have to get out of here. If he touches me, if I get just a bit of traction on my clit, I'm going to explode.

Just like last time. I can't let him know the power he has over my body.

"What the hell is up with you in the woods? Does rain and the smell of pine turn you on?" I yell.

He chuckles. "It does now."

"Oh God, let me up." My voice is hoarse. Men shout in the distance, flashlights stabbing through trees. Fear slams into me, sharp as the next smack. "Fine!" I shout. "I'm sorry about your car."

He doesn't stop. The spanking keeps coming, steady, almost rhythmic. Ten smacks, maybe more, every one leaving me breathless, my ass burning, heat curling through me in ways I can't ignore. The men are getting too close. I can't let anybody see me like this. Tears fill my eyes and slide down my face. "I said I was sorry."

Finally he jerks me upright, shoving me face down over the log.

This is not happening. It can't be.

His fingers find me and I moan, needing him so badly I don't care about my heart. Or the men getting closer. "Justice."

A zipper releases behind me while two fingers slide inside me. God. It's too much. I moan, pushing back against him.

"Ask nicely." He presses against me, his cock feeling huge.

"Please." The word is out of me before I even think.

He grasps my hips and powers inside me with one hard thrust.

I gasp, arching away, my hands falling to the wet moss.

"Shit," a man yells. "Sorry. Shit. Everyone back."

Heat rushes into my face.

Justice doesn't let up and hammers harder, hitting a spot in me that has my body arching. The mossy tree beneath me is hard against my ribs, but all I can feel is him. Inside me. Fast and hard, going deeper than I thought possible.

A trembling sets up inside me, triggering out, sparking nerves. I close my eyes as I climb, fast and wild, right to the crest. I hover, holding on, trying to keep control. He lands a firm smack on my wounded butt, and I break. My mouth opens in a silent scream as the climax sweeps through me, undulating in wicked waves that steal my breath. I ride them and then go lax just as he pounds one more time inside me, holding on, and shudders with his own release.

The rain drips around us as I come back into the moment.

He withdraws, and I moan, my body still trembling.

He pulls us both up, flipping me around and dragging the jeans up over skin that's already raw. The scrape makes me hiss, makes my knees buckle. I sway, wet hair plastered to my cheeks, chest heaving, legs weak in a way that's not just from exhaustion.

"Walk." His voice is gravel, and it vibrates down my spine.

I obey, stiff, furious, humiliated, my backside throbbing, the memory of his hand seared into me. I decide that I hate the forest. A lot. At this point, I'll always wear his damn handprint on my butt. Lights gleam ahead through the trees, his men staying out of sight. How embarrassing. Under my breath, I make myself a promise. Justice might think he's in control.

But one day soon, I'll kill him.

TWENTY-ONE

Justice

For a smart woman, sometimes Ella is way too reckless. What was she thinking heading into the forest with armed men all around her? Her sense of self-preservation isn't nearly what I expect. Plus, somebody shot a fucking missile at my place with her in the kitchen. I'm not sure who was the intended target. Could've been both of us.

I truly thought she'd behave herself tonight. The little brat.

She stomps inside my house and kicks off her boots, flinging mud. The woman is a mess. Leo follows her, looks around, and makes a beeline to hop on my sofa. He snuggles down and starts snoring instantly. Apparently fleeing my place took a toll on him.

"Go take a shower," I order, needing to check in with my men.

Ella huffs, turning to face me squarely.

A knock sounds behind me and I turn, opening the door to find Wynd. He's dressed in jeans and a dark shirt, no doubt patrolling the property. "I'm sorry to bother you, but I just got off the phone."

Ella sneezes behind me. If she caught a cold from running from me in the forest, she'll regret it. "Go take a shower," I order. Again. "What call, Wynd?"

He keeps his gaze focused on me and not the disobedient brat by the sofa. "Since we're having shipping problems, I've been in touch with the Kayrs operation, and they have some alexandrite." Wynd winces, his deep eyes darkening as he avoids looking at Ella. "They're willing to make a deal but want a stake in Malice Media in exchange."

I bark out a laugh. "Dage is messing with you. If the Kayrs family wanted into the social media game, they'd already be in it." Their powerful family has been around as long as mine, if not longer, and they stay out of the public light. Always. I wonder idly if they're making a move with the missile and then quickly discard the thought. Dage Kayrs would come at me in full sight. "Return his call, tell him I'm dealing with some shit, and ask what he really wants."

Wynd shrugs. "Dage is out of the country, and I've been dealing with Talen."

Just great. Talen is Dage's younger brother. I've never quite figured out their business structure, but after meeting Talen once, I figure he's the enforcer like I am. If they want somebody dead, Talen seems like he'd do the killing and grab an ice cream cone on the way home. Though, he's smart. It's possible they want to know more about crystals and how to charge them. Something tells me the Kayrs family could do it. "That guy would rather have his kidneys removed with a rusty butter knife than deal with social media." That much I can surmise. "He's messing with you and just wants money and not a social media platform. Probably a lot of money. Make a deal."

"Okay."

Ella sneezes into her arm.

"Bless you," Wynd says.

I glance at her. We've been in the rain a lot lately. "Go take a hot shower."

Wynd shuffles his feet. "Kaz also called in, and there's some chatter about Ella's unknown whereabouts coming from Rosalie Mooncrest. Alexei isn't involved yet, but . . ."

"Got it. Thanks." I shut the door and turn to face Ella. "Apparently you need to call your friend again and do a better job reassuring her this time. *After* you shower." I look pointedly at the mud she's dripping on the wood floor.

She shocks the shit out of me and punches me right in the gut. Oh, her fist glances off. But my temper still explodes.

"Fine." I drop my shoulder and lift her over it, allowing her to land hard and lose the air in her lungs. "I'll put you in the shower myself." The brat bunches her legs up, shoving her knees into my chest. I'm so over her attitude. I plant my hand on her ass. Hard. Once and then again. Her yelp is way too satisfying. Yeah, no doubt she's sore from both spankings. Just what will it take to tame this wildcat? "I promise my hand will outlast your butt, so you might want to try a different tactic." I stride through the house and up the stairs to my suite, kicking open the door and moving into the bathroom.

The place is all stone and wood with garnet and obsidian accents. I feel the power from both gems as I walk in, reach inside and twist the shower faucet, and ignore the struggling bundle over my shoulder. She's too small to go around punching people in the gut.

Appealing, though. She's fucking adorable with an exaggerated sense of her physical abilities. I'm starting to worry about her, and that won't do. Oh, mentally she's deadly. But physically she needs to learn not to punch people twice her size. I give her one more smack to the ass and flip her over, settling her inside the spray. One swipe of my hand has the shirt over her head, and I easily yank down the jeans, which she kicks toward me. They land in a wet slop at my feet outside the shower.

I can't help but stare. Her eyes have gone a cerulean blue with temper as the water washes the mud from her tight body. High tits, pink nipples, toned abs. Probably earned running away from computer system facilities she's hacked. Her skin is smooth and toned, and her legs long for her small body. I should leave her alone.

Then she punches me again. Aiming lower this time.

Shit. I slap her wrist away from my junk before she can make contact. "Damn it." I step inside and push her against the far wall. "Fine. You obviously need assistance." I tear off my shirt, kick my boots off, and rip off my jeans to follow them.

She leans against the dark stone wall, her breath panting, eyes darkening, cheeks pinkening. There's anger in those eyes—hunger, too. She doesn't want to want me . . . but she does.

I can work with that. "Stop trying to hurt me." I move into her, lifting her up against the wall. Her small gasp wisps between us. "You're not big enough or strong enough, and baby, I promise you're not actually mean enough." Oh, she's more than happy to punch me in the dick, but I don't think she's an actual killer.

The more I'm around her, the more I believe that

she didn't mean to nearly end Thorn. Although, I think she's fine with causing one of us to become sick. To have an irritating allergic reaction. "Now. Here's your one chance." I try to gentle my voice. She's been through a lot the last couple of days, the spankings the least of it. "Promise you'll behave, and I'll put you down, wash my hair, and leave you to have a nice and steamy shower."

My cock is painfully hard between us and now yelling at me. But I won't lie to her. God, she's pretty. Beautiful, even.

Her head goes back against the stone wall and she looks down her pert nose at me. "I don't see why you think you're in charge."

Surprise tickles through me. I nearly smile. "I'm the kidnapper. The kidnapper is always in charge."

"That's faulty logic."

"Faulty? I don't see how."

She arches a brow, water streaming over her lashes like she's some smug queen on a throne. "If you really had control, you wouldn't need to argue your case. The fact that you're trying to prove it means you're insecure."

I huff a laugh. "Cute. You should stop challenging me."

"Somebody has to," she fires back. "Otherwise you'll think it's okay to stomp around the forest spanking people."

My grin slips before I can stop it. "Careful, brat. You're making it sound like you enjoy the attention."

Her lips twitch, betraying her even as she tries to glare. "Don't flatter yourself."

"Not flattery. Observation." I lean just close enough to watch the water bead on her mouth. Her naked body is way too close to mine, and my heart starts to thunder. A craving slakes through me, and my voice roughens. If she keeps challenging me, this isn't going to end with her having a relaxing time in the shower. "You put yourself in danger, you get spanked. It's easy math."

She blinks. Once and again. "Don't act like you care if I'm in danger. You were just pissed you had to follow me into the muddy forest."

I pause and study her. That's hurt. There's definite hurt in her eyes, and she's trying to mask it. Not from the spanking. Not from me. The wound goes deeper than that. When was the last time somebody actually protected Ella Rendale? I'm sure Rosalie and Alana try, but considering they're both tangled up with mob bosses, I don't believe they have the best instincts. Even if one of those bosses is my brother. "I do care and truly thought you'd stay here safely tonight. I don't want you hurt."

She swallows and her gaze drops to my mouth before meeting mine. "Don't." Her voice quivers just slightly.

Interesting. Standing like this surrounded by steam and actually talking instead of fucking is getting tedious. I turn and drop us onto the bench with her straddling me, soft thighs sliding along mine. If she just lifts up and moves a bit forward, my dick could slam right home. "Don't what?"

Her hands flatten on my chest, and even that slight touch nearly sends me feral. "Play with me."

"I'd love to play with you." I lean down, my nose nearly touching hers. "But I'll never lie to you. Or manipulate you." She deserves better than that, and I don't have the fucking time to mess around. "You're right that I don't like disobedience, from anybody, but you got spanked because you put yourself in a dark forest surrounded by men with guns while having no idea where the fuck you were, especially when you intimated that you'd stay where I put you. You didn't. That's stupid and dangerous."

"So you care," she challenges, her lower lip barely protruding.

I'm trying not to take a bite out of that lip. "Yes."

"When did that change?" Steam winds around us, cocooning us and making her look ethereal . . . and vulnerable. Definitely in need of protection. "Just because we had sex?"

"I don't know." Why lie about it? "But it changed."

She curls her nails into my skin, biting softly. "You wanted to kill me."

I sigh. "No. I planned to lock you down on an island somewhere without electronics."

She jerks. "That's worse than death."

Yeah, I'm starting to get that. "Then you should start to obey me. If you enjoy sitting, that is." I've never been one to miss an opportunity.

"Not in my DNA." She's looking a bit too secure right now. "I think we need to make sure we have a deal. That we'll both stick to it. For sure."

Enchanting. Damn it. "Go on."

A pretty blush wanders across her chest, and I watch it, fascinated. Even her nipples turn a brighter pink. She clears her throat. "I'll help you with your server problem without giving you a code for a deadly virus, and you help me retake TimeGem Moments. I promise I won't ever attack your gems or servers again, and you promise you'll never kidnap me or lock me down on an island."

As a deal, it isn't bad. It's a start to negotiations, anyway. Although there's a glitch in her logic. "Who says I'm letting you go? If I keep you, there's no need to kidnap you again."

She rolls her eyes. So much for her being terrified by me. "Please. Do you want to put up with me long term?"

Amusement tracks through me. I ignore the voice in the back of my head wondering the same thing. "You have a point." I lift her by the hips, positioning her right where I want her. "How about we seal the deal?"

Her hands slide up and roll on top of my shoulders. Her nipples sharpen in front of my eyes. "You haven't agreed." She's breathless now.

"I know. I'm not taking those terms." Giving her plenty of time to stop me, I lower her onto me, trying to be gentle.

She winces as I stretch her, but she is wet. Needy. All hot and moist heat. Then she wriggles against me, leaning into me.

I slam her down until she takes all of me.

She gasps and arches, elongating the lines of her graceful neck. Her eyelids flutter closed.

I wait, my hands gripping her hips, my cock surrounded by her warmth. I'm not sure I've ever felt this good. Her voice only adds to my pleasure. Somehow. Her soft moans and gasps slide through me, licking me from within. There's no feeling like it.

She opens her eyes and her pupils widen in the steamy space. Her knees press down on the bench, on either side of my thighs, and she partially lifts up to slide back down. The sound she makes will accompany me to the grave. Soft and hungry, full of anticipation.

Then she pauses, her eyes wide. "One more term." Her voice is breathy.

I flex my fingers on her hips. "Name it."

"No more spankings."

I grin and reach around to clench her ass with both hands.

She hisses, and hunger glows in her eyes.

"Spanking turns you on." I lean forward, my grip firm, and suck a nipple into my mouth.

She arches and digs her nails into my shoulders. "It most certainly does not."

I gently bite her and move to the other nipple, noting her breath catching. She sounds proper and haughty. I bite the other nipple and then lean back to watch her eyes turn an even darker shade of blue. "I like spanking you."

She stills and pulses all around my cock. "That's, well, that's . . ."

"The way I want it." I kiss her, liking the softness of her lips under mine. "Behave and I won't spank you. It's as easy as that." Not in a million years can Ella behave. If I keep her, she'll have a sore ass every day.

I swallow. I'm not keeping her. But she's safer with me than without. I can't think about this right now, so I lift her up and gently slide her back down me.

She sucks in air and then starts to move on her own, her nails biting into me as she rides me.

I let her play for a while, setting the rhythm, until red edges in from the furthest reaches of my vision. I tighten my hold and direct her, yanking her up and pounding her back down. She goes soft in my hold. Submitting. Fire lunges through me, sizzling down my spine right to my balls. It zings around my body, landing in my chest. Somewhere.

The slap of flesh against flesh mixes with the spray hitting the wall, and I move her faster, feeling the second she's about to go over. I stop, holding her in place, my dick pulsing inside her.

She tries to lift up and I stop her. "What are you doing?" she groans.

"Taming you." This might kill me. I wait until her body settles and then I lift her, pushing her to the edge again. The second she's there, I stop.

Her head drops to my shoulder. "Justice."

"Yeah." I wait until she calms and then lift her again. "Look at me."

She does, her eyes glossy.

"Even when you're on top, I'm in charge. Understand?" I need to gain her obedience so she doesn't get herself killed. "Ella?"

She slowly nods.

"Say it."

"You're in charge." She tightens around me.

I move her, up and down, faster than she could do herself. She climbs, her eyes wide, and then finally goes over with a shattered cry. She tightens around me, hard and fast, gripping like we'll never be apart again. She bites into my pec, little mewling noises coming from her as her body shudders wildly.

I'm not far behind.

The climax nearly destroys me. I shudder through it, finally lowering her all the way and leaving her there with me still inside her. We pant together as the steam swallows us whole.

One thought hits me with absolute certainty. I have no clue what I'm going to do with Ella Rendale. Never in my life have I been the hero, not even of my own story, and I see no reason to start now. Heroes sacrifice. They let go for the greater good.

Fuck that.

I'm keeping her.

TWENTY-TWO

Ella

We move locations again, back to a city, when morning hits, and I'm going to miss the house in the forest.

I'm sore. In kind of a good way with a wisp of warning. My skin holds his teeth and finger marks. Justice is dangerous and sexy, and he is phenomenal in the sack. Or shower. Or forest. I've never been cold or clinical, notwithstanding my love for electronics and the hum of the Internet. I get attached to people, no matter how hard I try to keep my distance. Pure and simple. I've always known that for me, sex equals emotion. So I usually refrain and have made a lifetime out of remaining alone.

I don't want emotion with Justice.

I can't afford it.

As he shows me into yet another penthouse apartment in Silicon Valley, I note the distance between me and the sidewalk below. We're actually in San Jose, and I'm on the twenty-second floor. While I wouldn't mind attempting a Spider-Man escape, gravity would definitely win. "How many penthouses do you own in town, anyway?" The other one was more comfortable.

"This one is owned by a shell company, so it can't be traced. You're safe here for the day." Justice flips on lights as we go, showing a sprawling living room with floor-to-ceiling windows. Sunrise slams against the glass, flooding the penthouse in fire and shadow. Mount Hamilton catches the first strike of light, the observatory flashing against the peak. The rest of the range waits behind it, dark and steady.

San Jose stirs below us. Headlights thread through the streets, slow and uneven, the grid glowing as if the city is waking in pieces. From the twenty-second floor, it all looks exposed. Freeways pulse, buildings squat low, and the space between here and the ground stretches long enough to make my stomach tighten.

Leo snorts, looks around, and leaps over the back of a black leather sofa to settle down.

Justice watches him, his head cocked. I have to admit, the man has been much more patient with my new mutt than I would've expected.

"Stop thinking so hard." Justice points down the hallway. "I need to be in the city today, so you're in the city today as well. Extra safeguards are being put in place at my house, so for now, you're locked down here. Kitchen should be fully stocked." He points the other way. "Bedroom suite is that way."

Suite? As in singular? "Wait a minute—"

"Not in the mood, gorgeous." He rolls his neck, looking too dangerous in a black suit, crisp white shirt, and black tie. Apparently he has another meeting to attend. Being the head of the Irish mob probably takes a lot of time.

I like being called gorgeous because it's not true. Oh, Rosalie is gorgeous and Alana is beauty personified. I'm cute. Pretty enough. But definitely not gorgeous. However, I don't like being brushed off. "I don't care what kind of mood you might be in, Justice." My voice is surprisingly mellow and calm. Good. I need to keep control around this man. "We are not sharing a room." Yeah, I feel a little ridiculous considering the multiple orgasms I've had lately, but still.

"Right." He moves back to the elevator. "There should be clothing for you in the room and food for the dog in the pantry. I may be gone all day." He glances at his garnet and obsidian-encrusted watch. "There should also be a nice section of books to read in the bedroom."

I pause and look around carefully. There isn't a plasma television in the living room. "Um—"

"No electronics, Ella. Sorry." He doesn't sound sorry. Not in the slightest. If anything, he sounds . . . amused? "Can't have you escaping again. What kind of kidnapper would I be?"

He thinks this is funny? "No computers?" I breathe out, my ears ringing. This is hell. How dare he? He doesn't care about me at all.

"Nope. But there should be plenty of books for you. I told them to bring all new releases as well as a bunch of classics. Reading is supposed to support brain longevity, you know."

"I can't exactly help you with your problem without a laptop," I hiss.

He grins. Full on.

Holy crap, he shouldn't do that. That smile transforms his rugged face to something dangerously beautiful. I can't explain it. But the sight shoots through me, pebbling my nipples and softening my thighs. It's a good thing he's usually so grumpy. That grin should be outlawed. Or somehow captured for all time and used as the ultimate marketing tool.

The elevator door opens. Wait a minute. Where's the keypad?

He presses his watch. "I'll take you to Malice Media either tonight or tomorrow, if you're a good girl all day and don't cause me any problems. The elevator only works from my watch right now, so don't spend hours trying to find a hidden keypad. There isn't one."

"Well, that's dangerous," I mutter, fully planning on causing him every problem I can find. The condescending bonehead. "What if there's a fire?"

"Don't start one," he warns. "My men will get you out, but your ass isn't ready for another beating."

Oh, he did not. "I thought we had an agreement? Is this just a punishment?"

"We have an agreement and this is a punishment for wrecking my car. Behave yourself and you get freedom. Disobey me and you end up reading all day, which frankly, is good for you."

I can't come up with a bad enough threat that'll make him think twice, so I don't say anything. Then I glance at the sofa. "What about the dog? He needs to go out."

"Wynd will fetch him every three hours for some outside time. You'll stay inside."

I look around the spacious cage. "Where are you going, anyway?" Damn it. I don't care.

He studies me for a hard second. "I have a meeting with the owners of the three other social media companies."

I gape. "You what?"

"There's a fifth player on the board, and we need to take them out now. Plus, I want to know if anybody else is involved." He steps into the elevator, turning to stare at me. "Do you know anything about the new player?"

"Just that there is one," I admit. "I haven't been able to trace them back to any of the social media upstarts."

He runs a hand through his thick hair. "Neither have we. Also, early this morning, I hit back at TimeGem Moments with a fire to their main hub, Aquarius Social with a malware attack, and Hologrid Hub with a small explosion in Alexei's bar. Figured I'd make a statement."

My chin drops. "You attacked all three of them?"

He lifts a shoulder. "Barely. Just enough to let everyone know I could, and once I find out who's shooting missiles at me, then I'll take them out completely. I'm not sure it's one of them."

"I want to be there. I'm the rightful owner of TimeGem." I hope there's a badass suit in that room down the hall.

"No." He steps inside, presses something on the wall, and the door rolls closed. Jerk. What an asshole. I quickly survey the entire penthouse and find no electronics. Fine. If he thinks he can keep me here, he has totally underestimated me. He wants to punish me? That was a stupid move. I won't accept that.

My heart is getting involved and only his dick is. I know he's not a keeper. I will not spin daydreams about a guy who is just fucking me out of his system.

Jerk.

For three hours, I scour the place for what I need and then strip a couple of cords from lamps before plopping on the sofa with the latest Lexi Blake spy story. I love those Masters and Mercenaries. The elevator door, predictably, opens.

Wynd moves inside, his gaze seeking. "Truth be told, I wasn't sure you wouldn't try to burn the place down." He has a nice Gaelic accent that's thicker than Justice's, though his voice isn't as deep.

I sit up and place the book on the table. "I don't trust how efficient you'd be about saving me and the dog." There's no reason to be civil.

Wynd smiles and shoves a hand through his dark hair. "That's not kind." He whistles.

Leo looks up from the adjacent leather chair.

"Come on, boy," Wynd says. "Let's go chase a bird or two."

Leo stands and stretches before hopping down.

"Have you worked for Justice long?" I ask, rubbing the back of my neck. My eyes are scratchy. I sneeze. Darn it. I'm catching a cold from all the running through forests. I definitely need sleep.

"My whole life. We're distant cousins."

That's dedication. So I can't get out of here by flirting or bribing. Good to know. "Does he usually trap women in penthouses without a television?"

"Nope," Wynd says cheerfully. "I can honestly say you're our first penthouse kidnappee. I stocked the kitchen for you. If there's anything missing, you let me know, and I'll make sure you get it."

"Gee," I drawl. "You kidnappers are so kind."

"We try." He steps back into the elevator and partially turns, revealing a gun under his jacket. I'm sure it's not the only weapon on his body. "I also bought the books. If there's another one you want, let me know."

Isn't he accommodating? "Someday I'll come into a lot of money. Is there any chance you'd let me go for a hefty amount?" Might as well ask.

"Money doesn't do me any good if my head's removed from my body." He's still cheerful. "I also have a girlfriend, so don't embarrass us both by trying to seduce me."

I wouldn't know how. "Your girlfriend can't like your job."

"My girlfriend thinks I work for a social media company as a security consultant, which is mostly true. She doesn't know the rest of it." His blue eyes are earnest but knowing. Somewhat hard. "I should let you know that there's a lot of chatter coming out of Aquarius Social right now about your location. Searches being conducted. You might want to start practicing your breakup speech to Wesley Whisper. He's a decent guy, a good hacker, and I'd hate to see him floating in the ocean."

I gulp. "What in the—"

"I've known Justice a long time. He doesn't share." The dog lopes into the elevator and it closes.

What in the world did that mean? Justice can't be considering a long-term thing with me. The very idea lights my body on fire, and if I felt like being nicer to myself, I might allow a daydream or two. But why go there? I return to the book and read another chapter until Wynd comes back with a happily winded Leo.

"I'll see you in three hours," Wynd says.

"Whatever." I don't look up from the book.

The second the door closes again, I move, rubbing my eyes.

I already have the copper wire stripped from the lamp.

It coils warm in my palm as I drag a chair under the smoke detector and climb up. The plastic cover pops off easily.

Most people don't look at a building as a living thing. I do, and everything is connected somehow. "I have a plan, Leo." The dog just looks at me. It's a good plan. "I'm going to find a cure to the darn computer code I created, make it available to all four of the families, and then Justice can have the code. It's a win-win for everyone." But I need time and space to do that. Then maybe I can cure him, too.

Inside the smoke detector is a small board with two sets of wires. One pair feeds it power. The other ties this detector into a larger circuit that runs through every sensor on this floor and down to the fire panel in the basement. That's how the system keeps watch—one long loop of signals. If one detector stops talking, the panel just logs a fault. No sirens. No strobe lights. No warning to the men guarding the building.

I hold my breath and twist the copper onto the terminals, shorting the connection. The detector dies under my hand. The line goes silent.

Man, Justice is going to be pissed. Triumph filters through me. I know this isn't a game. But if it is, I'm winning. Kind of. Maybe for now.

That silence is all it takes. When the system loses contact with a unit, it frees an elevator for inspection. It's a built-in service feature, a way for a technician to ride up without triggering alarms. A loophole hiding in plain sight.

I climb down, my pulse steady and sharp. Then the elevator dings, soft and polite. The doors slide open and I rush inside, motioning for Leo.

He follows, panting happily, looking at me like we're

in for a great adventure. I swear, this dog has human qualities.

I laugh. Okay, this might be a game and I might be having fun. Justice shouldn't have said he was punishing me, and he should've left me with a laptop, at the very least.

Let's see him find me now.

Inside the cart, the buttons glow, waiting for me. Normally they'd be locked behind a keycard, but in service mode, the restrictions vanish. I press the button for the third floor since I'm sure there are guards on the bottom floor, and the car begins to descend silently. The guards down below have no clue.

The doors open onto an empty hallway, and we hurry out, headed straight toward the exit stairs. The stairwell door handle turns under my palm because the building codes require it. I step inside and jog down, each flight taking me closer to the street, closer to freedom.

Anticipation lights through me. Yeah, I'm challenging Justice, whether I admit it or not. Might as well be honest with myself. I broke his cage with nothing but copper wire and stubbornness. I guess he needs to know the real me, because I'll always be a challenge.

But I have to succeed this time, because I can't take another spanking. I just can't.

Leo and I emerge onto the busy street, and I run around the corner, studying my location. Perfect. Like in most places in Silicon Valley, I have a car hidden just several blocks to the north. "Come on, Leo. We need to run." We have three hours until they discover we're missing.

Well, unless Justice gets home first.

I shiver, duck my head, and run faster.

TWENTY-THREE

Justice

The warehouse district smells of diesel and old metal. The building we use doesn't look like much from the street—gray siding, flat roof, bulletproof glass dulled by dust. Nobody passing by would guess what waits inside.

The moment I step through the door, the lie peels back. Marble floors catch the low light, polished smooth from decades of use. Maple panels line the walls, warm and rich, beautiful. At the center sits a heavy round table, hand-cut, scarred by time. Four thick leather chairs circle it. No more than four. The old families knew better than to put power at one end and weakness at the other. Round means equal. At least on the surface.

I'm early, but so is everyone else. Not a surprise.

Alexei sits in black, shoulders loose but ready. His seat faces the door. I walk in and take the chair across from him. His eyes meet mine, steady, and he dips his chin in a small nod. I answer in kind.

To my left sits Mathias Beaumont, broad chest stretching the seams of his vest until the buttons look ready to give up. On Alexei's other side, Sylveria Rendale sparkles in diamonds. She wears a blue ball gown that belongs under chandeliers, not in a steel warehouse.

Her daughters are behind her. That's new. Usually it's guards only.

Alexei clears his throat. His voice slides calmly, the one sound in this room that doesn't hurt me. "I didn't much appreciate the attack, Beathach."

"I don't blame you." My reply is even. "I'd guess it took you ten minutes to clean up."

His mouth ticks up at one corner. "I figured it was a shot over the bow and assume it's a one-time deal." He keeps it casual, but I notice the open jacket. Easy reach for his weapon if the air shifts wrong.

"Yes," I agree. Unless he attacks first. I don't need to say that. He knows.

Mathias leans forward, and his voice grates when he speaks. "We didn't send that missile into your building, and we managed your attack on our servers easy enough. Which is what I assume you intended." The sound drives pain into my knees, sharp enough that I grind my teeth until it passes.

Yeah, I need them all to know I can get to them if I want. Message received.

"The missile wasn't mine, either," Alexei says. His voice leaves me steady. No pain. No heat.

"Or mine," Sylveria drawls.

I believe them. Which means someone else is moving against us. A fifth player, still in the shadows.

Mathias clears his throat again, and my knees flare white-hot. "We found a breach in our servers."

The ache lingers this time. I keep my face blank, fists pressed hard against my thighs until the pain dulls.

"As have we," Sylveria says quietly. Her voice grinds into me, rough, pressing deep in my kidneys until the ache blooms. I shift my shoulders, but I don't let the pain show on my face.

Alexei shrugs. His tone is smooth, merciful, giving me a moment of relief. "I haven't found anything, but I'll take a better look later."

Sylveria arches one eyebrow. "Good. My guess is that one of the baby social media companies has a decent hacker who's trying to get noticed."

"I know," I agree. "We're actively searching. If I find any information, I'll let you know. If we need to gather forces, which I doubt, we'll do so."

Alexei nods to a rough-looking Russian at the door. The man steps forward and places a folder on the table. Paper slides across polished wood, and the guards ringed around the room tense, hands close to weapons.

"Here's all the information we've gathered on a possible fifth company," Alexei says. "We've chased the trail around the world. It bounces everywhere, but the last trace goes back to Beijing." His mouth tightens. "I think it's here."

My man moves next, stepping forward to hand out folders.

Mathias reaches into his briefcase, his thick, gnarly fingers curling around a stack of his own. "This is what we have," he says. His voice grates, the scrape stabbing through my knees until I have to press them into the chair to keep from wincing.

Sylveria adds her folders, her voice rough, bruising across my kidneys. "I had one of my men put together what we've gathered. Between the four of us, we should be able to find this guy and kill him. We do not need more competition."

I gather my copies of the documents. Between the four of us, we should find this guy soon. "How about a wager?"

"Excellent," Alexei agrees, taking his stack. "First to find him gets sole social media coverage of the Silicon Shadows and Secrets Ball next year?"

Good bet. That will hurt the other three. "I'm in," I say.

Mathias hesitates and then straightens his shoulders. "Me, too."

Sylveria looks at all three of us. "You're morons, but I'm in. Why not?" She pivots and lowers her chin. "With your recent statement against all of us, I think you hit me harder than the other two, Justice. You attacked my facility."

"I was making my point about Ella," I answer, keeping my voice calm. "Stop coming after her."

Her eyes widen just a fraction.

"What about Ella?" Alexei asks. His voice doesn't hurt, steady as stone, and I meet his gaze.

"Why? Is your woman worried about her?"

"Yes," he replies smoothly. "She's quite concerned."

A grin tugs at my mouth. I like that he's honest, and it's obvious he cares. If I ever decide Ella has to disappear, I know who'll fight me for her.

"I wouldn't harm Ella," Alexei says as if reading my mind.

Ah. So he is in love. Good to know. When the mighty fall, and all of that. My eyes catch the panther tattoo sprawled across his neck, inked in black. The amethyst eyes shimmer as if they're alive, staring right back at me. It's good work, sharp and clean. He would've needed it in prison—to ground him, to keep him standing when everything else tried to break him.

"I'm not going to hurt her," I tell Sylveria directly, ignoring her daughters behind her. Corinda and Stacia perch on folding metal chairs hastily set up, nothing like the carved leather ones at the table.

Every one of us has guards scattered through the room. My own stand against the walls, hands near weapons, watching. Their guards mirror them. The air hums with tension, and the faint scrape of a boot against marble sounds like a gun cocking.

Since Sylveria hasn't answered, I hit the point home. "I meant what I said. Nobody harms Ella."

Mathias shifts beside me. His silvery-gray hair is thick, his eyes narrowing as they cut between me and Sylveria. His voice grates when he speaks, and pain shoots through my knees like knives digging under the joint. "Why would you care about her stepdaughter?"

"She's under my protection," I say, staring him down. I'm fairly certain he knows about the virus since he was present when we cured Thorn, although I doubt he understands it. He won't ask me about it in mixed company since the others don't know about it. "Ella's mine." It doesn't hurt to be explicit with these people.

Alexei barks out a laugh. The evenness in his tone

keeps me steady, though his words land sharp. "Are you serious? You're falling for the little sprite?"

"She's under my protection. That's all you need to know."

He chuckles, the sound colored with his Russian accent. "That's hilarious. I kidnapped her once. She got loose within hours."

I nod. "That's the difference between us. I left her with no electronics."

He winces. "She's not going to like that."

"No kidding," I mutter dryly. My gaze cuts to Sylveria. "Do we have any questions?"

"Oh no. I quite understand," Sylveria says. Her rough voice grinds into me, a bruising ache across my kidneys. I hold still. "I would like to meet with my stepdaughter at some point."

"That's right. You're having a server problem, aren't you?" I lean back, fingers against the table's carved edge. "I take it you need her."

The air shifts. She pats her hair into place. "We have business about the trust but can discuss it later." She smiles at Mathias. "The wedding was lovely, Mathias. Have you heard from Alana and Thorn?"

There had better not be a threat there. "They've touched base," I answer. "They're on their honeymoon and are not to be disturbed."

"Agreed," Mathias says. His gnarly hands shift restlessly on the table. "They deserve a little time off." He doesn't say it outright, but it's there. He wants his daughter far from whatever storm is coming. I can respect that. He clears his throat. The sound rips through my knees. "Sylveria, why do you need your stepdaughter's help?"

He's fishing for weakness, but she won't give it.

"Like I said," she answers coolly, "it's family business. We have some issues from the trust and will to settle."

Probably true, though I'll bet she's already drained the trust dry.

"I want my attorneys involved," I say, "to make sure Ella's protected."

"Oh my," Sylveria murmurs, and the roughness bruises deeper. "You really are enamored."

Enamored. A word I barely understand. "You'd better hope not."

"Is she working for you, Justice?" she presses, eyes sharp.

"None of your business," I answer.

Her smile is sly. "Well, if she works for you, she can work for me."

"I don't think she wants to work for you," I say evenly. "But I'll pose the question."

Mathias glares. "Justice, have you kidnapped Ella?" His voice rasps, stabbing pain back into my knees.

"Yes."

Mathias fidgets with his thick, gnarly hands. "She's dating Wesley Whisper from my company. If you kidnapped her, we should discuss it."

"Wesley can get in contact with her if he wishes," I say flatly. "They're no longer dating."

"Does he know that?" Alexei asks. His voice stays smooth, expression unreadable, the mask firmly in place. Controlled.

Is he amused? "I don't know, and I don't care." I focus back on him. "We've already had one high-society wedding. When is yours, Alexei?"

He doesn't pale, but he doesn't answer.

"Alexei," Sylveria says, her tone rough and bruising, "are you marrying Rosalie?"

Mathias leans forward, his brows rising.

For two of the most dangerous people on the planet, they sure like to gossip.

"If I do," Alexei says, glancing at his watch, "you'll be the first invited." He stands, graceful and calm, his chair sliding back on marble. His voice is steady, clean, giving me a brief reprieve. "It's been a pleasure." He strides out with his two men falling in behind him, precise and sharp.

Mathias rises next, patting his belly. "I really like Wesley. He does a good job for us. At least let him call Ella."

"Absolutely," I say. I couldn't care less what Wesley Whisper wants.

Mathias nods once, then strides out with his guards.

That leaves me with Sylveria and her daughters.

"Sit," Sylveria orders. Her rough tone presses into me, heavy in my kidneys.

Stacia takes Mathias's vacated chair, the scrape of metal against marble loud in the echoing space. Corinda joins her, folding her hands neatly on the table. Both young women are poised, calm, and watching me.

Corinda smiles, looking so much like her mother it's unsettling. Younger, beautiful, a sharper version of the same face. Blonde hair, blue eyes, lovely bone structure. She's the face of TimeGem Moments, and she seems to do a good job hitting parties and events. I think she has a few million followers and is an expert in makeup, movie lines, and the best cocktails. "Mother says you need a bride."

"Do I?" I ask.

Stacia flips her dark hair back, eyes sparkling. "Yes. Mother would like to auction us off as cattle. I'm not on board."

I like her. She's spunky. "I understand," I say. "But I'm not in the market."

Corinda leans forward, perfume light. "I've never looked for happily-ever-after. I've always thought a good business arrangement works for marriage. If you think about it, most arranged marriages last, whereas the silly love ones don't."

She's flawless in a white suit, makeup pristine. Pink lips, thick lashes, perfect nose. She'd be appealing to most. But right now, a little brat half my size holds my attention, and I don't see that changing.

"Would you stop trying to become the match of the century?" Stacia cuts in, her voice becoming irritating but not painful. "Alana already took that spot."

"Not if I can help it," Corinda says, her soft tone calming the room. She fixes her gaze on me. "What do you say?"

If I wanted a spouse who threw the best parties and knew the best people, she'd be perfect. Unfortunately, I don't care about either of those things. "I'm going to have to decline." I look at Sylveria. "Now that we're alone, I might as well tell you. Ella is coming for her company."

Sylveria's voice bruises me deeper when she rises. "You'll reconsider that since the company is mine. Not Ella's. My husband left it to me, and that's the end of it. Our servers run on diamonds."

But they were created to run on citrines. How easy is that to change? It's rare, that's for sure. I push back from the table, turning to Stacia. "You're delightful, and

I hope you marry for love." My gaze shifts to Corinda. "I understand your motivation and agree that most arranged marriages do work. I hope you find the person you're looking for, but it's not me."

"We'll see," Corinda answers, her smile sweet and sharp.

I glance at Sylveria. She adjusts her ball gown, glittering even here amid the steel and marble. Somehow, she still manages to look regal. I don't want to hurt her, but I will if necessary, so I give her one more warning. "Leave Ella alone. I don't want a war, but I'm ready." I stand and head outside, shutting the door behind me. My men move with me, two stationed close, watching my back. One of my black town cars speeds toward us, and I tense.

Wynd jumps out, his blue eyes wild and his tone low. "Ella and the dog are gone."

TWENTY-FOUR

Ella

I'm back in the tree, and Leo is sprawled under me, tongue lolling, content. We drove in a battered Toyota that blends into traffic, the kind of truck nobody remembers. I picked a path that ducks every camera I know about and a few I only suspect. Now I give the bird whistle and count to ten. Nothing stirs. That's fine. This isn't my usual hour, and if a lens tags me now, I'll have problems. I whistle one more time for luck, drop to the grass, and dust off my hands. The front desk won't let a dog in, so I need another approach.

The nursing home sits quiet, the big brick building stretched low and confident. I head toward the main doors, then cut left without breaking stride and follow the exterior until I reach the window I need.

A gardener looks up from across the lawn and then returns to tending his roses. I've learned that if I act like I know what I'm doing, folks usually don't bug me.

I tap the glass. The slats flip up, and my godmother

leans out, green glasses crusted with rhinestones catching the light. She pushes them higher, sees Leo, and softens. "Oh, what a sweetie." She props the window, hooks the screen out of the way, and waves me forward. "Bring him inside."

"That's the plan," I say. Leo looks at me, then at her, then back at me. He bunches his legs and slips through the opening like he's done it a hundred times.

I climb in after him and land hard on one knee—not nearly as graceful as my dog.

Aura grabs my elbow and steadies me while Magdalena's voice cuts from behind a monitor. "What exactly are you doing?"

I stand, brush grass off my pants, and watch Aura swing the screen back, slide the window down, and tug the blinds shut with quick, practiced motions.

Joslyn pivots in her chair, pale blue eyes that miss nothing locked on me. "Where have you been?"

"Kidnapped," I say. "Justice Beathach took me."

Aura's ring-heavy hand presses to her chest. "Are you serious?"

"Yes." Heat climbs my face before I can stop it.

Magdalena studies me, then the dog, then me again, her mouth tightening as if she's solved a problem she doesn't like. "You did not," she says.

Aura turns to her. "Didn't what?"

"Nothing," I say, too quick. "I didn't do anything."

Jos doesn't blink. "I doubt that." She tips her chin, unblinking. "Are you involved with Justice Beathach?"

"I'm not involved with him," I say. "He might have kidnapped me a couple of times." There are more pumpkins decorating the place than before, and several have been covered in orange sequins. The smell of fall, apples and ciders, spills from a couple of candles lit on the far credenza by the door.

"You didn't kiss him, did you?" Jos's voice is sharp, like she already knows the answer.

My cheeks blaze. "He kissed me."

Magdalena slides her glasses higher, pink sequins glittering across the frames she glued herself. She peers at me over the lenses, eyes narrowing. "Did you kiss him back?"

I shift on my feet. "I did." The words scrape out. I'd done a lot more than that. No way I'm giving them details.

Mag's chair creaks as she leans forward, her elbow on the desk, her hand fishing in the glass bowl beside her. She unwraps a caramel with neat, practiced fingers. "Well, how was it?"

I glance at the floor, then up, my voice light and shaky. "He's a good kisser." Oh, please don't ask for more details. Please.

Aura pats my arm, her thin skin soft and smelling faintly of rose lotion. "As long as all you did was kiss him, I suppose that's all right."

Oh, for the love of everything holy. "He's not that bad." I nod toward Leo, who sprawls contentedly on the rug. "He beat up a guy to save the puppy." Killed the guy, really.

Three pairs of eyes turn toward the dog. Jos studies him with her usual soft spot for animals. Mag tilts her head, sugar still melting in her mouth. Aura just smiles like glitter belongs in every corner of the world.

"He let you keep a dog?" Jos asks, disbelief edging her words.

"Not just *let* me," I say. "He helped me save him." My voice pushes too hard, like I'm trying to sell something

I don't quite buy. Justice might be decent with me, with dogs, probably with elderly women, but in the grand tally of life, his soul probably has some serious dents. It should worry me more than it does. "I kind of feel safe when I'm with him."

Aura gasps and claps her rhinestone-bright glasses up on her head. "That's how they get you, honey. They make you feel safe, make you feel special, and before you know it— "

"You're in the mob," Jos finishes flatly.

I laugh under my breath. "I don't think that's really how it works." Though both Alana and Rosalie ended up right there. Not in the business, but standing beside it. Rosalie's an attorney, a legitimate one, and Alana still fronts Aquarius Social with posts online, now branching into Malice Media. Neither of them has blood on their hands. Every instinct in me says their men would burn the world to protect them. I like that for them. "I can't gossip any longer. We need to get to work to retake my company."

I need the TimeGem powerful servers to cure the computer virus before anybody else gets a hold of it. Including Justice. Of course, I plan to cure him as well. Somehow.

Aura twirls a strand of her silver hair and eases back into her chair, sequined tracksuit sparkling under the glow of the string lights. She rolls closer to her keyboard, fingers poised. "I tracked what you sent. Whoever infiltrated the TimeGem servers knew what they were doing. I can piggyback on that, same as you. And I see you've already been in here."

The room hums with machine noise and little touches of defiance. Glitter clings to the carpet, catching the twinkle of string lights looped around curtain rods.

Mags nods. "We can take the system down whenever you want, but we need a plan."

Jos nods, fingers resting on the edge of her neat notepad. "If we take the diamonds out of commission, we have to make sure there are citrines ready to replace them, and you'll need to be there to charge them."

Mags taps her chin, squinting at the monitor glow. "Unless you charge them beforehand. Either way, we need them ready, and we need to be in the server room to do it."

I stiffen. I don't like the way they keep saying *we*. "How exactly are we going to do that?"

Aura smiles, and despite her rhinestone tracksuit and silver bun, it's wicked. "I'm working on that."

Mags exhales hard, her sequined glasses slipping down her nose. "I'd love to steal the diamonds. They're so . . . sparkly."

Aura tilts her head, considering. "I suppose we could. I know a good fence in Boise."

Jos leans back, crossing her arms over her white shirt. "There'll be some residual energy in the diamonds from Sylveria since she's the one charging them, but it'll fade. We could sell them on the open market. Think of the dogs we could save."

"I'd like that," I murmur. "Sylveria's hinted she needs my help a few times, but she hasn't told me what for, and I haven't hit her servers yet. Have you?"

Mags shakes her head. "Not yet. Someone else is already after them."

I grin despite myself. "I like that. I like that a lot."

Aura narrows her eyes, glitter flashing from her glasses. "Totally agree."

The monitors throw pale light across their faces—Aura

with her sequined sleeves, Mags with her candy bowl pushed to the side, Jos with her locket catching the glow. The whole room hums with electricity and age, these women plotting server raids like it's just another Tuesday.

"Do you want me to attack TimeGem?" Aura asks.

I love any idea that keeps these women working remotely. "Yes. Make Sylveria need my help, more than she already does."

"Then what?" Jos asks, folding her arms tight.

"Then I'll end up in the server room to help her?" I'm not sure about this plan.

Jos hops in her seat, looking adorable in a purple pantsuit. "Then we can plan a robbery?" Hope fills her faded eyes.

"Sure." I wonder if Justice will help. He's got the manpower. But considering I just escaped his penthouse, he's probably pissed. My butt still tingles, and I'm not up for another spanking. I'm pretty sure I'm bruised. "For now, I need to get to my last decent safe house to work. I'll finish opening the tunnel into their server. You can attack about four this afternoon. I'll clear the path for you."

"Excellent." Aura claps her hands, rhinestones catching the glow of the monitors. "I've been waiting to attack forever. I'm glad you're finally ready."

Me, too. With Justice on my ass, another player making a move, and Sylveria wanting me in her server room, I'm running on borrowed time. "I am so ready. Does anyone have a phone?"

"Of course. Do you want a burner or my regular one?" Mags asks, tugging open a drawer.

"Burner."

She rummages past stacks of candy bars, crystal

pendants, and a half-burned candle before tossing me a small black phone. "Who are you calling?"

"I'm texting Rosalie." That will have to do. I so do not want to talk about Justice with her while my godmother listens in.

My thumbs move fast. IT'S TIME TO FILE SUIT AGAINST TIMEGEM.

Rosalie has an entire case prepared—challenge of the will, challenge of the trust, fraud, theft. She's been waiting for my signal.

"She'll file it right away," I murmur.

The phone buzzes back: ARE YOU SURE?

YES. PLEASE FILE.

A flood of emojis rolls in—smiley faces, hearts, clapping hands—then: WHERE THE HELL ARE YOU? HAVE YOU BEEN WITH JUSTICE BEATHACH?

I return the text: I HAVE, AND I NEED TO TALK TO YOU, BUT NOT NOW. FILE THOSE PAPERS.

Three dots show, and then: FINE, BUT MEET TONIGHT. FIVE O'CLOCK. SANDBAG BAR BACKROOM. YOU AND ME.

I picture the routes in my head, dodging as much CCTV as possible, then send: ABSOLUTELY. SEE YOU THERE. I can get inside without being seen. Rosalie knows what she's doing. I toss the phone back to Mags.

"I'll destroy this in just a minute," Mags says easily.

"Thanks." I move back toward the window. "Would you all keep the dog for a bit?" It's easier to run without him.

"Of course," Jos says for the group, her fingers flying over the keys. "I'll order him food right now. And treats. Plus a few toys."

Leo flops down on her feet. Yeah, he's found a kindred spirit.

I don't blame him. I love this place and these women. The room hums with overlapping signals that include the faint whir of cooling fans, the snap of wrappers as Mags digs for another caramel, and the steady tick of the crystal-faced clock on the wall. String lights flicker above the curtained windows, throwing small halos across the cluttered credenzas. Aura's perfume bottles and bedazzled teacup sparkle under the glow, while Jos's workspace stays neat, her topaz locket gleaming as she makes another note in her tidy handwriting.

I gently pull the window screen free.

"Why don't you go out the main door?" Aura asks.

I shrug. "Dunno. I came in this way. Are you sure the cameras are still out?"

She rears back.

Oops. I lift up a hand. "I know they are. Sorry." I flop my leg over the sill and drop down on the other side, careful not to trample the flowers. "Thanks and I love you. Get ready to attack at four." I blow kisses, turn, and run across the lawn to the forest.

The trails are familiar as I move between trees to a small alcove where I usually hide my vehicles while visiting. There are no cameras anywhere near.

Reaching the truck, I open the door just as a gleaming town car tears around the bend and screeches to a stop at my side.

Two men jump out.

"Damn it." I shove the door, but the closest guy is quicker. His hand clamps on my arm, yanks me forward, and before I can twist free, he tosses me into the back of the town car. I hit hard, palms scraping the pristine carpet. The air smells like new car and real leather.

I push up, knees stinging. "Ah, shit."

Sylveria Rendale sits across from me in a blue ball gown, the kind that belongs at a gala, not here. The skirt is bunched at her knees, creased from the ride. A row of diamonds circles her throat, bright even in the dim car light. Her hair is pinned tight, not a strand out of place. "How are you, my dear stepdaughter?"

"Just great," I mutter, sliding onto the seat. "How did you know I was here?"

"I've been tracking Rosalie's calls and texts. Even though you used a burner phone, Rosalie didn't." Sylveria smooths her dress with long fingers, her nails painted red. "The best part is we're the only ones who know where you are right now. Most of the underworld still thinks Justice Beathach has you."

Well, fantastic. If I end up dead, he takes the blame. Darn it, Rosalie. We all figured she was so safe now protected by the Russian mob. Why hadn't I thought to give her a burner phone? What was I thinking?

I glance at the door. The hulking bodyguard wedges himself there, with his wide shoulders blocking the window, hands loose at his sides. Watching with no light in his eyes. Not even a glimmer. There will be no help for me from him. "I suppose you still want me dead," I mutter.

"I really do," Sylveria says, and then she smiles.

TWENTY-FIVE

Ella

Unlike the other social media companies, TimeGem Moments located its headquarters several miles outside of Silicon Valley. The building is a massive spread of metal and glass, two stories above ground and five more hidden below. The grounds are perfect, unnervingly so, with every hedge and path lined to precision. Statues glimmer as if they've been carved straight out of diamonds.

For a second I almost believe the sparkles. Then I wonder how the guards keep anyone from rushing in and prying the stones loose. I glance sideways at Sylveria, suspicion pressing against my ribs. The realization lands sharp. "Those aren't diamonds," I say, my voice catching. "I read an exposé on you a few years back. They swore the statues were covered in diamonds. The eyes. The nails. All of it. They're not diamonds. How did you fool the reporter?"

Sylveria doesn't flinch. She turns her face toward the window, her tone flat, almost bored. "A couple are real. You just don't know which ones we showed. The one the reporter saw was real. I told him the rest were authentic, and he wanted to believe that."

My father would've hated that. "Of course he did."

We roll up to the front of the building. Security cameras stare down at us from every angle, cold and unblinking. My stomach knots. "Are those on?" I try to keep my voice steady.

"I believe they're temporarily down," she answers carelessly.

"Wonderful," I mutter, though my palms are slick.

We ditch the car and walk inside, where the air feels thick, almost heavy with memory. Nostalgia twists at me, but it's poisoned. I remember coming here with my father, when things were still good. Before he married her.

If only he hadn't.

At the elevator, she presses her palm to the scanner, once to open, once more to close, and again to push the floor button. My chest tightens. My palm won't work here. I'm trapped without her.

The elevator descends fast, the walls humming as we drop. The space feels too small, the air too still, and every breath reminds me that I don't belong here right now. Not until I retake the platform. My pulse won't settle.

I'm almost grateful the hulking guy with the dead eyes isn't here. If I make it back up out of this place, I'll have to deal with him. For now, it's Sylveria at my side, her presence pressing in until I can feel it under my skin.

"What do you need from me, anyway?" My voice scrapes the air, sharper than I intend.

"We've had a breach in our system," Sylveria says. "And the diamond that powers the entire service seems . . . weakened."

I blink. What in the world? "Define *weakened.*"

"I can't." She lifts a shoulder, her tone flat. "When I try to charge it, I don't feel well."

My stomach twists. Holy crap. It sounds like the virus I uploaded to weaken Thorn. Except I haven't unleashed the deadly code into TimeGem's servers. I swallow hard. "Well. That's interesting."

The elevator doors slide open. Light spills out, soft and almost too pretty for what I expect. The floor looks polished and the place feminine. Potted plants line the corners, their leaves glossy and perfect, like someone wipes them down every hour. The air smells faintly floral, not chemical, and that throws me off.

I can't help but contrast this with the Malice Media hub. Yeah, totally masculine versus this feminine space. I stop just inside, taking it in. To the right, a seating area is arranged like a lounge—chairs angled, pillows in careful patterns, a coffee table gleaming without a single fingerprint. To the left, a wide glass counter stretches across the space.

Behind it sits Corinda.

I gape. "Corinda? What are you doing here?"

She preens, self-assured as always. "I can charge the diamonds." Then, as if she's dropping gossip instead of news, she adds, "Did you hear? Justice and I are becoming engaged."

A bolt of heat zings through me so hard it hits my toes. I stiffen. What the hell was that? I'm not jealous. I don't like Justice. "The poor man." My smile feels tight. "Is he ready to spend his life on magazine covers?"

She laughs. "I don't care whether he is or not. He'll look good on my arm."

I have to give her credit. She's always known exactly

who she is with her blonde hair piled high, confidence radiating as she leans back in her chair.

She rolls her eyes. "I don't work the desk. Give me a break. We cleared the floor since you were kind enough to come assist us with our servers."

Ah. There it is.

A double door in the mirrored glass behind Corinda opens. It's a definite upgrade from the last time I was here, and Stacia strides out. "Hey there."

Wow. It's a whole family reunion. "Hey, Stacia."

She looks at her mother and then back at me. "So she really did kidnap you, huh?"

I like her tone. "Yes."

Stacia shakes her head. "Mother. I thought we were just going to pay her. I think this whole kidnapping situation is a little too much."

Sylveria lowers her chin. "Stop contradicting me."

I think I could probably take all three of them. Then I notice the guards. Two at each corner, blending into the shadows. I actually have to look to find them. Nice. Very effective. The lighting in this place is phenomenally structured.

Sylveria gestures to the elevator. "All right, ladies. I'd like to speak with your stepsister alone."

"No." Corinda's voice is cool. "This involves all of us. I don't think it's a good idea to let her into our servers."

Stacia chirps in, reaching for her sparkly purse by the phone. Some of the cheap glitter drops to the cement floor. "Yeah. I don't think it's a good idea either. If the diamond is making the two of you feel ill, the gem might truly harm her since she doesn't have the affinity to diamonds that we do."

I feel like Stacia might be on my side. Even so, I have to hide my panic as I fight a sneeze. "The diamond is making you ill, too?"

Corinda nods. "Yes. When I try to charge it, I feel like puking."

"I'm not asking. Go." Their mother dismisses them.

Stacia rolls her eyes and walks around the glass counter toward the elevator. "Blink once if you need help," she says dryly.

Okay. Now I kind of want to punch her.

She chuckles and moves to the elevator, pressing her palm to the wall. It opens.

Corinda moves more gracefully around the counter and pauses. She's dressed in an unwrinkled yellow silk suit and looks pretty, I have to admit. "Just charge the diamonds, and I'm sure we can reach an arrangement," she says softly before moving into the elevator.

Stacia pauses. "Mother? We know she's here. If she disappears, I will cause a scene."

I blink. "Gee, Stacia. I didn't know you cared."

She shrugs, looking young and rather carefree in jeans and a button-down. High-end flannel. The blue brings out the blue in her eyes. "We're kind of family."

"I appreciate that," I say grimly. "I'd very much like *not* to be dead."

Corinda lifts a shaking hand to her head.

I frown. "How badly do you feel?"

"I just tried to charge the diamonds and I'm just feeling . . . I don't know. Tired."

"Don't charge the diamonds," I blurt.

Sylveria tilts her head. "Why not?"

"There's obviously something wrong with them." I

can't tell her about the virus, but I also don't want Corinda ending up dead. I'm not sure we could pull off the same feat with anyone else the way we did with Thorn when we saved his life, and Justice is still struggling. How am I going to save him? Plus, how did the virus end up in TimeGem, if that's what's going on here? Is there a different virus? Or a mutated one? "Let me discover what's going on with the servers before you try to charge them again."

Corinda pulls her sister into the elevator. "Nice try. We know you want to take over. We're not going to let you do that."

I decide not to answer, but my face must give me away, because she winks as the doors slide shut.

"What do you know about the diamond being weakened?" Sylveria demands, grabbing my arm and yanking me toward her.

I face her. "I don't know anything about your damn diamonds. I do know TimeGem Moments is supposed to run on citrines."

She rolls her eyes. "Whatever. Come this way." She turns, head high, still draped in that ridiculous ball gown.

"Do you ever dress down?" I follow, acutely aware of the guards posted in the corners.

"This is dressed down." She walks into the server room, and the moment I step inside, I feel at home. My gaze catches on a series of glass compartments set into the far wall. The middle one holds a tiara—citrine and diamond, but the glow is gone. It looks dull; lifeless. My breath catches. It has belonged in my family for longer than anybody can remember.

The tiara is exquisite. Large oval citrines burn golden in their settings, encircled by smaller diamonds that climb the delicate platinum frame. Even dulled, it's beautiful, regal. Once, the citrines would have shone like captured sunlight.

Then my gaze shifts to the center of the room. The diamond. Or rather, a structure made from several diamonds, massive, worth billions. They hum softly, as do the server banks surrounding them in tall columns flashing with yellow and white lights.

I step closer to the crown instead. I can't help it. As I near, the citrines flicker faintly, beginning to glow. I stop, my heart pounding.

"Wow," Sylveria says. "I always wondered about that."

"It's because the crown's mine." I wonder idly if my heirs, if I live long enough to have any, will be able to affect the citrines. I look back toward the diamonds. The centers are yellowed, but not with citrine color. It's sickness. "Somebody's infected your servers."

Sylveria nods. "No kidding." She lifts her wristwatch to her mouth. "Bring him in."

I pause. Interesting.

A side door opens. Two guards push in a bleeding, battered Wesley.

"Wesley," I whisper, moving toward him.

His gray suit is rumpled, one sleeve torn at the cuff. Blood trickles from his swollen lip down his chin, staining his white shirt. His knuckles are shredded, skin split and raw. A bruise is already spreading along his jaw, one eye puffing and darkening. His blond hair is damp, sticking to his forehead, but he's still upright, still steady. Relief pushes through my chest. He's hurt, but he's still breathing. "What is going on?" I demand, turning to Sylveria.

She shrugs. "I figured the two of you were working

together, know you're dating, and want to properly motivate you to help me."

I shake my head. "You kidnapped the head programmer from Aquarius Social."

"Yes."

I blink and panic. A sneeze takes me, and I cover my nose with my arm. Blinking, I sniff. "You do *not* want to go to war with Aquarius Social. You know they're aligned with Malice Media right now."

"I'm well aware." She doesn't even shift her weight. Does she have a clue how dangerous Justice is? She has to, right?

Wesley's eyes find mine. "Are you hurt?"

"I'm just fine." I look at his bruised, bloodied face. "Please tell me you did some damage in return."

"One guy is still knocked out."

A smile breaks out before I can stop it. "Good on you."

Sylveria's gaze slices across us both. "Figure out what's wrong with my diamonds, or you both die today."

I glance at the damaged stones, at Wesley, at the servers. He doesn't know what I did to Thorn.

He leans in, voice low. "Do you know what's wrong with the diamond?"

"It wasn't me," I say, answering the question he hasn't asked. All right, so he doesn't know, but he's smart enough to suspect. That's why I like him.

"Really?" His eyes darken as he studies me.

Man, he's cute. Not dangerous. Not like Justice. Just . . . good-looking, even broken up like this. "It wasn't me."

He winces. "Then we have a problem."

"No kidding." I glance over the servers, heat rising in

my chest. "If you want me to backtrack through this mess, I need full access, Sylveria."

"You're already logged in," Sylveria says. "I don't have a choice." She steps toward the door, skirts brushing the floor. "If you help me, I'll help you. Maybe we can reach an agreement for both of us to run TimeGem Moments. For now, you have two hours. If you haven't figured it out by then, I'm cutting off the oxygen to this room."

She doesn't wait for an answer. The door hisses shut behind her, locking us in.

The hum of the servers presses in, steady and cold. For a moment, it's just me and Wesley. He wipes blood from his mouth with the back of his hand, smearing it across his jaw, and breathes out slowly.

"Two hours," I say. "She makes it sound like a courtesy."

"I think she's serious." His voice is rough, worn at the edges, but steady.

We head toward the server bank. The room is lined with tall black towers, lights blinking in an uneven rhythm. The air is cool, too sterile, the scent metallic. Not healthy. Yellow and white indicators stutter where green should pulse.

I sit at the console, the glass desk humming faintly under my hands as the keyboard lights up. Wesley leans in close, close enough I can see the swelling at his jaw, the cut on his lip. He looks like hell, and something inside me twists. He doesn't deserve this.

Not after everything I've already done. We haven't slept together, and we weren't exclusive, but I still should've ended things before I slept with Justice. Not that I planned that. At all.

The screen fills with scrolling code. White text over black, endless strings of commands.

"There." Wesley's voice is sharp, focused. He points at a line of replication errors. "Cycle's broken. The diamond's not powering the secondary clusters."

"Yeah," I mutter, fingers moving fast over the keys. "But look at this. It's not just broken—it's blocked. Checksums don't lie."

He's quiet for a beat. "You've seen this before."

My chest tightens. The code is similar to the virus I uploaded to hurt Thorn, but it has been tweaked and dulled, as if someone took the edges off. I can still see the shape of it, the bones of what almost killed him.

"It looks familiar," I hedge, keeping my tone even.

Wesley studies the code, the glow of the monitor deepening the shadows on his face. "This isn't an outside attack. It's already inside, isn't it?"

"Yeah." I push deeper into the logs, scrolling through corrupted time stamps and half-erased functions. "It's not new. It's been sitting here for a while, feeding slow. That's why the diamonds are sick." But I see a few mutations where the virus has been slowed down.

Who mutated the virus? Is it possible they have a cure for it? For Justice, too?

"We need to pull it out before the whole system collapses." Wesley's voice is calm, practical, but I can feel the weight of his eyes on me. But he doesn't ask any questions.

I keep my gaze on the code. "We will. Just . . . don't touch anything until I've traced it back."

He leans back, running a hand through his hair. His knuckles are raw, bruises dark on his skin. He still manages a wry smile. "Bossy as ever."

The smile hits me harder than it should. Guilt flares sharp. I slept with Justice, and Wesley doesn't know. He can't know. This isn't the time. This isn't even the place. But the thought of him bleeding, trapped here with me, makes everything else taste sour.

I force my attention back to the terminal. "If I can find the entry point, I can strip it out."

"And if you can't?"

"Then we'll both find out how long it takes to suffocate in here."

He lets out a breath, low and steady. "No pressure, then."

I type faster, pushing past the guilt, past the weight of secrets. I can't let him see the truth, not about the virus, not about Justice. For now, all that matters is the code in front of me.

And the clock is already ticking down.

TWENTY-SIX
Justice

Fury clocks through me as I jump in the back of the town car, Wynd sliding in from the other side. My driver is a guy named Bronco, and it fits. He's large, broad, and armed. Funny thing is, it's actually his name.

I pull up my phone and start updating a fucking app I didn't think I'd need for a while. It's a good half hour from doing what I need.

"I'm so sorry," Wynd says.

I hold up a hand. "It's Ella. I should have figured. I had all electronics removed from the penthouse." I try not to smile, because it's fucking brilliant. And yet, she's out there, alone.

I press a couple buttons on my phone, instructing Kaz to find her.

We drive for nearly half an hour, almost to the penthouse, when Bronco stiffens.

"Hold on, boss," he says. "We have trouble."

I look up just in time to see another town car barreling toward us down the mainly quiet street.

"What do you want me to do?" Bronco's voice stays steady as his foot sinks deeper.

I pull my gun from its holster and glance at Wynd. "We play chicken."

"Sounds good." Wynd's grin is feral, even with the bruise.

Bronco lowers his head, engine screaming, and we surge forward.

Movement flashes in my peripheral—a streak of black cutting out of an alley and across the lane. Before I can process it, another car slams into us dead center, right between the driver's door and mine.

The impact throws me across the car. I smash into Wynd, my forehead cracking against the opposite window. Glass sprays. The car spins, metal groaning, tires screeching as the world tilts sideways. We slam into the opposing alley, the car crashing into brick.

For a moment everything goes black. Then . . . silence. Just the sound of glass raining down across the floorboards.

"What the fuck?" My voice rasps, raw. I turn, disoriented, as my door crumples inward with a groan of tearing steel. At least nobody is shooting at us this time.

I smash out the rest of the glass with my elbow and shove Wynd's door wide. I barely hit the ground before Alexei is there, gun jammed hard into my chest.

Blood trails down my face, sticky and hot, but I don't wipe it away. Fury rises sharp and fast inside me. I shift aside as Wynd stumbles free of the wreck. Bronco is still hunched over the wheel, motionless.

"He better fucking be breathing," I hiss, then square myself toward Alexei.

The barrel doesn't move. I keep my own weapon down, angled at the asphalt. No point in dying stupid.

His eyes are black fire, unblinking. It's only been a short time since we met, and he's still wearing the black suit and tie. I lean in, pressing my chest into the steel. If he wanted me dead, he should've made a move back in the warehouse. "What the holy fuck do you think you're doing?"

"Was it you?" His voice is low, lethal.

My skull pounds, blood dripping into my eye. "No." I don't even know what he's accusing me of. But it wasn't me.

"You don't know what I mean."

"I don't give a fuck what you mean."

He tilts the gun back a fraction, gaze locked. "You really don't."

"No, and if you don't lower that thing, I'll shove mine up your ass."

The grin that splits his face isn't humor. It's a predator baring teeth. "Somebody shot a missile into my new homestead ten minutes ago. I thought you were trying to make an even bigger statement than the one you made earlier."

"Rosalie?" My voice cracks more than I want to admit. "Is she alive?" I can't tell Ella that her friend is dead.

"She's fine. Everyone's fine." He lowers the gun. "It was the guest house that blew."

My chest loosens. Who is shooting missiles at us?

"Which means her seven boarders are moving into my house." His voice hardens, rising. "Seven old men. Eating my food. Breathing my air. Until I build them something else."

I blink. "What?"

He snarls. "She took them in years ago. From her old place. I promised her a roof, so I built them one. Now it's rubble, and they're mine until I replace it."

"Send them to a home."

His jaw tightens, teeth grinding. "That's not how it works." Then his eyes cut back to me. "You all right?"

"I'm fine." My head throbs, blood stings my eye, and my vision is edged in black. Part of me wants to shoot him for payback, just in the knee, but I have more pressing matters to handle right now. "I didn't bomb you."

"Yeah, I get that now." He takes a step back and looks at my damaged vehicle. "I owe you a car."

"You better not owe me a driver. Bronco." I look over my shoulder. "Wake up."

The man doesn't move.

"Bronco. His name's Bronco?" Alexei asks.

Bronco groans and pushes away from the steering wheel, his forehead bloody.

I breathe out. "You're paying for any medical bills, Sokolov."

"That's fair," Alexei says. "Do you need a ride?"

"No." I jerk my head toward a second car coming into view. My men are already out, weapons raised. Alexei's men spill from two additional vehicles, guns drawn as well.

"Everyone, weapons down," I say, voice hard. "I am not in the mood."

The barrels lower, but the tension stays wired tight. My face is throbbing.

Alexei clears his throat. "This is probably the wrong time, but I have a cousin I'd like you to meet."

I blink blood out of my eye and focus on him. "Excuse me?"

"She's cute. Russian. Dark hair, temper you wouldn't believe. She'll bear you many fine children."

My fist itches, but I stand still.

He steps toward his car. "Probably the wrong time, but it would be good if we could form an alliance. Marriage, family, that's how it's done."

"You want me to marry your fucking cousin?"

"That's the idea." He shrugs. "I'm sure Sylveria has approached you about her daughters."

I just stare and then cough out blood. "You fell in love with your own lawyer. Rumor says you're obsessed with her. That wasn't exactly an arranged match."

"She's one of a kind," he says reasonably. "And well . . . there is no 'and.' She's one of a kind. I couldn't let her go. I never will."

I understand his reasoning more than I should, because right now there's a pixie-sized blonde out of my reach. My gut twists. "I have things to do." I turn toward my vehicle.

"Ella Rendale isn't the one for you," he says suddenly.

I stop cold and turn back. "You want to die?"

"Not really." His voice stays calm. "But you know I can't let you align with TimeGem while your brother is tied to Aquarius Social. That would leave Hologrid Hub out in the cold. I can't let it happen."

I take a step toward him, glass crunching under my boots. My voice drops. "You go near Ella, and I will tear down everything you *love*."

I stress the last word. We both know exactly who he loves.

His smile fades, eyes hard now. "Then I suppose we understand each other."

Bronco groans again behind me. Wynd steadies himself against the car, still holding his ribs. The street is littered with broken glass and bent steel, engines ticking down as if nothing just happened.

I holster my gun, never looking away from Alexei. The night smells of gasoline and blood. My patience is gone. "I'm not using euphemisms, Alexei. I know where to hit you."

His eyes are already dark, darker still, until they look bottomless. "So it's like that, is it?"

"Yes," I say through gritted teeth.

"Huh." He looks more surprised than angry. "Then you'd better lock her down fast, because I'm sure I'm not the only one who sees her as a threat."

Ella is definitely a threat, and Alexei probably has no idea what she can actually do with a computer virus. I notice belatedly that his voice isn't cutting me, not the way it should, and he's been threatening me this entire time. It could be that Alexei, deep down, is a decent man, or maybe it's just that we're of the same mind. I've also noticed since I started whatever this is with Ella that words don't pierce as much. Maybe she's toughened me, or maybe she's softened everything else.

The woman has too much power. I need to check out that worthless penthouse for clues of where she's gone, at least until this stupid app finishes updating. Sometimes technology is such a pain in the ass.

"We can find another way to forge a connection between our companies," I say. "I don't want to do it through marriage. At least not with this generation."

"Apparently," he says, "that means your kids and my kids."

I think about it. "I'd be willing to consider that."

"Great." He doesn't even have a bride yet, but he's about to, so I can already see him planning ahead.

"Are you going to tell Rosalie?" I'm rather curious how brave he is with the lawyer.

"Hell no. That's something that comes up in about twenty years." He glances again at my demolished vehicle. "Send me a bill." With that, he turns and walks to the back of his dented car. The door slams, the engine growls, and he drives off without another word.

Wynd sags against what's left of our car now that he can finally breathe. "Are you sure we shouldn't just follow and shoot him?"

"It's a definite possibility," I say, finally wiping the blood from my face. I gingerly touch the cut above my eyebrow. It doesn't feel too deep. A bandage will do.

I move toward my other vehicle just as Bronco lurches out of the driver's seat, blinking hard, his balance off. He sways, head darting side to side, trying to place himself.

I glance at Wynd. "Are you okay?"

"Yeah." He rolls his shoulder. "Rattled my brain a little, but I'll live."

"All right. You need to get Bronco to a doctor. He's definitely concussed. Could have internal injuries too."

Wynd brushes glass off his pants. "I'm on your six."

I stare at him. "Right, because I may need help checking out my penthouse."

He rolls his eyes. "We didn't think we'd get hit by a car today, now did we?"

"No. That's fair."

And they had shoved us into an alley to box us in clean.

I whistle at two of my men. "Get Bronco to the hospital. Keep me updated."

They rush forward, taking him by the arms, steadying his bulk between them.

I turn to Wynd. "Secure us another vehicle."

He glances at me. "Do you want to change clothes?"

"No. We don't have time. Let's go."

When I find Ella, she's going to learn that this isn't a game, even though I suspect she feels it is. She better be safe.

TWENTY-SEVEN

Ella

"I know you're good at this," Wesley says to me, "but you seem familiar with this particular code. Have you, ah, seen it before?"

"It looks somewhat familiar, but I don't know why." I sit back as I lie to him. "I think I purged it from the system."

He sits close beside me, glancing over his shoulder at the diamonds. They still glow with that sickly yellow tint, as if the sickness in the code has seeped into the stones themselves.

"I don't think I can restore the stones," I say.

He leans back, eyes flicking toward the sealed door. "We're coming up on the two-hour deadline, and this place is airtight."

"I know it is," I murmur. "Hopefully she doesn't want to kill us today."

"I think she would love that," he mutters.

I almost smile. "We didn't save the diamonds now, did we?"

His gaze sharpens. "Did you do that on purpose?"

Of course I did it on purpose. I lie smoothly. "No. I can't save the diamond. She's going to need citrines if she wants my help with the energy."

He appraises me. "Won't that give you an in to the entire system?"

I shrug. "Not if she locks me out of the computer."

The hum of the servers fills the pause. The room is colder than I first noticed, the air biting my skin the longer we sit. Rows of black towers line the walls, blinking in uneven rhythm, throwing off pulses of pale yellow light. It feels less like a server room and more like a machine breathing around us, steady, endless, watching.

He leans over, brushing his knuckles across my cheek. The touch is unexpected, and guilt stabs me hard. "So I've been thinking."

Oh, crap. A pit drops in my stomach and I turn to focus on the stones. Away from him. The diamonds dominate the center, their jagged edges catching every glow from the monitors, shadows crawling across the floor in fractured patterns. The chill isn't just from the air system. It's from the energy itself—wrong, unstable, turning this place into a tomb.

He doesn't take the hint. "Ella, I think it's time for us to take the next step. I know you like all your safe houses and running around town, but would you consider moving in with me?"

My mouth is suddenly dry. He's smart, he's sexy, he's tall, blond, brilliant. "I can't."

His eyebrows arch. "Is it because of Justice Beathach?"

I choke, coughing hard even though there's nothing in my throat. I clear it fast and then sneeze. Twice. "Why would you say that?"

"Bless you. I saw you two dance together at Alana's wedding."

"Oh," I say lamely. I had even forgotten he was there.

Wesley shakes his head. "You know he's a killer, right?"

"I do know that." I don't know what else to say.

I like Wesley. I like him a lot. It has been fun dating him, and it could have been even more fun if I'd let it go farther. But with Justice, it's different. Messy. Dangerous. Half the time I want to kill him, and the other half I'm tearing his clothes off. I ripped them off once already, and the memory makes my chest burn with guilt. Even worse, I'm enjoying this game we're playing. My brain needs the challenge, and so does Justice.

I know there's more to life than passion and sex. I know that. Wesley is hot. He's steady. He's brilliant. But he isn't Justice.

"Why is it?" he asks.

I've been lost in my own head. "What?"

"That girls choose the bad boys. Not just the slightly reckless bad boys, but the bad, killer-monster-to-their-souls men beyond redemption."

"I don't know," I admit. "I'm not choosing Justice." My body might have done that, but it doesn't mean we're going to end up together. We don't get along that well.

"Then why not give us a chance?" Wesley asks. He's so reasonable.

I don't have an answer.

He studies me for several moments. I like his attentiveness. I always have. But even so, I can't stop comparing him to Justice, to the way Justice looks at me, the way his gaze burns straight through me. Maybe there's something seriously wrong with me.

The hum of the server room fills the silence between us. Cold air pushes out of the vents above, steady and biting, wrapping around my arms until goosebumps rise.

Wesley leans in. "You know Justice helps run the Irish mafia, right?"

"Yes." I sigh. "I am aware of his job."

"Then why in the world would you want to get involved with him?"

It's such a good question. "I'm not. I think you and I have nothing to do with anybody else. I like you, Wesley. A lot."

He leans back in his chair and groans. "Oh no. Not the 'I think you're a great guy, Wesley' speech."

I wince. "You are a great guy."

"Oh God, Ella, stop talking." He runs a broad hand through his sandy blond hair, leaving it ruffled, making him look annoyingly adorable. "What do you want?"

It's a good question. A fair one. "I don't know."

"You can't possibly want an Irish mobster who kills people for fun."

"No. I really don't." I swallow. "The whole killing-for-fun thing has never appealed to me. But I don't think that's Justice." Oh, I realize that he's killed people, but I don't think he has any fun with it.

"You don't know him." Wesley snorts. "Honey, I've been in this business my whole life. I know him." He sobers. "Besides him being a very poor choice for you and an unsafe one, you've got to step back and look at the larger picture. Alana and Thorn are married. That means Aquarius Social and Malice Media are aligned. Although you're on the outs with Sylveria, you are TimeGem."

The weight of it hits me all over again. Wesley has no idea about the virus, no idea how close I came to tearing everything apart already. If he knew, he wouldn't be looking at me with that steady calm, wouldn't be asking me to choose him. His world is neat and rational. Mine is cracked down the center.

I shift in my chair, pretending to focus on the screen in front of us. The code scrolls by, endless lines of white against black. My hands hover over the keys, but my mind is caught between the cold hum of the servers and the warmth of Wesley's hand brushing mine only minutes ago. He doesn't realize how much I'm hiding. He doesn't realize how much guilt I'm choking on.

And I can't let him.

He leans back, his chair creaking, as he continues drawing lines together for me. "If you and Justice end up together, that aligns TimeGem and Malice. That leaves Alexei Sokolov out in the cold. He won't allow that to happen. He'll take out one or both of you."

My money's on Justice in that fight. The thought is instant and unwelcome. Truth is, I have no idea. They're both mob bosses. Maybe they'd kill each other. What I do know is that I don't ever want to be on the opposite side of Rosalie.

"I don't look at life that way," I tell him.

He tilts his head, a small smile tugging. "I know. You're all heart."

"No, I'm not. I'm all brain," I shoot back. "I'm phenomenal with computers."

"Yeah, but I still think that's your heart," he murmurs.

The words sink into me, sweet and painful all at once. I draw in a long breath. "Wesley, I just think—"

He lifts a hand, cutting me off. "No. We're not breaking up while we're trapped in this server room."

I fall quiet. The truth is, I'm not sure we've ever been

anything real. We never agreed to be exclusive. But he watches me, steady and certain, and the weight of that gaze presses on me until my chest feels tight.

He places his warm hand over mine. "I need you to think about this carefully, okay?"

"Okay," I whisper.

The door unlocks with a heavy click, the sound sharp over the hum of the servers. Cold air rushes across the floor as Sylveria strides in, her gown sweeping behind her. Two guards shadow her, silent and alert.

I lift my chin and give her my coldest stare. "We tracked a computer virus through your system and neutralized it. But I can't do anything about your diamonds, which were somehow infected by this virus." Playing dumb doesn't sit well with me.

Her gaze slides to the center of the room where the stones pulse with that sickly yellow. "A computer virus infected my diamonds?" Her lips press into a white line. "That's unacceptable."

Ha. If she only knew. "It's worse than that. I'm concerned that the virus has also infected you. If so, it could spread to any diamond you use." I'm so curious.

"That's ludicrous. Humans can't catch a computer virus." She squares her shoulders, eyes locking on me. Thoughts flash across her face as she no doubt thinks it through. As someone who exchanges energy with a stone, she knows their power. I can see the acceptance when it hits her. "Did you do this?" she snaps.

"I didn't." The words are sharp, and for once, they're honest. I didn't do it this time. "This wasn't me. I don't know who did it, but there's only one way to find out. Do you have another diamond you could try to charge?"

"Of course I do." She sweeps across the room to a recessed storage panel. Her palm unlocks the seal, and she pulls out a diamond the size of a marble. It gleams faintly in her hand.

The server fans whir faster, filling the room with a low rush of air. Wesley leans forward, his chair scraping against the concrete, gaze fixed on Sylveria. My own pulse picks up, a sick twist of dread and curiosity.

She draws a breath and centers herself. Energy stirs, faint at first, then stronger, and the gem flares with a soft glow. For a second, it's almost beautiful. Then a crack splinters across the surface, and the glow yellows, bleeding from the edges inward.

Wesley glances at me, his jaw tightening.

"It's compromised," I say. "You now carry the virus."

Sylveria closes her hand around the fractured stone and opens it again. The crack remains. She frowns. "I caught a virus from a computer. Did you know this could happen?"

"Yeah," I mutter. "I've seen some data that it's possible." Of course I know all the data, but she doesn't need to realize that. I didn't think it would happen like this. "At least it's not killing you."

"A computer virus can't kill a person," she says.

Oh, how wrong she is. "Who the heck knows? We've never truly understood how humans exchange energy with crystals."

She stares at the damaged gem. "So now I can't charge the diamonds." She speaks slowly, as if testing the words.

I do imagine that would suck. "Have Corinda and Stacia tried to charge the damaged stones?"

"Corinda has," Sylveria whispers, paling. Her blue eyes shoot sparks.

"What about Stacia? Can she charge diamonds?" Wesley asks.

Sylveria's nostrils flare. "Yes, but not with the skill I have. She doesn't have enough of a connection to the gems to be the sole charging force."

The hum of the servers grows louder, a steady pulse in the walls. I shift my weight, keeping one eye on the diamonds in the center. They glow faintly, yellow where they should burn clear, and the sight twists my stomach.

"There might be a cure for your virus," I say. "I just don't know what it is." That much is the truth. There's no way I can duplicate what Alana did to save Thorn. I don't have that connection with Sylveria or with diamonds.

She walks to the cabinet, her gown whispering over the floor, and pulls out a citrine the size of a bowling ball. The beauty gleams under the sterile lights. "I guess you're going to have to charge this, aren't you?"

My blood starts to hum, and I have to fight every instinct in my body not to connect to the stone. "I'm not going near that."

"Excuse me?" She looks stunned, and so does Wesley.

Yeah, I would freaking love to charge a citrine here. "I have no idea what's been infected and what hasn't. If I'm going to charge a citrine, it's going to be one I acquire, not one that comes from you. Every gem in this place might be infected, and I'm not willing to risk that."

She smiles, cold and deliberate. "I could just suffocate and kill you."

"You sure could," I say cheerfully. "But that leaves you up shit creek, doesn't it? Unless you think Stacia can take over full time for you." I'm bluffing. If I have to, I'll charge that citrine. She probably knows it.

She studies me for a long moment, her fingers still curled around the citrine. Then she smiles, all teeth, as she places it gently on the desk next to the computer. "I guess that's up to you, then." She sweeps toward the door and steps outside, her skirts brushing the floor. The lock engages behind her with a sharp click.

At first, nothing changes. Then the vents overhead shift, the hum turning hollow. My next breath catches in my throat, thinner than the last.

Wesley meets my gaze. He doesn't have to say a word. We both know what she's done.

The air is already running out.

TWENTY-EIGHT

Justice

We park in front of the Cinderfalls Community Home, and I cock my head. Why in the world would Ella be here? I've investigated her before and haven't found any connection to this place. What if she just dropped the dog off, figuring he'd be safe at a nursing home? Damn it. I take a deep breath.

Wynd fidgets in the front seat. He doesn't like me driving. I'm an excellent driver, but somebody already rammed a car with me in it. Twice. I suppose my being dead when Thorn gets home wouldn't bode well for Wynd.

"This is weird," he says.

"I know." I drive around the front and park at the far end, looking at a long span of lawn.

He stretches his hand on his leg, and I note cuts on his knuckles from the crash earlier. We're both still bloody. "Do you want me to go inside?" he asks.

"No." I check my phone again. The dog is definitely here. I had him chipped but hadn't installed or updated the app soon enough. It had taken too much time. Keeping my temper in check, I zero in and widen the screen. The dog's on the other side of the compound. I hit reverse and follow the curved path all the way to the east side of the building, where another long lawn stretches out with trees on either side. It's a peaceful place, and with the leaves turning golden and red, it screams cozy autumn. All the pumpkins and decorations lining the front don't hurt.

"How close can you pinpoint with that thing?" he asks.

I stare at the blip on the screen. "Just this. I can get to the east side of the building, but I can't tell you what room the dog's in."

"Movement." Wynd cocks his head. "Maybe it's that room."

I lean forward to see an elderly woman swing her legs over a windowsill and pop out. Before she exits, she tosses a huge duffel to the grass with a solid thud that carries across the lawn. This is different. She's dressed in a bright pink velour tracksuit with matching tennis shoes and a scarf over her gray hair. She reaches in and assists another woman out, this one with gray-white hair and a blue tracksuit.

The dog leaps out after her, runs a tight circle, and then sits, panting happily. My shoulders go tight at the sight of him. Leo. All right. Now where the hell is Ella?

Another woman emerges, this one in jeans and a button-down shirt. She also looks to be in her seventies or so, and the other two women help her to the ground.

"Who are they?" Wynd asks.

"I don't know." I keep my hands loose on the wheel and watch the trio steady themselves, the pink tracksuit lady planting her feet near the duffel. The dog glances back at the window, then at them, then at the trees, waiting for a cue. I breathe in slow and let the quiet press against me until it sharpens my focus.

I lean even closer to the window, waiting for Ella to hop out. She doesn't. Instead, the first woman, the one in neon pink, reaches up and gingerly slides the window down before hefting the duffel bag over her shoulder. She stumbles and then rights herself.

"What do you suppose is in that bag?" Wynd asks.

"I have no idea." My voice is sharper than I intend. Where is Ella?

Wynd reaches for his door handle. "Do you want me to intercept them?"

"No. Let's see where they're going."

They glance around, quick and cautious, then take off at a surprisingly fast clip across the lawn and into the tree line. I wait until they disappear on the trail before reigniting the engine and following along the forest's edge to the main road. Trees crowd close on either side, shadows stretching longer with the fading light. The quiet feels loaded, pressing in against the glass.

A clearing opens ahead, and I catch sight of the women climbing into a car. At first glance it looks too big, too heavy, but then the details register. Chrome fenders catch the dusk. The body is a pale seafoam green, paint polished within an inch of its life. Whitewall tires. Wide bench seats. A Buick Electra from the sixties.

The thing shouldn't even be running, but it purrs when they slam the doors. Somebody's babied it—waxed, polished, kept hidden away until now. Lace curtains twitch in the back windows, and a sun-faded hula girl wobbles on the dash. It's a car out of time, but they slide in like it's always been waiting.

Wynd whistles low. "That's . . . something."

"Yeah," I mutter, watching the taillights flare. I keep driving, letting them ease onto the road behind us, heading the opposite way. Once they're clear, I swing a sharp U-turn and fall in behind, far enough to stay out of their mirrors.

My hand finds the button on the dash, and I call Kaz.

"Hey, Justice," Kaz answers, his voice cheerful. He's been a lot nicer since Ella lit into him. He doesn't even sound smug today.

"Hey, I need you to do a search on the Cinderfalls Community Home. Three women, all in their late seventies. They came out of the east side window. I don't know who they are, but they're tied to Ella."

"Sure." The sound of typing filters through the speaker.

We merge onto the interstate, headlights flashing past, the tires humming steady under us. "Call me back when you have something." I click off.

The road winds through Silicon Valley, then spits us out the other side to a long stretch of property outside of the city.

"They're going to TimeGem?" Wynd mutters.

"I don't know." I ease back, following discreetly. My pulse jumps when their Electra slows at the entrance to the long drive and pauses, taillights glowing red in the dusk.

I slow down at a distance, keeping my car angled toward the shoulder so they can't catch my headlights in their mirrors. The Electra idles at the entrance to TimeGem. The property sprawls for acres, a sweep of manicured forest and glass walls beyond the gates. The place is designed to look open and modern, but I know better. There are cameras everywhere.

I tap my phone to get Kaz again. "Hey, is there any

way you can cut the feed to the security cameras around TimeGem?"

"Of course." Kaz sounds affronted.

I watch the old car. "I figured it'd be difficult."

"Eh, not that difficult." His keys clatter fast through the line. "Well, this is interesting."

My jaw tightens. "What?"

"They've already been cut. The cameras are down."

I breathe out, low. "Can you tell when they were taken offline?"

More typing comes over the line. Silence stretches with the Electra still frozen up ahead. My pulse keeps time with the tick of my engine.

"About three hours ago," Kaz says finally.

So, within the window of Ella disappearing. "I don't like this."

The Buick shifts, brake lights flashing, and then it rolls forward, away from the gate. I follow at a careful distance, tension coiled so tight my shoulders ache.

I glance at the dash. "Kaz, do you have anything yet on the elderly women?"

"Not yet. I'm not finding any connection to Ella, but I'll keep digging."

"Thanks." I end the call.

The women turn off the main road and disappear under the trees. I keep going and then swing into the first shoulder I can find and kill the engine. The forest presses close, shadows stacked deep between the trunks. The air is colder here, carrying the damp bite of leaves and earth. I step out, Wynd on my heels, both of us armed and ready.

We move silently through the trees until the clearing

opens ahead. The women are already at work, the duffel bag spilled open at their feet.

"Holy shit," Wynd whispers.

I agree. Weapons. Not a couple of old revolvers or hunting rifles. Serious hardware. An FN SCAR with a collapsible stock, matte black and immaculate. A short-barreled Benelli M4, the tactical grip worn from use. I catch the gleam of an HK VP9 pistol, extra mags lined up in a neat row. Beside them sits a stubby grenade launcher that looks like it's been oiled within the last week.

And in the middle of it all, absurd and glittering under the weak light, a tactical knife with a sparkly pink handle. Razor sharp, polished, deadly. Somebody took the time to bedazzle murder.

"Jos," the woman in pink says, voice brisk, pointing at the woman in jeans. "You take the grenades. I dropped 'em last time."

I stiffen.

"What I wouldn't give for a rocket launcher," Jos mutters. "Didn't you have one of those, Aura?"

"Oh yeah. In the trunk," the woman in pink replies cheerfully, walking over and popping it open.

The casual way she says it makes the hair at my neck rise.

"Should we stop them?" Wynd asks.

I don't answer. I'm not entirely sure what we should do.

Leo turns and barks at me, sharp and happy. That's enough.

All three women whip around, weapons already raised.

I step from the trees, Wynd trying to cover me. I shove him back. "Ladies." My voice carries.

"Justice Beathach." The woman in pink hardens her

jaw. Papery skin, delicate lines, but confident with the Ruger trained steady on me. "What are you doing here?"

I cock my head. "You first."

"None of your damn business," the woman in the blue tracksuit says. Sparkles adorn her collar. She's the only one whose name I don't have.

Aura nods. "That's exactly right, Mags. Beathach, you get out of here." She waves her gun for emphasis.

"I don't think so." I keep my tone even. "Is Ella in TimeGem?"

The women glance at each other. I take two more steps forward, and three guns snap toward me in unison.

Leo gives a happy bark and bounds over, tail wagging.

Aura frowns, her arched brows drawing together. "Leo, don't be nice to him. He's the bad guy."

The dog grins up at me anyway, tongue lolling, and my chest loosens despite myself. I keep walking until I'm close enough that one twitch could put a bullet in me. Wynd flanks my side. I don't want him hurting any of these women, so I cut him a look. He nods once, sharp. If he moves, he'll disarm, not destroy.

"Don't you be looking at us like that." Mags straightens, chin up. "We could take you both instantly. We haven't shot you on purpose."

"I appreciate that." My voice stays calm. "I'm going to ask again. Is Ella inside TimeGem?"

Aura's mouth tightens. "Yes. She was kidnapped earlier, and we've come to get her."

Fire rushes through me, so I go stone cold. "How do you know she was kidnapped?"

They hesitate. The silence stretches, and I let it.

Finally, Mags shrugs. "We might have cameras placed

around the outskirts of Cinderfalls. We saw her get taken. This was the earliest we could get our gear together."

"It's been a while since we've broken somebody out of a facility," Aura adds, dead serious.

I scrub a hand over my jaw. If TimeGem wants a war, they've got one. Right now, I need to get Ella out of there while she's still breathing. She'd better still be alive. "Who are you?"

"I'm her godmother." Aura straightens bony shoulders.

Okay, then. I have no record of that. For now, at least I know she's not an obvious threat to Ella. "All right. How about this? I'll go get her out, and you stay here."

"Not a chance in hell." Aura lifts her delicate chin, grip steady on the gun. "We're going."

I obviously don't have a choice. Giving a small nod to Wynd, I go for the gun.

TWENTY-NINE

Ella

The air is definitely disappearing much too quickly. My chest feels tight already, every inhale thinner than the last. I scan the walls, searching for vents, but I don't see any. They're probably hidden high up, tucked into the corners where shadows cling.

Wesley moves to the door and runs his hand along the seams, slow and deliberate, looking for a way out that we won't find. A small panel slides open above the frame and a camera blinks to life, the red light sharp in the gloom.

"Are you ready to charge the citrine?" Sylveria's voice slices through the speaker, tinny and smug.

Oh, now I'm pissed. "You can't seriously be considering killing us."

She chuckles, low and ugly. "I would actually like to work with you. But if you're not going to help me, I'd rather you were dead."

"If I do help you, you could still kill me," I mutter.

"True," she allows. "But that's not what I want." The sound distorts through the camera, metallic and detached.

Now I'm fighting her and my own urges. Everything inside me wants to touch that citrine. Connect to it. I turn toward Wesley. "How much do you know about how we exchange energy with crystals?"

"I know enough," he says. His voice is steady, but his eyes flick to the ceiling like he's counting our breaths. "I wouldn't be able to program Aquarius Social the way I do if I didn't understand what Alana does. I mean, let me rephrase that. I don't understand, but I comprehend there's some sort of energy exchange."

"Have you ever tried it?" I press. There have to be a lot of people out there who have the gift. It just makes sense. It feels good to finally speak of this, even in a death box. We've avoided the subject so far, too secretive, too dangerous, but he can't be completely in the dark. Not with his job.

He grins despite the air thinning. "Yeah, I've tried it. I didn't charge anything. Maybe it was the wrong crystal."

"Excuse me," Sylveria cuts in. "You've got about three minutes of oxygen left. Do you really want to have this conversation right now?"

My pulse spikes. Three minutes. I glance at the citrine across the room, the size of a bowling ball, its golden surface glittering under the harsh light. It has to be ten pounds at least.

Wesley catches my gaze. "Do you know most people don't have any idea that exists?"

"I know." My lips curve despite everything. "The world thinks the Malaga Citrine is the largest citrine ever mined. Eight point eight pounds. Twenty thousand carats or so." The truth is bigger. Much bigger. "The four families have been mining and hiding gems for millennia. People wouldn't believe some of the sizes we've found."

The sparkling yellow pulls at me. I can't resist any longer. I walk to it, each step heavy as my lungs ache. My fingers close around the gem, warm and thrumming with power. The minute I connect, energy rushes through me, flooding my hands, racing to my earlobes, surging into my brain. The tingling builds until I gasp, the sound raw and sharp in the thinning air.

I let natural power fill me as I walk to the center of the room and place the citrine where the diamond had been.

She doesn't feel diseased to me, although none of us really understand how this virus works. For all I know, it could've jumped from the diamond to the citrines or bled into any other gem nearby. Viruses don't obey rules, not digital or physical.

I nod once. "Wesley, go ahead and hook the citrine into the servers."

He shakes his head, jaw tight. "I don't think it's worth it. I have no idea what's going on or how viruses are moving from rocks to people, but I've surmised that much." Even so, he retakes his seat. His fingers hover over the keyboard, then curl into a fist.

"It's too late," I tell him, and the words scrape my throat. As if on cue, a thin whistle cuts through the silence. Fresh air hisses down through vents hidden somewhere in the ceiling. I pull a deep lungful and feel the tightness in my chest loosen. At least the bitch turned the oxygen back on.

I spread my hands across the surface of the citrine, unwilling to let go. "Come on, Wesley. It's too late for me to stop now. I've already touched the stone."

The surface thrums under my palms. Heat pools against my skin and spreads upward, quick and electric. I plant my feet shoulder-width apart, rolling my neck until it cracks. It's been far too long since I exchanged energy with a rock this size, and my body is starved for it. My fingertips prickle, my calves twitch, and even my toes curl against the floor as the current sweeps through.

Wesley grumbles, a sound buried low in his chest, but he starts typing anyway. His fingers fly now, keys clicking in sharp bursts as he types in the code that links the center console to the entire system. I catch the set of his jaw in the glow of the monitors. He doesn't like this.

Neither do I.

Most people have no idea how much strength a gem like this holds. They think jewels are for wearing, admiring, locking away in a museum. They don't understand a stone this size can fuel an empire, power every corner of a social media network, while keeping the world distracted and hungry for more.

I lift my chin toward the blinking camera. "If I'm doing this, you might as well make it worthwhile. Have Corinda and Stacia start posting on TimeGem Moments right now. They can share good memories with other users and capture energy." Every time somebody clicks "capture now" or "like" or "save," more energy transfers into the system. If I'm going to do this, I want it all. Because this entire company is going to be mine again.

"I understand," Sylveria replies. Her voice rattles through the speaker, distant, warped. "They're already on it."

"Good." I close my eyes, steady my breath, and let the energy in. It rushes through my hands like molten gold, zipping into every nerve ending, racing along my veins until my entire body sings. The hairs on my arms rise, then flatten again under the invisible pressure.

The crystal glows, a blinding yellow, and light fractures across the room in jagged shards. My chest expands with it, my pulse hammering in my throat.

"You good?" Wesley asks.

I don't answer. I can't. The power is too much, too wonderful. Maybe I'm feeding a virus into my blood, maybe I'm sealing my own end. But even if I am, this is the way I want to go.

The door clicks open and Sylveria strides inside. I'm too caught up in the energy exchange to care. The hum still thrums in my bones, every nerve buzzing. I can feel her presence press against mine, sharp and invasive, and I see it in her posture.

I've never seen her really try to charge a diamond until earlier, and the little she pulled then was nothing compared to what's swirling around me now. The air pops with static, heating in jolts that make my skin prickle. My hair lifts, floating for a moment before falling again as the energy whips through the room.

I spend a good twenty minutes with the citrine, pushing and pulling, until finally I step back, lungs burning, chest wide open. I feel full—too full—and turn to face them.

Wesley pivots in his chair. His jaw goes slack. "Holy fuck."

"What?" I ask.

"Your eyes. They're gold. Yellow."

I blink hard. I've never looked at my reflection while charging, and I haven't handled a crystal this size in too long. "Really?"

"Yeah." He blinks several times, as if trying to convince

himself it's real. "Do Alana's eyes turn aqua when she charges the aquamarines at Aquarius Social?" He stands so fast the chair tips backward. "Oh God. Don't tell me Thorn's or Justice's eyes turn red when they charge their garnets."

"I don't know," I admit. "I've never paid attention." My pulse stutters. "I don't think so. But what do I know?"

The air between us crackles. Wesley looks like he's holding a secret he never wanted.

"So what's your plan now?" I ask Sylveria.

Before she can answer, an explosion rocks the base. The entire room shudders like it's alive, and a shockwave rattles my bones.

"Ah, crap." Wesley lunges from his chair and yanks me aside, shielding me with his body. "What's happening?"

I swallow, heat and ash already filling my lungs. "I have an idea." I glance over at Sylveria. "You might want to let us go."

Her face drains, pale as wet chalk. Another explosion tears through the space, the boom echoing until the walls vibrate. Ceiling panels rip loose and crash to the floor in a storm of dust. Wesley pulls me clear of the collapse, his grip bruising, his breath harsh against my ear.

A third blast roars. I hear the outside elevator doors blow apart an instant before debris shoots across the open entrance to the reception area.

Justice and Wynd walk inside, bloody and cut. They fill the space, moving like a storm that's already decided the damage. Justice has Corinda in a headlock, her feet dragging against the floor, while Wynd presses a gun to Stacia's neck.

"What did I tell you?" Justice asks, his voice so low it shakes the air.

I shove out of Wesley's arms on instinct, panic clawing

at me. Then I realize he's not talking to me. His eyes burn straight into Sylveria, who oddly has a yellow tinge bleeding into her pale cheeks—same as the damaged diamond.

"I haven't hurt her," she says, too calm, too collected.

Justice growls. A real growl. The sound reverberates off the walls. "I told you she was under my protection, and I also told you what I'd do if you hurt her."

I edge away from Wesley, every instinct screaming at me to get small, get out of the line of fire. "I'm not hurt," I blurt. That's the truth. For all that I don't like Sylveria or her daughters, I don't want them dead. Not really. "Would you please let go of Corinda?"

"I actually don't mind being in his arms," Corinda says, smiling as if she enjoys being dragged into chaos.

"He's got you in a headlock," her sister snarls.

Wynd slowly eases the gun away from Stacia's neck, but his grip on her arm looks painful.

Stacia tilts her chin toward me, calm as a statue. "I've had worse first dates, to be honest."

A laugh bursts out of me, sharp and inappropriate. I sneeze quickly. Now I'm panic sneezing? The whole thing is too ridiculous.

"You're all going to be arrested," Wesley growls, stepping in front of me. He plants himself between me and the group, body taut, ready to take on all of them. "This is not happening. All of you need to go. Now."

Anger swells from Justice as he walks toward us, still holding Corinda. "Get out of my way."

Wesley clenches his fists. "No. I know all about you. Ella is too good for you."

"We agree. Now move," Justice snarls.

"No." Wesley winds back his arm.

Justice is faster and lands a punch, nailing Wesley in the face.

Wesley drops hard.

"Justice!" My scream tears out of me as I rush toward Wesley.

"Leave him." Justice's voice is brutal, final. "You touch him, he dies."

I skid to a stop, breath heaving, my hands shaking at my sides.

Wesley forces himself to sit upright. Fury carves lines into his face. "What the hell?"

Fire burns in Justice's eyes. "Don't ever get between Ella and me." The words are so dark, they crawl up my spine like ice water.

I gulp.

Justice shoves Corinda toward her mother, that deadly gaze on me. "You. Here. Now."

My feet move before I can think, before I can stop myself, obeying him. Going to his side.

"Wait." I turn and rush to the back of the room, my lungs still raw from smoke and dust. My hands fumble with the latch until the glass door gives way. Inside, the crown sits bent and battered, one side caved in like it's taken a fist from God himself. Even so, the citrines embedded along the rim spark to sudden life, flaring bright in a way that makes my throat tighten. Good Lord, they're glorious.

The energy I'd drawn from the larger crystal still rides me hard, and it flows through my arms into the crown as if the pieces were waiting for me all along. The glow sharpens, facets catching light that shouldn't exist in this wreck of a room.

I grab it and turn to hustle past the center console,

crown cradled against my ribs, then pause. What am I doing? Instinct takes over. I reach out and heft the citrine from the console, its weight solid and burning against my palm and forearm.

"What are you doing?" Sylveria takes a step toward me, her voice sharp, but Justice pivots. Just enough to shift his weight, just enough to remind her he's there. She freezes.

"I'm taking this," I say, smiling without humor. I pause near Wesley, crouched in pain but still upright. While I want to soothe him, I don't want to see him get hurt worse.

"I pulled the punch," Justice cuts in flatly. "He's fine. Get up."

Wesley pushes to his feet. His face is gray, but he doesn't buckle.

Justice doesn't even look at him—he turns that molten glare on Wynd. "Borrow a car and take him to a doctor. He's bleeding and it's not from me." He turns back to Wesley. "Find an excuse. If you call the cops, Wynd will shred your skin from your body."

My stomach lurches. I want to help Wesley, but I want him alive more. How badly had Sylveria hurt him? I hadn't even asked. So I force myself to move, hurrying toward Justice, fury burning bright in my chest.

He stares at Sylveria. "You might want to run. I haven't decided what to do with you yet. A tropical vacation is a good idea." He points to the exit, so I move and step over broken panels, twisted metal, and what looks like a set of old keys half-buried in dust. None of it makes sense, not here, not now, but I don't stop.

"We are going to talk about this," I snap at Justice. Then I notice the weapon in Wynd's hand. My stomach flips. Recognition slams me cold. "Wait a minute. I know that gun. Where's Aura?"

Justice herds us toward a revealed stairwell beside the mangled elevator doors. "That's another reason you need to hurry. Your godmother is stuck in the trunk of an old Buick."

The words knock the air out of me. Aura. My godmother. In a trunk.

I stumble into the stairwell without protest, still clutching the crown in one hand. Wynd eases the citrine away from me, his face unreadable, his grip careful but firm as he keeps a gun on Wesley, who limps along beside him.

"She's in a trunk?" My voice cracks on the word.

"Yeah," Justice says grimly as we start the climb. "And she's going to be pissed."

THIRTY

Ella

I am so angry with Justice I can barely think straight. My pulse hammers, my hands still twitch from the kidnapping, and my chest feels like it might explode. We just walked the women back to their suite at Cinderfalls, and they're flitting around, talking about supper.

Mags clicks her tongue. "Really, Justice. You ruined a good rescue by punching Wesley in the face. Jealousy is bad." She hands him a bag of cookies. "But you did save our Ella, so there's hope for you."

Jos nods. "You're lucky we let you leave us in that trunk."

I barely keep from snorting.

Aura sighs. "You were a little slower about it than I'd like." She hands him a tea sachet. "It's my favorite blend. Have some later."

Justice takes the tea and cookies, looking lost. "Thank you." He glances at me. "We have to go."

I kiss them all and leave Leo with them before following Justice out to his car as darkness falls. It has been a long day. "I can't believe you locked them in a trunk." I slide inside.

He does the same and starts the engine. "According to them, they let me." He chews thoughtfully on a cookie.

The three women seem to rather like him now. How is that? He put them in a damn trunk and left the dog in the back seat. What if we hadn't made it back?

"I can't believe they gave you cookies," I mumble. "Is Wesley all right?"

"Yes. I didn't break his jaw, but Sylveria's goons broke a couple of his ribs." Justice glances at me. "You're not dating him."

I know that. In fact, I broke up with him. Well, I guess Wesley didn't let me say the words. But still. I turn back to the window for the rest of the drive. The silence is thick. Out of the corner of my eye, I glare at the side of Justice's face, memorizing every bruise, every cut, every speck of blood that doesn't belong to him.

The tension between us is a live wire. If either of us breathes too hard, the car might explode.

We finally reach Justice's skyscraper that houses Malice Media and his once-destroyed penthouse. The repairs are impressive. Money talks. He parks outside, ushering me in the backdoor as one of his men handles the vehicle. We're in the elevator before I can breathe. The hum of the motor fills the silence, a steady drone that grates on my nerves.

I can't hold back any longer. "How could you lock them in a trunk?"

Justice's gaze flicks toward me. "What the hell else was I supposed to do? They were loaded to fight, and they were coming in with grenades. They'd all be dead if I hadn't put them in that trunk."

"You could have taken them back to the nursing home," I mutter, arms crossing tight over my chest.

"I could have," he agrees, his voice sharp, "and they would've escaped again. Give me a break."

I grind my teeth, because he's right. "All right. You have a point." The words taste sour, but I choke them out anyway. "And you didn't hurt them. You did keep them safe." I think about Mags, her stubborn grin and her bad habit of throwing grenades when things go sideways. I've tried to get her to stop using explosives on jobs, but she doesn't listen. It's probably best Justice never finds out how often they've blown things up. Sure, they never kill anyone, but accidents happen.

My voice rises before I can stop it. "Why did you punch Wesley? He was trying to protect me."

Justice glances at me. Blood smears his cheek, his neck is bruised, and his knuckles are raw, split open like he punched through glass. His expression doesn't flicker. "I think I was pretty clear about that," he says mildly.

"All he did was step between us. He was trying to protect me."

Justice's gaze sharpens. "That's not his job. It's mine. He's lucky I pulled the punch."

My skin is buzzing, my pulse pounding, and I can't believe the gall of him. "I don't know what you think is going on between us, but it's not. You don't own me."

"The fuck I don't."

My head jerks so hard I'm pretty sure I put out a disc. "Excuse me?"

"You heard me." There's fire in his tone now. Even though his voice stays calm, mild almost, every nerve in my body tries to take the heat. It's too late for that. Not only am I furious with him, I'm jacked up from finally exchanging energy with a decent-sized citrine. My body is still humming, alive and raw.

We walk through the cleaned-up penthouse, which is impressive, and he pushes open the door to his room. "Get changed."

"No," I say flatly.

"That's it." He grabs me, one hand sliding into my hair, fingers threading through and his palm cupping the back of my skull. The pull sends a sharp sting down my spine, oddly erotic but with a bite that leaves no question who's in control. With that grip, he propels me straight into the bathroom and flips on the light.

"Haven't we already done this?" I mutter.

"You are such a brat."

The smack to my ass actually hurts, the sharp crack echoing in the tiled room. "Hey—"

"Do it, or I'll do it for you." He rips at his bloody clothes, peeling them off with rough, sure movements.

"Fine." My voice scrapes. I'm covered in dust and blood and particles from the explosion. Every inch of me feels coated in grime. I yank off the ruined clothes and step under the warm spray. The water pours down my shoulders, sluicing away dirt and tension almost instantly. God, it feels good.

He follows me in without hesitation and nudges me aside so he can wash the blood off his face and hands. The water runs red for a moment before circling down the drain. I angle my head, studying him from the corner of my eye.

His body is spectacular—pure muscle, hard steel, unyielding. His shoulders look like they could hold up the weight of the building.

My gaze catches on the cut above his forehead. "You probably need stitches."

"I don't need stitches. Just a Band-Aid."

He's probably correct. If he's been exchanging energy with garnets, and obviously he has, since Thorn's out of town, his healing properties will be elevated. Yet another side effect of the gifts we've learned to enhance through the years.

He looks at me, eyes sharp through the steam. "Now's about a good time for you to say thank you."

No way. "For what?" I snap.

"Saving your damn life."

"My godmother would've handled it." I tap a finger on my lip, letting the water bead and drip off my chin.

He snorts.

I chuckle, my body relaxing. "We need to talk. Sylveria is infected in a different way than you are, and not from *my* virus."

His eyes darken. "Are you sure it isn't the same one that's in me?"

"Yes. I was in the TimeGem servers for a while and memorized the code. I can send it to Kaz and he can check. I think there's a slight variation, to be honest."

He nods. "Yeah, that makes sense with the attacks against us all." He reaches out, grabs the shampoo, and starts lathering my hair. His fingers work strong and slow, and I fight the urge to lean into him. I really don't want to give him the satisfaction of knowing how good this feels. Tingles spark across my scalp and wander down my body, loosening muscles that have been tight for hours. I close my eyes, surrendering despite myself.

"Just because this feels good doesn't mean I like you," I mumble as warm water glides over me.

"I don't like you either. Yet."

His hands are gentle now, working through my hair with a patience I didn't know he had. When he's done, he rinses me clean, then scrubs his own hair and face while the spray slides down both of our bodies. Heat from the water mixes with the warmth between us until I can't tell the difference. My chest tightens as I step into him, drawn against every ounce of better judgment I have left.

He grabs my hair rougher this time, yanking my head back to take my mouth in a kiss. The contact is brutal, devouring. Heat surrounds me, fills me, consumes me. God, the man can kiss. His mouth takes control, and his body presses powerful and sure, all around me, demanding I yield.

"Hey, Justice," a voice calls out, muffled through the door.

Justice freezes. "What the fuck?"

"Sorry. Sorry." The voice—Irish sounding, I think—rushes out the words. "We have police detectives here. They're threatening to call in the SWAT team if they don't speak with Ella Rendale."

My eyelids fly open.

Justice growls low in his throat. "Fine," he calls out. "We'll be out in a minute. Keep them in the living room."

"Gotcha."

I step back, skin still humming. "Detectives?"

"Who knows. I can't imagine Sylveria called anybody, but she has to be scared of what I'll do to her for kidnapping you. She's not stupid." He shuts off the water, ushers me out, and grabs a towel. Then he attacks me with the fabric, drying me thoroughly, every swipe more possessive than the last. By the time he's finished, I'm panting, my legs shaky under me. His smile is wicked, dangerous, and he bends low, sliding the towel down to my feet. He dries them, slow and deliberate, before pressing a kiss high between my thighs, on my clit, on his way back up.

"Hey," I gasp, shoving at his shoulders.

"Hey, yourself." His grin softens into something almost playful, and for a second, I want to jump him all over again.

Something in my gaze catches him, because he tackles me onto the soft bathroom mat, cushioning my fall with his strong arms.

I gasp. "What are you doing?"

"You." He presses against me, slowly penetrating me.

I gulp, trying to concentrate. "The police are here."

He keeps powering inside me, so big and strong above me. "So?"

So? Seriously? "It's the police." I try to push him away but instead widen my thighs to take more of him. He feels so good against me.

"I figure I should tell you that I'm keeping you." With one final thrust, he shoves all the way inside me, balls deep.

I arch against him, my nails scraping down his chest. Panic takes hold inside me, but my body is already quaking around him. "This is temporary, remember?" I gasp out.

"Not anymore. I'm done fighting this." He pulls out and then powers back inside me.

I can't think. Not when he's taking me like this, his eyes a deep brown with those intriguing flashes of copper. "You're just caught up."

"Hmm." He kisses me, his mouth hot as he continues to thrust.

I let him take me over, my mind going quiet.

Then he stops.

My eyes focus. "What are you doing?"

He cocks his head to the side, fulling embedded in me. "Waiting for your agreement."

"Ha. Like you need agreement. What if I don't give it?"

"Then you don't come."

My mouth gapes open. That isn't what I expected. I tighten around him, enjoying the flare in his eyes. "The police are waiting."

"I'm waiting." He slowly, torturously, pulls out of me and slides back in. He grasps my wrists in his much larger hand and lifts them above my head, trapping them against the floor. "I'll make you scream until you agree. One time, two times, it doesn't matter."

My abdomen turns over, and wetness spills from me. "The police will hear."

"Good. They can come watch." His expression turns wicked.

I know not to challenge him, because he'll accept. My body feels strung tight. I wrap my legs around his waist. "Let me get this straight." I'm panting but I can't stop. "You've gone from wanting to fuck me out of your system to fucking me into submission."

His nips along my jawline. "Close enough." He pulls out, shoving back in, making me arch again because it's just too delicious. Tortuous. Determined. His gaze captures mine. "I won't hurt you, Ella. More importantly, I'll never let anybody else hurt you. Mercy isn't in me. I'll never hesitate. I promise."

My heart stutters. Actually pauses in my chest. "I don't know if I can trust like that."

He bites my earlobe.

I shudder.

"I'm not giving you a choice." With that, he starts

hammering inside me, pushing me up, holding me when I detonate. I cry out his name, my eyelids closing as sparks fly behind them. He locks inside me, his body tightening as he joins me.

I blink my eyelids open.

He grins. "I could've gone a couple more times for you, but the cops are here."

I'd forgotten. Just for a second.

He withdraws and pulls us both to our feet, carrying me into the main room to toss on the bed. "Get dressed."

"Stop being so bossy." I roll off and hurriedly go through the stack of clothing he's bought for me. I yank out a pair of jeans and a soft white-and-pink-checkered flannel. Girl cut. My fingers tremble as I button it up. I have no clue how he knows my size, but every piece fits perfectly. Socks follow, then brown boots that feel right. When meeting the police, one should wear boots. "Do cops usually show up here?"

"Never. The fact that my men let them up to the apartment says something." He runs his hands through his thick, dark hair, brushing it away from his face. The gesture is rough, impatient, and Lord help me, I notice the lines of his cheekbones, the cut of his jaw. He's handsome. Strikingly so. If he ever lost Malice Media, he could probably model.

Then I really study him. No. Probably not. Models lean boyish with a hint of edge. Justice is all edge, all dangerous weight. There's nothing boyish about him.

"What?" he asks, catching me staring.

"Nothing." I shake my head, breaking free of the thought. "Let's go."

He's already pulled on jeans and a dark gray T-shirt that stretches across his chest in a way that makes me want to curse. He pads barefoot toward the repaired hall.

Barefoot. I swear it's a power move to meet the police in his own living room without shoes, as if to prove he doesn't need them.

Me? I'll take the boots. Just in case somebody needs kicking. Or I need to run.

We almost reach the living room when he grabs my hand. His grip is solid, immovable. I try to pull free, and he just tightens, dragging me with him.

"Why the fuck are you in my apartment?" Justice asks without preamble.

Two people stare at us. One is an oversized man, trench coat straining across his gut. The other is a slimmer woman in a fitted black suit. It's sharp, expensive, and she wears it like armor.

"Sorry to bother you," the woman says. "I'm Detective Caldwell, and this is Detective Ashner." Her eyes flick from my wet hair to Justice's damp mess and then back to me.

Heat rushes into my cheeks.

"We were in the shower," Justice says unnecessarily.

Oh, man. My fists curl.

"I see," Detective Caldwell replies, her voice neutral, but her gaze sharp. "If you don't mind, we'd like to speak with you separately."

"I mind," Justice says.

This is odd, but I'm feeling impish. "I don't mind at all," I say cheerfully.

He gives me a look. I give him a smile. I'm done letting him dictate everything. I'm not entirely sure how far I can push him, but I want to find out.

"I prefer to stay here," he says.

"That's too bad," Detective Caldwell returns. "Ms. Rendale, we'd like for you to come with us."

I think about it.

Justice cocks his head, staring at me. His expression is unreadable, and I honestly don't know what he'll do. I don't know if he'll take them out or let them walk, and that uncertainty twists in my gut. My guess is not—surely people know where these detectives are—but it has been a long day, and even if I get free, at some point Justice is going to catch up with me again.

"I think I'll stay put." I cock my head. It's a good thing Justice's men somehow fixed the place quickly. "Why are you here?"

"How'd you get that bruise on your forehead?" Detective Caldwell asks suddenly.

My hand twitches toward the mark. I hadn't really thought about it. I must've been hit by one of the falling ceiling tiles. It felt like debris was everywhere when Justice had blown his way into TimeGem. I force a laugh. "A rough pickleball match."

"Pickleball?" Her voice drips with disbelief, and her eyes narrow as she studies me, then they cut to Justice. "You both are pretty battered and bruised for not having any problems."

"I was in a car accident," Justice says, his tone even, almost bored.

She squints, stepping closer. "I didn't read a report about that."

I angle my head, and my stomach flips when I see the long scrape, purple bruising spreading across his skin. That definitely hadn't come from a car. That had occurred during the explosion when he rescued me.

"It happened too fast and I didn't see the other car," Justice deadpans. His expression doesn't change. "It's been a rough day. You have one second to tell us why you're here."

I plaster on a smile. This is really weird. "What's going on?"

Ashner's phone rings and he answers it. "Yep. We're here now just waiting for you to call."

I glance at Justice. His face is stone, no expression at all.

"Are you sure? Okay, thanks." The detective slides the phone back into his pocket, then turns and walks toward us. His shoes click sharp against the polished floor.

"What's going on?" I ask again.

He looks straight at Justice. "We've had a witness file a report attesting to the fact that you murdered Horace Whimple and buried his body at your estate. We're executing a search warrant right now, so we thought to bring you in at the same time."

I shake my head. They were making sure we stayed put until the warrant was served? Horace is dead? Who'd kill him? "That's ridiculous," I blurt out.

"Why?" Detective Caldwell demands, her focus snapping to me. "Are you saying your boyfriend here is too innocent to kill anybody?"

I cough out a laugh because I can't help it. "No." We all know who Justice is. "I'm saying he'd never be dumb enough to bury a body on his own property."

Justice gives me a look. "Stop trying to help."

Fair enough.

"Listen, Mr. Beathach." The trench-coated detective's tone hardens. "You're going to have to come down to the station with us. I suggest you call your lawyer on the way."

THIRTY-ONE

Justice

We're sitting in the drab interrogation room, Fergus as my lawyer. He's old and pissy, and besides being my accountant, he once practiced law. I have tons of lawyers on retainer, but right now, I just want him.

I glance at the door, feeling Ella outside. Right outside in the company of Wynd. He met us here after dropping Wesley at an urgent care, and he has instructions to zip tie her to the doorknob if she tries to move. I'm done treating her gently. She'll have a guard on her until I decide what to do with her. Letting her go doesn't appeal to me, and neither does constantly chasing her all over the damn country if she gets irritated. Or just wants freedom.

I hate that she was in Sylveria's den and could have easily been killed. I don't know what to do about Sylveria, and that gnaws at me, but right now Horace Whimple is my concern.

The interrogation room tries to bully me and fails.

The steel table is scratched and sticky at the edges, while a dent the size of a fist sits near my elbow. The mirror carries a smear someone half-heartedly wiped.

Detective Caldwell sits across from me, calm on the surface, shoulders tight. She taps one light pink nail on the battered table. She has been asking questions for fifteen minutes, and I'm already bored. "We know Ella Rendale was cheated out of her inheritance."

That may be true. "Perhaps, but I'm not sure how much she was cheated. It's my understanding that she plans to sue for her rightful place." I keep my voice casual. Although knowing Ella, she'll blow the whole place up first. I rather like that about her.

Detective Ashner leans against the far wall and tries for menace. He looks tired. I imagine his job isn't easy, and today it shows. He watches me the way a bouncer watches a door he knows will not hold. "Your understanding? Come on, man."

I appreciate his attempt to be my buddy in this place. Cold breath from a ceiling vent slides across my forearms, and a camera winks red in the corner. The chair complains every time I shift. Tile pops under boots in the hall, and somewhere a copier coughs. It smells of damp paper, anxiety, and lemon disinfectant that never met a lemon.

"Obviously, you and Ms. Rendale are in a relationship," Caldwell says. The tone lands accusatory. Fluorescents buzz above with a faint hitch that turns seconds into static.

"Well, we obviously took a shower together," I say. Their voices are barely bothering me, and I have to wonder if it's because I've been around Ella so much.

Caldwell's gaze sharpens. "Are you in a relationship with Ms. Rendale?"

So they're trying to make Ella my motive for killing Horace. Interesting. "None of your business."

Fergus sits forward so his chair legs squeal. "My client isn't here to answer personal questions," he says, voice low and steady. He places a gnarled palm on the rough table.

"The hell he isn't," Ashner bursts out. "We have a dead body on his property by the ocean."

"I don't believe you found a body," I say. "I think you have a report, and somebody is wasting all of our time." I can't imagine anyone would dare bury a body out at my actual home. Although I have been distracted lately, and my men are scattered over different areas. I haven't been home enough, so I guess it's possible. Whoever did so will bleed. For quite a while.

The light flickers and steadies. Caldwell's gaze never leaves my face. "You own one of the most powerful social media companies in the world," she says, tapping the table again. "I'm sure your security system at your private residence is impressive."

"I have three registered firearms," I say. "That's all I need." The plastic seat creaks when I shift, and the vent hums a steady line across my wrists.

Her brows pull together. Her nail ticks against the steel table and keeps time with the fluorescent buzz. "You don't have cameras. CCTV. Everywhere?"

"No," I say. "I value my privacy, Detective. I assume you do too." The ceiling camera's LED blinks its slow red pulse and I toss it a smile. Just for the hell of it. I don't know anything about the detectives yet, but I will by the end of the day. Kaz is already on it.

Caldwell glares. "You're telling me you have zero cameras on your private estate?"

I watch the vein now pulsing near her temple. "Cameras are too easy to compromise, even with our protections. You build a firewall and someone beats it. Then you build another and someone else tests that. I don't need the risk or the noise." I hold her gaze and say nothing for a beat. "I don't want anyone watching me drink coffee on my deck in the morning. It's simple, and it's true."

The detectives don't need to know this, but I don't even leave the place exposed to overhead collection. Mature canopy covers approach lanes. My roofs use a matte, low-reflectance ceramic coat that cuts visible and near-IR glare. We track satellite pass windows from TLE data and schedule outdoor movement when skies are empty.

She shakes her head. "I don't believe you."

"I don't need your trust," I say.

Fergus fidgets beside me, and a chair leg grates. He straightens his dark blue flannel, neat about the line of it. He slicked his hair back for the city.

"You're looking good, Fergus," I say.

Pink touches his cheek and he gives me a quick glance. "Thanks. It's been a while since I dated anybody." He studies Caldwell. "You're pretty young, but I like your levelheadedness. Are you free?"

Surprise touches her eyes. She recovers and sets her mouth. "Knock it off, counselor."

"I apologize. Like I said, it has been a while." Fergus turns to Ashner. "You look like you need a nap."

I keep my expression flat and my breathing even. Control is a habit.

Caldwell smiles. "I've heard rumors of a missile attack and a firefight in the middle of my town, right around Malice Media's headquarters, but you know what? There are no police reports. Do you find that odd?"

"Sure do," I agree. "You can't believe rumors, Detective."

Her brow wrinkles. I have more power in this world, and she doesn't understand. That makes her likeable.

A soft knock lands on the door, and Ashner crosses to it. What now? He opens it, leans into a whisper with someone in the hall, then comes back with a smile he almost hides.

I keep my pulse even. Cheerful news for him is bad news for me, most likely.

The latch clicks as the door seals. Chair legs scrape somewhere down the corridor and fade. "The cadaver dogs earned their steaks today. We found a body," Ashner says, not looking so tired now.

"Are you serious?" Fergus shakes his head.

"Yep. Found the body of Horace Whimple on your property out by the ocean. Buried about seven feet down. Just seven," Ashner says. He adjusts his belt and squares to me, pleased with himself.

I keep my face neutral. "Somebody was in a hurry." I look to Caldwell. "Before you ask, no, I didn't kill him. I don't know who did, and I don't know how he ended up on my property."

One of her eyebrows arches, and suspicion fills her eyes. Does she believe me? I think so. Not because I'm trustworthy but because I wouldn't be that stupid.

Ashner clears his throat. "Maybe you're paving the way for your girlfriend so she can retake TimeGem Moments. That tracks for you, doesn't it?"

It tracks. I don't hand that to him. "I wouldn't put a body on my land. Besides, Horace Whimple doesn't own any of TimeGem Moments."

"You're wrong," Ashner replies. "He owns ten percent."

I didn't know that, so the fact isn't public.

Fergus shifts beside me, and his chair gives a quick squeal.

"You don't really rely on public records, do you?" Caldwell asks. She flips a page in her notebook. "If there was an agreement in place, even one kept from those of us who aren't billionaires, you'd have known."

"I didn't know about this," I say. "What documentation do you have?"

"We don't need to share that with you right now," Ashner says. He drags a chair two inches and parks on it. "You have motive and opportunity to kill Whimple, and the body was found on your property. Tell us the truth."

"I have," I say.

Fergus gives one small shake of his head and sets a legal pad square to the table edge. "Who's your witness?"

"We don't need to tell you that," Ashner replies.

That means the tip is anonymous.

Fergus meets my eyes and nods once. "An anonymous tip like that won't hold up in court and you know it," he says. "I'm not even sure it gives you probable cause. Did you have anything else before you searched the property?"

Caldwell steeples her fingers and lets the question hang. A door shuts somewhere beyond the wall. I lace my fingers together and rest them on the table so they do not move. The mirror gives me my own posture and nothing else. Ashner rolls his shoulders and tries for weight.

I let the pause work for me. Control is habit. If they had more, they'd have led with it. I count three slow breaths and hold her gaze. The room waits for their next card, and I let them deal it.

"We had probable cause, as I said," Ashner says.

"I don't know about that." I'm done with this. "You had an anonymous source who made an accusation. With that, you got a warrant to search an entire piece of land way outside of town?"

Ashner sets his knuckles on the table. "We were told exactly where to look. That gives us credibility. The warrant was for a very small patch."

That sounds reasonable. I'm done talking. I need to get Ella alone and safely away from this mess, and we still haven't discussed the fact that she hijacked my fire suppression system.

Fergus stands, his chair feet rasping across the floor.

Ashner blocks the way with a flat palm. "You're not going anywhere."

"Are you going to arrest me?" I stand, towering over him. He's probably only six feet tall.

He swallows.

Detective Caldwell pushes away from the table and

rises with economic motions. "I don't think we need to arrest you at this point, especially since it would cause a media frenzy. Surrender your passport, and we'll continue to build this case against you."

She doesn't think I killed him. I can appreciate that. She knows I'm smart enough not to bury a body on my own property. Passport surrender means they want control of my range and time. It also means they don't have what they want yet.

Like I need a passport. "Of course," I murmur.

"Who do you think killed him, if it wasn't you?" she asks. The question is predictable.

"I have no idea," I say. "If I were looking, I'd guess Sylveria Rendale got pissed at her lover for some reason. She'd bury a body on my property."

Caldwell closes the file with two fingers. "We'll interview her stepdaughter, Ella Rendale, next."

"No," I answer.

Caldwell smiles. "I don't think that's up to you."

"Let's go." Fergus steps to the door and holds it open. I move into the hallway with him. Ella stands next to Wynd, blowing her nose.

I'm worried the run through the rainy forest has given her a cold. The woman needs sleep.

Rosalie Mooncrest strides toward us, flanked by Alexei's men in a tight, practiced formation. Polished shoes hammer a steady beat on the tile. The corridor narrows under their approach.

Ah, fuck. How did Ella get word to her friend?

Rosalie lifts a hand. "Ella. I'm here." Her black hair is loose over her shoulders. She wears cherry red lipstick and a navy suit, looking sharp and professional, even at this late hour.

"Thanks for coming," Ella says. "Sorry no drinks tonight."

Detective Caldwell steps out from behind me. "Ms. Rendale? We'd like to speak with you."

Rosalie moves in front of Ella and angles her shoulders to block the lane. Alexei's men come alert and space out along the wall. "I don't think so," she says. "I need to speak with my client before she talks to anyone, and you have no right to hold her." She cuts me a quick smile. "Hi, Justice. How's it hanging?"

I don't like this at all. "Ella, you're coming with me," I say.

"I don't believe so," Rosalie murmurs. "She's coming with me."

Alexei's men tighten their formation. Hands hover near jackets.

Wynd shifts his weight toward Ella and stiffens when two guards slide a half step forward.

Ella gives me the sweetest smile imaginable. "It's been fun, Justice, but I'm going to go."

She knows I won't throw her over my shoulder in the middle of a police station. I take one step closer and keep my voice low. "I strongly recommend you come with me. We have a lot to discuss."

"Nope," she says, chipper as ever, and threads her arm through Rosalie's. "Like I said, it's been fun." She turns with a quick grin. "I'm starving, Rosy. Have you eaten dinner?"

I watch her and Rosalie walk down the hall, the line of Alexei's men sealing around them.

Lightning flashes outside.

Wynd looks at me, waiting. "What do you want me to do?"

"At the moment, nothing," I say dryly. If nothing else, I can count on Alexei's men to keep her safe. At least until I get my hands on her. That woman is forever escaping me. It's impressive—and irritating. She's got a sweet ass as she walks away, though. "I'll talk to her another day. Let's go." Yeah, I make sure the cops hear my last word.

We follow the stream toward the exit. Outside, news vans already crowd the darkened street, ignoring the pouring rain, cameras with bright lights pointed at the doors. Horace's death is a big deal.

"What's the plan?" Wynd whispers, glaring at the bright lights showing the entire area.

I keep walking toward the darkness, through the storm, and lower my voice. "If Rosalie gets her to Alexei's compound, I won't be able to reach her, so we take her first. Map their route and find the spot we can take her from the car."

"Gotcha," Wynd says.

We reach my car and I slide into the back seat. "Put the word out that I don't want Ella or Rosalie harmed in any way."

Wynd looks down. "Understood. My car's around the corner, and I'll bring Fergus with me. I'll have people in position. Where do you want to be?"

"Oh, I'm going to be in the car that takes her," I say. That little brat's freedom just ended.

A pattering splits the air. What the hell?

I stretch out of the vehicle, and the driver tosses me a Sig before ducking. A battered white van careens by the cars parked at the curb, the passenger spraying bullets.

People scream, duck, and run. Reporters take cover and start recording almost instantly.

I turn to see the car with Ella and Rosalie slam into a light pole.

The gunman turns the weapon on them.

"Ella, get down!" I bellow, already on the move.

THIRTY-TWO

Ella

"Out. Get out." I shove Rosalie with all my strength as she opens the car door, and she falls to the ground, her skirt splitting up the side. "Get by the tire," I order, panicking. The bright lights around the station don't allow us to escape into the darkness.

Gunfire erupts all around us.

She grabs my arm and yanks me out, pulling me toward the tire. Then she calmly lifts a small gun from a strap at her thigh and levers up, shooting back.

Bullets pierce the trunk of the car, and I wrap my arm around her neck, dragging her down and out of the way. I look up, seeking shelter.

Justice is running full out toward us, blood on his cheek, firing toward the van as he moves.

The world stops. Holy crap. Danger and fury cascade from him, and his dark gaze remains on me. I can't move.

Rosalie struggles beneath me. "Let go of my neck," she croaks.

I release her. "Stay down."

The wheels of the van screech as it turns the far corner, and then cars rev up in pursuit.

Justice reaches us and he crouches. "Are you okay?" He gently wipes dirt off my chin, his eyes a wild brown flecked with lighter tones.

"Yes." I gulp as Rosalie sits up next to me.

Alexei's men surround us. I can't breathe.

Justice looks around. "Anybody hit?"

Police pour out of the station as reporters clamor toward us.

I don't see any blood. There's a lot of damage, especially to the cars, but nobody seems to be dying.

Justice must make the same determination, because he visually checks Rosalie over, nods, and then lifts me right off the ground, cradling me against his rock-hard chest.

"Hey," I protest.

"Stop," Rosalie says, jumping up and grabbing his arm.

He looks at her, then over his shoulder at the men behind her. "Either shoot me or get the fuck out of my way." He starts moving toward Wynd and his bullet-riddled vehicle, where his larger-than-large driver is already pulling away from the curb. Steam hisses through the holes in the hood, and the vehicle seems to be limping, but it rolls toward us.

"Ella?" Rosalie asks.

I look over Justice's shoulder to see her panicked face and wide eyes. There's a scratch on her chin. Had I almost just gotten her killed? Tears fill my eyes, and I bat them away. If I ask her, she'll have her bodyguards shoot Justice. Right here by the police station, and I think they'll do it. "Justice?"

"I'm not letting go. Make a decision." There's no give in his voice or hold, and he keeps walking. Shoulders up, body relaxed, gait graceful as he tries to get us out of here before the police stop us.

I don't want Rosalie hurt. "I'm fine, Rosy." I make sure my voice is loud enough for the now-staring cops to hear. "Justice and I need to talk. I'll call you later. I promise."

She wavers and pushes strands of her dark hair away from her face.

Wynd opens the backdoor of the car and Justice slides inside, still holding me. The door is slammed shut, and the car peels away from the curb. Wynd must be staying to deal with the police.

"Take us to the bar while the house by the ocean is swept. I want the grounds completely searched," Justice says to the driver.

I take several deep breaths and let myself lean into Justice's strength. Just for a second. I can feel his steady heartbeat beneath my shoulder and I look up at his dark eyes. "How are you calm?"

He lifts one eyebrow. "That's what you ask me?"

I blink. "Um, yeah." Okay, so he's pissed. Of course. Somebody just shot at him. At both of us. "What are you thinking?" Probably about revenge. But who was the shooter?

"That I didn't spank you hard enough *last* time."

The words take a second to register. Probably because the heat is roaring through my head, and the sound of my own blood boiling fills my ears. Wait a second. "What?" My brain feels like it's surrounded by clouds. Filled by them. Buildings are flying by outside. How fast are we going? "Justice?"

He flips me to face him, my thighs falling on either side of his. One swipe of his hand down my front has buttons flying in every direction. I gasp, but he grabs the center of my bra and yanks me toward him, his knuckles brushing my breasts.

I really can't breathe now. My nipples flare wide awake and shoot from relaxed to diamond hard. Just like that.

His mouth is close to mine, and his eyes blaze fire. Like the real kind.

Oh. He's mad at me. The whole leaving with Rosy and not with him situation. And he'd just ripped my shirt with his driver in the front seat. There's no divider. "Um." My gaze drops to Justice's lips. Full and firm.

His fingers twist, tightening my bra painfully.

I suck in air and lean closer to him, instinctively trying to ease the pressure. "I don't like the caveman act," I croak.

Something changes in his eyes. Like a hidden monster flicking closer to the surface. "Don't you, now?" His voice is silky. Challenging. Pissed.

I'd swallow but my throat is dry. Completely. "No." I try to make my voice firm, but I'm still breathy. Who wouldn't be? The guy's deadly. "We have enough going on right now," I whisper. "Let's deal with all of that." Like with whoever's trying to kill us.

He pulls me even closer. "I'm dealing with you. First."

Oh, God. What does that mean? His free hand somehow releases the button and zipper on my jeans in another smooth motion. Before I can protest, he has two fingers inside my panties, sliding them inside me. Not gently. He seems to like to do this. I suck in air and move against him, already wet. Heat fills my face at that. Dark red spirals beneath his cheekbones at the same time.

I stare at him, my mouth opening. The driver is right there. We're speeding way too fast through town. His fingers are *inside* me.

"Say my name," he whispers, his heated breath warming my mouth.

"Justice," I whisper instantly, overcome.

Triumph and hunger glitter in those eyes now along with pleasure. At the sound of my voice. His name. The situation, probably. "If this is what it takes to make you obey, I'm all in." He scrapes his nail across my clit.

I bite my lip to keep from crying out. Panic fills me along with the most erotic sense of danger. My clit has a mind of its own as I move against his hand.

"Who owns you?" His mouth is on mine now, and I can feel his lips move.

I shake my head, holding my breath. I won't give him that. Not here. Not now.

The car lurches to a stop, and my shoulders relax. I realize a second too late that there is no safety. Somebody outside the car opens the door and Justice moves us out and into the drilling rain, his fingers still inside me. He tosses me over his shoulder, his fingers working now, his other hand now on my back, keeping me in place.

Rain drills us and chills me. I try to struggle, and he

adds a third finger to the others, stretching me painfully. Then we're inside.

"Don't disturb us," he orders.

Oh, man. He really doesn't care who sees us doing anything. Everything. Doesn't care a whit.

I'm flopped over his back, my hair covering my face, and I don't look up from a worn wooden floor. Don't want to know who sees. The smell of peanuts fills my head. We move into another room and he kicks the door shut with one foot. He leans forward, and a bunch of papers and notebooks as well as a laptop crash to the floor.

He flips me over onto my back and I land on a desk, shoulders and then my head as he rips off my jeans and panties. He crouches and his mouth is on me. Hard. His thumbs dig into my thighs, spreading them, and then he sucks my clit into his heated mouth.

Fire lashes through me. I cry out, an old desk chilling my butt. It's not enough. Too much. I can't think. He nips and licks, not gentle, bringing me to the brink. Right to the edge. Then he backs off. Once and then again. I'm sweating, moving, needing. I can't think. My ears tingle. His grip is bruising, and his mouth deadly.

He lifts up, his chin on my clit, as he releases my thighs. "Keep them open or I'll spank your pussy until you're raw."

A mini orgasm nearly takes me and my thighs tremble. But I stay still. So I don't see his hand move until it's clasped around my neck, partially raising me.

I grab his solid arm out of instinct.

"Hands. Down." There's no give in his tone, and his face looks carved from rock. Hunger glows in his eyes along with that darkness that terrifies me. Yet I've never wanted anyone or anything this badly.

I dig my nails into his forearm.

His fingers tighten on my neck until my air is cut off. Tears fill my eyes and I scratch him, fighting. He doesn't relent. Finally, the room swimming around me, I drop my arms to the desk. His hold relaxes.

I suck in air, gasping, my body on fire. The orgasm to end all orgasms hovers right there, out of my reach. As if my body is waiting for his command.

His gaze hasn't left mine. Then his fingers tighten again, taking the air. My nails curve against the worn desk, but I don't lift them. Not again. I can't breathe. Approval fills his eyes. He marginally relaxes his hold. My very life is in his hand. One hand. "Beg me."

The order barely permeates. "Please." For air? For an orgasm? For life? Maybe for all three?

He stands and pulls me upright at the same time. "My jeans. Now."

I'm like a robot, obeying commands. Can't think. Can only feel. I release his button and pull down his zipper. He's rock hard behind the jeans. Commando. I push them down as far as I can and he takes care of the rest, releasing my neck to tear off his shirt.

It occurs to me that I can move back.

He watches me as if reading my mind.

I don't move. The long span of his chest, muscled and cut, fills my view. Bullet holes, a couple of them, knife wounds, and whip marks are evident. Beauty and death, all in front of me. The symbol of Malice Media is tattooed over the myriad of scars there.

He slides a hand between my legs, cupping my butt,

and lifts me. With one hand. His other grasps my hips and flips me, leaving me on my hands and knees on the desk.

"Um."

Grasping both of my hips, bruising me, he shoves inside me with one hard push. To the hilt. I cry out, pain and pleasure swamping me, his hands keeping me from falling forward.

He grasps my hair and jerks my head back, leaning over until his mouth is at my ear. "One sound only from you. My name. Only. Understand?"

Tears fill my eyes. If he doesn't start moving, I will plan his death. With a lot of pain. I'm smart enough not to say that. "Yes."

"Say it." That hand releases my hair and wraps around my neck, his thumb tight against my trachea.

"Justice," I moan.

He starts to move then, hard, in and out, hammering with full control, one hand on my hip yanking me back into him. The other hand stays in place. Controlling my breathing. My life.

The pounding is loud in the small office, flesh against flesh. Electricity zings through me, and I'm helpless in his grip. Slowly, his fingers tighten. I'm climbing, so fast, so hard, but I can't breathe.

My vision darkens from the edges. I dig my hands into the desk, trying to push against him. To breathe. I'm so close.

He releases my neck and I explode. I scream his name, live wires edged with barbed wire uncoiling inside me, ripping through every nerve, taking me over. My head drops as the fire-tipped waves pummel through me, taking me somewhere else. Don't know where. I shudder wildly, coming down, just as he clamps himself deep inside me, his body jerking behind me.

I gasp in air, panting, tears sliding from my eyes.

He stops. Still inside me.

Wow. Just wow. What just happened?

He withdraws and turns me over, facing him, my butt on the old desk. My body jerks in aftershocks. One broad hand grasps my neck, gently this time, as he leans over and pulls me to him, placing a kiss on my trembling mouth. He looks primal, like an animal stripped to its nature, appeased. For now. "You're never leaving me again. Tell me you understand."

"Justice—"

He cuts off my air and then relents. "Tell me."

He's demanding forever. Not giving me a choice. I know who he is. Do I want to go back to life without him? Without this? Oh, he scares the shit out of me, but when the bullets were flying earlier, he ran through them to get to me. To protect me.

"I'll keep you safe, Ella. Anybody comes for you, they die and they die bloody. Hard. You're mine." It's like he can read my mind. His grip is still there. Enough to remind me. "I'm not going back. Neither are you. I'm also not waiting for you to reason it out. Now tell me."

I lick my lips and enjoy how his eyes flare. I'm ready to take a chance. A risk. I don't want to be alone anymore. I don't want to be without *him.* "Fine, but I want romance. Fun. True partnership where you completely let me in." My mouth is running now, and I hope I'm being clear with what I want and need. I figure this is the only chance I'll get to make sure he understands. "I want it all, Justice." All of him? Yeah, I'll take that.

"You can have it all. Your place is here. With me."

"Okay." I exhale slowly. I haven't had a place in way too long, and this one is seriously sexy. "Also, once in a while, I want gentle."

Now one dark eyebrow rises. "That was."

THIRTY-THREE

Justice

Rain threads through the trees in steady lines, a quiet stitchwork that pulls the forest around me tight. The ocean barrels loudly from the other side of my home, and salt hints in the air. The porch roof catches the fall and turns it into a soft drumbeat above my head, and for the first time in too long, I feel settled.

I know my men patrol the trees around me, and I trust the front gate is well protected. But the woman sleeping in the house behind me, *my* woman, has me content.

Part of me wants to awaken her just to listen to her voice and feel the pleasure on my skin. But after I took her in the bar office last night, I brought her home and spent all night marking every inch of her. Making sure she knows where she belongs.

With me.

I take a sip of the coffee, and morning steam lifts past my face. The brew tastes dark and clean. My bare feet rest on the wet wood of a lower step, cool as river stone, and I enjoy the fresh rain-soaked air.

My phone buzzes, and I pull it from my pocket, glancing at the screen before answering. "Hi, Thorn."

"Were you in a shootout on the police steps yesterday?" he snarls.

"I'm fine, brother. How are you?" I ask lazily.

He goes quiet for a moment. "Justice. What's going on?"

"Somebody wants either Ella or me dead," I say, not believing anybody had aimed at Rosalie. This is about us. "I've got it handled. You've got more time on your honeymoon, and you have to stay there. I don't need to worry about one more person taking on bullets." If somebody's after me, they're after Thorn too.

"Is it Alexei?"

This is an answer I know for sure. "No."

"How do you know?"

"Because Rosalie was in the crossfire."

Thorn is silent again.

I can't blame him. This sucks. "I don't think it's Mathias, and I made it clear to Sylveria what I'd do to her if she attacked Ella or me again, and I blew up TimeGem Moments pretty good, so she knows I'm not fucking around." I already texted him about that mess. "So it's someone new trying to make a name."

"Are we still finding ghost hints in our server?"

"Yeah." I have Kaz trying to track whoever it is, but I've been dodging bullets in the meantime. "Whoever's new isn't a very good shot," I mutter.

"Maybe you're just good at avoiding death, brother."

I smile. His voice is warm and steady, the way it's been since we were kids. Bliss suits him. "How's Alana?"

"She's been on Aquarius Social posting videos all morning. We might be having a bit of a contest."

"You might be?" I ask.

He snorts. "Yeah, I think I accidentally challenged her to see who could get more likes through the day."

"You're never on Malice Media," I retort.

"Yeah, I'm losing." He doesn't sound too sad about it.

The least I can do is help him out. "I can call Kaz and have him get some of our influencers working hard today."

"Hey, that'd be great."

"We don't have anybody as good as Alana," I admit.

His chuckle rolls over the line. "I know, but still, I'd like to at least give her a run for her money." He sighs. "I hope you know how difficult it is for me to stay here and not come home."

"I do."

"We saw Ella on the media during the shooting. Where is she now? Alana wants to know."

I think through my options and then, since this is my brother, I go with the truth. "She's here with me, where she's staying."

Silence beats across the line. Finally, he speaks. "So we go to war with Alexei?"

I blink, surprised, and watch a jay hop between a couple of trees. "It's that easy?"

"If Ella's who you want, then yeah. It's that easy."

I rub my chest. For so long it's just been Thorn and me, and he's always had my back. But to hear him say he'll go to war with a Russian mobster because of the woman I've chosen—that's something. "Actually, I think Alexei's okay. We talked the other day."

"You talked to Alexei?"

"Yeah. He wants to maybe forge an alliance with the next generation. I told him we'd be open to it."

Thunder cracks in the distance.

"Are we open to it?" Thorn asks.

Hell if I know. "Maybe, but if it keeps us from going to war for a while, we could at least talk about it. Who knows? Maybe your kid and Alexei's kid will fall in love."

"I don't see that," Thorn says. "How about your kid and Alexei's kid fall in love?"

"I'm not sure I see that either." It was one thing when I was speaking hypothetically, but now that I know exactly who the woman will be to carry my kids, I'm not sure I'll let them go to the Russian mob. If nothing else, I bought us some time before war. We might as well enjoy it.

"I should probably tell you that Horace Whimple's body was found on my main property by the ocean. Close to your place," I murmur.

"Excuse me?" Thorn asks.

I tell him the whole story. "It's over about a mile from the house, cordoned off, still a police crime scene. I searched my house and the rest of the grounds and couldn't find anything."

"So some anonymous source called it in and buried the body on your land?"

Isn't that convenient? "Yep."

"Have they done an autopsy yet?"

"Today," I say. Rain drips from the porch roof. I wipe my knee where it splattered and take a sip of coffee. "Of course, even if the killer planted evidence that links the death to me, it'll be gone." We have contacts in the coroner's office.

I listen to the silence. This is Thorn trying to convince himself not to come home and take care of things.

"I've got this," I tell him. "You need to trust me."

"I do."

The absolute truth in his voice warms me in a way most people will never understand. My condition leads to this as well as to pain. I guess there has to be some balance.

Thorn clears his throat. "Justice, take care of these problems, would you?"

I finish the coffee. "Of course. Enjoy your honeymoon."

"Are you sure Ella's the one?"

I chuckle. "I'm absolutely positive."

"Good." He sounds pleased. "Bye."

The line clicks off. I text Kaz instructions to get all of our influencers moving and see if we can spark activity today on Malice Media. With the most advanced algorithm out there, we should at least give Alana somewhat of a challenge. I'd like to help my brother save face, even though he didn't seem to care much about it.

Kaz doesn't answer. That's odd.

My phone buzzes again from a blocked number. I accept the call but don't say anything.

"Are we at war?" Alexei Sokolov's voice comes through calmly.

I sigh. "Because of Ella?"

He's quiet. Quiet for two beats. "No. What's wrong with Ella?"

"She's mine. That's concrete. So if we're going to war

because of our connections to TimeGem and Aquarius, let's do it." I wouldn't mind a decent fight, to be honest, but I'd rather a bunch of good men didn't get killed.

He sighs. "I'm not willing to go to war over that at this moment, considering I'm marrying your woman's best friend. I thought we had a deal with the next generation."

"We might. Especially if you have a daughter," I say.

His slight growl tells me he doesn't like that.

"The future is years away," I note.

"Maybe," he says. "But we're at peace right now. Or at least I thought we were."

I scrub a hand through my hair. "You're going to have to be clearer than that, and don't speak Russian." I add a Gaelic insult on the end, just to have some fun.

"I don't speak Gaelic," Alexei snaps.

He's been cranky since somebody tried to blow up his homestead.

"What's going on, Alexei?" I ask, keeping my temper.

"I've got you and one of your men on video close to my place when the rocket was launched."

I rock back. "Bullshit. That can be faked."

"Doesn't look fake," he returns. "Was it you?"

Is he messing with me? "You know it wasn't."

"I don't know that."

I don't have time for this. "Fair enough. What do you want from me?"

"You come show me how this is fake and I'll let it go. If not, expect a bomb coming your way, and I'm talking the entire Malice Media infrastructure."

I wince. I really don't want Malice Media blown up while Thorn's on his honeymoon. "Fine. If your computer gurus can't figure it out, mine can. Meet at my corporate headquarters."

"Oh no. Mine," he retorts. "You come to Hologrid Hub."

"My computer guy is the best, and he works from Malice. He knows the system. I give you my word that you'll be safe."

Lightning zaps close to the tree line. "Fine, but I'm bringing firepower," Alexei says. "I'll be there in an hour." He clicks off.

God. Russians are cranky.

The door opens and I hear movement as Ella steps outside, wrapped in the comforter. I glance up. She's beautiful in the morning light, her eyes the color of sapphires, her hair wild and mussed around her shoulders. She looks more pixie than ever, and I'm hit by the raw need to protect her, to keep her safe.

She hesitates, then walks over and flops into my lap. I catch her and hold her close.

"Good morning." I kiss her, going deep.

She kisses me back, sinking into my chest. "All right, now you need to talk," she murmurs, sleepy.

I'm not much of a talker. Even so, her voice smooths over my skin like a balm.

"Tell me about your mom," she says.

I automatically lapse into Gaelic, then catch myself. "Sorry. She was beautiful, kind, smart, and fun." I tighten my arms around Ella. "You would've liked her. She treated Thorn like he was hers too, and he loved her as much as I did. She created the best games for us all to play."

I pause, trying to remember the good parts of my

childhood. Our father didn't like us much—he was pretty much a bastard—but my mother, his second wife, made life enjoyable. "She brought brightness. Her voice was sweet and soothing. It could heal. Different from yours, but still kind."

Ella caresses down my neck. "I've been thinking about how my voice eases you. If you look at my energy as citrine, and yours as obsidian and garnet, I'm kind of light to your dark. I think it's possible that you and I exchange energy as well, and mine is healing to you."

That's sweet and makes sense. "What's mine to you?"

Pink blooms across her face. "Irritating."

Ha. That's not why she's blushing. Amusement filters through me.

My phone buzzes. I sigh, reaching for it, hoping Thorn hasn't changed his mind. The number's unfamiliar. I put it on speaker. "Who's there?"

"Hi, it's Wesley Whisper."

Ella frowns. So do I.

"How'd you get this number?" I ask.

"I'm a computer programmer," he snaps. "So here's the deal—"

I stiffen but let him speak.

"I think you've kidnapped Ella. I'm on my way to the police station, and when I get there, I'll not only file a missing person's report, but I'll tell them you blew up TimeGem and committed battery on me."

"I don't like being threatened, Wesley."

He coughs. "That's too bad, because I'm going to save her if it's the last thing I do."

Ella sits up. "Wesley, I'm here. I'm sorry things ended the way they did, but I haven't been kidnapped."

I kiss her forehead. Nice of her to step in, though I'm already thinking I'll have to kill the guy.

Unfortunately, she must read something on my face, because she frowns and shakes her head. "I'm trying to save your life here, Wesley."

"I don't care about my life," he retorts.

That I can understand. I'd die for her, too.

"Either you meet me and talk this out, or I'm going to the cops. I don't believe you're not under duress," Wesley says.

Ella rolls her eyes. "I wouldn't lie to you under duress." Her cheeks pink slightly because we both know she'll do whatever I want with enough encouragement. She glares at me. I smile. God, she's cute.

"All right, Wesley," I say. "We'll meet with you—"

"Not you," he breaks in.

Maybe I'll just beat the shit out of him. "Oh yeah, me. If you don't drop this, you're going to end up dead." I don't think he's recording me, but if he is, I'll deal with it later. "We'll meet you in half an hour at the Malice Media headquarters." I can deal with him before Alexei arrives. "You'll get fifteen minutes, and if you still want to go to the cops, I'll make sure you do it in a coffin." I end the call.

"That really wasn't nice," Ella says.

"Are you kidding me?" I retort. "After the two meetings, let's go shopping. See how nice I'm being? I'm letting you meet with him first." I want to go ring shopping. I'll surprise her.

Even her frown is sexy. I want to get her naked again. Now. "We're meeting at your office," she says. "If you ask anybody to kill him, they will." She's not wrong. She leans up and cups my face, running her palm over the whiskers I didn't bother to shave this morning. "Promise me you won't kill him. He's a decent guy."

"Have you slept with him?" It shouldn't matter, but I want to know.

"Nope," she says cheerfully. "We dated a little bit, but it just wasn't there."

She probably just saved his life. "So long as he gets the message he can't go to the police," I warn.

"I know. I'll talk to him."

"I'll be there."

She leans up and kisses my neck. The woman is seriously touchy, and I'm shocked by how much I like that.

"I hope I didn't force you into this," I surprise myself by saying.

Her instant laughter fills me like joy. Or what I figure joy feels like. "You weren't exactly subtle, but I do want to stay. I like you, Justice." She glances down at my neck. "You make me feel safe. I've never felt like this. Not really."

Her sweetness does something to me that feels new. Good. I shift my weight and pull out a bracelet from my back pocket to clasp around her wrist. "Saw it the other day. Thought you'd like it."

She breathes out, circling her wrist so the citrines and garnets catch the light. "It's beautiful. Thank you."

My phone buzzes again. Have I ever been this fucking popular? I might have to turn the damn thing off. I lift it to my ear. "Beathach."

"Hey, it's Bronco. I'm at Malice Media's headquarters and am supposed to meet with Kaz about security. He's not here, and he's not answering his phone."

"That's unusual. Find him." I stand, still holding Ella. "Also put extra security in the lobby. I'm on my way, and the Russian mob is coming to tea."

Now all I have to do is convince Wesley to leave Ella alone without killing him and pissing her off, deal with the Russian mob to avoid a war, and keep the cops from arresting me for the murder of a man I didn't like.

What could possibly go wrong?

THIRTY-FOUR

Ella

Justice and Wynd flank me as we slip through the back door into Malice Media's main reception area in the middle of the city.

I already miss the house by the ocean, but we'll stay there again tonight.

The hinges click shut behind us, cutting off the hallway's shadows, and a rush of cool air greets my skin. The lobby spreads wide, polished and calm, not a single mark of the bombing left. Marble tiles shine beneath recessed lights, pale cream streaked with gray veins. The space smells faintly of pine polish and new fabric, covering any trace of smoke or ash that might have lingered.

Clusters of couches stretch across the room, angled toward sleek black tables. The arrangement feels calculated for more business than comfort. Every piece carries garnet accents and obsidian trim—thick bases on lamps, carved edges along the tables, inlays along the chair legs.

Dark stone gleams against pale walls, pulling the eye and grounding the luxury.

I tug at the hem of my new dress, a soft blue that skims my knees. The fabric moves lightly with each step, brushing against my thighs. My new citrine necklace glitters warm yellow at my throat, catching flashes from the overhead lights. It matches the bracelet that fits snug against my wrist, the gems alive with fire whenever my hand shifts. Their brightness cuts through the obsidian around us, a burst of color against all the shadow.

Presents from Justice. I've never been pampered by a man before and am surprised by how much I like it. Love the jewels, really.

I bite back a sneeze. Am I catching something or what? Sleep would be nice.

Justice doesn't slow. His long stride keeps us moving, the black fabric of his jacket stretching over shoulders built for command. Wynd matches his pace on my other side, every step a silent echo, his gaze sweeping corners and doorways. Their presence forms a wall, one I didn't ask for but can't shake off, solid enough that each breath feels steadier.

We cross half the lobby before Wesley pushes up from a couch tucked in the far corner. The movement draws every guard's attention for a split second. He's tall, shoulders broad despite the sling binding one arm tight to his chest. The bruises across his cheekbone and jaw stand out under the lights, purple and green cutting against tanned skin. His other hand stays loose at his side, steady and in control. Even injured, he carries himself with a confidence I admire.

I aim a look at my man that says more than words, and Justice's mouth twitches in response, the only crack in his carved expression. The warmth in his eyes is quick, quiet, gone before anyone else notices.

"Wesley, how are you?" My voice lifts, clear enough to roll across the marble and bounce back faintly.

"I'm fine. I'd like to speak with you alone." His words stay even, steady, though he closes the space between us with careful steps.

Justice and Wynd stiffen. Their shoulders square, weight settling in unison, both ready to shut him down before he gets close.

"No." Justice's tone is final.

Enough of this. "Would you stop?" Frustration threads through my voice. The men stationed at every corner stand locked in place, their gazes flicking between us, tension coiled. The whole room feels wound tight, waiting for the next move. "Give me a break, would you?"

"No." Justice's answer is short, sharp, the word cutting as clean as his expression.

"Come on, Justice," I murmur. "Let me just speak to Wesley for a minute." I have to reassure the poor guy so he doesn't get himself killed.

Justice's jaw ticks, but he doesn't move. The polished marble under his shoes gleams with reflections from the overhead lights, and the faint hum of the air system fills the silence. He watches me longer than I expect before the tightness in his shoulders eases just a fraction. Patience isn't his natural state, but he's edging toward it with me. I doubt anyone else ever sees that.

Two guys behind the wide reception counter shift,

catching Justice's eye. The counter is brushed steel with obsidian edges, and they stand behind it in matching dark suits, the kind that conceal weapons. One of them jerks his chin, a silent signal that they need Justice's attention.

"Fine." Justice steps closer to Wesley, a smile curving his mouth with no trace of humor. "You touch her, I'll break both your hands. Got it?"

Wesley lifts his brows. "I don't touch people unless they want it."

"Good. Because she doesn't." Justice's hand lands on me with a quick pat, sharp enough on my backside to make heat rise in my face. Then he turns, his long stride carrying him toward the guards. Wynd moves with him as a silent shadow at his side.

I watch them cross the lobby, their tall frames cutting through the expanse with lethal grace. Yeah, Justice will pay for that pat later. Maybe.

Wesley gestures, and I walk with him to one of the sofas. The leather cushions dip as I sit, the surface cool against my thighs. Beyond the wide windows, rain streaks the glass in silver rivulets. The storm outside blurs the city into gray lines and moving shadows. The panes shimmer faintly, reinforced, maybe bulletproof.

"I have a gun in my boot." Wesley leans closer. His powder-blue three-piece suit strains against the sling at his shoulder. "Just say the word."

"What word?" I fight a nervous laugh. "We're surrounded by at least ten guns right now, Wesley. We wouldn't make it."

"For you, I'd try." His gaze holds mine, smart and earnest, so open I feel guilty.

I draw in a slow breath, the scent of rain and leather wrapping the moment. "I like you a lot."

"I like you a lot too." He leans forward another inch but doesn't close the space. Smart man.

"But just as a friend," I add, letting the words settle. "We weren't going anywhere. We share code. We share computers. That's it."

His jaw tightens. "I'm plenty of girls' dream guy. I know that. But I want you." His gaze flicks over me, not lingering where it shouldn't. "You're gorgeous, yes. But even if you weren't, your brain . . . no one talks tunneling or network paths with me the way you do. Don't you see how perfect that is?"

I glance across the lobby. Justice stands in profile, black suit cutting sharp against the pale marble. His attention stays on the guards, but I know he's tracking my every move.

Wesley follows my gaze, his face hardening. "You can't have fallen for the mob boss. Have you?"

To put it mildly. The rain outside beats harder, blurring the view beyond the glass. "I have." The truth is simple. "I'm sorry, Wesley. I hope we can still be friends."

His wince confirms that my appeasement falls flat. "I think you've been brainwashed and this is Stockholm Syndrome." His tone sharpens as he pushes to his feet.

I rise too, the leather seat creaking. "You don't have to insult me. You just complimented my brain. I know what I'm doing. Thank you for your friendship, and I really do hope you find the right person for you."

He towers over me when we're both standing, his suit pulling across his shoulders. Justice dwarfs him in presence, but Wesley's height is undeniable.

"I can't let you give up your life like this." His hand flexes at his side.

"I'm not giving up anything," I murmur. "Thank you, but I think it's time we moved on."

A piercing shriek rips through the lobby. The sound bounces off the marble walls, shrill enough to make my pulse spike. I jolt, and Wesley spins fast, eyes wide.

Justice and Wynd are already moving, their bodies cutting a path toward me with lethal speed. Another scream follows, high-pitched, ragged, words spilling in rapid Spanish. My ears catch the rhythm but not the meaning.

We move together toward the noise at the back of the lobby and reach the hallway. Justice plants himself in front of me, his broad back a wall. "Stay here."

"Why?" I ask, moving with him anyway.

The corridor narrows, lined with open doors. Cleaning supplies sit in plastic bins, mops leaning against tiled walls. The fluorescent lights buzz overhead, cold against the shadows pooling along the floor.

A fifty-something woman wearing a pink maid's outfit stumbles backward, hands trembling as she points, her voice breaking.

Wynd catches her by the arm, steadying her, and guides her toward the open lobby.

As we step closer, something shifts. A dead body slides forward from one of the closets, hitting the floor with a soft, sickening thud. Brown hair spills across the tile, strands catching the light. The air stills.

I stop short, the metallic tang of blood reaching me before my eyes take in the rest.

Justice's chin lowers, his jaw set hard.

"Oh my God." The words scrape out of me, barely audible. "That's Sylveria Rendale."

The hole through her head leaves no question as to her death. Her skin is pale, blood staining her temple and trailing along the floor. She is lifeless in a light blue silk suit, her one foot bare and the other wearing a red-bottomed navy blue heel. She will never move again.

Sirens wail in the distance, growing sharper with every second. The rising pitch cuts through the lobby, echoing off the marble walls until the sound feels like it's inside my skull.

"Damn it." Justice's voice is pure grit. "We were set up." His head snaps toward Wynd. "Take Ella. Get her out the back door and to my place by the ocean since it's been cleared. Keep guards on the whole property, including Thorn's place, until I get there. Got it?"

"Yes," Wynd answers, already signaling the men stationed by the windows. Boots pound against the floor as bodies shift into formation, dark suits moving like pieces on a chessboard.

I can't stop staring at Sylveria. Dead. On the floor. She'd hate being on the floor and missing one shoe. Just hate it. "Wait." My voice comes out raw.

"No." Justice doesn't look at me. His tone leaves no room to even argue. "I want you out of here."

I gag as I breathe in the coppery smell of Sylveria's blood. The soft strands of hair fanned around her face look delicate against the gore. The wound in her head is merciless, a blackened circle that robbed her of everything in one instant. She despised me. I never liked her. Still, seeing her sprawled and ruined sends a spear of nausea slicing through me.

Justice's hand shoves at my arm, pulling me off balance. "Move."

"I'm going with her," Wesley blurts out.

"The fuck you are," Justice snaps, fire in every word. His body angles forward, broad shoulders tense as a bowstring.

Outside, tires screech, rubber burning against wet pavement. Sirens wail closer now, red and blue lights strobing against the windows in dizzy bursts.

"Go!" Justice roars, the command cracking the air. Guards scatter, voices low but urgent, hands on weapons. The energy shifts into something sharp, electric, and on the verge of exploding. "Somebody fucking find Kaz," Justice barks, scanning the lobby. "He should be here." His voice vibrates with rage as he cuts toward the corridor.

Wynd answers without looking up. "The cameras are still down."

The weight of the moment presses in—sirens screaming, rain hammering the glass, blood pooling across the white tile, and the body of Sylveria Rendale lying as proof that everything just changed.

I touch Justice's arm. "That's what the reception guy was telling you? That your cameras are down?"

"Yeah." His mouth flattens. "Not good."

Somebody knocks loudly on the outside door.

"Go." Wynd grabs my arm, his grip firm, and we cut down the hallway and away from the lobby, toward a hidden elevator tucked around the corner. Guards shift aside to clear a path, radios crackling low as orders snap back and forth.

The steel panel blinks faintly when Wynd presses his

palm against the scanner. The hum of machinery answers, low and mechanical. I eye the glowing panel. I need my biometrics added to this system. Just in case. Malice Media has too many secrets not to poke at.

Wesley shadows us. I shake my head at him, but he doesn't fall back. The elevator doors slide open with a hiss, and we rush inside.

Wesley steps in behind me.

"I'm going to have to kill you," Wynd mutters, steel in his voice.

"I'm making sure she's safe," Wesley growls back.

My eyes start to water and I sniff, fighting another sneeze. I need cough drops.

Wynd slams a button, and the doors close. The car drops fast, humming around us. His gun is out in one smooth motion, barrel lifting.

I raise both hands, palms open. "No. Don't shoot him."

"I don't have a choice." His eyes are hard and steady.

"Yes, you do." My voice cracks sharp across the small space. "Seriously. Right now we need to get out of here before the police reach us. For some reason." Why? I could've handled the police. "Though, shouldn't I make a statement?"

Both men shake their heads, in perfect unison for one odd second.

"She's your stepmother who stole your inheritance," Wynd mutters. "Everybody knows that. We need to get you out of here until Justice figures out what happened."

"Agreed," Wesley says.

I hate leaving Justice with the cops. He runs hotter when I'm not beside him, and I swear he steadies when I speak. Maybe my voice can help him deal with his usual pain. The thought flickers through me, warm, then the elevator jolts to a stop.

The doors slide open into the hidden garage, cold concrete stretching under harsh fluorescent lights. The air reeks of motor oil and burned rubber. The floor is solid with no hint of the burned and collapsed tunnel beneath it. Man, they'd repaired at least this part of the garage quickly. A town car idles ahead, exhaust curling thick and acrid in the stale space, next to a quiet SUV.

I step out first with Wynd and Wesley close in at my sides.

Then the world explodes.

A body barrels from the shadows and slams into us with bone-cracking force. My lungs empty in one shocked gasp as I'm thrown sideways. Fists and elbows cut the air—thuds, cracks, wet grunts filling the garage. The sound of flesh meeting flesh, the scuff of boots on concrete. Someone's elbow smashes my temple, white pain bursting through my skull, and I crash against the metal side of the SUV.

Gunfire pops, sharp and deafening in the enclosed space. Shouts ricochet, tangled with groans of pain.

Dizzy, I drop, the floor trembling beneath me as my vision swims. "Justice," I whisper, the word torn and weak.

Another gunshot. Another grunt. Then hands—rough, unrelenting—clamp around me, dragging me up. My head lolls, body too heavy, too slow. I can't see who has me. The grip tightens, hauling me like I weigh nothing. The thought of Bronco slams into me. He's massive, a truck in human form. If it's him, maybe it's rescue. Or maybe not.

I fight for clarity, for breath. My limbs flail weakly against unyielding arms. A trunk door screeches open, metal on metal, and I'm heaved inside.

I slam against hard carpet, bouncing twice before collapsing flat. The air tastes of grease and rubber. A lid slams shut above me. Darkness swallows me whole. My fingers brush my temple to find swollen skin, no blood, but an already rising lump.

A sick twist tightens my chest as the truth settles in.

I'm in a trunk.

And I don't know who put me here.

THIRTY-FIVE

Justice

This place is a complete shitshow. My men edge toward the wide glass doors, weapons ready, muscles tight. I raise a hand, sharp enough to stop them as I move into the lobby, pleased Ella has gone the opposite direction. "Let 'em in." They step back, eyes still locked on the flashing lights outside.

I glance at the dark cameras in the corners. "Also, somebody fucking find Kaz." My voice carries through the marble, echoing off polished walls.

Uniformed cops barrel in, guns drawn, boots squeaking on wet tile. Their radios crackle, the smell of damp wool and rain-soaked leather cutting through the sterile polish of the lobby.

"The body's at the end of the lobby down the hallway," I tell them, motioning toward Sylveria. "Nobody's gonna shoot you."

They don't look convinced. Can't blame them. My reputation precedes me, and it's not soft.

An older officer steps forward, easily pushing eighty, though his frame is still lean and wired with muscle. His mustache and gravelly voice give him a Sam Elliott edge, the kind of man who's fought his share of battles. "Mr. Beathach, I'm to wait with you until the detectives arrive."

I point to one of the plush seating areas. "Have a seat."

"Sure thing." He lowers into the leather with an impressive grace.

My shoulders loosen for the first time in minutes. At least Ella's out. The thought steadies me. She's mine to guard, mine to keep. Nobody takes what's mine and walks away breathing.

I sit.

"Who found the body?" he asks.

I point to the crying woman in the corner already speaking with officers.

Fifteen minutes later, the detectives finally show. I'm not surprised to see Ashner and Caldwell again.

She's buttoned into a navy suit with a pink shell beneath, boots polished to a deep brown sheen. He's still in that trench coat, dark circles carved deeper into his face than last time.

They glance at me first, walk to the back hallway to see Sylveria's corpse, which I assume is still sprawled across the polished floor.

They return, and the Sam Elliott look-alike stretches to his feet and crosses over to speak with my men behind the desk. Detective Caldwell takes the seat across from me, the leather creaking under her weight. Detective Ashner stays standing, chin lifted, eyes cutting down.

"This is a terrible coincidence," Caldwell says, her voice flat but sharp.

My gaze sweeps the lobby again, expecting Kaz to walk through a door. Any fucking door. Where is he? "Isn't it, though?"

"Yes, but the good news"—Caldwell's eyes flick upward toward the corners of the ceiling—"is this is Malice Media. I'm sure there's CCTV everywhere."

"It's my understanding the cameras are out," I answer.

Her stare drags back to me, slow as a blade sliding free of a sheath. "Are you kidding me?"

"Oh, if only I were." I lean back, calm on the outside, heat simmering beneath. Why would anybody shoot Sylveria in the head and then tuck her into my damn closet? The timing stinks. "We have witnesses but no video. She fell out of the closet when the cleaning lady found her," I say evenly, pointing to Gertrude. She's sobbing into the chest of a uniform, voice rushing in Spanish, hands cutting frantic arcs through the air.

Caldwell studies me harder this time, suspicion bright in her dark eyes. "I didn't think you were dumb enough to bury a body on your own property." Her tone is low, almost a murmur, but sharp enough to slice.

"I'm not."

"Maybe you are. Maybe you're trying to look dumb."

I force myself to remain relaxed. "Not my style." My watch ticks faintly as I glance at it. Every second drags heavily against me. Whoever's making a move is doing it hard. Right now.

Ashner pulls a stick of gum from his pocket and slowly unwraps it. "Do you have somewhere to be?"

"Always." I lean back, shoulders loose. "Before you ask, I have no idea who shot Mrs. Rendale and dumped her in the lobby closet of my building."

"That would make sense," Caldwell says, "except the cameras are down."

"Obviously," Ashner mutters.

Caldwell shakes her head. "You've got one of the most intricate systems in the world. Are you telling me just anybody can shut it down?"

Around us, my men hold steady, but the police outnumber them. Too many twitchy fingers near too many triggers. One wrong move, and I'll be nothing more than a red stain across the white marble. "No," I admit. "It's incredibly difficult to infiltrate my system." Which leads to the real question—where's Kaz? His absence gnaws at me, especially since my system has gone dark. Did somebody get to him? Take him?

Ashner and Caldwell keep pressing, their clipped words and irritating voices scraping at my patience. But none of it slices deep. My skin doesn't burn, doesn't split. Not today.

It's Ella. It has to be. Something about her, her voice, her kindness, her energy, somehow has eased the pain always around me. I think she's correct in that her energy and mine complement each other. Belong together.

"Where is Ella Rendale?" Ashner asks suddenly, his gaze sweeping the room.

I wondered when they'd get to her. "She went shopping."

"She's not—" Caldwell cuts herself off with a short snort. "You let her go shopping by herself?"

I meet her gaze without blinking, my jaw steady, shoulders squared. "I don't have her on a leash and chain," I say evenly, though the truth is closer than I'd admit. "She chose to go shopping. I can't tell you where she is right now."

"Why don't you call her?" Ashner plops the gum in his mouth.

"I'd rather not. If I'm going to tell her that her stepmother is dead, I'll do it in person." My voice stays mellow but my jaw's locked tight.

Caldwell runs her palms down her perfectly pressed navy slacks. Her nails gleam a brighter pink today, catching the light like lacquered glass. Interesting. She breathes out before speaking. "Here's the deal, Mr. Beathach, you're coming down to the station with us."

The heavy glass doors shove open again. Fergus shoulders his way inside, green flannel damp with rain, Carhartt jeans stiff, brown boots scuffed from work. His dark hair is slicked back. "Sorry. Took me a while to get through that mess outside." He shakes his head, water droplets flying. "Not only do you have police everywhere, the news vans are here. Somebody tipped them off, boss."

"Great," Caldwell and I mutter at the same time.

Fergus moves forward, his gaze sharp. "From my understanding, based on what our men said on the way in, the cameras went down this morning, and then the cleaning lady found the body. The police were already en route, and the press was parked outside before anyone even knew what was in the closet." He checks his watch, gold catching the fluorescent glare. "Somebody set this up."

Ashner chomps his gum again. "Maybe your client set this up. It's almost too obvious he's guilty, right? That's a decent defense, don't you think, Caldwell?"

Caldwell tilts her head, a stray strand of dark hair slipping from her bun to frame her cheek. She'd be pretty if she weren't gunning to put me in a cell. Not for me, not for anyone tied to me.

She flips her notebook closed with a neat snap. "Well, Mr. Beathach, you are being detained. You're coming down to the station with us either on your own or in handcuffs." Her eyes cut toward the glass doors. Outside, news vans jockey for curb space, umbrellas bump, and camera lights flare white against rain-slicked pavement.

"I'm fine either way." I smile, slow, and pull my phone from my back pocket, the case warm against my palm. "You might want to take a look at this."

"What's this?" Caldwell asks.

I hadn't planned on sharing this information. "Cameras. Installed at my personal residence yesterday."

Fergus's head snaps up. "You did?"

"Yeah. Didn't tell anybody." My tone stays even. "With a body showing up there, I figured it was time."

Caldwell takes the phone and scrolls, face unreadable except for a twitch at the corner of her mouth. The blue of her suit catches the overheads, and her nails flash a hot pink when her thumb moves.

"As you can see," I say, "there I am arriving with Ms. Rendale last night. Timestamped. There we are leaving this morning. Plenty of angles. No window for me to kill Sylveria Rendale and stash her in a closet on my own property."

"These could be doctored." Caldwell's gaze lifts.

"Sure." I take the phone back. "Your email?"

She gives it, and I send the files. "Run them through every analyst you trust. My word stands. It's real."

Fergus exhales, shoulders loosening under rain-damp flannel. "Never thought you'd put cameras out there."

"Didn't have a choice." The lobby smells of lemon polish, wet wool, and the faint iron thread of death. "We need to know who is getting onto my property and leaving bodies." More importantly, I need eyes on Ella at all times.

Caldwell snorts. "You can afford to hire somebody to kill, you know."

I give her a smile. A real one. "I'd never ask anybody to do my dirty work for me, Detective. That I promise you."

She swallows and visibly shakes herself before her chin goes up.

Questions keep coming for another half hour. They cycle the order, poke the same corners, try to catch a flicker. I give them nothing new. Radios chirp. A tech's flash pops near the closet. Evidence markers sprout across the tile like small yellow teeth. The coroner seals Sylveria into a black bag, zipper rasping, then a cart squeaks away toward freight doors.

Caldwell stands, straightening her slacks. "I want everyone out of this lobby. Our techs need the entire space."

I stand as well. "Fine by me."

The front doors push wide. Alexei Solokov strides in with two men tight at his shoulders. Their collars are crooked, hair damp, jackets creased from elbows in the crowd. Rain beads on his coat and rolls down to the floor in neat drops.

"Mr. Sokolov," Detective Ashner says, stepping forward, trench coat swinging. "We'd like to discuss a couple of matters with you." He tucks his gum to one side of his mouth and waits.

"Not now." Alexei doesn't spare him another look. His gaze finds me across the room and holds. There's calculation there, and a heat that ignores the chill in the vents. "Justice," he says, voice even.

"Yes, detectives," I tell them without taking my eyes off Alexei. "I'll be in touch."

Caldwell's jaw works once. "I want you at the station later today for a formal interview. Don't make me detain you." She signals her team. Uniforms start funneling people toward the doors, hands light on elbows, voices clipped but controlled. Outside, a siren winds down.

Yeah, she doesn't have enough to take me in with my alibi in her email. Not right now, anyway.

Fergus edges closer, boots leaving damp ovals on the marble. "You want Sokolov in the conference room?" he asks under his breath, glancing at Alexei's guards, then at mine.

"No. We're going downstairs," I say. "Sound good?"

Alexei adjusts his cuffs, brushes water from his sleeve, then nods once toward the interior hall.

I don't give the cops another glance. I turn and head toward the elevator, Fergus tight on my right, Alexei and his two men shadowing me with steps that echo across the marble. Their boots leave damp streaks on the floor from the storm outside. The lobby's air is thick with polish, copper, and the faint sting of rain every time the glass doors open.

"Wait a minute," Caldwell calls after me. Her voice is sharp enough to crack through the hum of voices behind us.

"Nope." I put my hand on the plate. The scanner warms under my palm, then the elevator doors slide open with a hiss. She'll need a warrant for the other floors.

We step into the car. It's a good-sized box, steel walls reflecting too much tension. The fluorescent strip above buzzes, throwing hard shadows across the men crowding inside. The air grows close, heavy, a mix of aftershave, damp wool, and gun oil. Too much testosterone, too little space.

The doors close.

"What the fuck's going on?" Alexei asks, his tone clipped, almost casual, though his eyes are sharp. One of his men shifts beside him, adjusting the strap of his shoulder holster.

"Sylveria Rendale was found dead in a lobby closet." My words drop into the silence.

Alexei stills. For a beat, the only sound is the grinding of the elevator cables as we descend. "No shit?"

I nod once.

"Did you kill her?" he asks.

"No, and I don't know who did. My cameras are down." I don't like that fact. "I can't find my computer guy. Kaz."

Alexei shrugs, but the movement's too loose, too deliberate. "I know all about Kaz and have never found a hint of disloyalty to you. But, maybe he did it."

The laugh I force out is short and sharp. "Kaz? No. He's loyal to the bone."

The doors part with a low chime, spilling us into the server floor. Cold air hits my face, smelling of ozone, solder, and dust baked into wiring. Towers of servers hum in tight rows, their blinking lights throwing pulses of green and blue across steel and concrete. The sound is constant and low, like a growl that never fades.

Kaz's chair is empty. His console dark. The emptiness there is louder than any alarm.

Alexei's mouth tightens. "If your guy isn't here, why am I?"

"I'm not a novice," I answer, already striding to an isolated machine that isn't connected to Malice Media or even the internet. I want to get this over with so I can go reassure Ella. At least Wynd got her somewhere safe. "Plug in your damn drive."

Alexei fishes out a black thumb drive, rolls it across his knuckles, then tosses it to me. I catch it, shove it into a port on the unit that's safely disconnected from my garnet.

The screen flickers. A video loads showing grainy night footage of a Jeep rolling up in front of Alexei's place. Two men climb out. Both masked.

The first is clumsy, steps uneven, shoulders hunched like he doesn't belong in his own skin.

The second rounds the hood with measured purpose. A rocket launcher gleams against his back. "That's you," Alexei says. "It's your watch."

"It's not," I breathe out. "Mine has more garnets." I watch the man as his arm shifts, wrist turning, and the ink on his skin flashes under a streetlight. I freeze. My pulse thunders in my ears. “Holy fuck,” I murmur. Betrayal feels like knives down my torso. “I know him.”

Alexei leans closer, his men tensing at his sides. “Who?”

My head tips back, rage sliding into place like a blade locking in. “We need to find Ella. Now.”

THIRTY-SIX

Ella

I'm bouncing out of unconsciousness along with the car bumping over uneven roads. The trunk rattles around me, the carpet rough under my cheek, the air stale and hot. It smells faintly of leather polish mixed with gasoline, with a trace of citrus air freshener trying and failing to cover it. Every jolt slams my head against metal, pain sparking at my temple. My ankle throbs, sharp and angry, though I don't remember twisting it. Panic scrapes through my chest.

Who threw me in this trunk?

I try to think through the options. I'm not even sure who the guy who hit us was. Just how well do I know Bronco? Was he there? I don't know what happened. I really don't. My thoughts keep sliding, foggy and uneven, as the car rocks me hard against the side. Two huge sneezes take me, and my head throbs. My nose hurts. It feels more like an allergy attack than a cold, and I don't have any medicine.

Justice. His face swims across my mind. I need him. Now.

Finally, what seems like hours later, we come to a stop. I roll forward into the front of the trunk and crack my elbow. Pain jerks up my arm.

The trunk opens and bright light blinds me. A hood shoves down over my head, coarse fabric scratching my face. "Hey!" I yell, reaching out and scratching at air. My entire world spins, black and suffocating, as hard arms grab me and lift me against a solid chest.

His smell isn't one I know. Not like Justice. It could be any of the men I was in the elevator with. My body presses against muscle, the beat of his heart steady through cloth. His footsteps pound, echoing on hollow pavement. My eyes water. Are we in a parking garage? It smells like damp concrete, motor oil, and old exhaust.

A ding echoes. I sneeze into the hood. Gross. We step into an elevator. I hear the doors close. I thrash, twisting, but he's too strong.

"Justice is going to kill you for this." My voice is muffled through the hood.

He doesn't answer.

"*I'm* going to kill you for this." The words burst out, and raw fury ripples through me along with fear. Terror, really. I reach up, but one beefy hand locks around my wrist, pinning me in place. I slam my shoulder against his chest. He doesn't even grunt. Jerk.

The elevator lurches. We're descending. I yelp, sharp, because I had expected to rise. No. We're going down. Crap. So that's where they bury the bodies.

"Who are you?" I demand. I blink rapidly, though there's nothing to see. My head pounds, my ears ring.

Every breath tastes of fabric and oil. The doors part, and cool air rushes around us, lifting the edges of the hood.

I sneeze again. Darn it.

He walks across a hard surface. The hum of machines thickens, low and steady. I'm dropped into a chair, metal biting through the seat of my dress, and the hood is yanked off.

Corinda stands in the middle of the TimeGem server chamber, hands hovering over a diamond that glows faintly with a tinge of yellow. She steps back. Pale. Her eyes shimmer a faint yellow and her fingers tremble hard. The place has been cleaned, but damage still shows on the walls and floor.

"Corinda?" I snap, mouth dry, tongue thick as cotton.

My stepsister's hair is a tangled mess around her shoulders, but her green sweater and jeans look neat, as if she'd dressed down for a casual day instead of a kidnapping. Sure, we don't like each other, but how could she do this? Does she think I killed her mom? Does she even know that Sylveria is dead?

I turn . . . and see Wynd. My breath catches. Not Wynd. Not Justice's friend and cousin. Confusion blankets me before reality slaps me hard. "Bastard," I hiss. Then I turn my head and sneeze again.

Wynd shifts left, his gaze locked on Corinda. His presence fills the room, the weight of it pressing the air thinner. His voice cuts through the hum, low and certain. "Did you get it charged?"

Not in a million years would I have guessed it was him. My breath snags, and for a second the ache in my temple dulls under the shock. Wynd. Standing here like he belongs. My chest tightens, panic breaking through the haze, and I start to stand.

His gaze snaps to me. "If you move, I swear to God, I'm going to beat the shit out of you." He shifts more to the left, body angled toward Corinda, as if I'm already handled. "Answer me, Corinda. Is that diamond charged or not?" His voice is colder than I've ever heard.

Corinda looks down at the diamond, its glow wrong and sickly, already streaked with yellow, though it should be fresh. Her hands tremble so violently she can barely keep them open.

I shake my head, heat rising in my throat. "How long have you been trying?"

Her eyes flick to me, glassy, and her voice is dazed, hollow. "All night."

"That's what you get for being a murderous kidnapper," I fire back, my chest tight with disbelief. I know she's ambitious and maybe even ruthless. I never thought murder fit in the picture. My voice scrapes raw. "Did you kill your mother?"

Corinda pales further, the yellow light catching her skin until she looks carved from wax. Her hands drop to her sides, useless, and her bottom lip trembles.

I drag my eyes back up to Wynd, the sight of him still a hammer against my skull. "It had to be you. Nobody else could've gotten Sylveria's body inside the Malice Media structure."

"Yeah, I dumped her body, but I didn't shoot her," he says carefully, eyes locked on Corinda, voice edged like steel.

"Corinda," I whisper, stunned. My pulse stutters. I'd

like to say nothing surprises me anymore, but this—this does.

Her shoulders curl inward. "You don't understand." Is she in shock?

I would be if I killed my own mother. "No, you're right. I don't." My gaze bounces between the two of them, the diamond's faint hum clawing up my spine. "What is this? Some lovers' thing gone horribly wrong?"

Wynd glares at me. "I am so fucking tired of you."

Is there any way I can reach Corinda? "I don't know much about people and energy," I mutter, forcing air into my lungs, "but I think he's using you." My fingers twitch against the arms of the chair, searching for leverage. Because someone who could kill her own mother isn't going to help me, but maybe I can make her turn against him, somehow?

Of course he's using her. A side door clicks open and Stacia strides in, her heels sharp against the concrete. She has that stupid sparkly purse at her elbow. Cheap glitter falls on the floor as she moves, and I fight another sneeze. So it is allergies.

Wynd lights up like someone jammed a live wire into him. "Hey, baby, things are going exactly like you said."

My jaw drops. "Stacia?" I turn my head and sneeze, then look back at the purse. The fucking glitter purse. That's why I've been sneezing lately? Wynd has been hanging out near it and bringing cheap glitter into my world?

She glances at me first, then at Corinda slumped near the diamond, then finally at Wynd. She moves against him, leaving glitter on his arm. Her smile is sharp enough to cut. "We're tired of being second fiddles around here. I'm taking over TimeGem, and we're going after Malice Media for Wynd."

I cough, air jagged in my throat. "You're going to take out both Justice and Thorn?"

"I am," Wynd says, lifting one shoulder in that lazy way that makes my stomach twist. "I'm a distant cousin, and I can charge garnets." He grins. "Justice will think Kaz took you. Not me."

Fear makes my ears heat. "What did you do with Kaz?"

"You don't need to worry about him any longer." Wynd's tone is too calm. "His body will never be found, unlike yours. Unfortunately, I'll be the one to find you, and I'll comfort Justice before I slice his throat."

"You get to shoot this one," Stacia says to him, eyes bright. Then her mouth curves in a cruel smile. "Shooting Mother took more out of me than I thought. That bitch fought."

Corinda stumbles, her knees buckling. She falls into a chair, head rolling forward as if the strength's been drained from her.

"Did she just pass out?" Stacia asks, tilting her head.

"Yeah," Wynd murmurs. "We've been forcing her to charge for about fifteen hours, and I think she might need a break." He turns and crushes his mouth against Stacia's in a hard kiss.

"I want to gag." The words rip out of me before I can stop them. Every time I've sneezed or had my eyes water, Wynd has been around. I didn't realize it until right now. "I take it you gave Stacia that ugly-ass purse?"

He grins. "Yep. The next one will be diamonds."

Stacia smirks when she pulls back. "You always thought

I was the nice one. The funny one." Her eyes gleam. "But I'm also the one with the brain, and we weren't going anywhere with my mother, you, and the Beathachs in our way."

What assholes. I try to make sense of any of this. "Wait a minute. The guy who tried to kill me in my safe house? That couldn't have been you. You were outside and you saved me from him."

"Yeah, I hired that guy," Wynd said. "He was supposed to bring you here to charge the citrines as well as the gems I stole from Justice. I have a couple of beautiful alexandrites for you to try." He glares. "I felt Sylveria's guy behind me, so I had to shoot my friend and get hit in the head. Just to keep my cover. It's your fault."

Wow. I actually thought he was a decent guy. "You two haven't thought this out. Charging the gems isn't that easy. If you somehow take out Justice and Thorn, you won't be able to handle the garnets, Wynd." How stupid is he?

He shrugs. "I can charge them for a few years, and we'll have a bunch of kids. Some of them will charge garnets, some the diamonds."

Stacia's smile is thin. "We can make it until then. If we have to keep good old Corinda with a chain around her ankle for the rest of her life to charge diamonds, we will."

I look at Corinda and can see that she's more devastated than exhausted now. Her lashes are wet, and there's a smear of dirt along her jaw that makes her look young and fragile. She's still out, head rolling to the side. I press my palms to the arms of the chair until my knuckles go white. "How could you kill your own mother?" I rasp again.

"Oh, please." Stacia waves a hand like she's shooing a

fly. "That bitch didn't want anything to do with me. She thought Corinda was her ticket to a billionaire. I don't need either one of them." She snorts. "You know that mother is the one who tried to kidnap you with the big firefight on main street, right?"

"I wondered," I mumble. "But she wanted me to charge the citrines, so she didn't send the missile into Justice's penthouse."

Wynd smiles. "That was me. I thought to take Justice out first and Thorn later."

I can't breathe. "So why send a missile into Alexei's home?" That doesn't make sense.

Stacia looks at me like I'm a moron. "Mother did that. She figured Alexei would blame Justice, and they'd kill each other. Or at least, one of them would die. Same thing with the gunman at the courthouse. She truly wanted to take them all out."

Wynd slides an arm around Stacia's waist and pulls her into him. "You're so smart, baby."

The pet name makes bile rise in my mouth. "Murderers don't get to be called baby," I spit.

Stacia laughs, all sharp edges. "I wish we could keep you locked away here like Corinda, but Justice will never stop looking for you, so you have to die." Walking across the room, she opens a cupboard. "After you do me a favor, of course."

She pulls out a fat citrine the size of a bowling ball and places it on the desk next to Corinda. The gem throws back a mellow, honey light that makes my vision swim. The sound of the servers thrums underfoot, a slow, steady throb that seems to sync with the gem's pulse.

The citrine calls to me. How am I going to get Corinda out of here? If someone told me two days ago I'd be trying to save my stepsister, I'd have told them they were nuts.

Stacia grabs a broom from the corner and, without touching the diamond herself, shoves the pedestal hard. The gem tips, slides, and clanks off the stand, landing with a dull thud on the console. Dust lifts. Corinda coughs, her lashes fluttering.

"Our system is clear of the virus," Stacia says, voice flat. "But apparently it lives in my dear sister. She can't charge a diamond without infecting it."

Wynd nods. "Everyone else is safe. It appears that when you destroyed the virus in the system last time, you created firewalls. Our servers are fine."

Damn it.

Stacia stares at me. "Can you take the virus out of Corinda like you did the servers?"

"Most viruses aren't curable," I say. My jaw hurts where I hit the trunk. Alana had cured Thorn, but they have a connection that's beyond this world. I can't duplicate that with Corinda. However, I don't want to die right now. "But I can try. I'll need time within the system." Maybe I can contact Justice somehow.

"I'll think about it. For now, it's time for you to charge this little puppy," Stacia says cheerfully, eyes bright as knives as she fetches the citrine and turns to place it on the pedestal.

I frown. "Why would I do that? The second I do, you'll kill me."

"We're going to kill you anyway," Wynd says, casual as morning coffee, "but it's up to you." His gaze rakes me head to toe. "I can make it fast, or I can take my time. Slow. Have some fun."

Slow chills prick my skin. "Do you have any idea what Justice is going to do to you?" I blurt before the thought can be tamped down.

Wynd smiles, and whatever playfulness he had disappears. "No one will ever know it was me, Ella. I've got it covered. Kaz's last thought was a regret for being such a pain in the ass all these years."

The name hits me like a punch. He killed Kaz.

Wynd snatches my hair and throws me toward the citrine. Agony rips across my scalp. I slam into the console, bounce off metal, and land on my knees. Pain blooms in my palms and legs from the impact.

He stands over me, gun already out. "I'll shoot Corinda in the throat, then you in the foot, then the other foot, then your shoulder, then the other shoulder," he recites, voice calm, methodical.

I lift a hand. "I understand. You're going to keep on shooting me."

"Yep." He leans in. "If that doesn't work, I'll take your clothes off and convince you another way."

My gaze jerks to Stacia. She doesn't even blink. "Aren't you two in love?" I snarl.

"Definitely," Stacia says. "But you do what you've got to do. Now start charging that crystal. Our entire system needs the power."

I stand on shaking legs and place my hands on the gem. The stone is warm, buzzing faintly under my palms. Heat travels up my arms, a hum under skin.

Corinda coughs behind me. She sounds like her lungs are full of water.

I press harder and force my will into the task, thinking of Justice, of Alana and Rosalie, of my godmothers, and of whatever little life I can salvage for Corinda if I live through this.

"Wait a sec. Who killed Horace?" I ask.

"Me." Wynd shrugs. "Horace was in the way. I buried him at Justice's just to fuck with him."

"You're sick," I breathe.

Now I just have to figure out a way to get Corinda and me out of this before Wynd makes good on his threats. I look up and he smiles.

"This is going to be fun," he promises.

THIRTY-SEVEN

Justice

Fergus, Alexei, and I ride the elevator down to my secret garage. The air feels heavy here, metallic with oil and old smoke, the kind of silence that makes every footstep echo. The doors slide open and the first thing I see is Bronco, slumped on the pristine concrete, pale and still, the car gone but my SUV waiting beyond it. Wesley Whisper is on his knees beside him, shaking him, trying to wake him.

"What the fuck?" I move toward them. "Wake up, Bronco." He's out cold.

Wesley looks up. "He got shot twice. By Wynd."

I nod. "Wynd is the enemy." Words I never thought I'd say, but I saw him on that video. I know the tattoo on his wrist.

Alexei barks orders into his phone.

I lean closer. Blood is caked up Bronco's neck in a dark, sticky trail glinting under the fluorescent light. "Is he breathing?"

"Yes," Wesley says. "I'm not sure what happened. The elevator door opened, and he attacked Wynd. The guy went ballistic." Wesley's bleeding from a cut beneath his eye and there's what looks like a bullet wound near his collarbone.

"How bad are you hurt?" I ask, my breath heating.

He wipes blood off his chin. "Dunno. I've already called an ambulance, but they don't know how to get here."

"I'll open the door. Tell them to come around back." I need to find Ella. "You tried to save her?"

"I did," Wesley says. "I love her."

"That's too bad." My voice is flat. "She's mine, but I owe you one. Thanks for trying to save her. Get Bronco to the hospital."

Wesley nods and hauls Bronco up with raw, shaking effort. He staggers toward the massive door.

I run and jump into the SUV and punch the button to open the door.

Alexei climbs in beside me, sliding his phone into his jacket pocket as Fergus barrels into the back seat.

"You good for this?" I ask.

"Yes," Alexei says grimly. "I'll help you get her back. Where would Wynd take her?"

The door is taking way too fucking long. I pull up the map on my phone, scroll, and shove it into his hands. "She's the blue dot."

He blinks down at it, then looks up at me, his eyes dark. "You chipped your woman?"

"No. I chipped the dog. She's got a bracelet with a tracker in it."

"Smart," he says.

The engine roars to life.

"Don't tell me you don't have Rosalie covered," I say.

He smiles without answering.

"That's what I figured."

The door is only halfway open when Kaz crashes into it and crumples to the ground. The sound is sharp, like a sack of bricks hitting steel.

"Holy shit." I leap out and run to him. He's bleeding from everywhere, streaks of red glistening under the harsh garage lights. Dirt covers him, head to toe, thick in his hair. The metallic tang of blood cuts through the smell of grease and gasoline, and for a second I almost choke on it. His clothes are shredded, caked with dirt, and his skin feels clammy when I grab his shoulders. I lay him on the pavement, his body twitching once before going slack.

"It was Wynd," Kaz mumbles. Blood bubbles from his lips, thick and wet. "He shot me and buried me in the old lot on Blarney Street. I wasn't dead. Asshole."

I press my hand on one of the bullet wounds. He's bleeding but not enough. Is he almost out of blood? "How?"

"Dug my way out." His voice is barely there. "Grabbed a lady's phone, meant to call you but got Bronco. She took the phone, and I had to get here."

He walked five blocks bleeding to death. So that's why Bronco attacked Wynd. He must've been coming up to tell me when the elevator door opened.

"I got him," Wesley calls, still feeling for Bronco's pulse. "I hear sirens now." He moves to drag Kaz inside the garage and out of the rain. "How many times you shot?"

"Dunno," Kaz whispers. More blood slips from the corner of his mouth. His swollen eye is shut tight.

"Thanks," I tell Wesley. "Get them help." If we survive this, I might have to hire the guy. I give one last, long look at Kaz. "Stay alive." I jump back in the vehicle and push down the gas pedal. The SUV surges forward into the night. Alexei holds the phone out. The blue dot looks solid. We go after it.

"Where are they?" I ask Alexei.

He thumbs the screen, eyes narrowing. "They're at TimeGem."

I pause. "TimeGem?" But Sylveria is dead.

"Yeah." He nods. "Besides Wynd, did you recognize the other guy from the video?"

"No. Probably hired muscle." He was clumsy. I slam the accelerator. The SUV rockets forward, the world on either side of the vehicle blurring into streaks of gray and green. Panic chews through my chest, raw and unfamiliar. I've never felt this before. Wynd has Ella, and he likes to play with his prey.

"I didn't see this," I mutter.

Alexei shakes his head. "We never do. It's always the people closest to you, isn't it?"

Not really. My brother would never do this. I don't think Kaz would, either. Ella's a complete brat, but she'd never betray me.

I wrench the wheel, pulling off the interstate toward TimeGem Moments headquarters. Asphalt rattles under the tires. We round a curve down the quiet street, and suddenly there's an old Buick in front of us. "What the fuck?" I swear.

Alexei glances at me. "What?"

"Her godmother's in there."

Alexei leans closer to the front window. "Huh?"

"I don't know," I growl, leaning on the horn.

The dog lifts his head in the back seat and presses his nose against the window, his tail visibly wagging.

"Her godmother's a dog?" Alexei mutters.

"Shut up." I cock my head. Through the Buick's dusty rear window, I see Aura behind the wheel. I honk again. She ignores me.

I press the gas pedal and nudge the Buick's bumper.

She slams her brakes and whips the wheel, spinning into a tight 180 before sliding to a stop on the shoulder. Dust explodes around her.

I hop out of the SUV.

The Buick's driver's door bursts open, then two more. Three women climb out, each one leveling a gun at me. I see a Ruger, a Glock, and a Ladysmith, all black steel in the sunlight.

"What the hell are you doing out here?" I yell. I can't remember the last time I raised my voice.

They're all dressed like some strange corporate color wheel. Mags wears bright yellow, Jos is in fluorescent green, and Aura sparkles in eye-popping blue.

"What do you think we're doing?" Jos snaps. "We're going to get our girl." They look like a deadly yoga class for seniors.

I swallow hard. "How do you know where she is?"

Mags shifts in her yellow suit, looking uncomfortable. "We've been hacked into all the cameras of the four social media companies for years. We saw her brought in by your man—the one who's with you all the time. He lifted her out of the trunk and put a hood over her head. She was alive."

I shove panic into the distance. "Alexei and I are going in. Fergus, you and the ladies are going to provide cover from outside. Got it?"

"No," Aura says flatly. "We're going in."

Jos yanks her green pants up, ready to move.

"If you go in, you're just going to get in my way," I say, letting them all see the killer in me.

"You need backup," Aura fires back.

Alexei takes one step forward, and he pretty much looks like death. "I'm his backup."

The women glance between us, back and forth. Finally, Aura lowers her shoulders. "All right, but we're covering the entrance. If anyone comes out that isn't you, we're shooting. And if you're not out in fifteen minutes, we're coming in."

"That seems fair," Mags says.

I pause. "Aura? Do you still have the rocket launcher in the trunk?"

Alexei swears something in Russian under his breath.

"Of course." Aura smiles widely, moves to the back, and brings me what I need.

Alexei and I jump back in the SUV and I hit the gas.

"Are they serious?" he asks.

"Yeah, they're serious." I left Fergus with them on purpose. He might be able to stop them, but I don't know. Either way, I don't want him caught in the crossfire. I glance at the Russian. "Are you sure you want to do this? This isn't your fight."

"I want to help. Rosalie will be heartbroken if anything happens to Ella. Besides . . ." He lifts his shoulder. "I like her. She's sweet."

"That she is," I say. "And she's all mine."

I stomp the accelerator and swing the SUV around the gate. Guards shout, rifles bark, and I duck as bullets tear into the metal. Glass shatters, and sparks fly. I don't care.

My woman is in there.

THIRTY-EIGHT

Ella

My arms ache, my ears ring, and I'm filled with as much citrine power as is humanly possible. I've exchanged energy for at least fifteen minutes, and the world is singing. It's too bad I can't shoot this power from my fingertips and take off Wynd's head.

Corinda has awakened, but she sits like a husk in the chair, not moving. The hollows in her cheeks look like they were dug with shovels and are so dark I can barely tell if she's still in there. She blinks but doesn't seem to see anything.

"How can you do this to your own sister, Stacia?" I step away from the stone. The power throbs through me. I might be invincible. Probably not to a bullet, though.

Stacia is busy playing with Wynd's butt and snuggling into his side. At least that looks like where her hand is. The way his pants tent kind of confirms that fact.

"Oh, please," Stacia says. "We were never close. She

was Mother's favorite. Always has been. The truth is she's dumber than a box of rocks."

"I don't think she is," I retort. "I think she just has different ambitions than you. You're fucking evil. I've never met anyone who would kill their own mother before."

"It was me or her," Stacia says. "She was slowly killing me by edging me out. She wanted Corinda to take over and bring in some billionaire new husband. Her money was on Justice. You know she planned to kill you, right?"

I swallow. My fingers are tingling. "Yes. I'm aware of that. I really don't think it was very nice of her, but I wouldn't have shot her in the head."

"You would have," Stacia says cheerfully, and the casualness sends a chill down my spine. "You just won't admit it." Her sigh sounds heavy and fake when she looks up at Wynd, her gaze adoring. "We can't exactly keep her any longer. Justice is going to come looking."

"Are you sure you don't want to kill her?" he asks like he's making dinner plans.

Stacia looks at me, then back at him. "I'd rather you did it. I shot my mother."

When he looks at me, his eyes are dead. "You want me to shoot her?"

"No." She shrugs. "I want you to make it more personal."

I take a step away from them.

"Oh, yeah?" Wynd sounds interested.

I shake my head. "How can you do this to Justice? He's like a brother to you."

"No, he's like a brother to Thorn," Wynd says. "I'm

the hired help. I have royal blood in my veins just like he does. The garnets can be mine."

I cough out panic. I'm sure he doesn't have half the power needed to charge them, and he's too egotistical to know it. "You're going to drive two social media companies into the ground."

"We can handle it until kids arrive," Stacia says, patting her flat stomach. "I've heard kids as young as three can charge."

"Even so, that's years away," I snap. "Do you have any idea how Aquarius and Hologrid will take you down by then?"

Wynd shakes his head. "I've been coming for them for a long time."

"Yes," Stacia says. "We've been infecting servers left and right. You have no idea how weak the infrastructure is on both Aquarius and Hologrid Hub. I'm in their systems."

I blink. "You can code?"

"Of course I can code," she snaps. "What do you think I've been doing this whole time? Just going to parties, having fun with Corinda, and posting on social media?"

"Well, yeah," I say, stunned. Apparently we underestimated Stacia the same way the world underestimated Alana. I should have known better.

"Don't worry," Stacia says. "I've done plenty of damage."

She doesn't know I already found the routes and corrupted them.

I swallow and try not to sneeze. That stupid purse is too close. "If you can code, do you know where the virus came from?"

"I have no idea." Stacia stares at me. "I figured you created it."

"No." Not the mutated one, anyway. If I can get to a mainframe, I can clear her out completely. She's not nearly as good as I am. She didn't have Aura, Mags, and Jos training her all her life. My mind goes to the women. I have to get out of here. Who will take care of them?

I think of Justice. I think of what we could've had. I fell hard, and I fell fast. I love a guy who can break someone else's neck with his own hands, and I never told him. Oh, I'll put up a good fight, but Wynd is twice my size. While I feel the power of the crystal, it doesn't give me extra strength.

"I'd very much like for you to strangle her now," Stacia says cheerfully.

I take another step toward Corinda. The idea of Wynd's hands around my throat makes me want to gag. I back toward Corinda and grab her arm. "You need to wake up now. Help me."

She looks up listlessly. "Huh?"

"Get up. We need to fight." I bite the words through my teeth.

She looks at me, then at her sister, and then she pushes herself up as if her body is ninety years old.

"There you go," I say.

Stacia actually laughs. "Nah, we're going to let you live. You have a purpose to serve, so why don't you just sit down and behave yourself?"

"You are such a cunt," Corinda slurs. She wavers on her feet. "I can't believe you killed our mother. You're going to die a horrible death." The words are soft, fragile.

Her voice is weak; speaking has tired her out. I can't count on her much for an assist.

I scan the room for weapons. The only thing I can see is a pen. I grab it.

Stacia watches me and laughs.

It's funny until I stab her in the eye. I brace my feet and get ready to lunge just as the barely repaired elevator door blows open. The whole room stutters.

Justice. He came for me.

I grab Corinda instinctively and push her behind the pedestal as the doorway fills. Justice and Alexei stand there like two different kinds of storms.

Justice hits first. He reaches Wynd and tackles him, bringing him down hard. Alexei moves for Stacia, but Stacia yanks a gun from her side and shoots him. Alexei jerks back, blood spattering across his face, shock written all over him. She laughs, and a knife flashes out of nowhere. Alexei's right hand moves as he throws, the blade spinning wildly, embedding perfectly in her throat.

She falls back, the gun clattering from her hand. She clutches at the knife, gurgling, and falls hard. I watch as her body shudders, convulses, and then the light leaves her eyes.

Alexei frowns and grabs his upper chest.

I move Corinda over to him. "How bad?" I ask.

"I don't know," he gasps. He collapses to his knees. "Kind of hurts."

Oh shit. I look over at Justice, but he's busy pummeling the ever-living shit out of Wynd. Wynd's face is hamburger meat. I'm not sure there's a nose left I recognize. Justice looks up, fury all over him, blood splattered across his face.

"I think Alexei took a bad one," I say, holding Corinda as best I can. She's barely steady.

Justice turns and punches again. One more blow snaps down on Wynd's face. I hear bones crack, a percussive cascade, then the body shudders and goes still. Justice, his face splashed with blood, moves toward us. "Are you hurt?"

"No, I'm good," I say, though my mouth's dry.

Alexei tears his jacket off and looks down at the wound. Blood pours from him, pooling dark on the floor. Sirens and alarms burst to life above us—blares and the sound of men running, boots on stairs echoing through the shafts. "Shit. Hold on."

"Guns out," Justice says.

Alexei pulls a pistol from his boot. Justice pulls his too. I run over and grab the gun Stacia dropped, the cold metal slick with her blood.

"We can't just keep shooting people," I say, the panic making my voice thin.

Alexei's eyelids flutter.

"No," I cry out. He can't die. Rosalie will be crushed. I stand and run into the server room, carrying the citrine out to place beside him.

"What are you doing?" Justice asks.

I gulp. "I'm not sure." I plant my hand on the crystal and the other over Alexei's heart. It's beating slowly and not as strong as I like. I shut my eyes and think of Rosalie. Of her sweetness and her loyalty. Of her being my sister. A hum sets up around us.

"Holy shit," Justice murmurs.

I tap into his energy, pulling strength from him. From the garnets and obsidian gems on his watch. I mentally picture a strong amethyst stone, Alexei's stone, and shove healing power into the man.

He gasps and sits upright. "What the hell?" He looks down and then presses a hand against his still-bleeding wound.

I shudder and sit back. At least I bought him some time.

"More soldiers are coming," Corinda says listlessly.

"You're right," Justice says, his voice calm as he raises it so the oncoming men can hear him. "Wynd and Stacia are dead. The new owners of TimeGem Moments, Ella and Corinda, are alive. We're taking them up the elevator. Anybody that comes at us dies."

He hoists Alexei over his shoulder. Alexei drops his head back and groans as blood runs down his temple, streaking the Russian's cheek. I wrap an arm around Corinda and guide her toward the elevator. Her legs are shaky, but she moves.

Hopefully we can get out in time. The alarms keep wailing. Footsteps close in. I can feel my heart hammering like it's trying to escape my ribs. We press our backs to cold metal and wait for the doors to close on whatever comes next.

The elevator doors shut, and I look up at Justice, a brutal man with blood splashed across his deadly angled face.

He came for me.

THIRTY-NINE

Ella

I'm in the hospital waiting room, happily eating vanilla ice cream while Aura, Mags, and Jos dig into their own cups. Leo is at my feet, tail thumping, licking something that looks an awful lot like a pup cup. Dogs aren't supposed to be in the hospital, but when they tried to make him leave, Justice changed their minds without even standing up. I don't want to know how he did it.

"Everybody good?" Fergus asks, looking up from a root beer float like he's discovered a new religion. I have no idea where he got that in a hospital. He's planted at the table and keeps eyeing Mags. I'm not sure how I feel about that, or the fact that my godmother called Merlin to make kissy noises earlier.

"We're all good," I say. "What's the news?"

Justice walks into the room, blood still across his neck. "Kaz is still in surgery to remove another bullet, but the doctors are optimistic. Alexei was shot through the clavicle. The bullet missed his heart by millimeters and he's going to be fine. Rosalie's with him and his room's well-guarded. He's yelling at the nurses, so I think he'll be out soon. Bronco's got a pretty bad concussion but can go home tomorrow. Wesley's been stitched up from a bullet wound and is still professing his love for you."

I wince. "He did try to save me, and he got everyone to the hospital in time."

Justice shakes his head. "He was rather helpful today. I don't want to have to kill him."

I'll take that as a win for now. "Corinda?"

"She's dehydrated and in shock," Justice says, looking around at the various occupants of the waiting room like he's not sure how he got into this situation. "Should be okay in a couple of days."

I shudder. "I can't believe Stacia killed Sylveria and was ready to sacrifice her sister." Tears try to prick my eyes and I push them back. "I'm sorry about Wynd. I would've never suspected him."

"What about the police?" Fergus asks.

"We gave statements and pretty much told the truth," Justice says dryly. "There's CCTV of everything. Plus we've got statements from Aura, Mags, and Jos." He glances at them. "By the way, you three have very impressive resumes. The police nearly snapped to attention when I used your names."

Mags smiles and gives Fergus a sly wink. Aura claps her hands and chuckles with delight. Jos just digs a new hole in her ice cream.

I've been mulling a few things over, especially since they admitted to finding me because of the CCTV at TimeGem. "It's time for you to confess."

All three of them pause, two with spoons almost to their mouths.

"To, ah, what?" Aura asks.

Just how much do they have to confess? "About the virus? The newest one that infected the diamonds." I narrow my gaze.

"Oh." Mags waves a hand in the air. "Yeah, that was us. We knew you'd eventually want to take down Sylveria, so we weakened her diamond and her by using a mutated version of your virus. It wouldn't have killed her, just so you know."

Aura smiles. "That also made you necessary to her, so she'd stop trying to kill you."

Jos nods. "Win-win, as they say."

Do they really say that? I sigh.

Jos snorts. "That Kaz kid? He's pretty good. He cyber attacked us back, and it burned a bit. For a short time."

Aura lifts her head. Mags catches her breath.

"What?" Jos asks.

I blink. Once and then again. Justice stills. I swallow. "Kaz attacked you *back*?"

"What the fuck?" Justice mutters.

"Justice. Language," Aura says, pressing her lips together.

I shake my head. "No. Wait a minute. Don't change the subject." My head starts spinning.

"What subject?" Jos asks innocently, smiling at Leo.

I can't breathe.

Justice lowers his chin and glowers at them.

Mags is the first to break. "Oh, all right. The fifth player on the board? The one messing with everyone a little bit? That was us."

"You three?" Justice growls out.

Aura smiles at him like he's a prized pupil. "Of course, dear."

I shake my head. How does this make sense? "Why?" It's the only word that comes to mind.

Aura blushes.

Jos looks at her ice cream.

Mags winks at Fergus.

I wait. My chest hollows out because I'm not breathing, so I force my lungs to work. "Ladies?"

Aura's eyelashes flutter. "Fine. That Wesley is a nice man, but you walked all over him. We figured you needed somebody . . ."

"Stronger," Jos finishes for her.

"Much tougher," Mags agrees, her gaze sliding over Justice.

Aura blows him a kiss. "You and Justice worked together to figure it out. Plus, not going to lie, we had a lot of fun messing with these so-powerful companies. For goodness' sake."

I gape. "You did all of that to matchmake Justice and me?"

"We'd do anything for you, sweetheart," Aura assures me. "Getting him named bachelor of the year wasn't easy, you know."

He moves for her, and I hold up a hand. "Wait. You three offered to take him out for me."

Justice's chin goes down.

Aura chortles. "Yes, and you declined our offer. Of course."

I can't breathe. I stare at my man. "Before you get pissed, how in the world did you find me today at TimeGem?"

Justice strides right at me, graceful and unhurried,

reaches for me, and lifts me to sit in his lap. He cradles me like I'm fragile, and the room shrinks to the space that exists between us. Everything inside me settles. I snuggle in, because why not? The guy rescued me again and, okay, I kind of love him.

"How?" I ask again.

"I'll always find you." He leans over and kisses me, and the three women sigh around us. What romantics. I bet he has a tracker in my jewelry. In fact, that makes perfect sense.

Aura clears her throat. "You owe me a rocket launcher."

I jolt.

Justice pauses and then nods. "That, I do."

I frown. He is not giving her another rocket launcher.

"Considering I'm surrounded by most of your family," he says, smiling, "how about we just do this now?"

I blink. "Do what?"

"We're going to get married."

"Yay!" Mags chirps. Jos smiles into her ice cream. Aura claps, which is the least surprising reaction.

"I might even wear a dress," Jos says, eyes bright.

Happiness engulfs me. "You're supposed to ask."

He looks at me. "I don't think so. You'd try to weasel out of it."

"I would not." I grin.

"We're getting married. Say the words, Ella." His voice lowers and takes on that same command tone he used the other night. It slides across my skin and awakens something.

"Fine. We're getting married, but we're throwing a bash. I want a wedding fit for a princess." I even have a tiara to wear.

"You've got it," he says.

"I'm sure Alana will figure out a way to show the world," Mags says.

Justice blinks. "Oh wait. I guess you'll figure out a way to make TimeGem the key? I think it's yours now. This is going to get complicated."

"You like complicated," I murmur. He must, right? Or he wouldn't have just proposed.

"No, I don't." One of his dark eyebrows lifts. "That's why I live in a house by myself in the middle of the woods."

"Now with me and a dog," I add. Well, until I run again. I'm sure he'll catch me. It'll be fun, though. I rub my palm along his whiskered jaw. "When we healed Alexei earlier? I figured out how to heal you. We just need to combine the right stones and energy."

"Yours and mine," he says softly.

Yeah. Exactly. "We can try later today."

Aura clears her throat. "You know, we were talking to Ella about how Alexei's built a guest house for Rosalie's boarders. It was blown up."

Justice's voice goes short. "Yes."

"You would never let anything like that happen, would you?" Mags asks softly.

"Of course not," Justice says, and the answer is so automatic it makes the rest of us smile. "You're saying you want a building on my property for you three to live in?"

Mags grins like she's won something.

Aura folds her hands and speaks like it's common sense. "Just think how much safer you'll feel close to us instead of working from afar."

Justice's bronze skin pales a fraction—if that's possible.

I wrap a hand around his chin and kiss him once. He doesn't soften, exactly, but I feel it in the way his jaw eases. "I'll think about it," he grumbles.

I take that as a yes. If a year ago someone had told me that Alana, Rosalie, and I would be engaged or married to some of the most dangerous men alive, I'd have laughed. I never thought I'd find love like this. I never thought there *was* love like this.

"Just for the record," I murmur, because some of my family is here and the moment feels big enough to spill, "I do love you."

Tears flash in Aura's eyes.

Justice presses a kiss to my nose and smiles, a little resigned but real. "I love you, too."

I grin. "This is going to be fun." I'm teasing him, but he's everything. Oh, he's a little rough, and plenty dangerous, but he came for me. Through bullets, through fire, through pain.

Might as well give him forever.

EPILOGUE

Ella

I'm about as happy as I can be as I post once again on TimeGem Moments and ask all of my millions of new friends to capture the moment with me.

"Stop gloating," Alana grumbles next to me.

I can't help it. I upload and then look at her, stunned as always by her beauty. For the Silicon Valley Shadows and Secrets ball this year, she's wearing crimson with her brunette hair up high on her head. Her eyes sparkle. "It's not my fault our men made the bet and I won." I guess Justice kind of won, but he said I did, so here we are. "Plus, I need to catch up with you. I'm still getting in the groove of owning TimeGem."

Beautiful ball gowns and dangerous-looking tuxedoes move all around us. The champagne is flowing freely, and the music is soft and romantic.

Rosalie glides toward us, easily holding three glasses of champagne. She hands them to us. "Is she still gloating?"

"Yes," Alana grumbles.

Rosy is wearing blue this year, and she looks like a princess with her amethyst jewelry.

"All right," I say. "You can start posting."

Alana grins and immediately does so.

Rosy takes a sip and shakes her head. "That means I need to post on Hologrid Hub, you know."

Yeah, I know. I turn and watch as Rosalie's seven elderly boarders, all dressed to the nines in different colors of tuxedoes, flirt with my three godmothers. I figure they've all earned the title.

Aura looks lovely in pale blue, Mags in bright pink, and Jos in a green dress. They've danced with each of the men, and at the moment, there seems to be a bit of a scuffle between two of the guys. It's cute, and I figure they'll work it out.

There's a twittering, and we turn to see our men make their way to us from the bar. Yeah, I want to twitter, too. The trio is something to look at. Dark, dangerous, deadly.

Justice's gaze meets mine, and he prowls toward me.

I swallow. In a tux, he's even more primitive looking. I'm not sure how.

He reaches me and leans down to bite my earlobe. "Say something sweet."

I grin. "I like your face."

His nostrils flare, and pleasure glitters in his eyes. "I like yours." His eyes sweep my pale yellow gown that's encrusted with citrines. "You're beautiful, princess."

"Thank you." I glance down at the massive citrine, garnet, and obsidian engagement ring that's heavy on my finger. It's beautiful. We tried several times to cure him of his virus, but it had taken his brother returning home and adding his energy to the moment to actually do it. Justice is now healed and at one hundred percent. Voices still bother him, but they don't cause physical damage. And my presence helps even with the irritation, which makes me feel lovely. It really does.

Much to his dismay, I also finally created a code to counter any computer virus, and I've already shared it with the four families. We're safe. For now, anyway.

Thorn stands behind Alana and pulls her against his chest.

Alexei is next to Rosalie, standing like he always does, as if just waiting for somebody to try to take her. They won't.

My attention is caught by Corinda over by the flower arrangement, looking beautiful in a light purple gown. She's speaking with a tall man with broad shoulders. "Who's that?"

"My cousin, Saveliy," Alexei says smoothly. "I just arranged their marriage."

I swallow. "What?"

Justice nods. "Corinda is in. This creates an alliance between TimeGem and Hologrid Hub, and it helps everyone."

I need to speak with her later, and I will. We're becoming close, and I don't want her to sacrifice herself. "I take it he's a billionaire?"

"Nearly trillionaire," Alana says. "He's handsome, too."

I guess. I'll check in with her later.

Justice takes my glass and puts it on a table. Then he wraps an arm around my waist, lifts me, and walks over to the dance floor to set me down.

"You could ask for a dance, you know?"

He leans down and kisses me. Hard. Firm. Sexy. "Behave yourself, brat. We both know what I can do to you on a dance floor."

Heat fills my face. Because he's right. "You behave, or I'll make a run for it tonight."

His hand spreads across my lower back. "Feel free. I haven't spanked you nearly enough lately."

Heat flows into other places on my body now.

My friends and their men start dancing around us, and I lean into Justice, finally feeling like I have a home. "I love you."

He holds me tighter. "You're everything, Ella Rendale. All mine."

Exactly.

ACKNOWLEDGMENTS

Some stories rise from ash and quiet endurance, shaped by patience, pressure, and the belief that change can come even when the night feels endless. This darker retelling of Cinderella would not exist without the many people who helped bring it to life. I sincerely apologize to anyone I may have unintentionally forgotten.

To Tony, my constant and my anchor, who stands beside me through long nights and looming deadlines. Your strength, patience, and unwavering support steady me when the clock feels dangerously close to striking twelve.

To Gabe, my brilliant civil engineer, whose logic and problem-solving skills I can always rely on, and to Karlina, my artistic visionary, whose creativity and passion remind me that magic often hides in unexpected places. I am endlessly proud of both of you.

My sincere thanks to my agent, Caitlin Blasdell, for believing in this darker world and for guiding this series with such care, and to everyone at Liza Dawson Associates for their continued support.

Thank you to my editor at Kensington Publishing, Elizabeth May, and to the entire Kensington team who work tirelessly to turn ideas into finished books. My gratitude goes to Alexandra Nicolajsen, Steven Zacharias, Adam Zacharias, Alicia Condon, Lynn Cully, Jackie Dinas, Jane Nutter, Vida Engstrand, Sarah Selim, Barbara Bennett, James Walsh, Justine Willis, Andi Paris, Kristin McLaughlin, Kait Johnson, Kelsy Thompson, Catherine Kenny, and Sydnee Thompson. After publishing more than forty stories together, I am grateful to work with such a talented and dedicated group of professionals.

A special thank you to the Rebels, my fierce and loyal street team, for championing these stories and helping them reach readers. A huge thank you as well to my social media wizard Anissa Beatty, and to Rebels Madison Fairbanks, Joan Lai, Gabi Brockelsby, Leanna Feazel, Kimberly Frost, Karen Clementi, Asmaa Qayyum, Jeanne Ortego, and Heather Frost. Your enthusiasm and support keep these stories alive long after publication.

Thank you to my publicity teams at Book Brush and Writerspace for the creative tools and support that help bring my vision to life and connect these stories with readers in meaningful ways.

To my family, friends, and loved ones who have stood by me through late nights, moments of doubt, and every deadline along the way, thank you. Gail and Jim English, Kathy and Herbie Zanetti, Debbie and Travis Smith, Stephanie and Don West, Jessica and Jonah Namson, and Chelli and Jason Younker, your encouragement and belief in me mean more than I can say.

Finally, thank you to the readers who were willing to step into the ash and darkness of this retelling and trust that something transformed would emerge. Grimm Bargains walks a darker path, and I am deeply grateful you chose to follow it. I hope this Cinderella story stays with you long after the clock strikes twelve.

DON'T MISS OUT ON THE OTHER CAPTIVATING GRIMM BARGAINS BOOKS, SET IN THIS SEDUCTIVE WORLD OF MONEY, POWER, BILLIONAIRES, AND THE DANGEROUS DESIRES THAT DRIVE THEM . . .

Available now!

HEADLINE
ETERNAL